InvestiGATORS
Take the Plunge

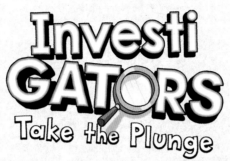

Investi GATORS
Take the Plunge

written and illustrated by
John Patrick Green

with color by **Aaron Polk**

First Second
New York

To my biggest fan.

Wait, scratch that... To my air conditioner.

First Second

Copyright © 2020 by John Patrick Green

Drawn on Strathmore Smooth Bristol paper with Staedtler Mars Lumograph H pencils, inked with Sakura Pigma Micron and Staedtler Pigment Liner pens, and digitally colored in Photoshop.

Published by First Second
First Second is an imprint of Roaring Brook Press,
a division of Holtzbrinck Publishing Holdings Limited Partnership
120 Broadway, New York, NY 10271
All rights reserved

Don't miss your next favorite book from First Second! For the latest updates go to firstsecondnewsletter.com and sign up for our enewsletter.

Library of Congress Control Number: 2019948198

ISBN: 978-1-250-21998-5

Our books may be purchased in bulk for promotional, educational, or business use. Please contact your local bookseller or the Macmillan Corporate and Premium Sales Department at (800) 221-7945 ext. 5442 or by email at MacmillanSpecialSales@macmillan.com.

First edition, 2020
Edited by Calista Brill and Rachel Stark
Cover design by John Patrick Green and Kirk Benshoff
Interior book design by John Patrick Green
Color by Aaron Polk
Printed in China by Toppan Leefung Printing Ltd., Dongguan City, Guangdong Province

10 9 8 7 6 5 4 3 2 1

Chapter 1
INVESTIGATORS!

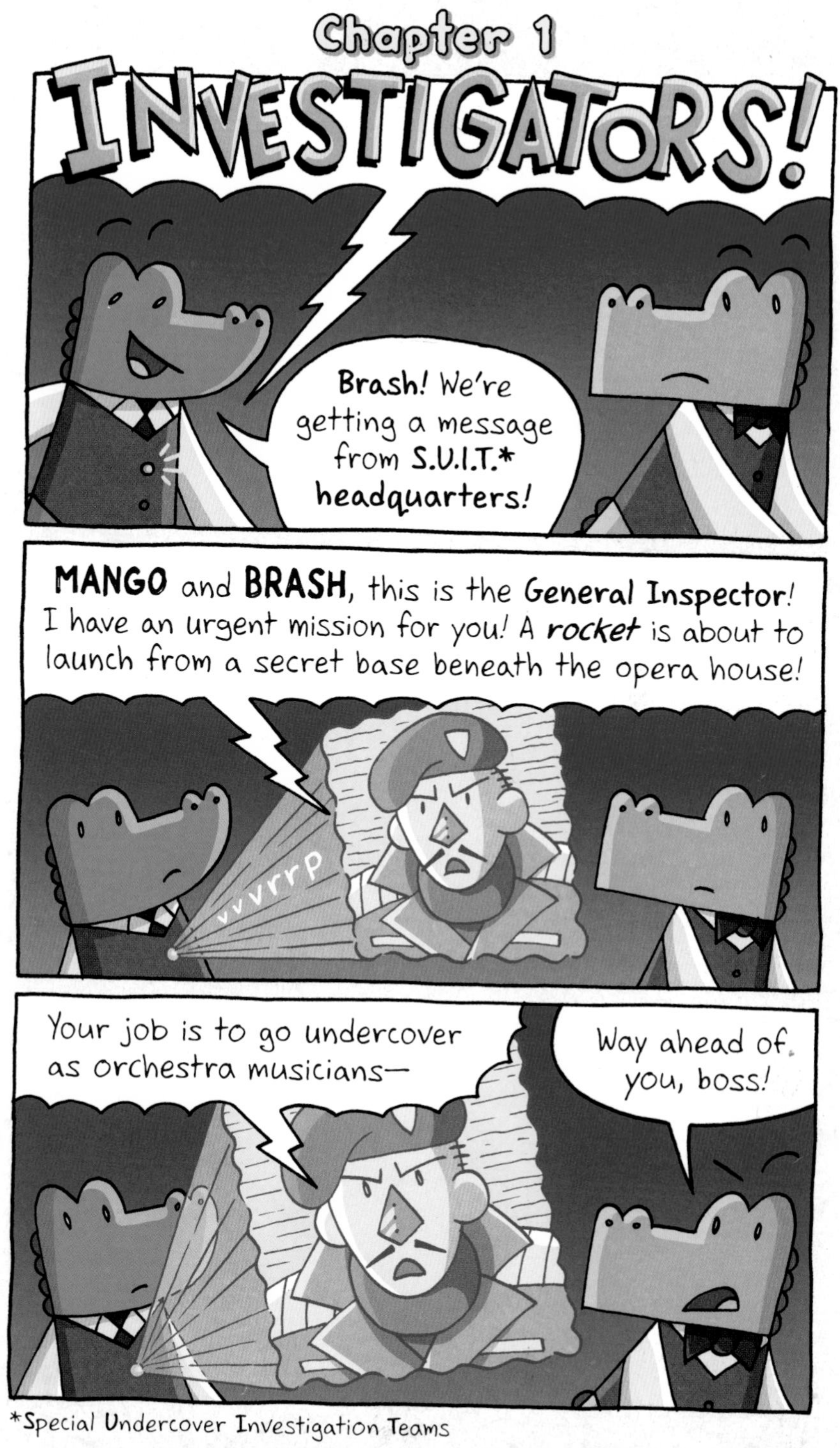

Brash! We're getting a message from S.U.I.T.* headquarters!
MANGO and BRASH, this is the General Inspector! I have an urgent mission for you! A rocket is about to launch from a secret base beneath the opera house!
vvvrrp
Your job is to go undercover as orchestra musicians—
Way ahead of you, boss!

*Special Undercover Investigation Teams

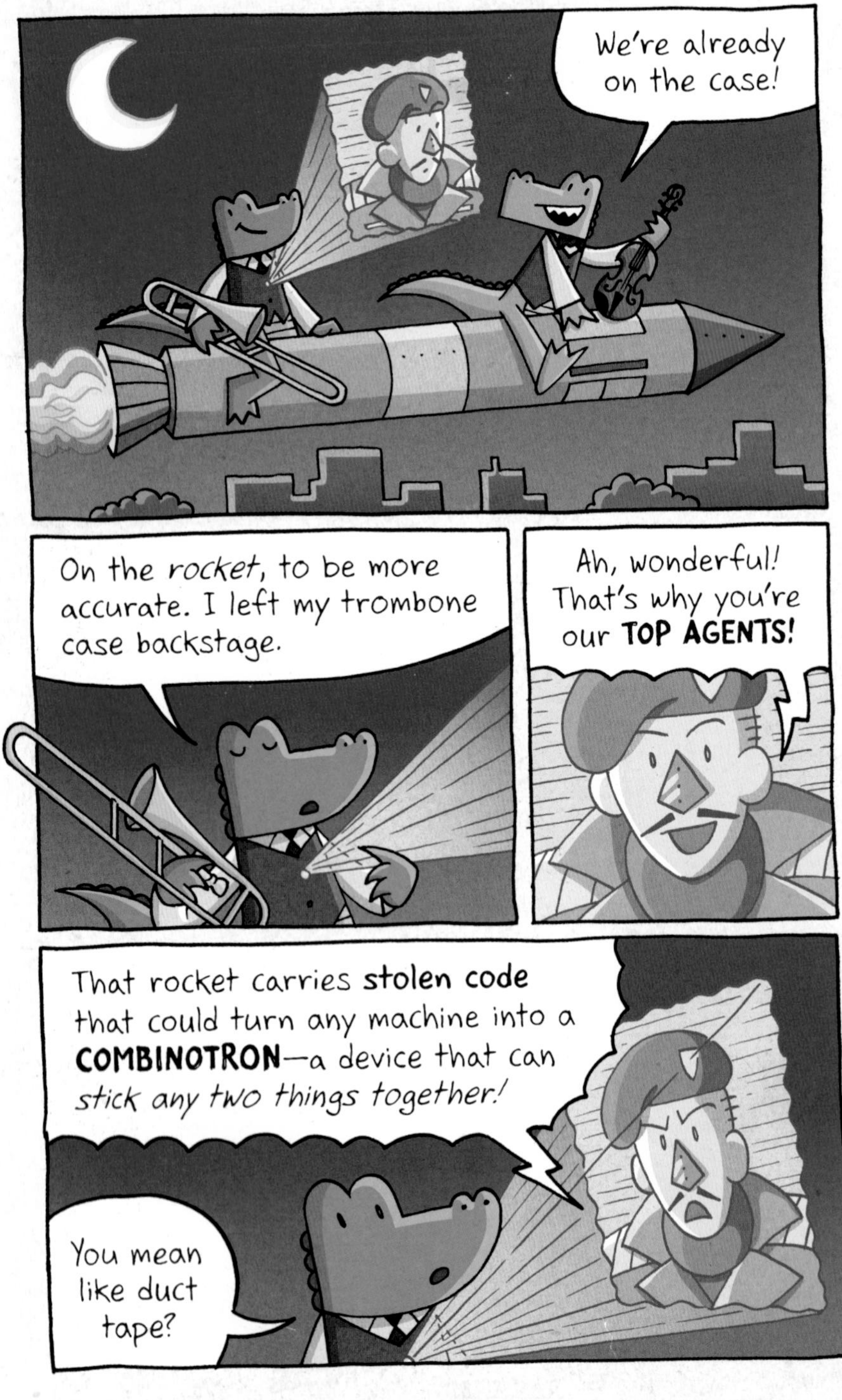
We're already on the case!
On the *rocket*, to be more accurate. I left my trombone case backstage.
Ah, wonderful! That's why you're our **TOP AGENTS!**
That rocket carries **stolen code** that could turn any machine into a **COMBINOTRON**—a device that can *stick any two things together!*
You mean like duct tape?

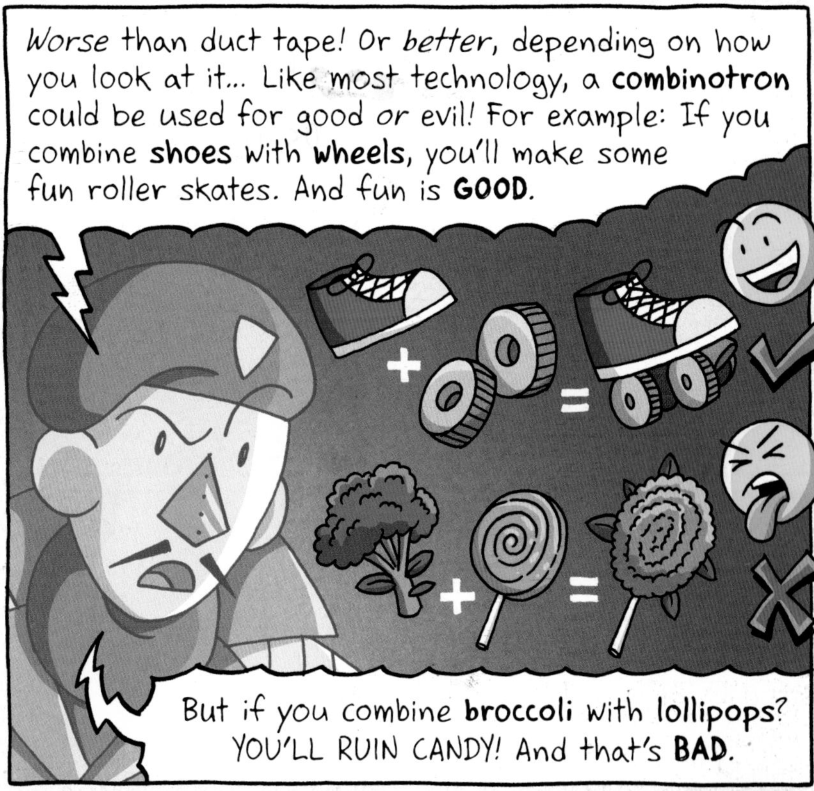
Worse than duct tape! Or *better*, depending on how you look at it... Like most technology, a **combinotron** could be used for good *or* evil! For example: If you combine **shoes** with **wheels**, you'll make some fun roller skates. And fun is **GOOD**.
But if you combine **broccoli** with **lollipops**? YOU'LL RUIN CANDY! And that's **BAD**.

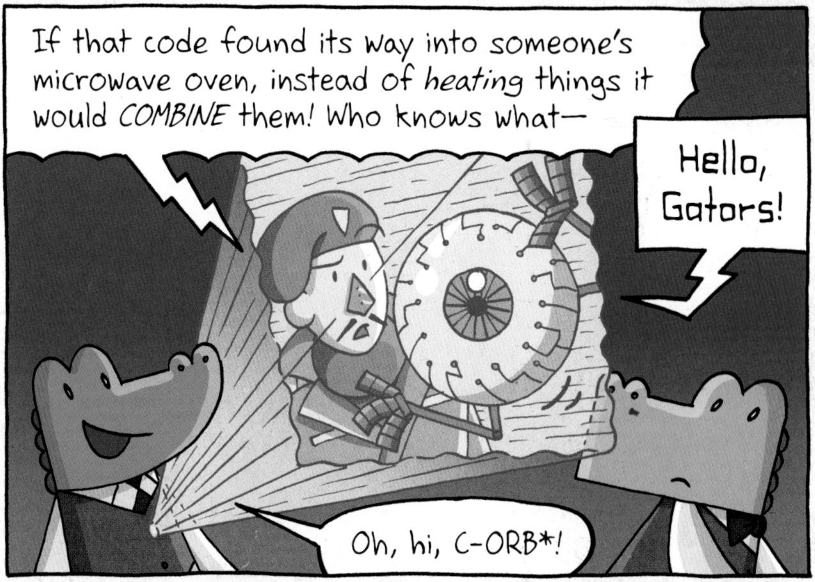
If that code found its way into someone's microwave oven, instead of *heating* things it would *COMBINE* them! Who knows what—
Hello, Gators!
Oh, hi, C-ORB*!

*Computerized Ocular Remote Butler

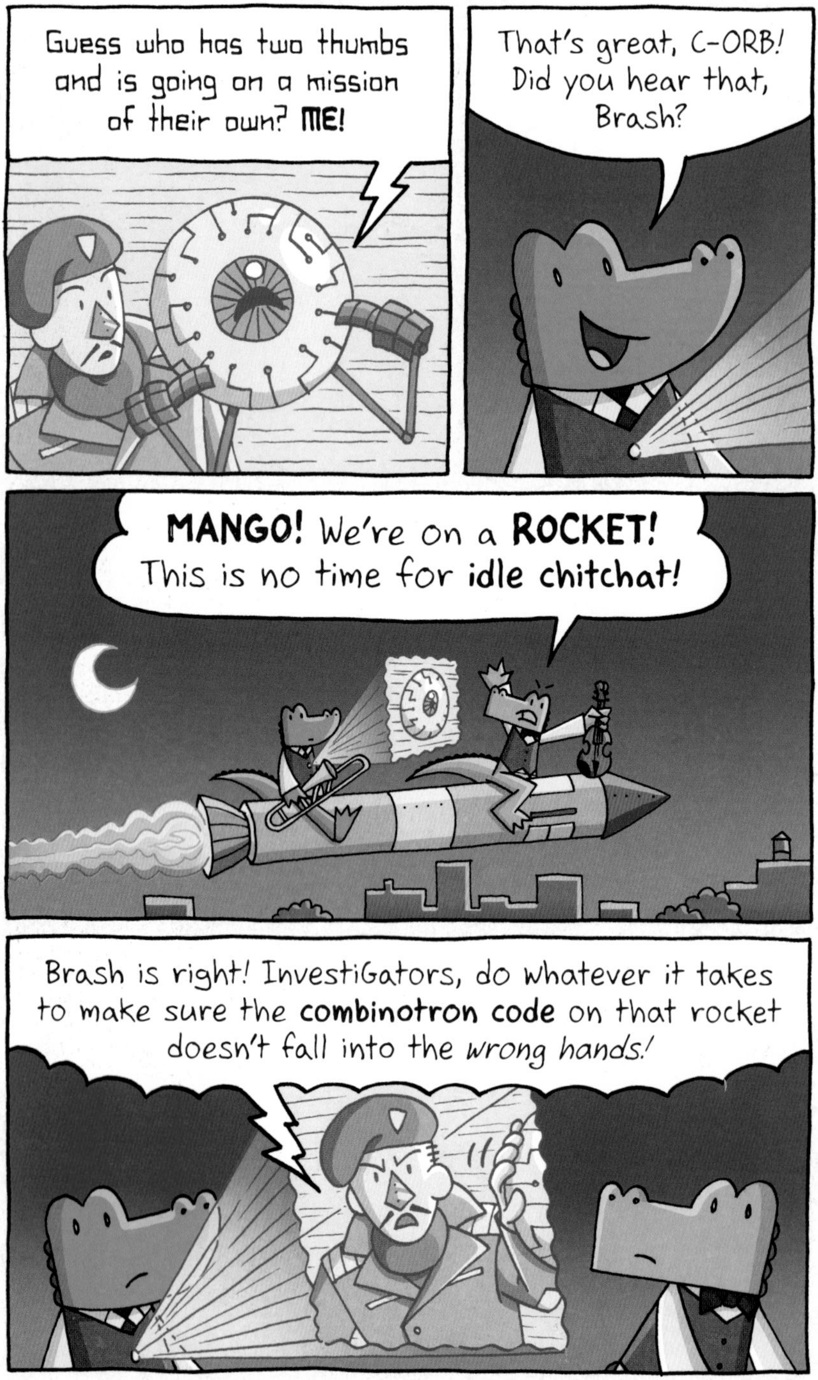

Guess who has two thumbs and is going on a mission of their own? ME!
That's great, C-ORB! Did you hear that, Brash?
MANGO! We're on a ROCKET! This is no time for idle chitchat!
Brash is right! InvestiGators, do whatever it takes to make sure the combinotron code on that rocket doesn't fall into the wrong hands!

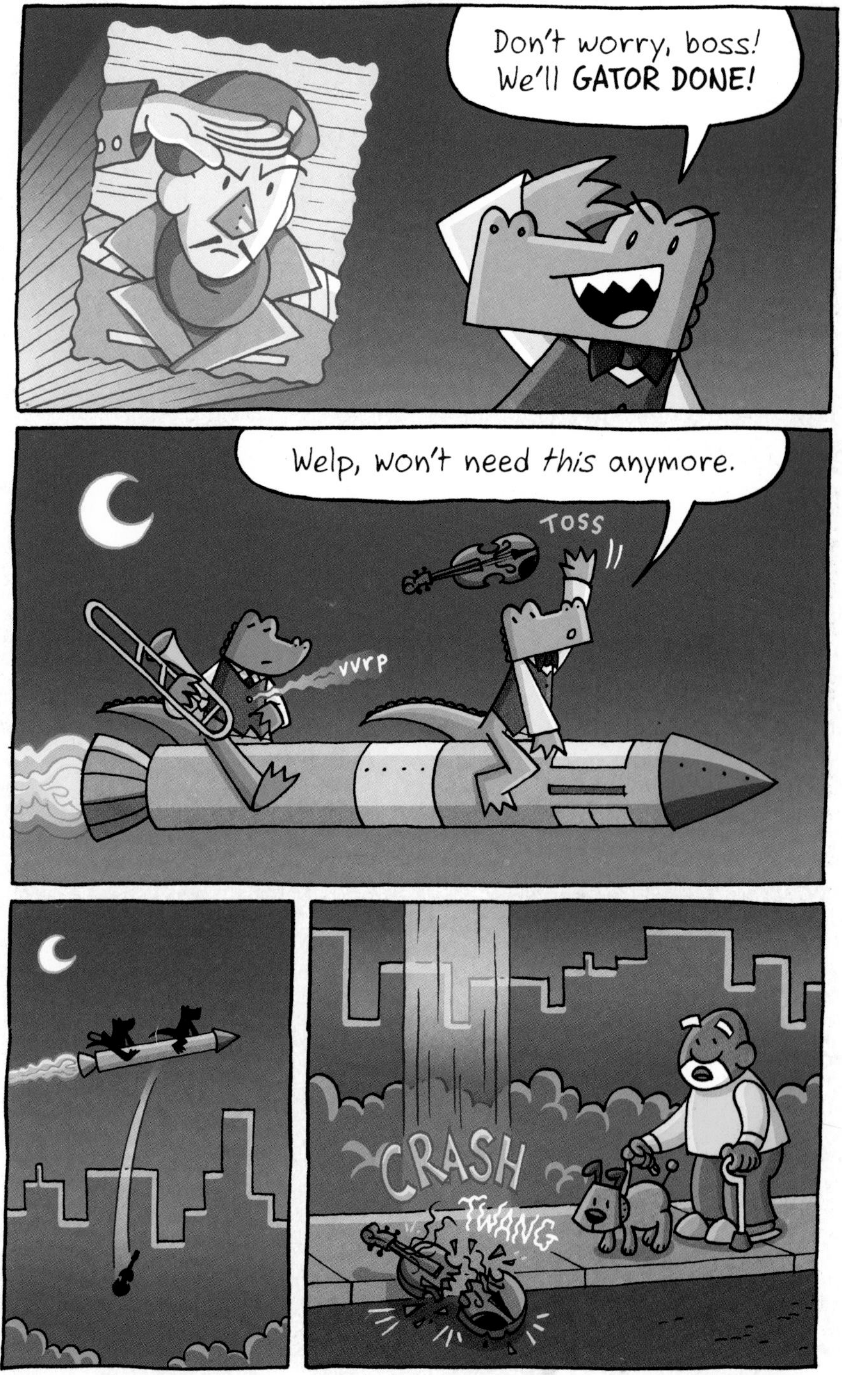
Don't worry, boss! We'll GATOR DONE!
Welp, won't need this anymore.
TOSS
VVRP
CRASH
TWANG

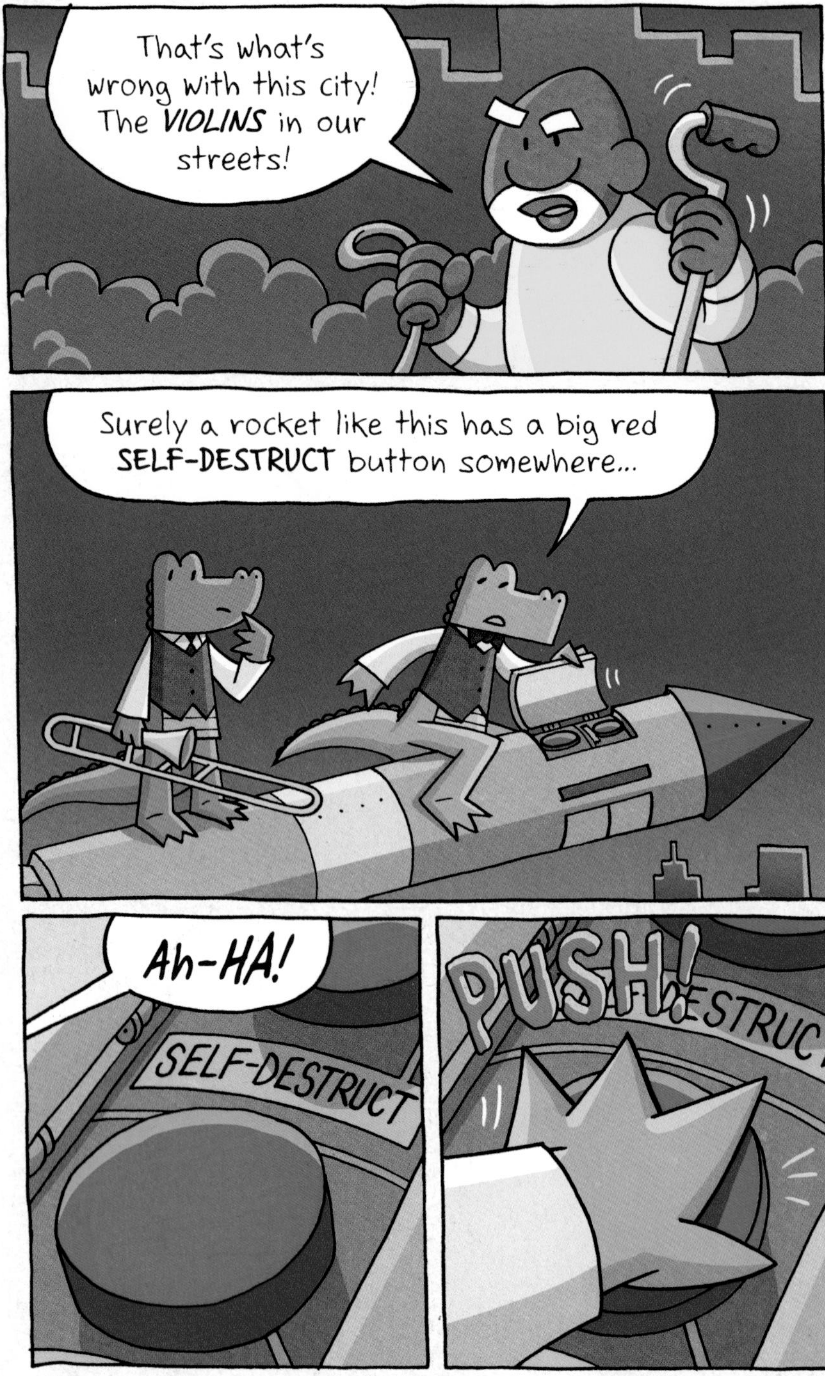

That's what's wrong with this city! The VIOLINS in our streets!
Surely a rocket like this has a big red SELF-DESTRUCT button somewhere...
Ah-HA!
SELF-DESTRUCT
PUSH!

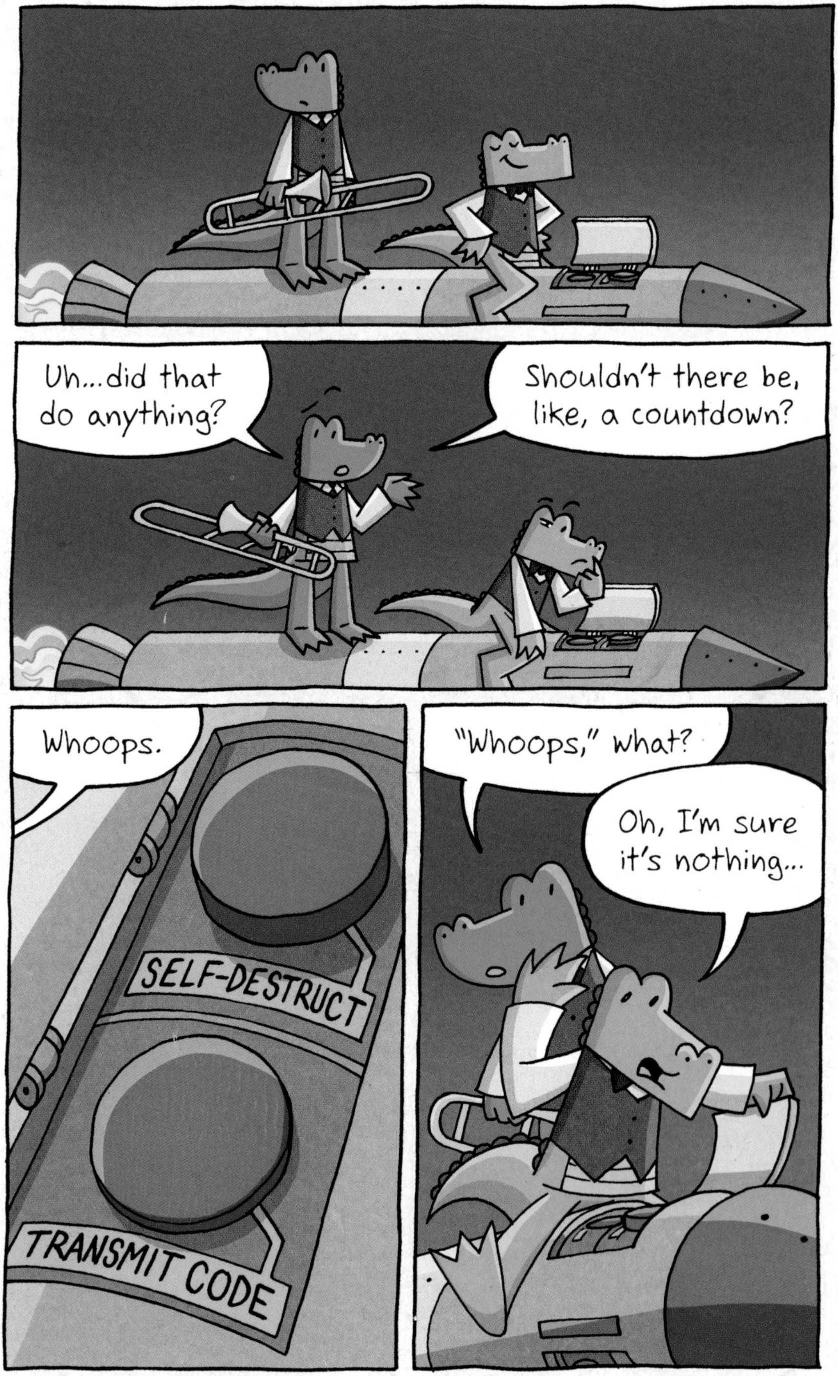
Uh...did that do anything?
Shouldn't there be, like, a countdown?
Whoops.
SELF-DESTRUCT
TRANSMIT CODE
"Whoops," what?
Oh, I'm sure it's nothing...

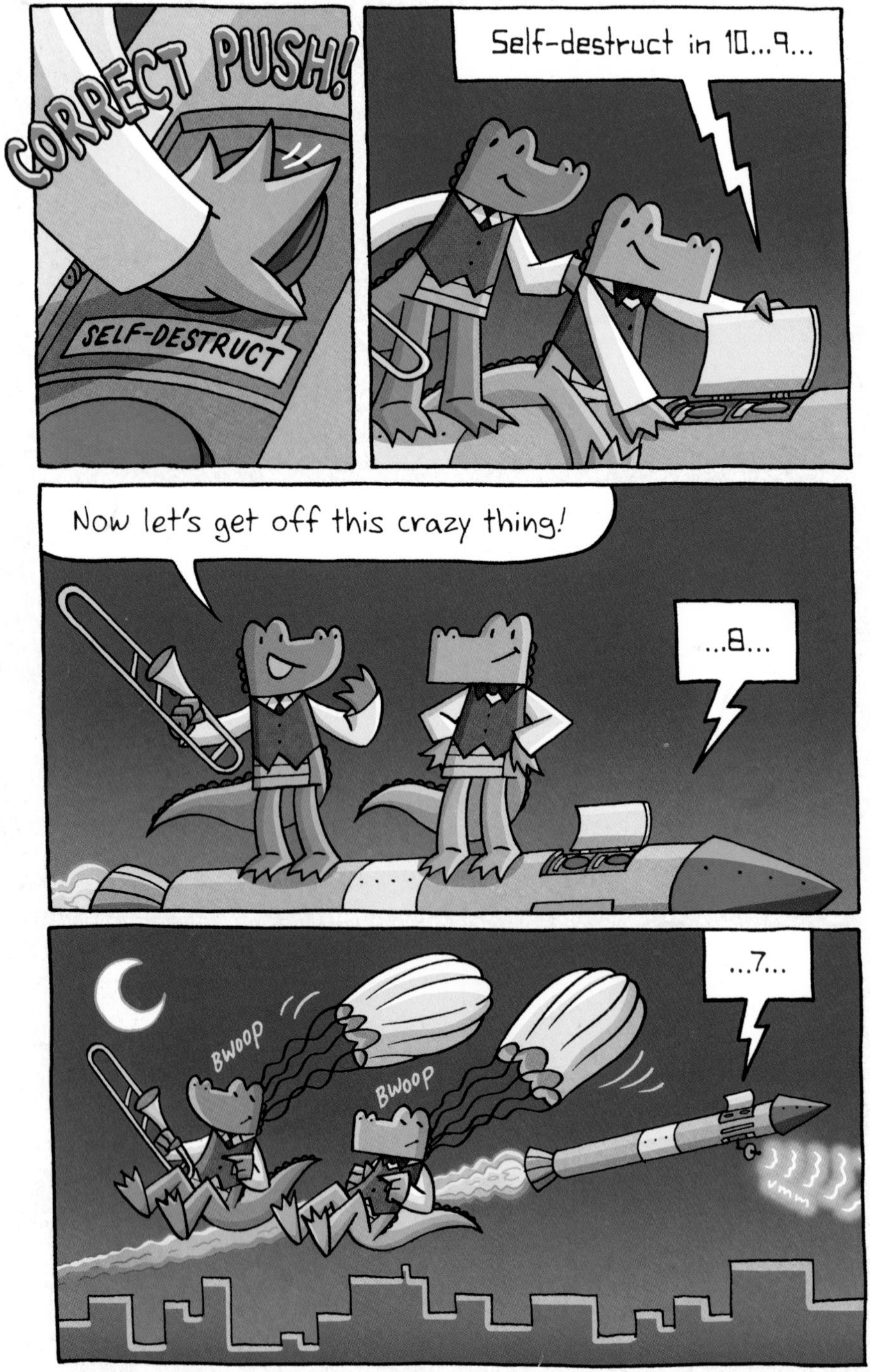
CORRECT PUSH!
SELF-DESTRUCT
Self-destruct in 10...9...
Now let's get off this crazy thing!
...8...
...7...
BWOOP
BWOOP

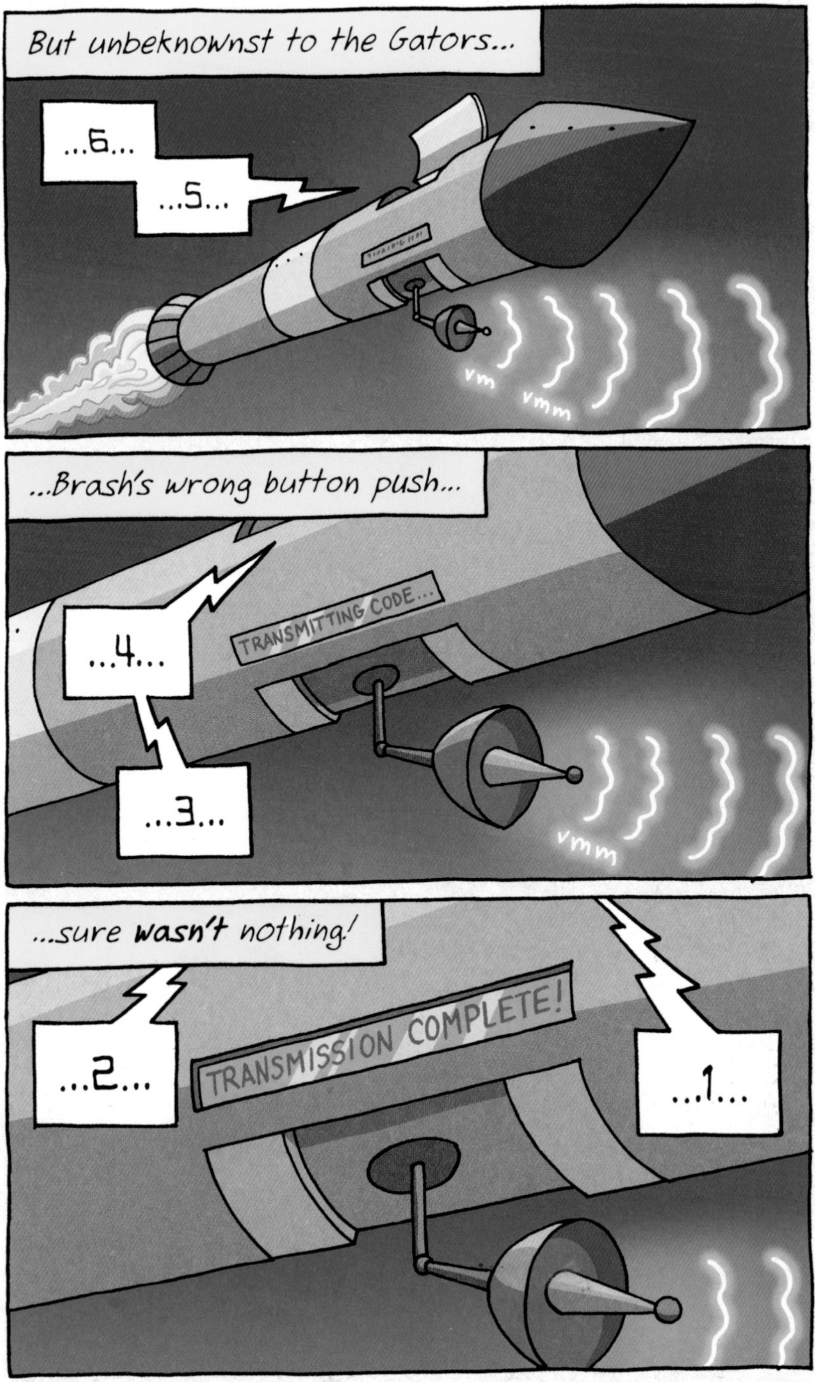
But unbeknownst to the Gators...
...6...
...5...
vm
vmm
...Brash's wrong button push...
TRANSMITTING CODE...
...4...
...3...
vmm
...sure **wasn't** nothing!
TRANSMISSION COMPLETE!
...2...
...1...

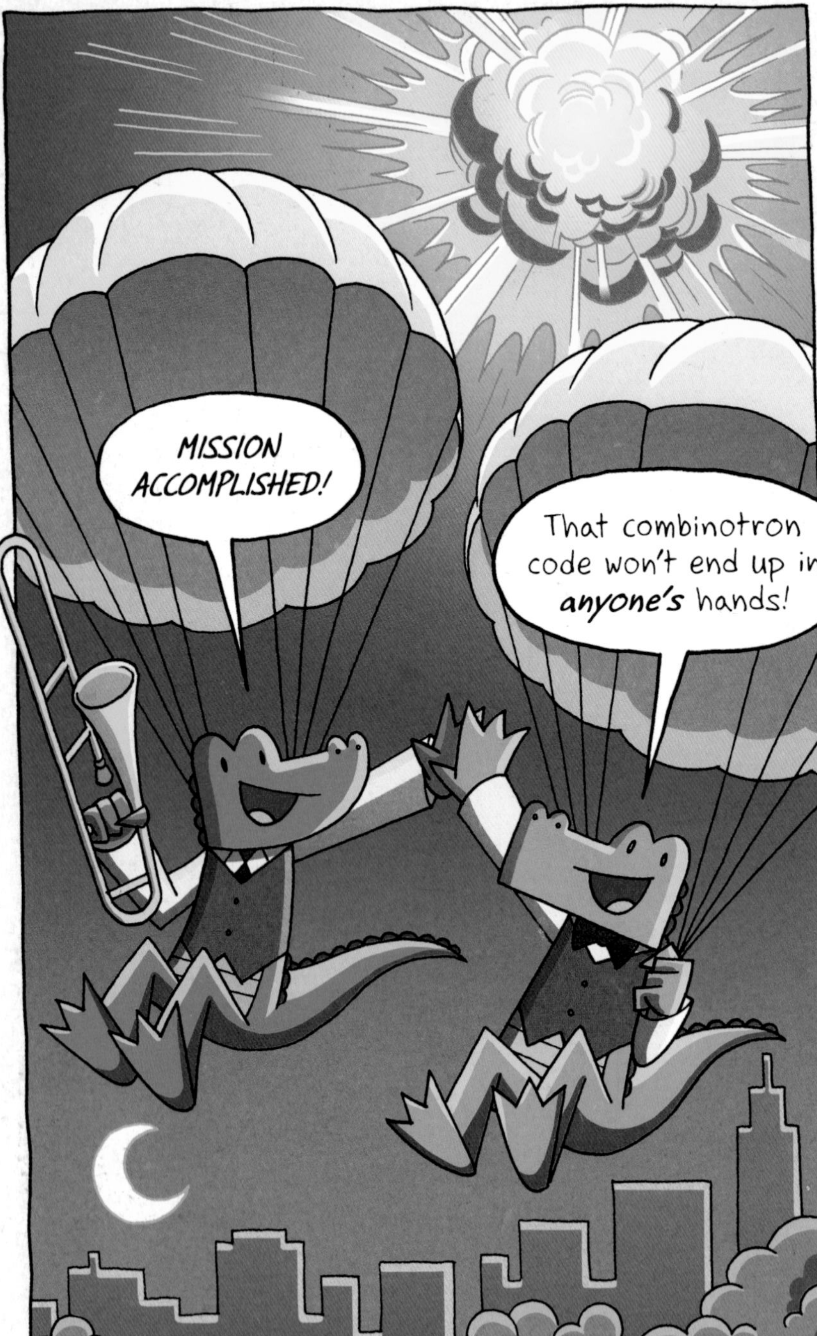
MISSION ACCOMPLISHED!
That combinotron code won't end up in **anyone's** hands!

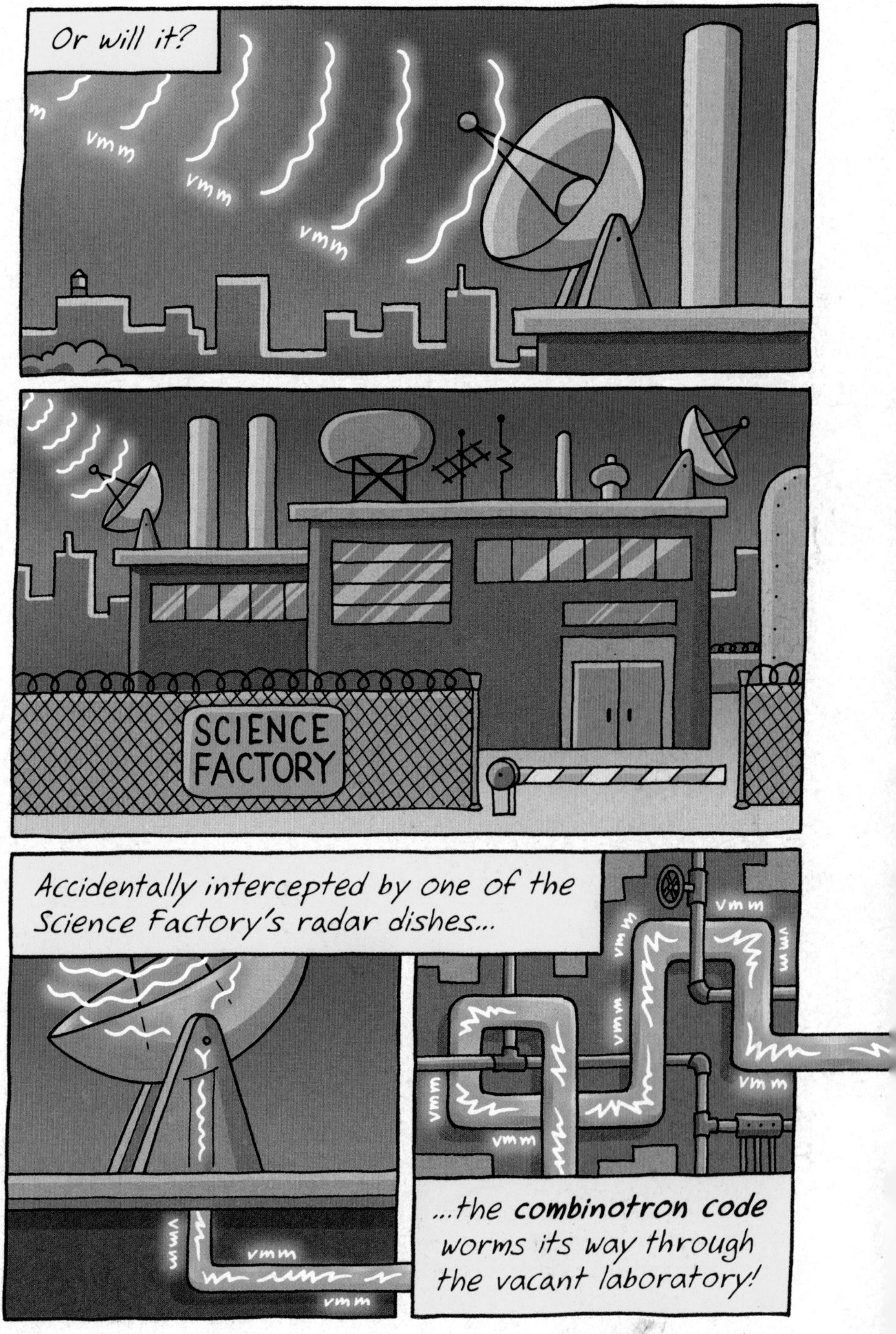
Or will it?
vmm
vmm
vmm
SCIENCE FACTORY
Accidentally intercepted by one of the Science Factory's radar dishes...
vmm
vmm
vmm
...the **combinotron code** worms its way through the vacant laboratory!

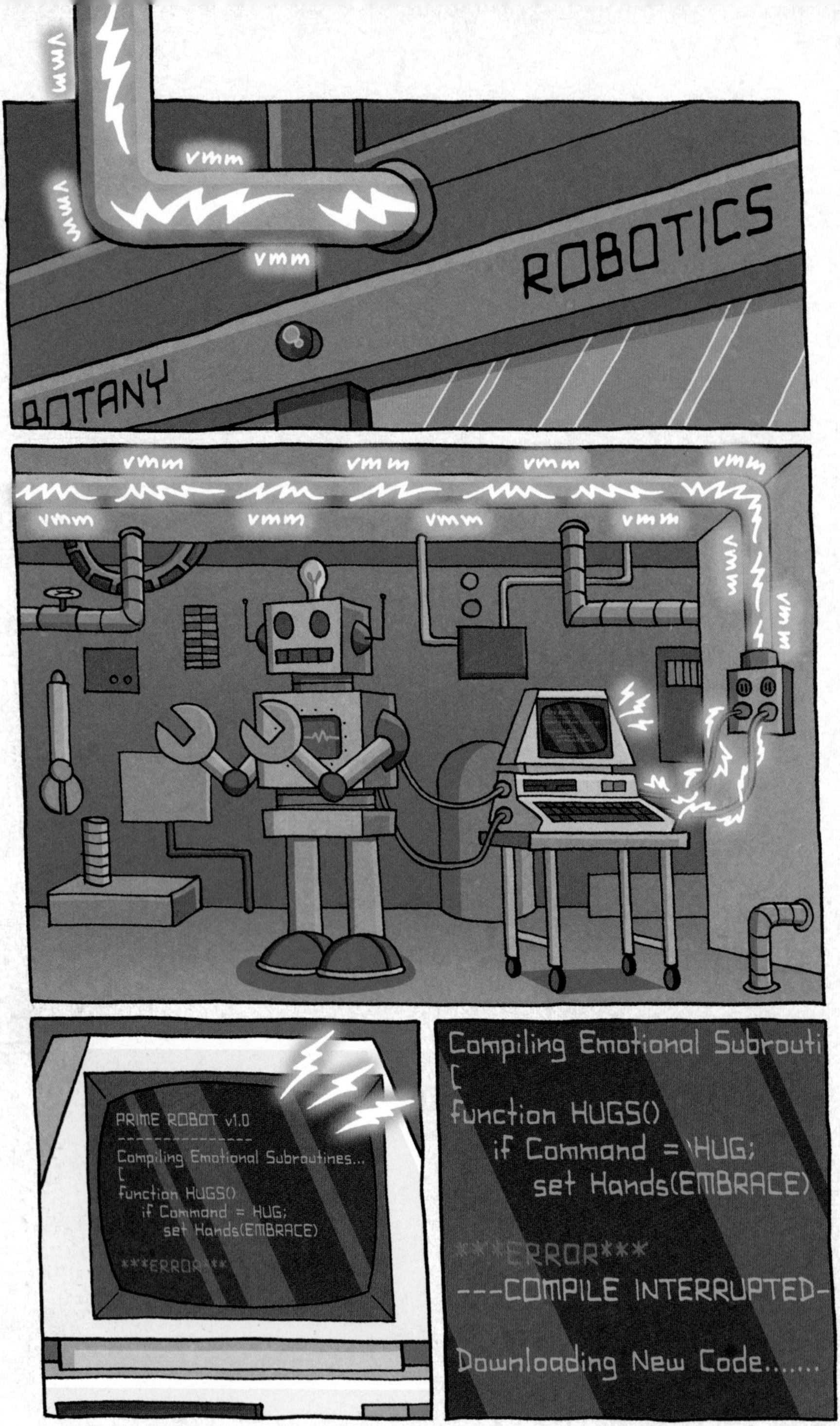
vmm
vmm
vmm
vmm
ROBOTICS
BOTANY
vmm vmm vmm vmm
vmm vmm vmm vmm
vmm
vmm
PRIME ROBOT v1.0

Compiling Emotional Subroutines...
[
function HUGS()
if Command = HUG;
set Hands(EMBRACE)
ERROR
Compiling Emotional Subrouti
[
function HUGS()
if Command = 'HUG;
set Hands(EMBRACE)
ERROR
---COMPILE INTERRUPTED-
Downloading New Code.......

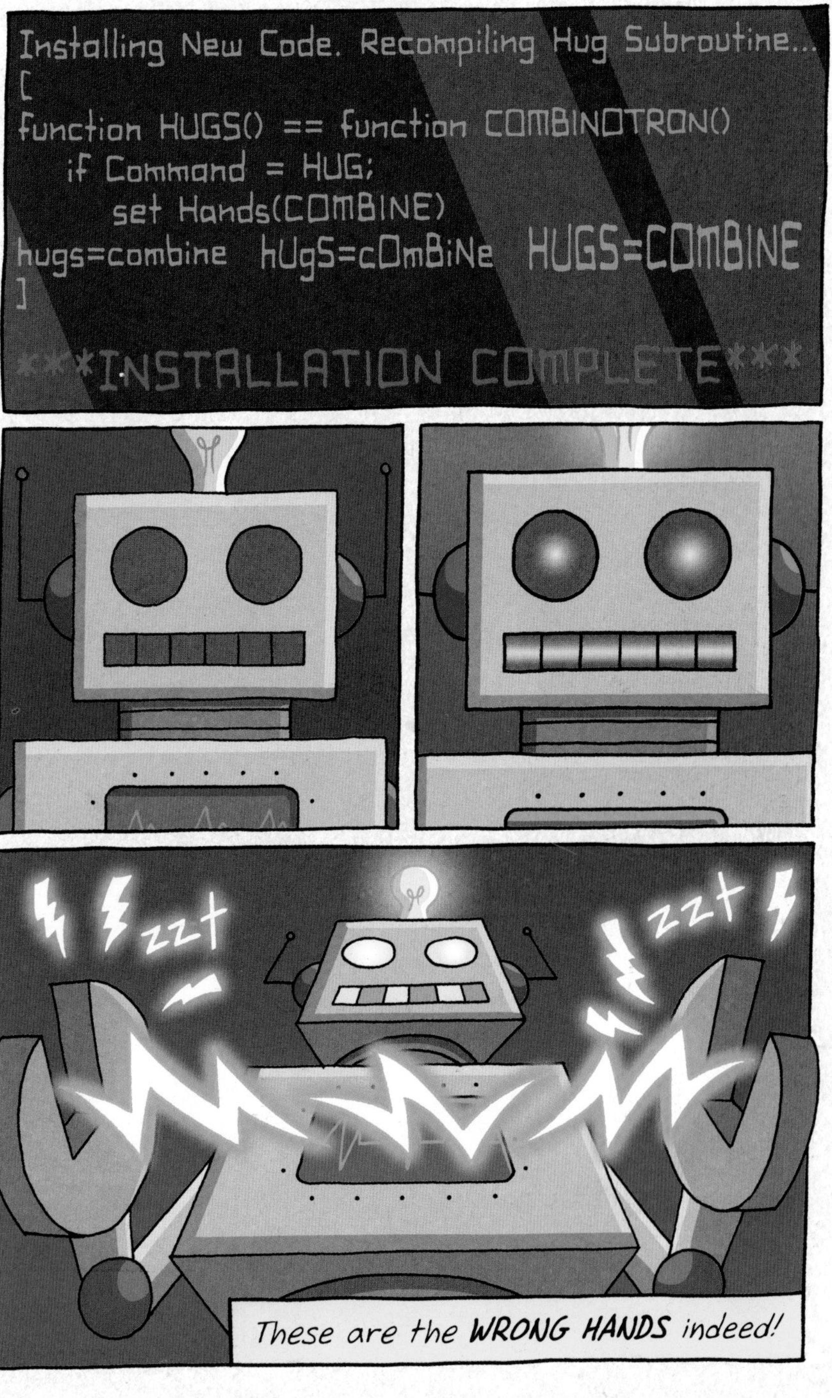
Installing New Code. Recompiling Hug Subroutine...
[
function HUGS() == function COMBINOTRON()
if Command = HUG;
set Hands(COMBINE)
hugs=combine hUgS=cOmBiNe HUGS=COMBINE
]
INSTALLATION COMPLETE
zzt
zzt
These are the **WRONG HANDS** indeed!

Chapter 2

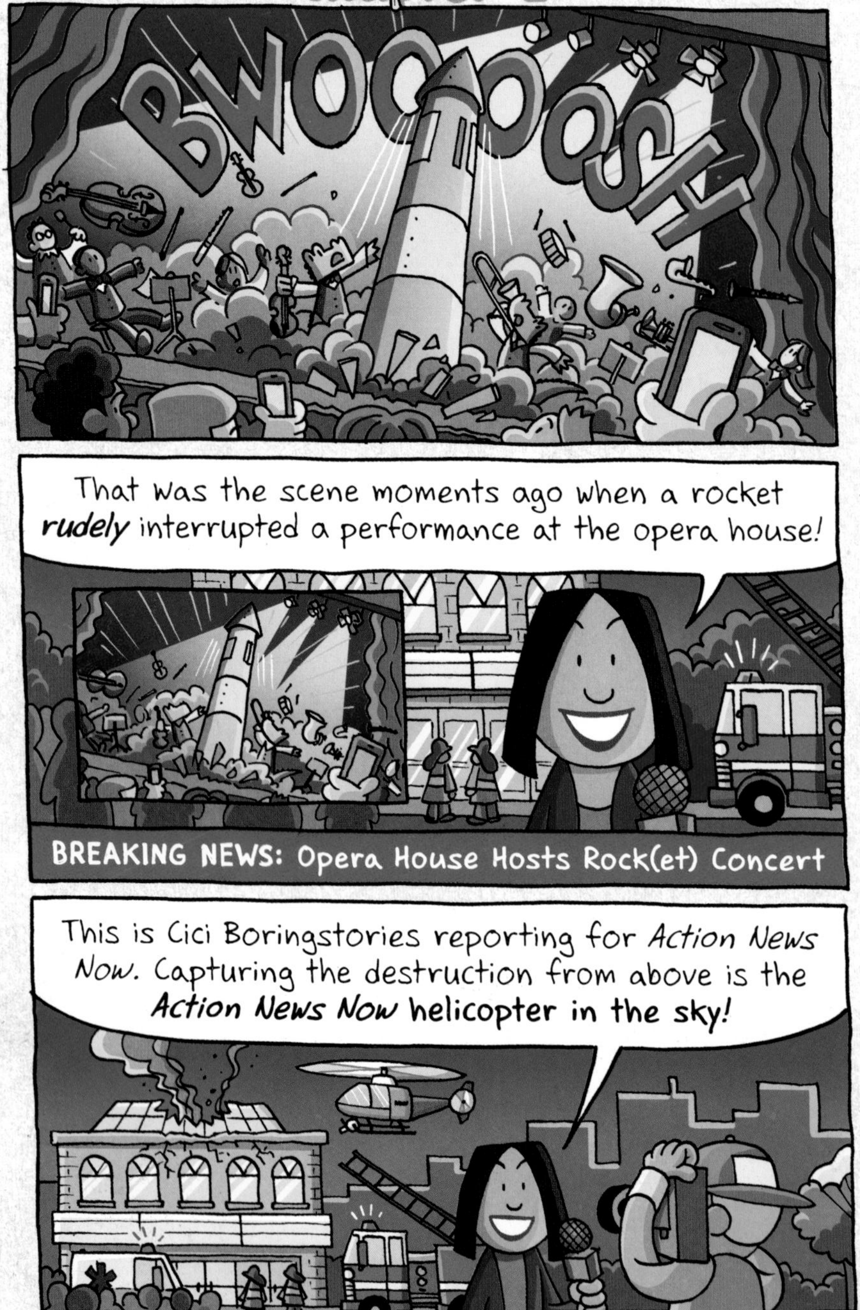
BWOOOOSH
That was the scene moments ago when a rocket *rudely* interrupted a performance at the opera house!
BREAKING NEWS: Opera House Hosts Rock(et) Concert
This is Cici Boringstories reporting for *Action News Now*. Capturing the destruction from above is the **_Action News Now_ helicopter in the sky!**

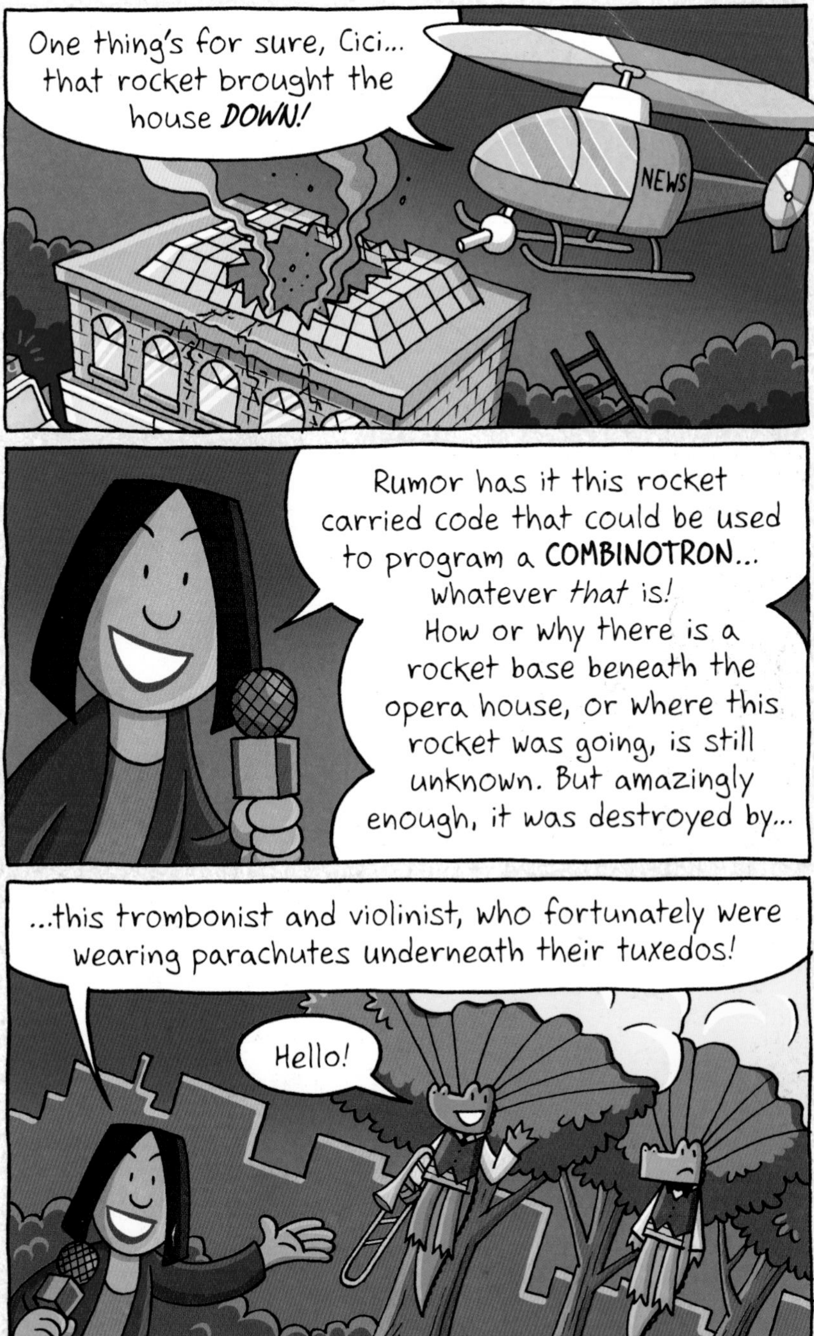
One thing's for sure, Cici... that rocket brought the house **DOWN!**
NEWS
Rumor has it this rocket carried code that could be used to program a **COMBINOTRON**... whatever *that* is! How or why there is a rocket base beneath the opera house, or where this rocket was going, is still unknown. But amazingly enough, it was destroyed by...
...this trombonist and violinist, who fortunately were wearing parachutes underneath their tuxedos!
Hello!

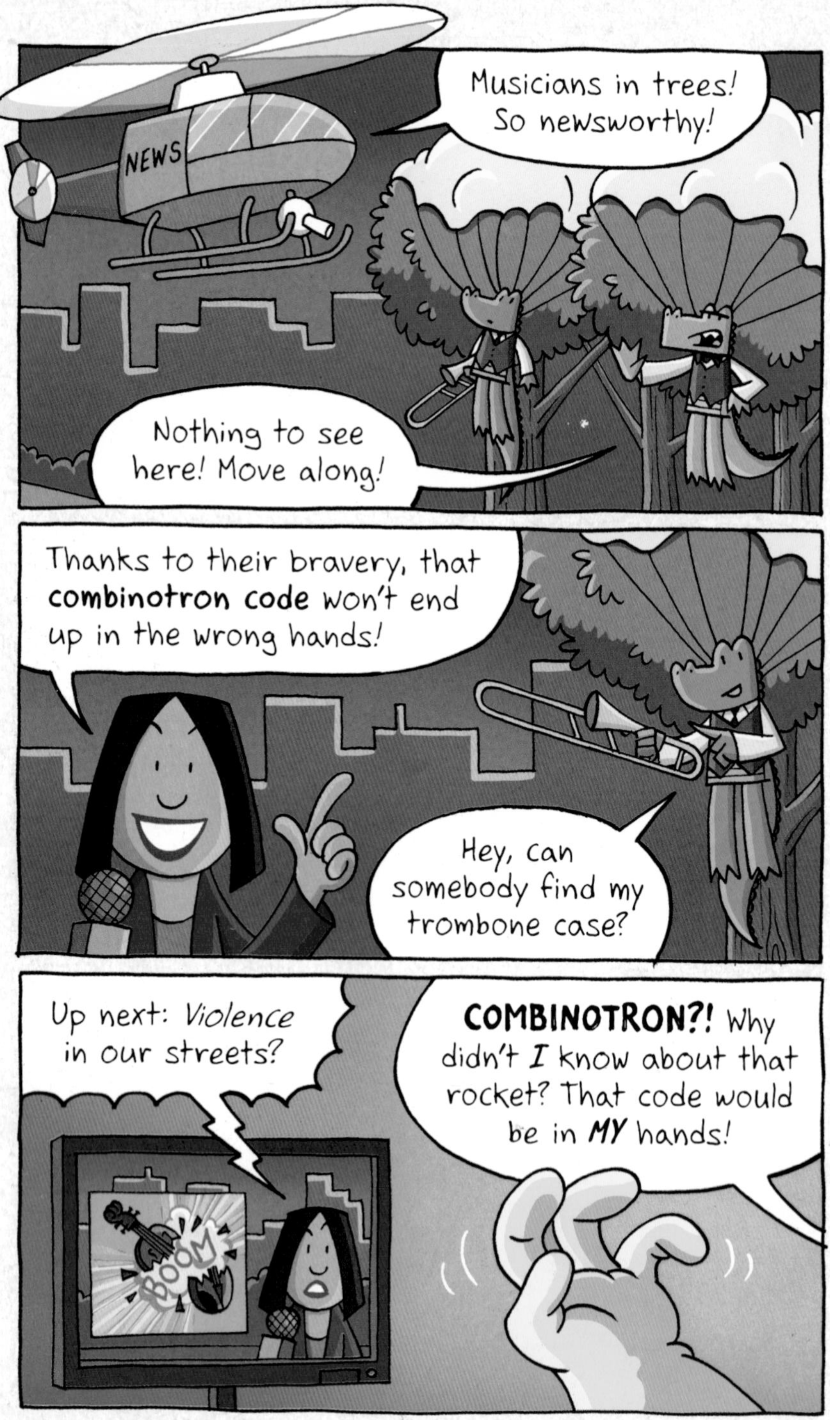
NEWS
Musicians in trees! So newsworthy!
Nothing to see here! Move along!
Thanks to their bravery, that **combinotron code** won't end up in the wrong hands!
Hey, can somebody find my trombone case?
Up next: *Violence* in our streets?
BOOM
COMBINOTRON?! Why didn't *I* know about that rocket? That code would be in ***MY*** hands!

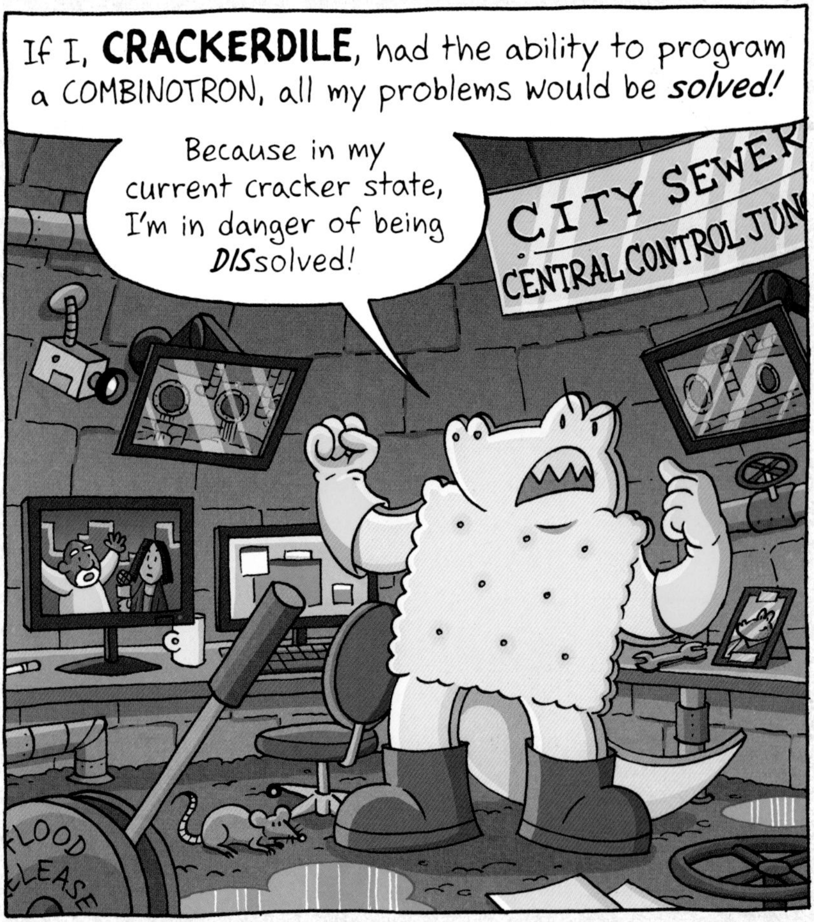
If I, **CRACKERDILE**, had the ability to program a COMBINOTRON, all my problems would be *solved!*
Because in my current cracker state, I'm in danger of being *DIS*solved!
CITY SEWER
CENTRAL CONTROL JUNC
FLOOD RELEASE

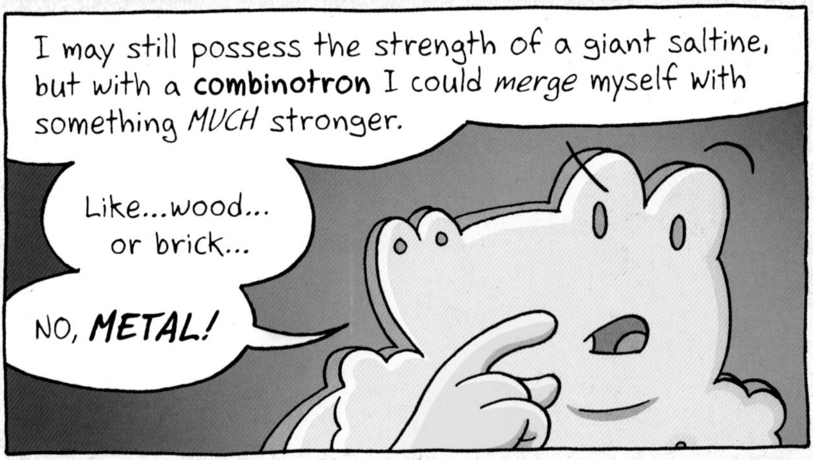
I may still possess the strength of a giant saltine, but with a **combinotron** I could *merge* myself with something *MUCH* stronger.
Like...wood... or brick...
NO, ***METAL!***

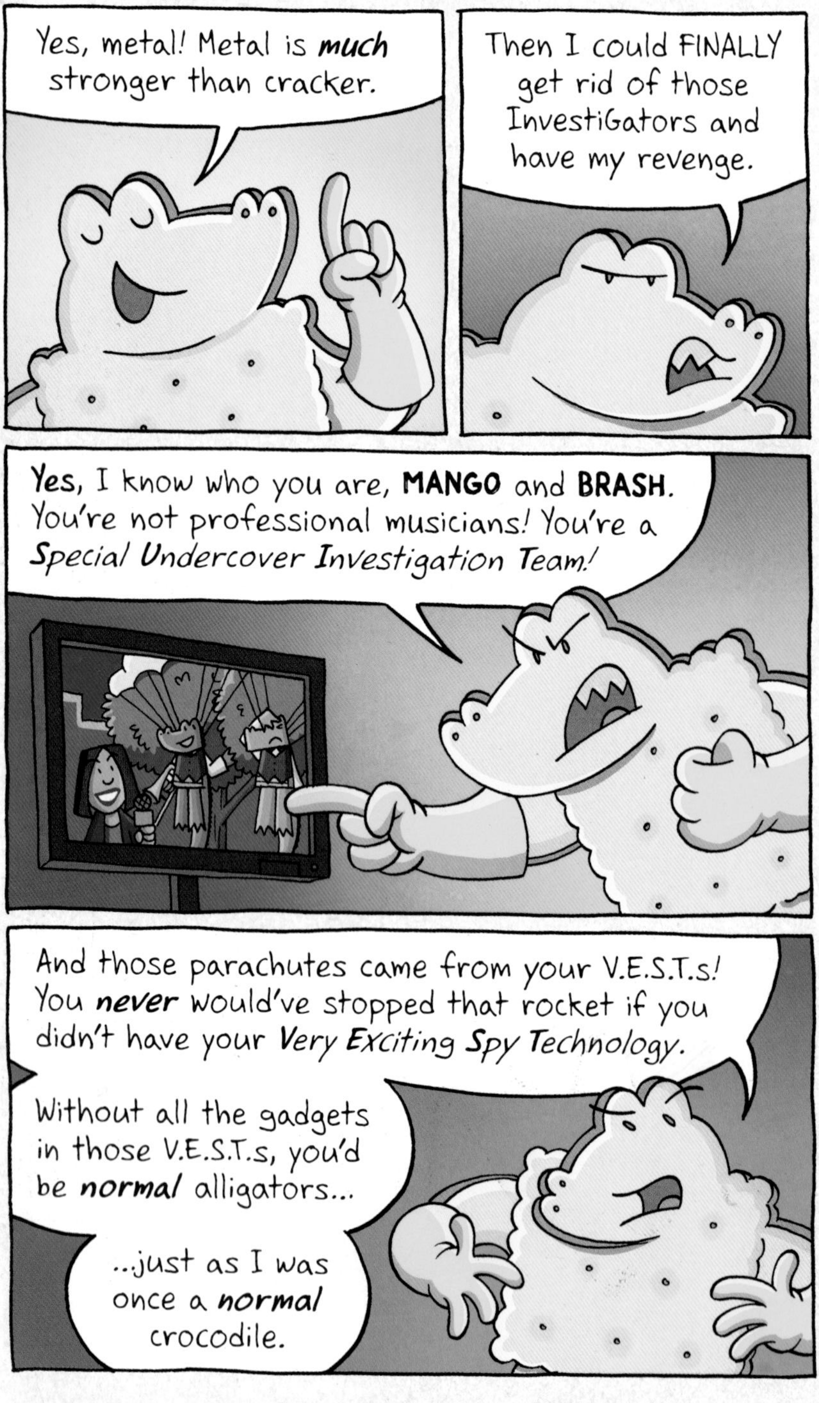
Yes, metal! Metal is **much** stronger than cracker.
Then I could FINALLY get rid of those InvestiGators and have my revenge.
Yes, I know who you are, **MANGO** and **BRASH**. You're not professional musicians! You're a *Special Undercover Investigation Team!*
And those parachutes came from your V.E.S.T.s! You **never** would've stopped that rocket if you didn't have your *Very Exciting Spy Technology*.
Without all the gadgets in those V.E.S.T.s, you'd be ***normal*** alligators...
...just as I was once a ***normal*** crocodile.

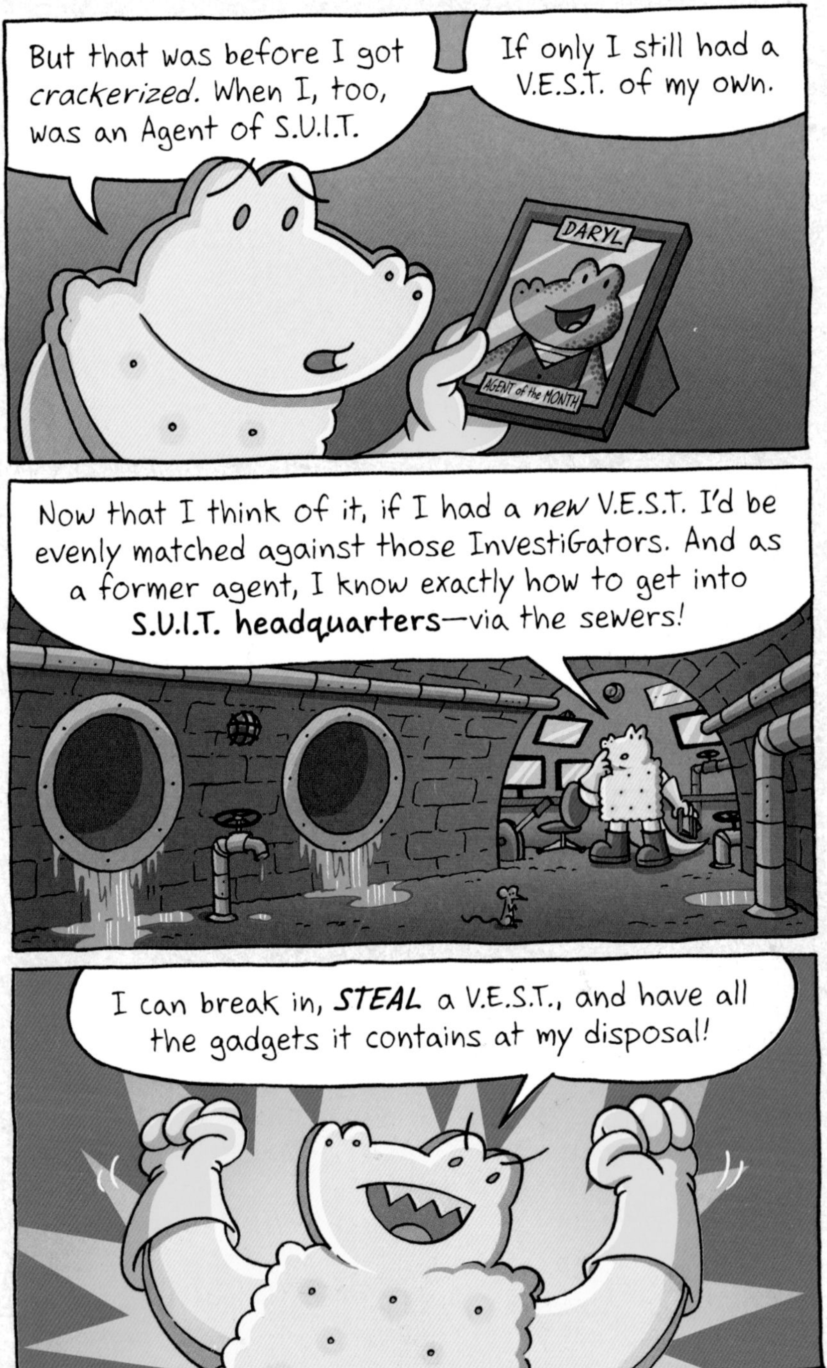
But that was before I got *crackerized*. When I, too, was an Agent of S.U.I.T.
If only I still had a V.E.S.T. of my own.
DARYL
AGENT of the MONTH
Now that I think of it, if I had a *new* V.E.S.T. I'd be evenly matched against those InvestiGators. And as a former agent, I know exactly how to get into **S.U.I.T. headquarters**—via the sewers!
I can break in, ***STEAL*** a V.E.S.T., and have all the gadgets it contains at my disposal!

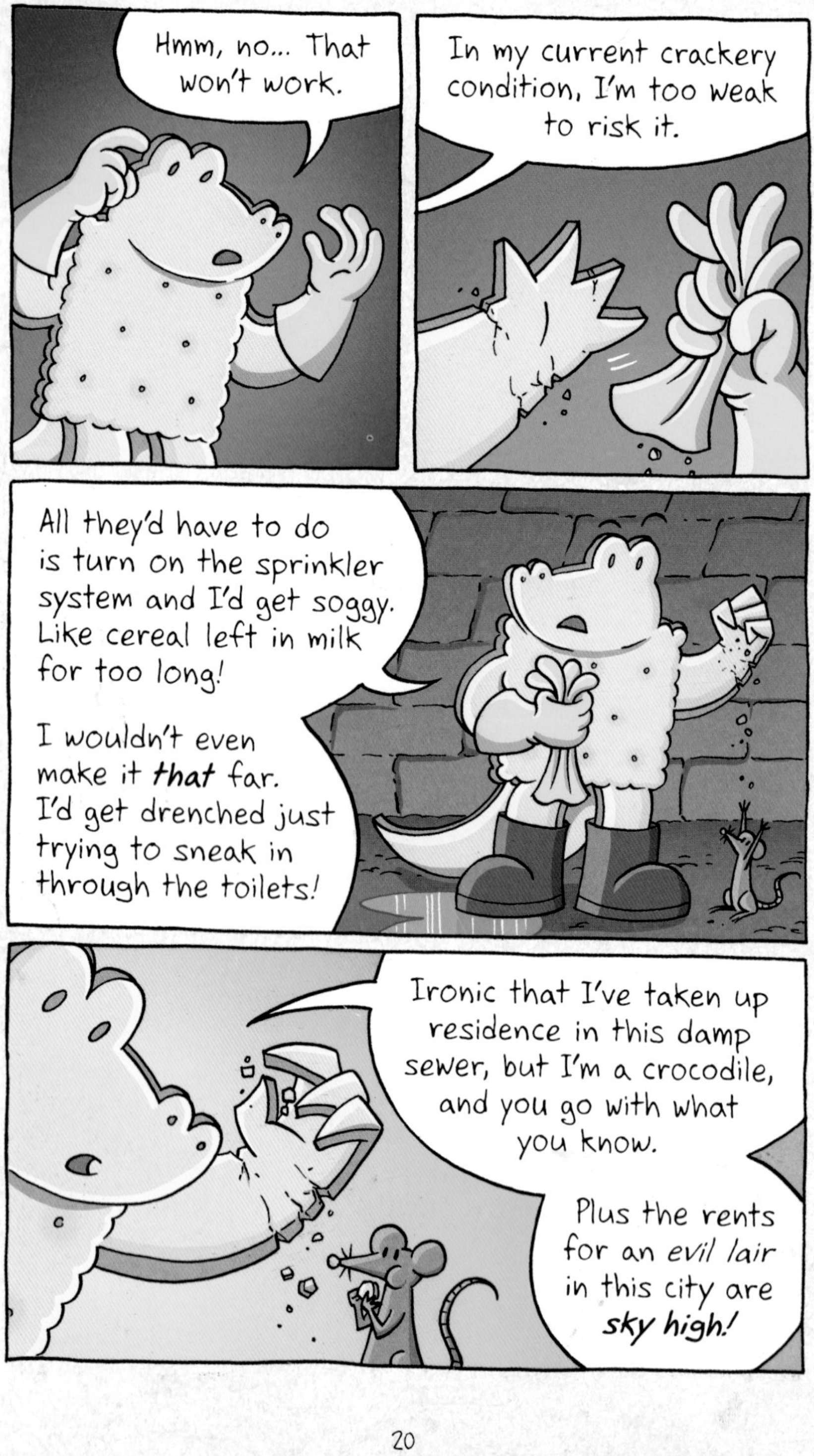
Hmm, no... That won't work.
In my current crackery condition, I'm too weak to risk it.
All they'd have to do is turn on the sprinkler system and I'd get soggy. Like cereal left in milk for too long!
I wouldn't even make it ***that*** far. I'd get drenched just trying to sneak in through the toilets!
Ironic that I've taken up residence in this damp sewer, but I'm a crocodile, and you go with what you know.
Plus the rents for an *evil lair* in this city are ***sky high!***

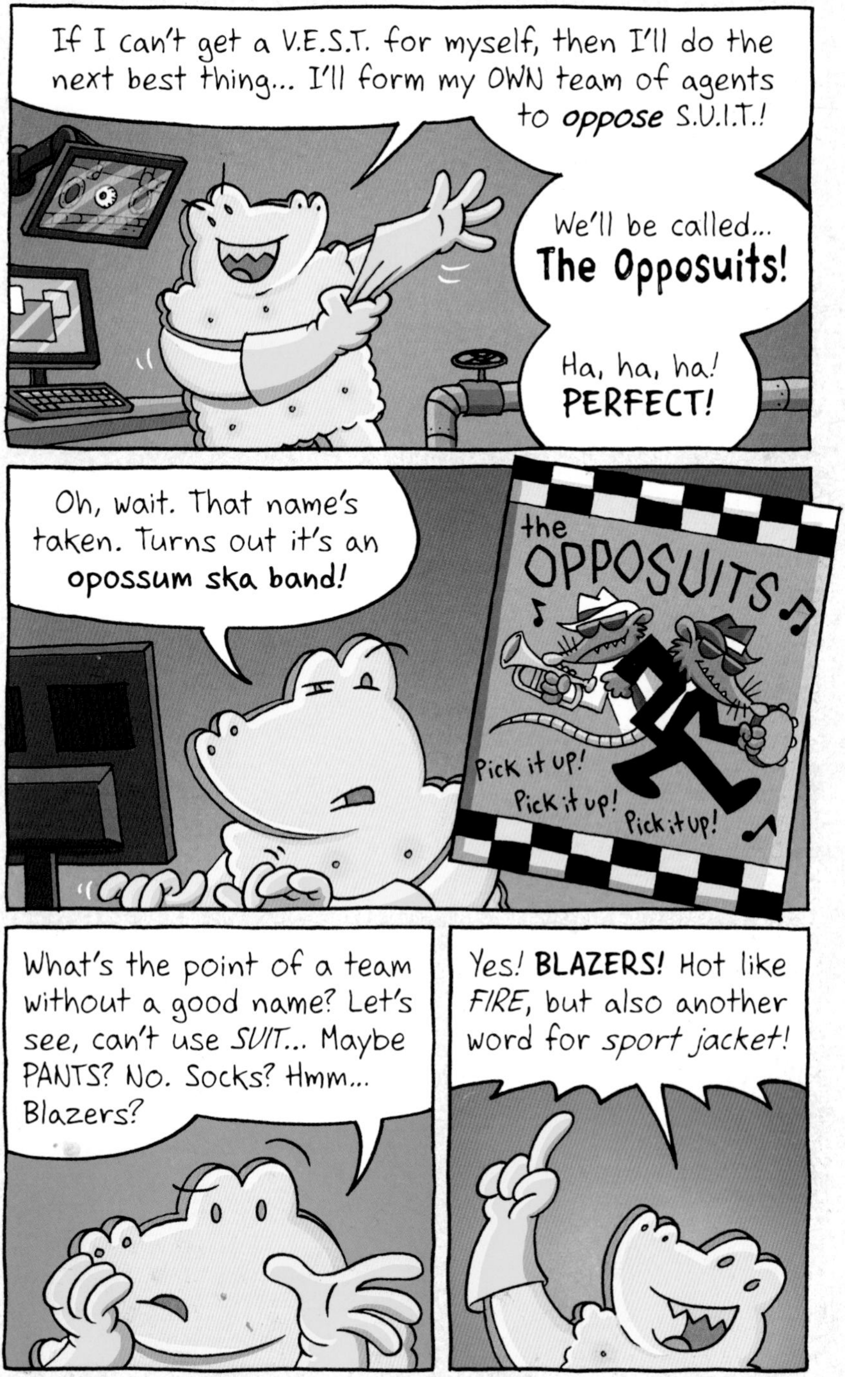
If I can't get a V.E.S.T. for myself, then I'll do the next best thing... I'll form my OWN team of agents to *oppose* S.U.I.T.!
We'll be called... **The Opposuits!**
Ha, ha, ha! **PERFECT!**
Oh, wait. That name's taken. Turns out it's an **opossum ska band!**
the OPPOSUITS
Pick it up! Pick it up! Pick it up!
What's the point of a team without a good name? Let's see, can't use *SUIT*... Maybe PANTS? No. Socks? Hmm... Blazers?
Yes! **BLAZERS!** Hot like *FIRE*, but also another word for *sport jacket*!

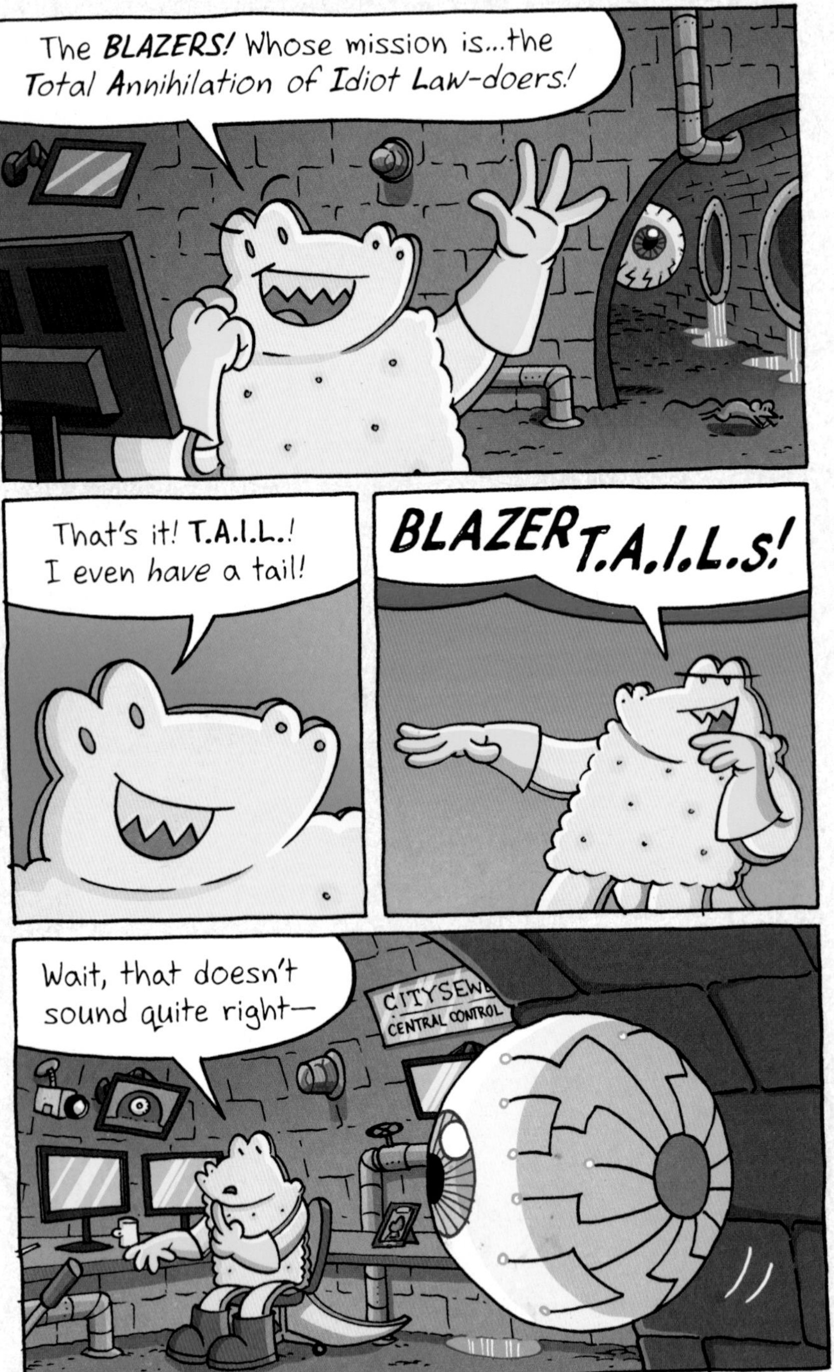
The BLAZERS! Whose mission is...the Total Annihilation of Idiot Law-doers!
That's it! T.A.I.L.! I even have a tail!
BLAZER T.A.I.L.S!
Wait, that doesn't sound quite right—
CENTRAL CONTROL

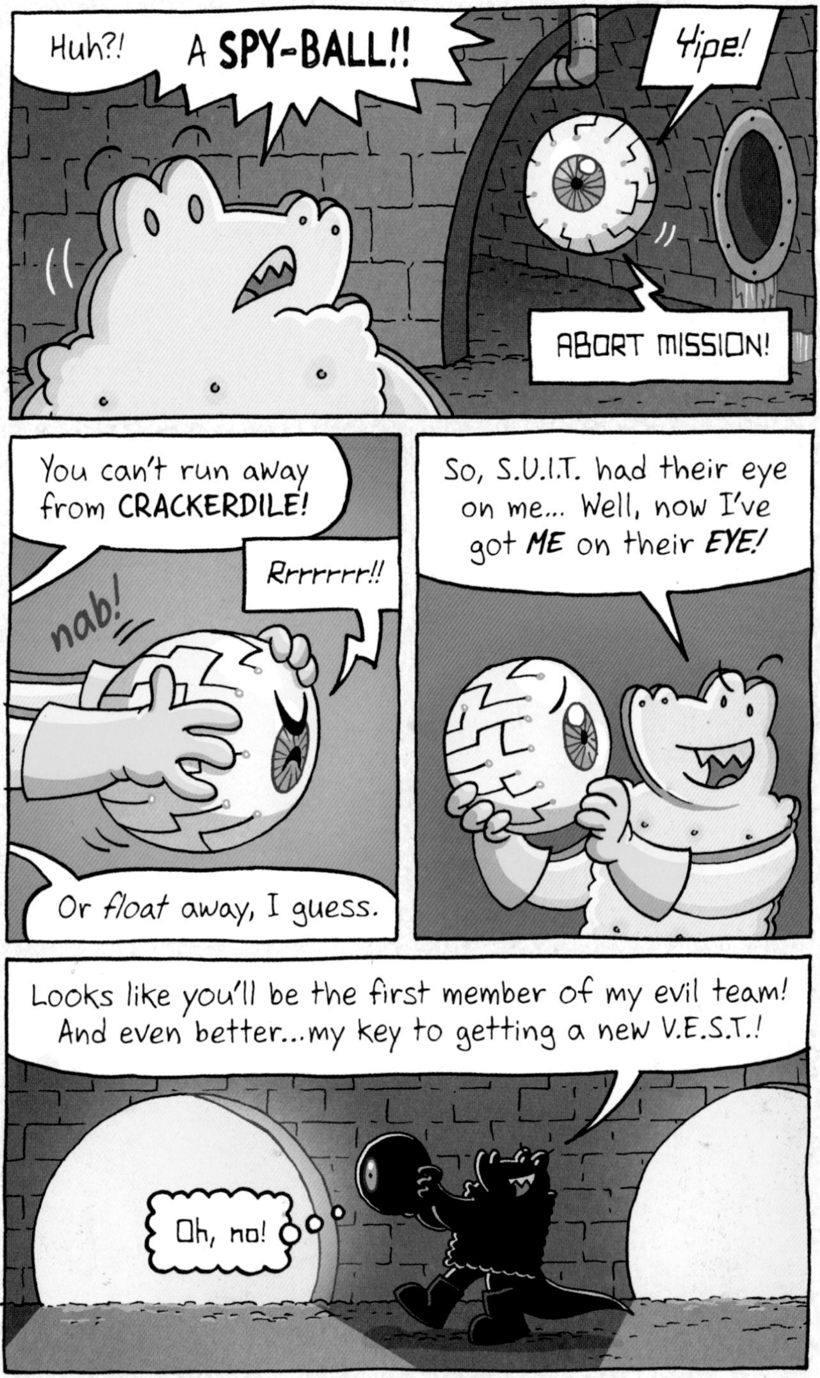

Huh?!
A SPY-BALL!!
Yipe!
ABORT MISSION!
You can't run away from CRACKERDILE!
Rrrrrrr!!
nab!
Or float away, I guess.
So, S.U.I.T. had their eye on me... Well, now I've got ME on their EYE!
Looks like you'll be the first member of my evil team! And even better...my key to getting a new V.E.S.T.!
Oh, no!

Chapter 3

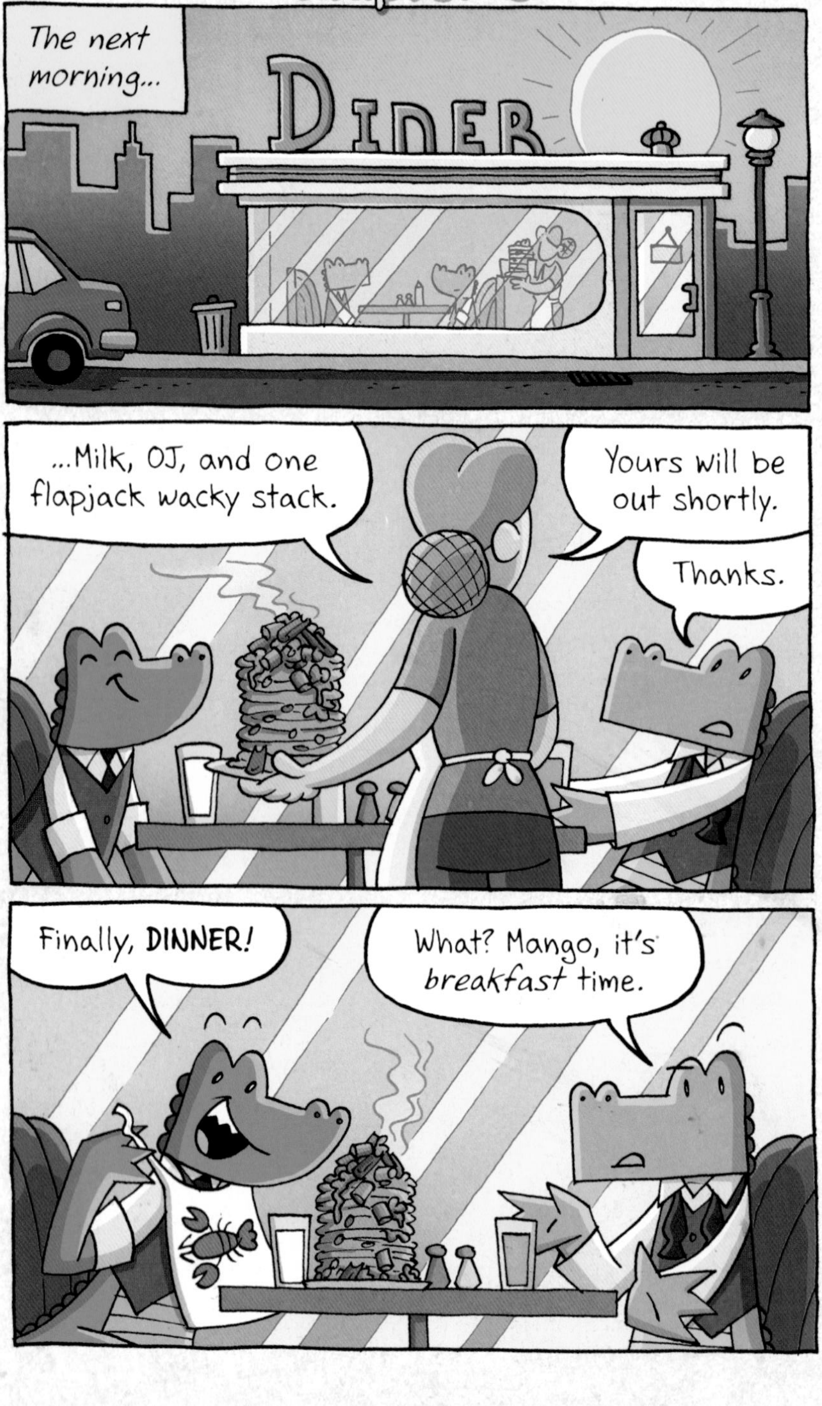

The next morning...
DINER
...Milk, OJ, and one flapjack wacky stack.
Yours will be out shortly.
Thanks.
Finally, **DINNER!**
What? Mango, it's *breakfast* time.

Exactly! Breakfast is the most important meal of the day. Which is why I also eat breakfast for LUNCH and DINNER.

Okaaay...

Shlorp

But since we were stuck in a tree all night, I missed out on yesterday's dinner.

So now I'm having last night's breakfast dinner for breakfast today!

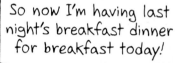

You want some, Brash? It's got pumpkin, rhubarb, jelly beans, garbanzo beans, franks 'n' beans—

No, thanks. I'll wait for my chilaquiles.

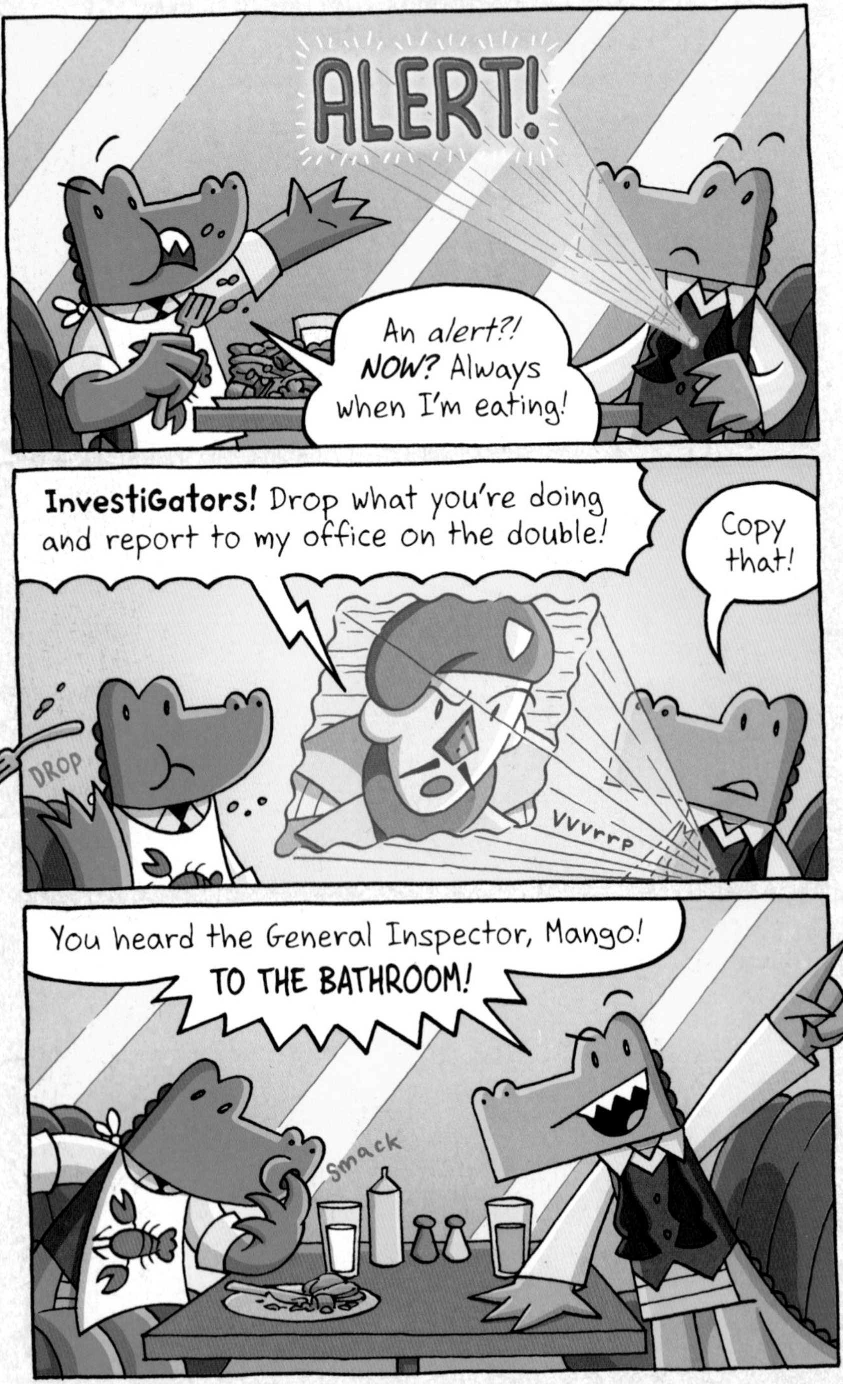
ALERT!
An alert?! NOW? Always when I'm eating!
InvestiGators! Drop what you're doing and report to my office on the double!
Copy that!
DROP
VVVrrp
You heard the General Inspector, Mango! TO THE BATHROOM!
smack

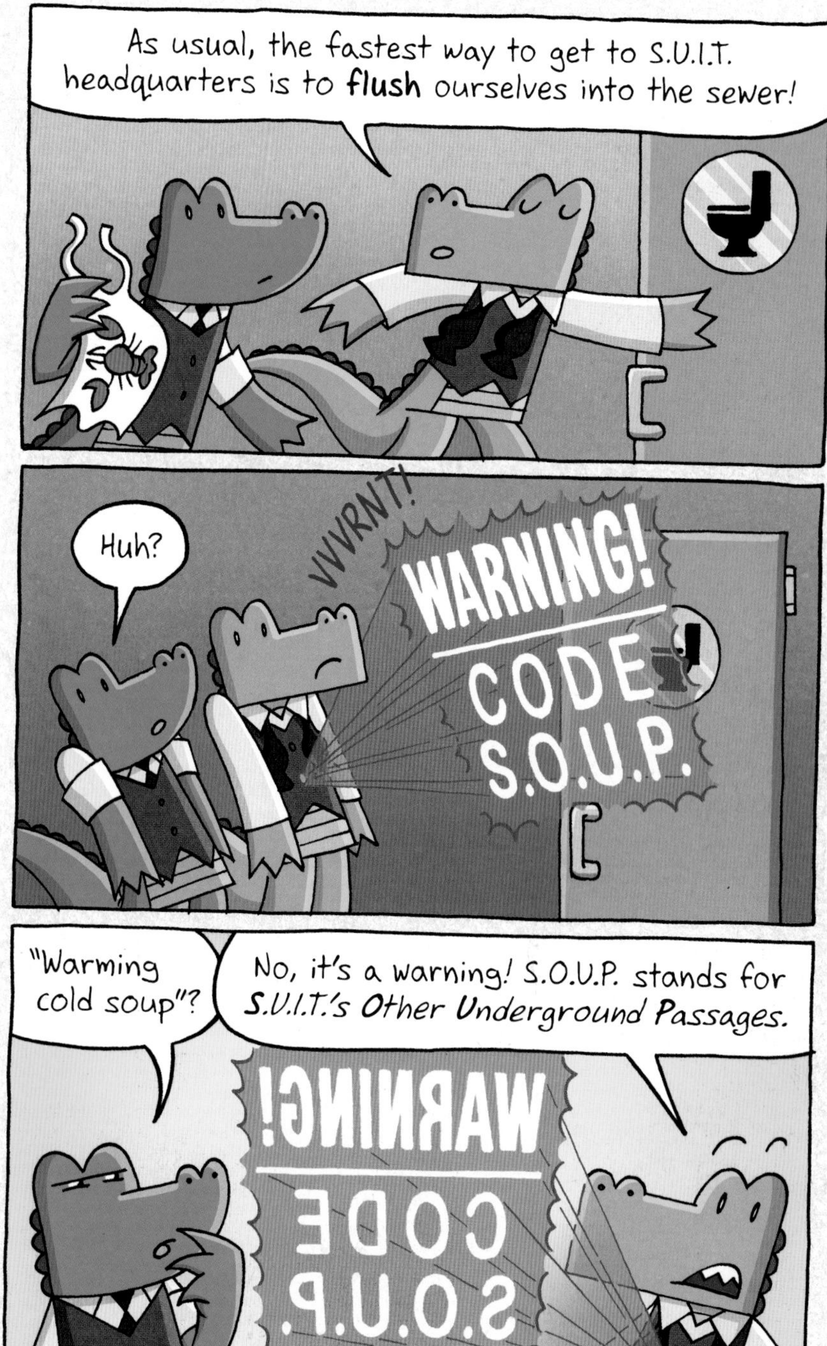

As usual, the fastest way to get to S.U.I.T. headquarters is to **flush** ourselves into the sewer!
Huh?
VVVRNT!
WARNING! CODE S.O.U.P.
"Warming cold soup"?
No, it's a warning! S.O.U.P. stands for *S.U.I.T.'s Other Underground Passages.*

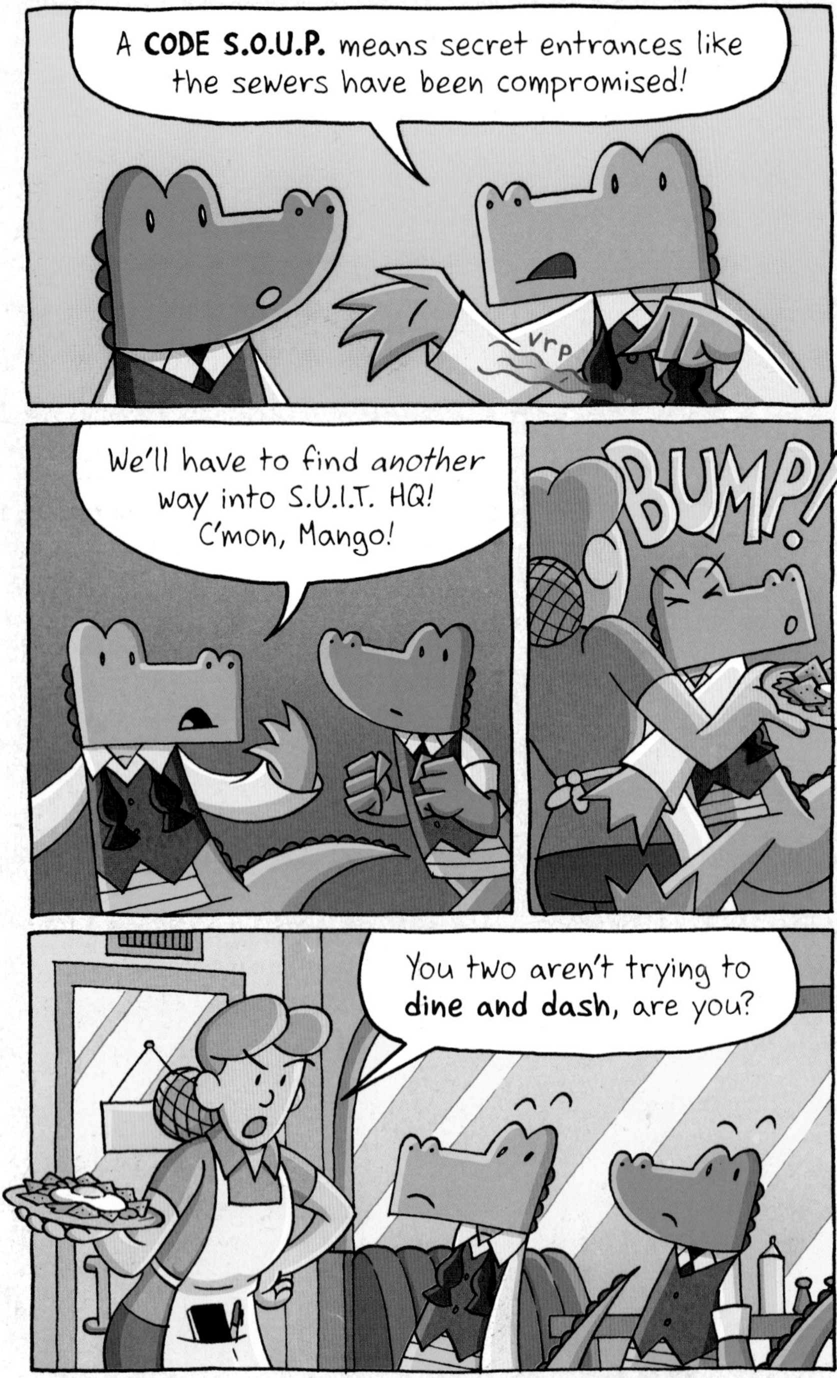
A **CODE S.O.U.P.** means secret entrances like the sewers have been compromised!
VRP
We'll have to find *another* way into S.U.I.T. HQ! C'mon, Mango!
BUMP!
You two aren't trying to **dine and dash**, are you?

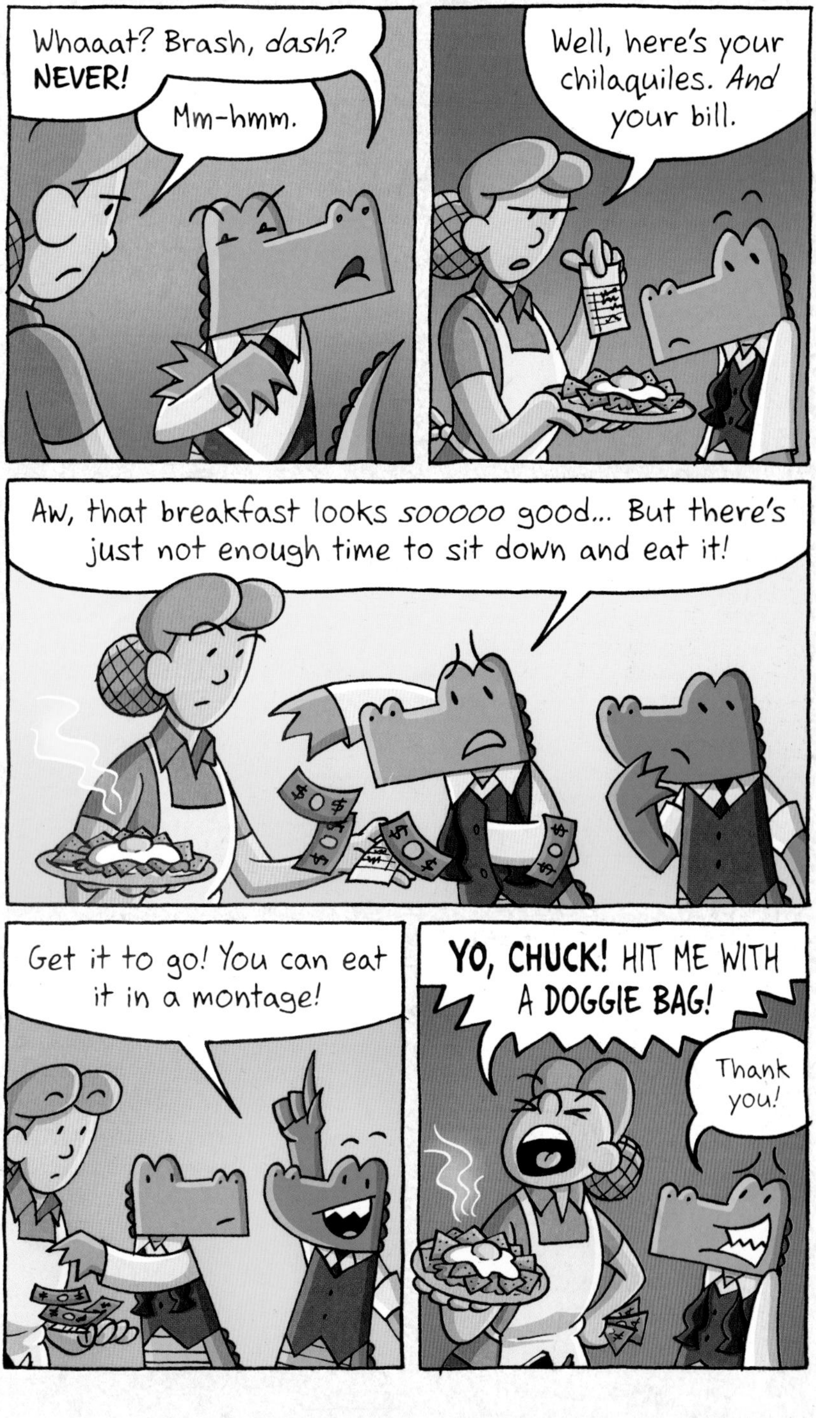
Whaaat? Brash, dash? NEVER!
Mm-hmm.
Well, here's your chilaquiles. And your bill.
Aw, that breakfast looks sooooo good... But there's just not enough time to sit down and eat it!
Get it to go! You can eat it in a montage!
YO, CHUCK! HIT ME WITH A DOGGIE BAG!
Thank you!

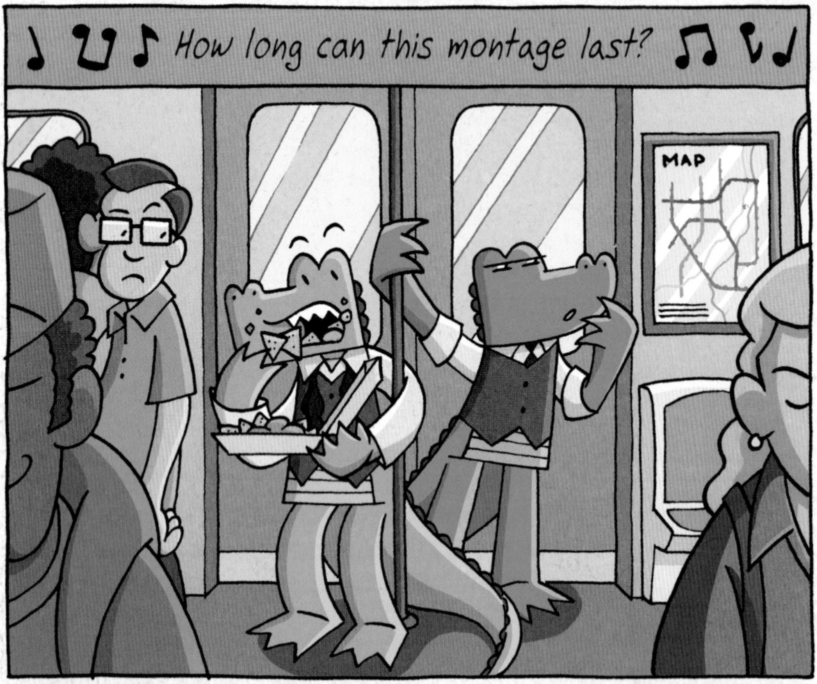
How long can this montage last?
MAP

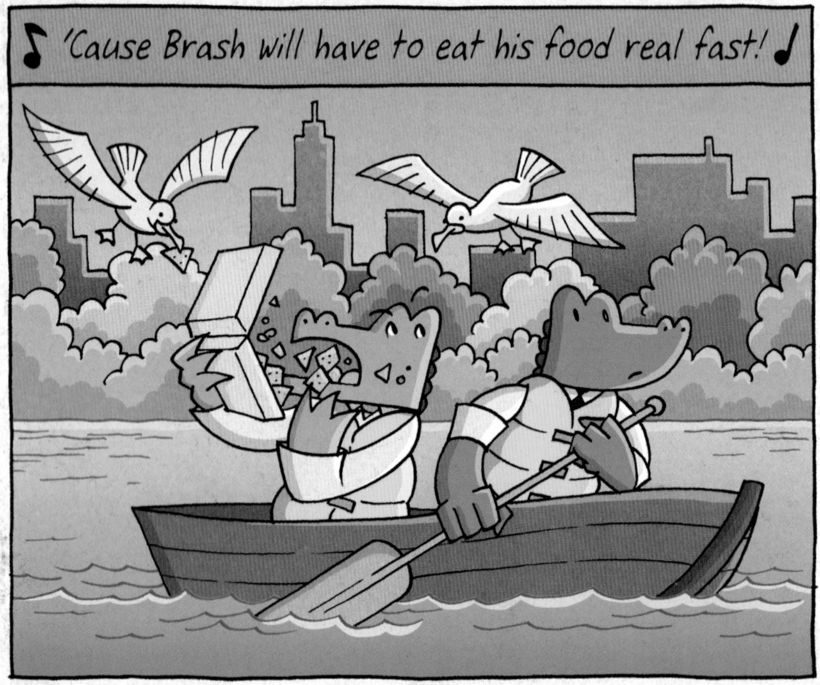
'Cause Brash will have to eat his food real fast!

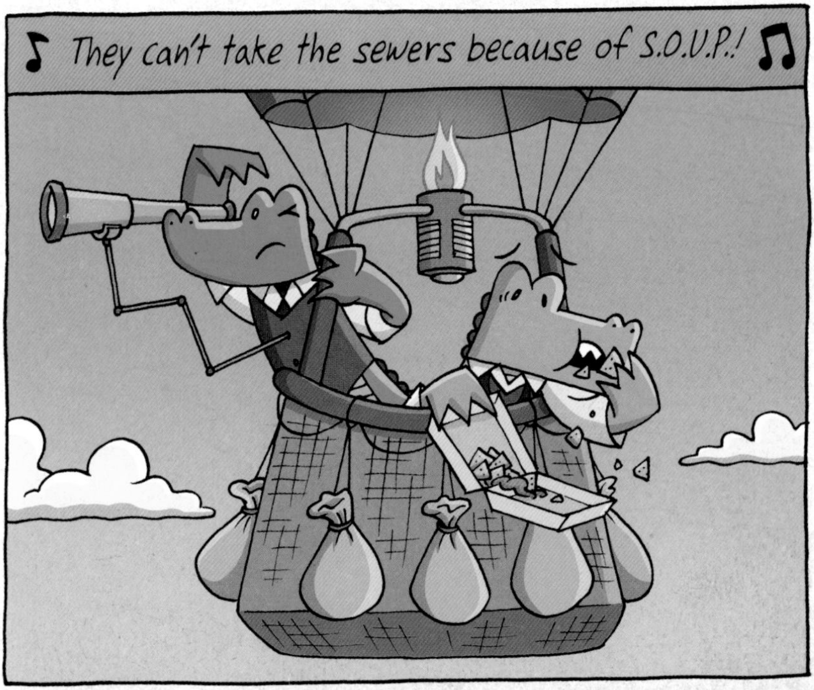
They can't take the sewers because of S.O.U.P.!

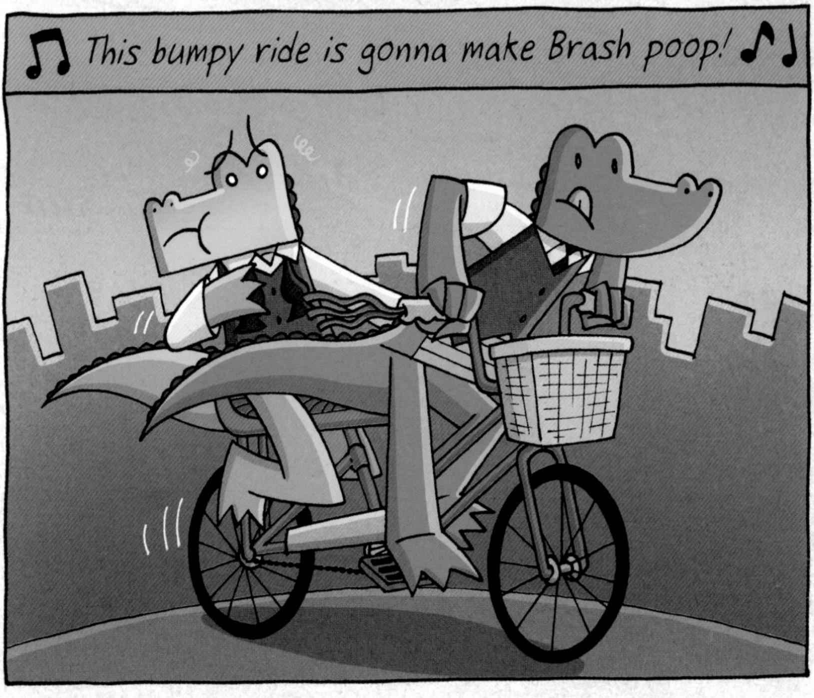
This bumpy ride is gonna make Brash poop!

Chapter 4

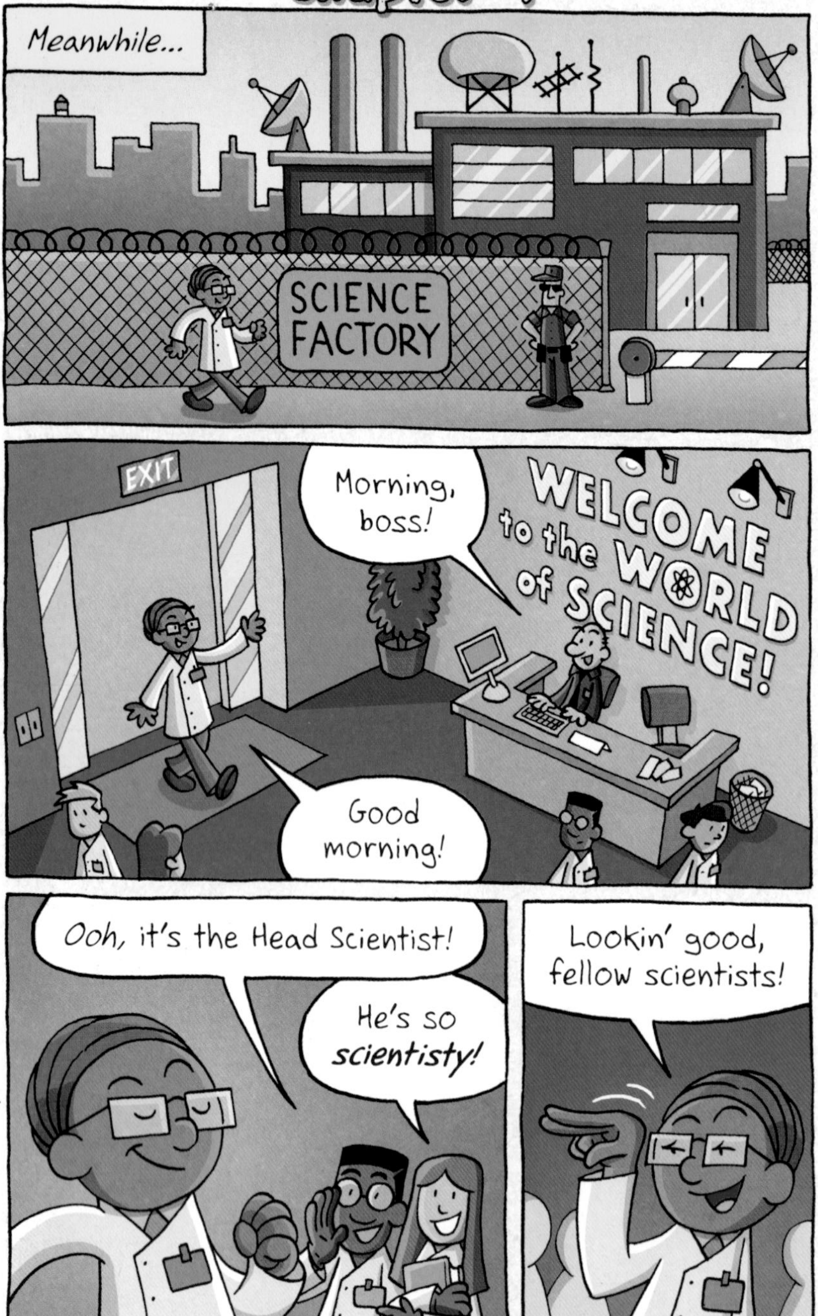
Meanwhile...
SCIENCE FACTORY
EXIT
WELCOME to the WORLD of SCIENCE!
Morning, boss!
Good morning!
Ooh, it's the Head Scientist!
He's so *scientisty!*
Lookin' good, fellow scientists!

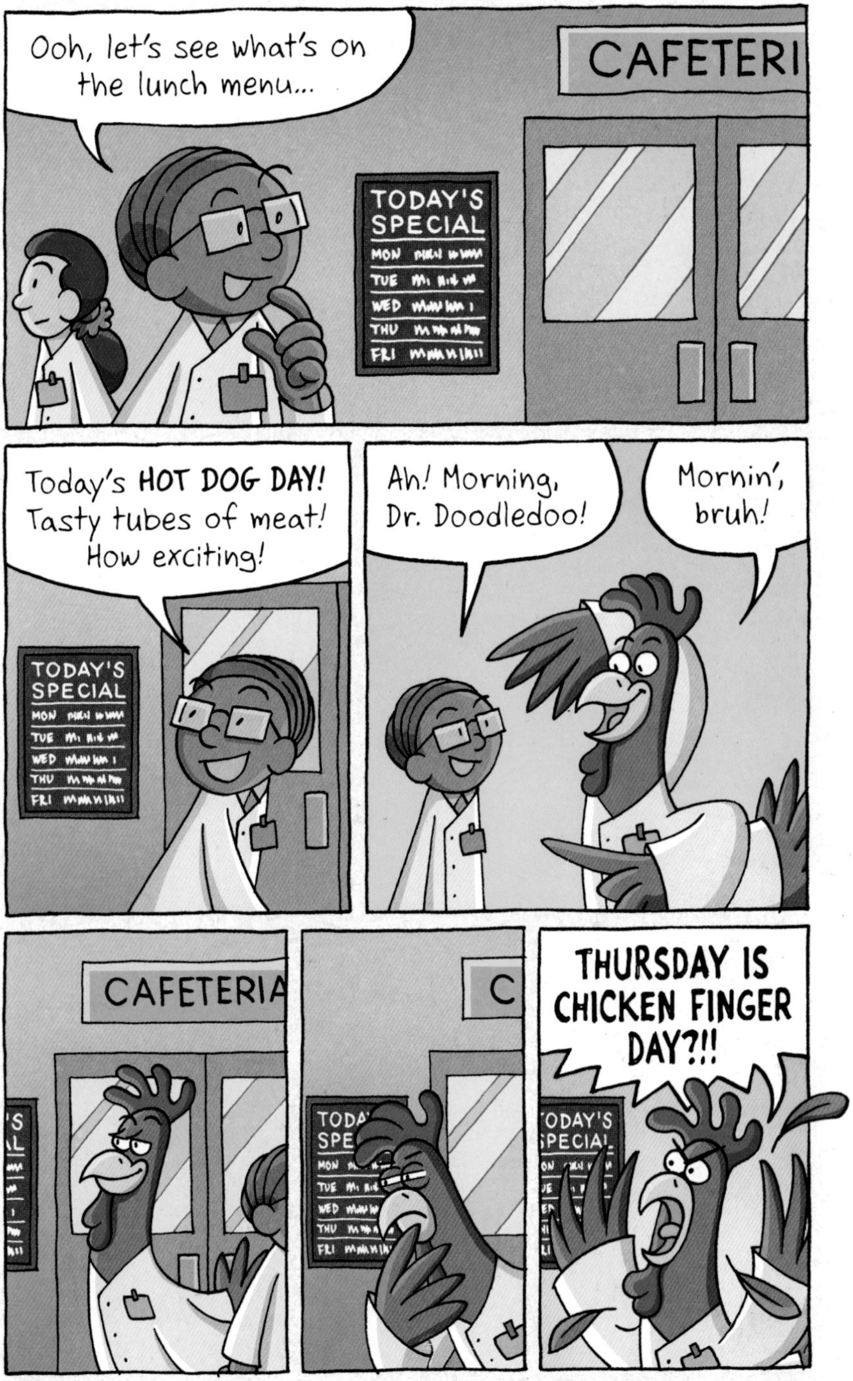
Ooh, let's see what's on the lunch menu...
CAFETERI
TODAY'S SPECIAL
MON
TUE
WED
THU
FRI
Today's HOT DOG DAY! Tasty tubes of meat! How exciting!
TODAY'S SPECIAL
Ah! Morning, Dr. Doodledoo!
Mornin', bruh!
CAFETERIA
THURSDAY IS CHICKEN FINGER DAY?!!

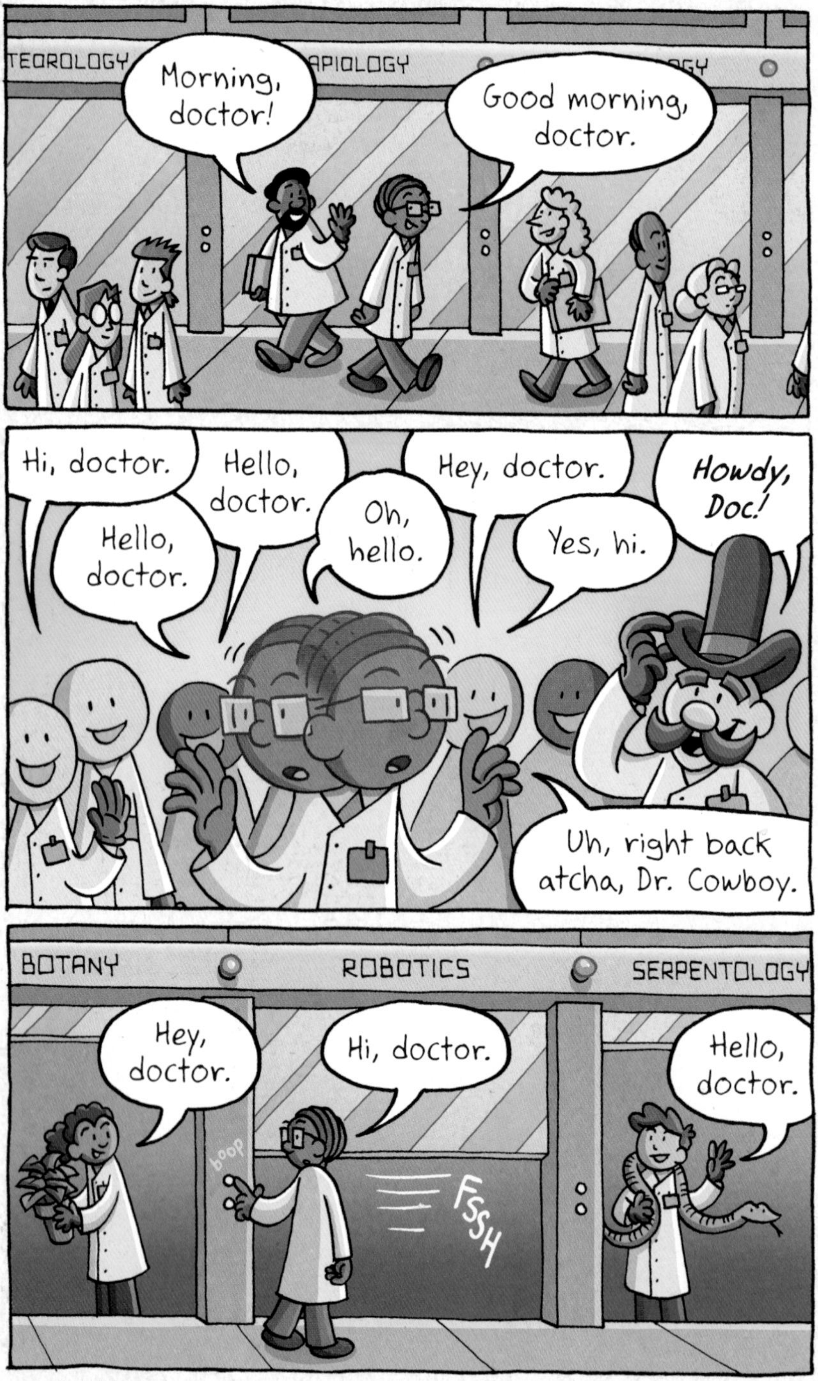

TEOROLOGY
APIOLOGY
Morning, doctor!
Good morning, doctor.
Hi, doctor.
Hello, doctor.
Hello, doctor.
Oh, hello.
Hey, doctor.
Yes, hi.
Howdy, Doc!
Uh, right back atcha, Dr. Cowboy.
BOTANY
ROBOTICS
SERPENTOLOGY
Hey, doctor.
Hi, doctor.
Hello, doctor.
boop
FSSH

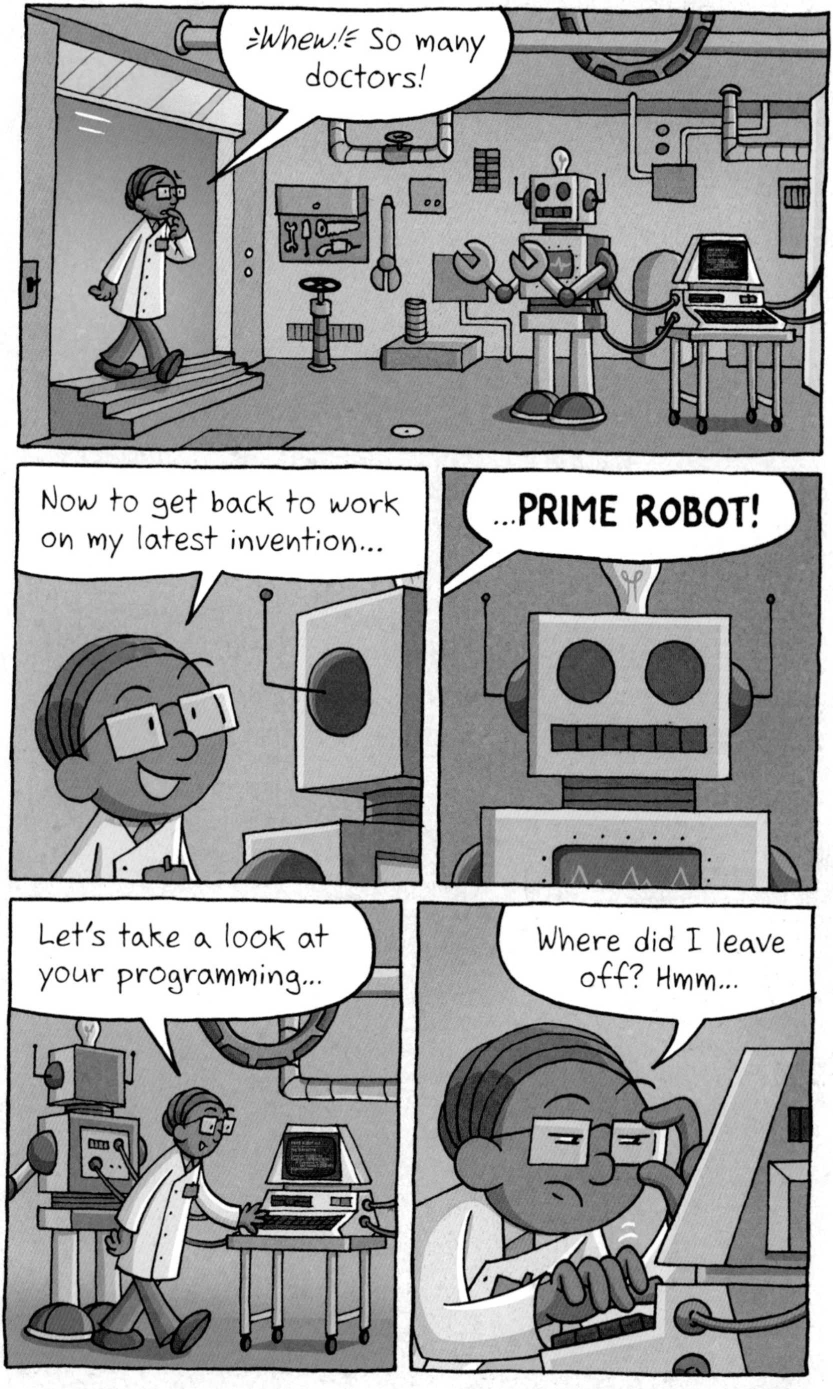
Whew! So many doctors!
Now to get back to work on my latest invention...
...PRIME ROBOT!
Let's take a look at your programming...
Where did I leave off? Hmm...

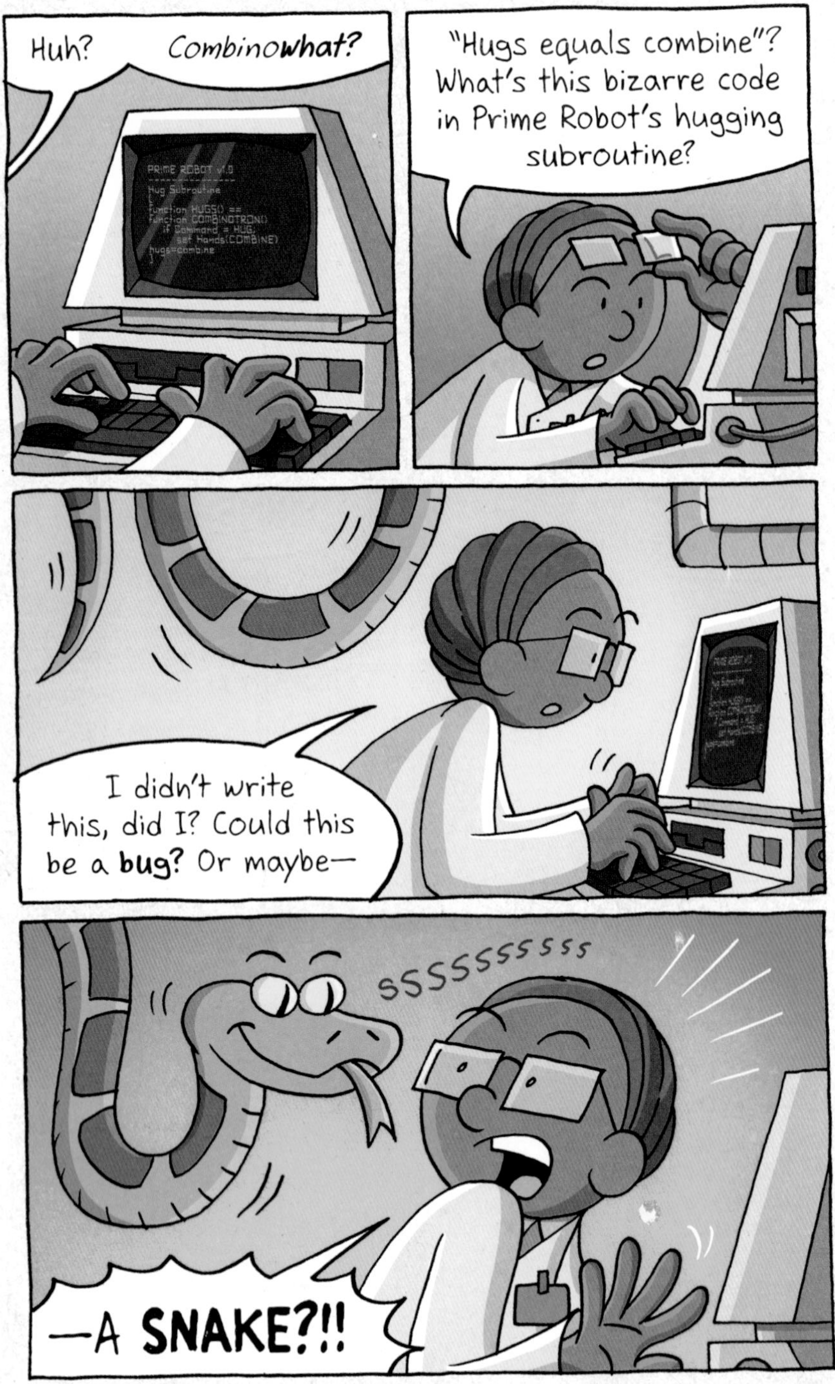
Huh? Combinowhat?
PRIME ROBOT v1.0
Hug Subroutine
function HUGS() ==
function COMBINOTRON()
if Command = HUG;
set Hands(COMBINE)
hugs=combine
"Hugs equals combine"? What's this bizarre code in Prime Robot's hugging subroutine?
I didn't write this, did I? Could this be a **bug?** Or maybe—
SSSSSSSSSS
—A **SNAKE?!!**

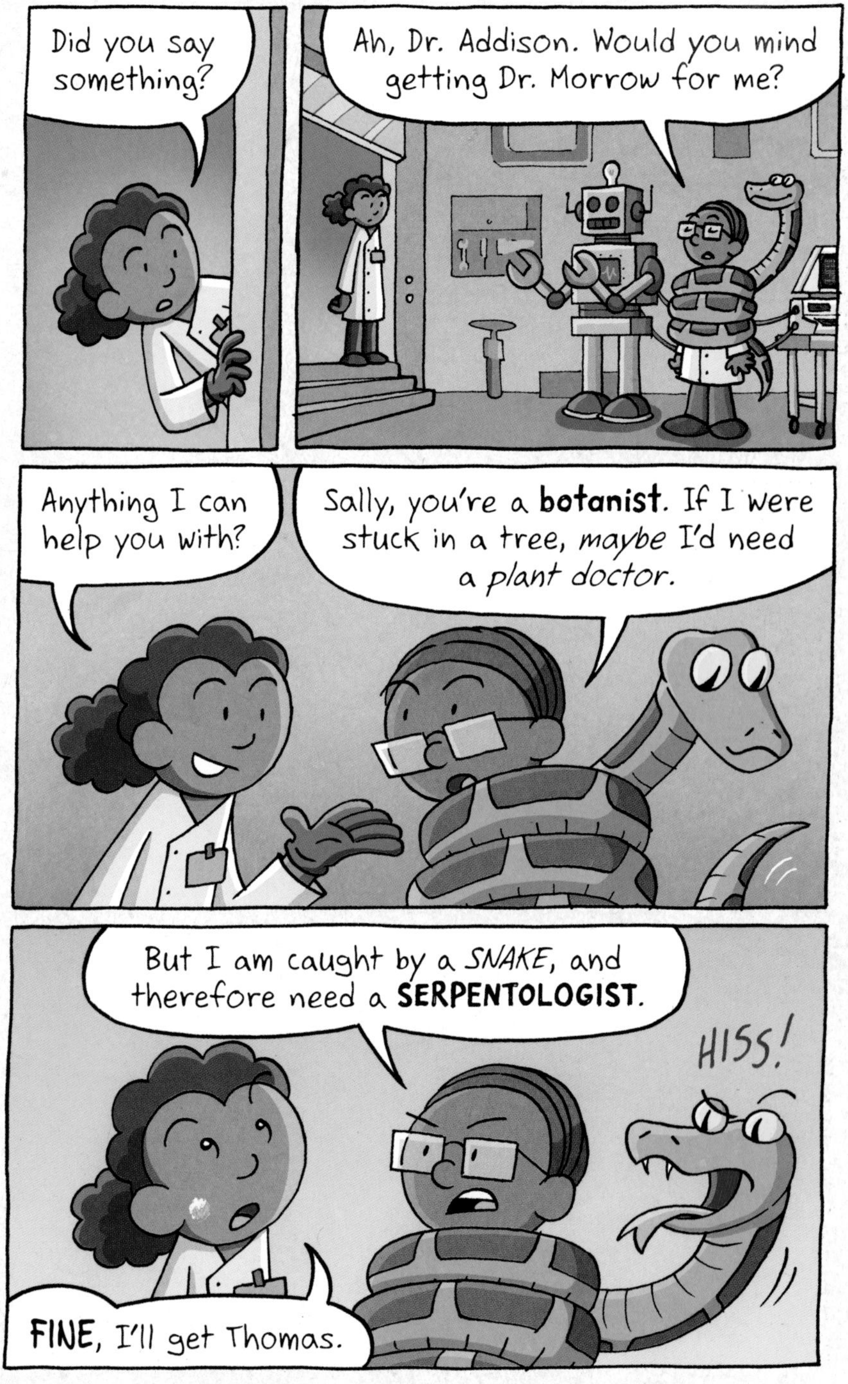
Did you say something?
Ah, Dr. Addison. Would you mind getting Dr. Morrow for me?
Anything I can help you with?
Sally, you're a **botanist**. If I were stuck in a tree, *maybe* I'd need a *plant doctor*.
But I am caught by a *SNAKE*, and therefore need a **SERPENTOLOGIST**.
HISS!
FINE, I'll get Thomas.

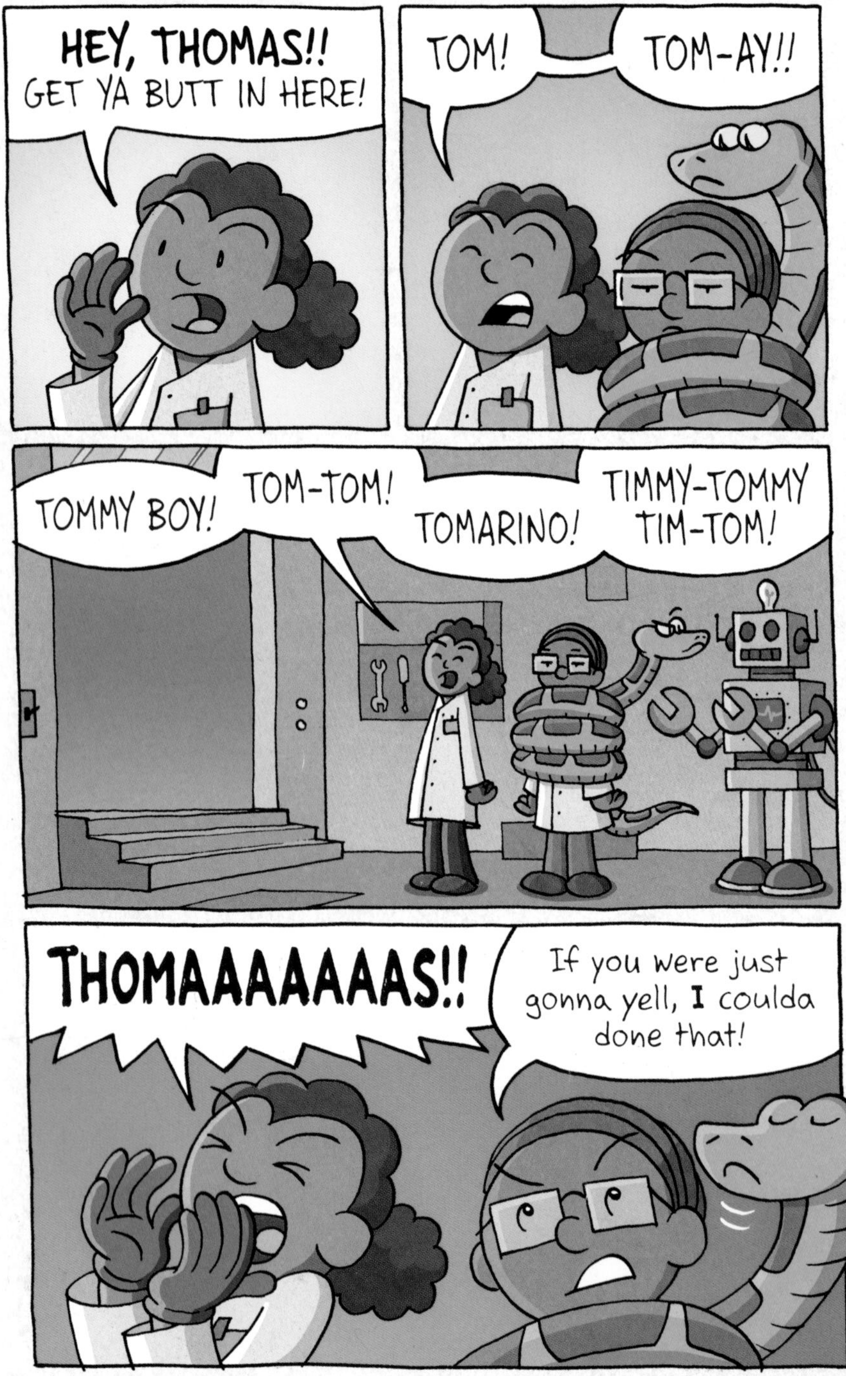
HEY, THOMAS!! GET YA BUTT IN HERE!
TOM!
TOM-AY!!
TOMMY BOY!
TOM-TOM!
TOMARINO!
TIMMY-TOMMY TIM-TOM!
THOMAAAAAAAS!!
If you were just gonna yell, I coulda done that!

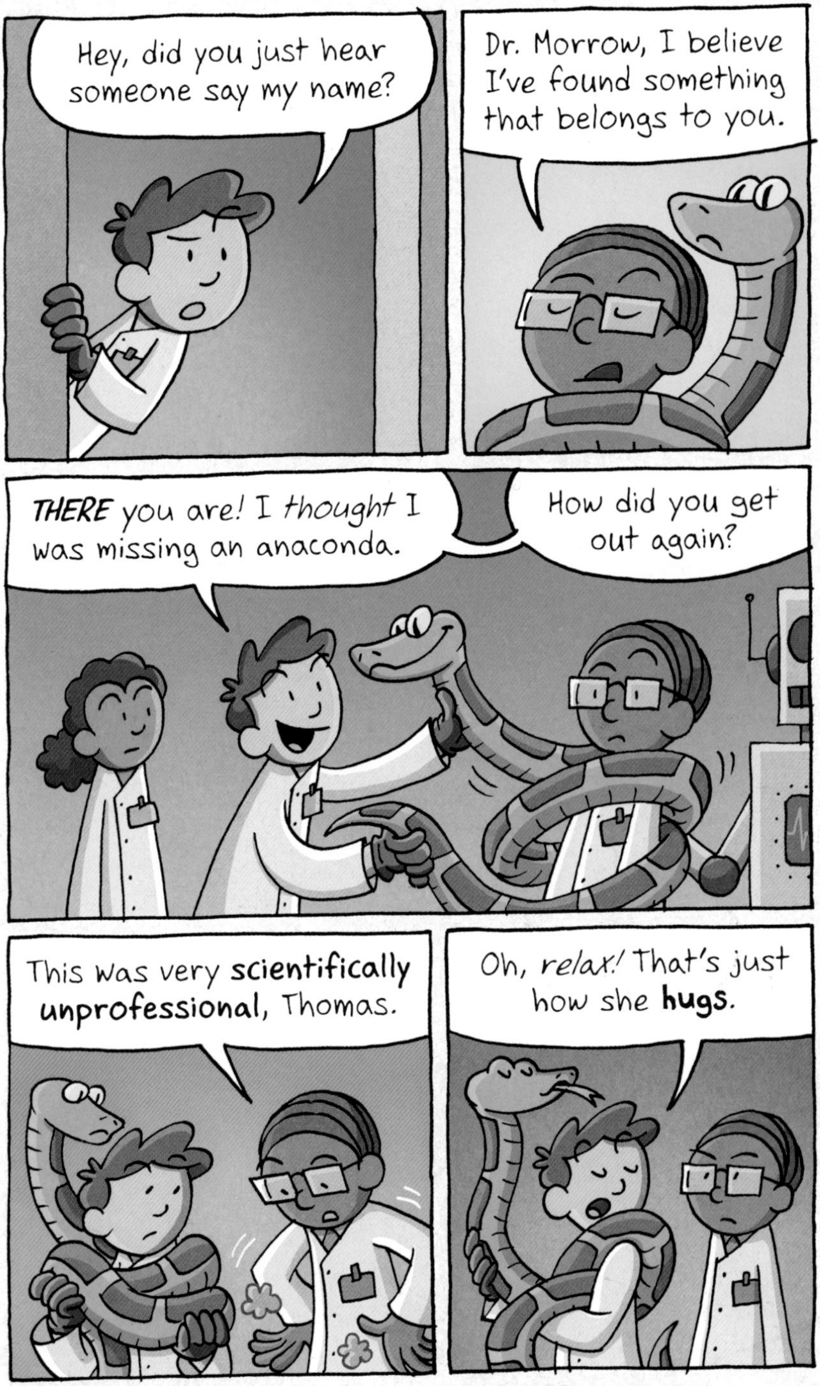
Hey, did you just hear someone say my name?
Dr. Morrow, I believe I've found something that belongs to you.
THERE you are! I thought I was missing an anaconda.
How did you get out again?
This was very scientifically unprofessional, Thomas.
Oh, relax! That's just how she hugs.

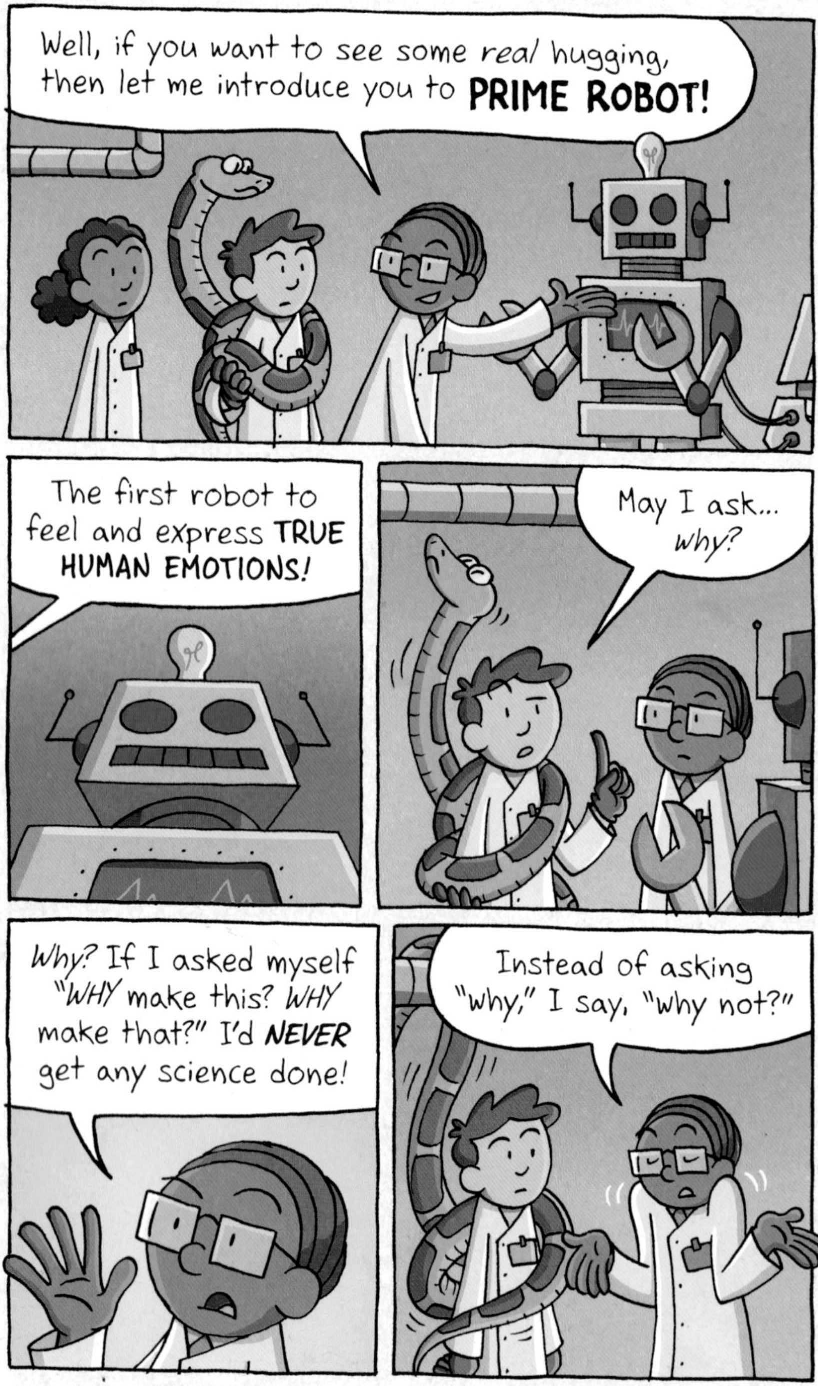
Well, if you want to see some *real* hugging, then let me introduce you to **PRIME ROBOT!**
The first robot to feel and express **TRUE HUMAN EMOTIONS!**
May I ask... *why?*
Why? If I asked myself "*WHY* make this? *WHY* make that?" I'd ***NEVER*** get any science done!
Instead of asking "why," I say, "why not?"

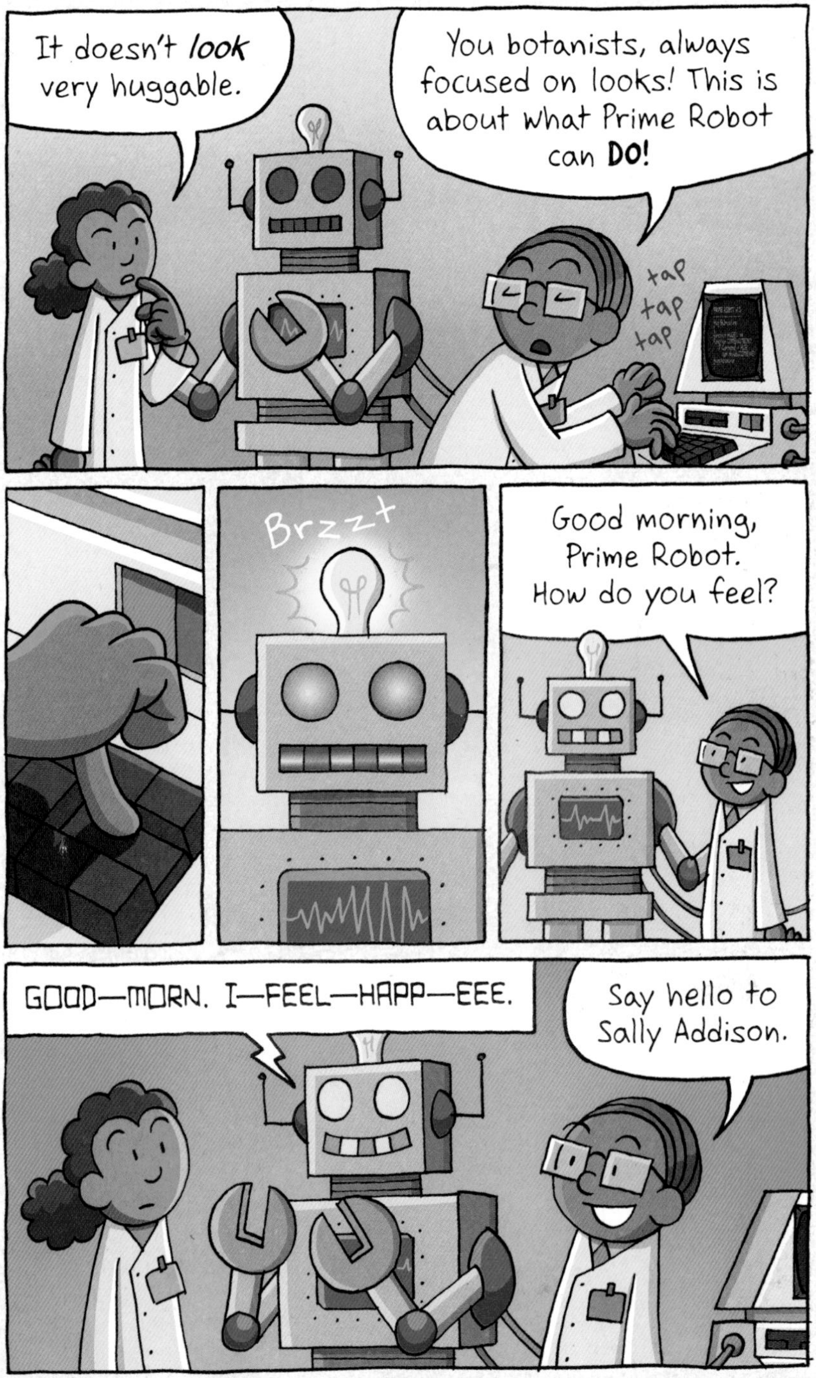
It doesn't *look* very huggable.
You botanists, always focused on looks! This is about what Prime Robot can **DO**!
tap tap tap
Brzzt
Good morning, Prime Robot. How do you feel?
GOOD—MORN. I—FEEL—HAPP—EEE.
Say hello to Sally Addison.

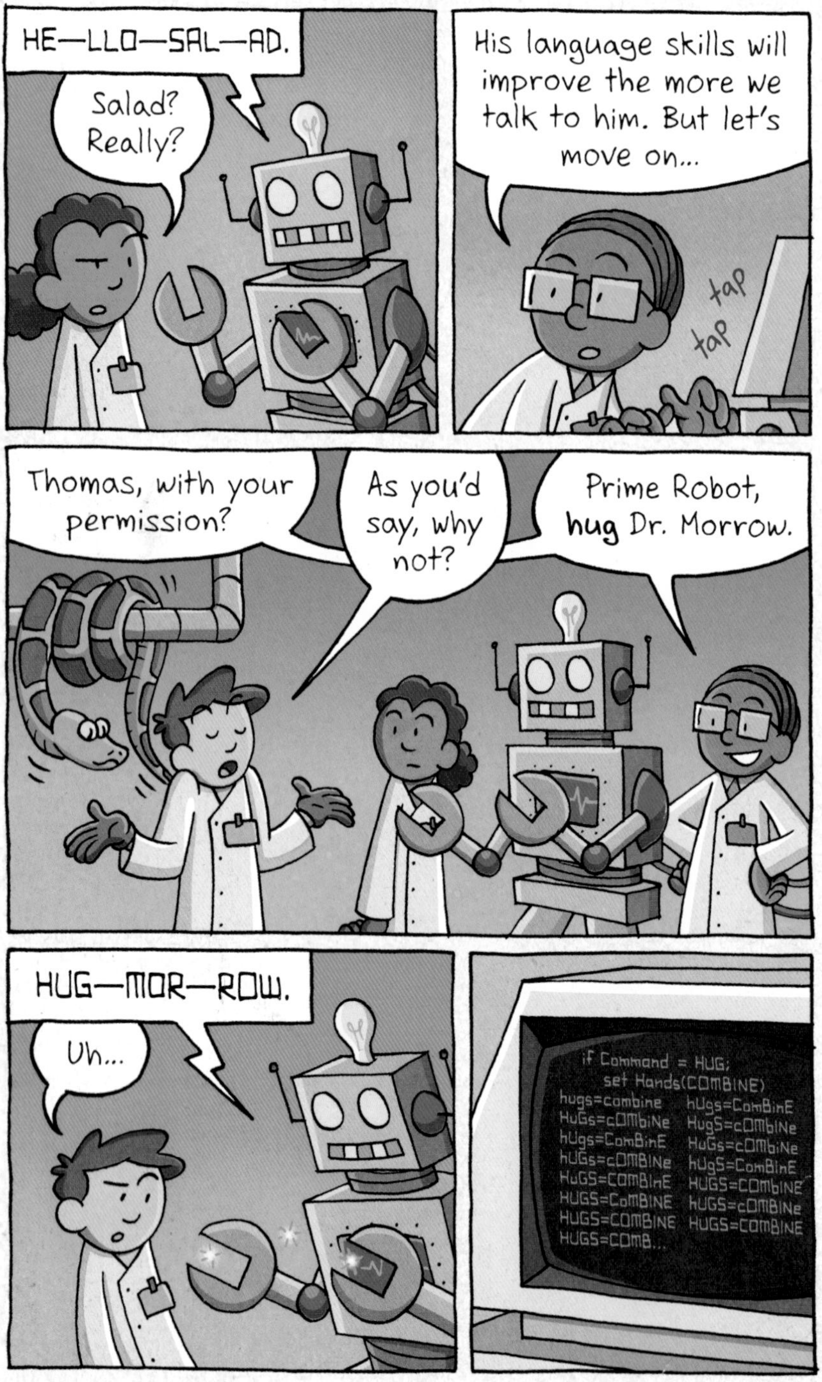
HE—LLO—SAL—AD.
Salad? Really?
His language skills will improve the more we talk to him. But let's move on...
tap tap
Thomas, with your permission?
As you'd say, why not?
Prime Robot, **hug** Dr. Morrow.
HUG—MOR—ROW.
Uh...
if Command = HUG;
set Hands(COMBINE)
hugs=combine hUgs=ComBinE
HuGs=cOMbiNe HugS=cOMbINe
hUgs=ComBinE HuGs=cOMbiNe
hUGs=cOMBINe hUgS=ComBinE
HuGS=COMBInE HUGS=COMbiNE
HUGS=CoMBINE hUGS=cOMBINe
HUGS=COMBINE HUGS=COMBINE
HUGS=COMB...

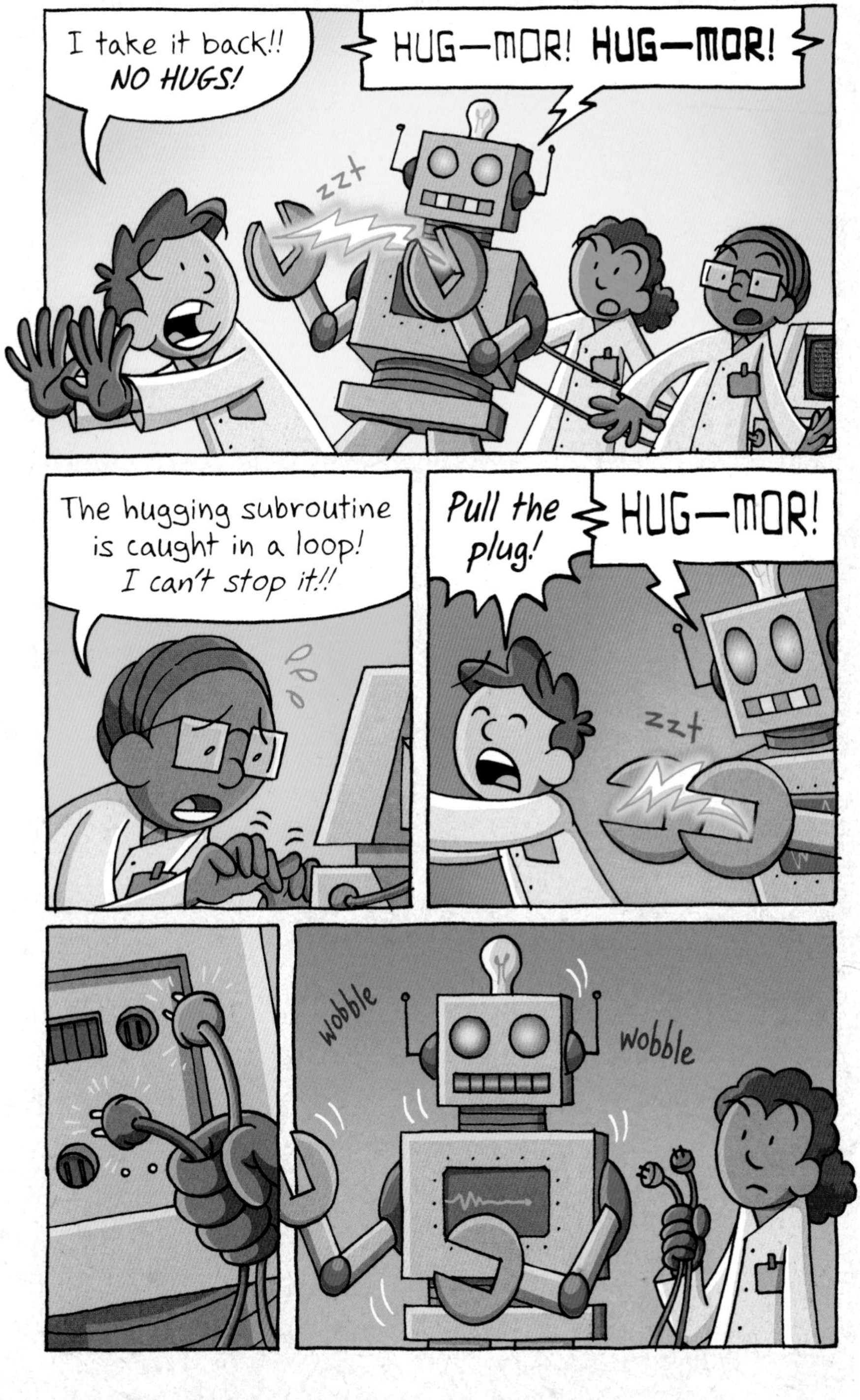
I take it back!! NO HUGS!
HUG—MOR! HUG—MOR!
zzt
The hugging subroutine is caught in a loop! I can't stop it!!
Pull the plug!
HUG—MOR!
zzt
wobble
wobble

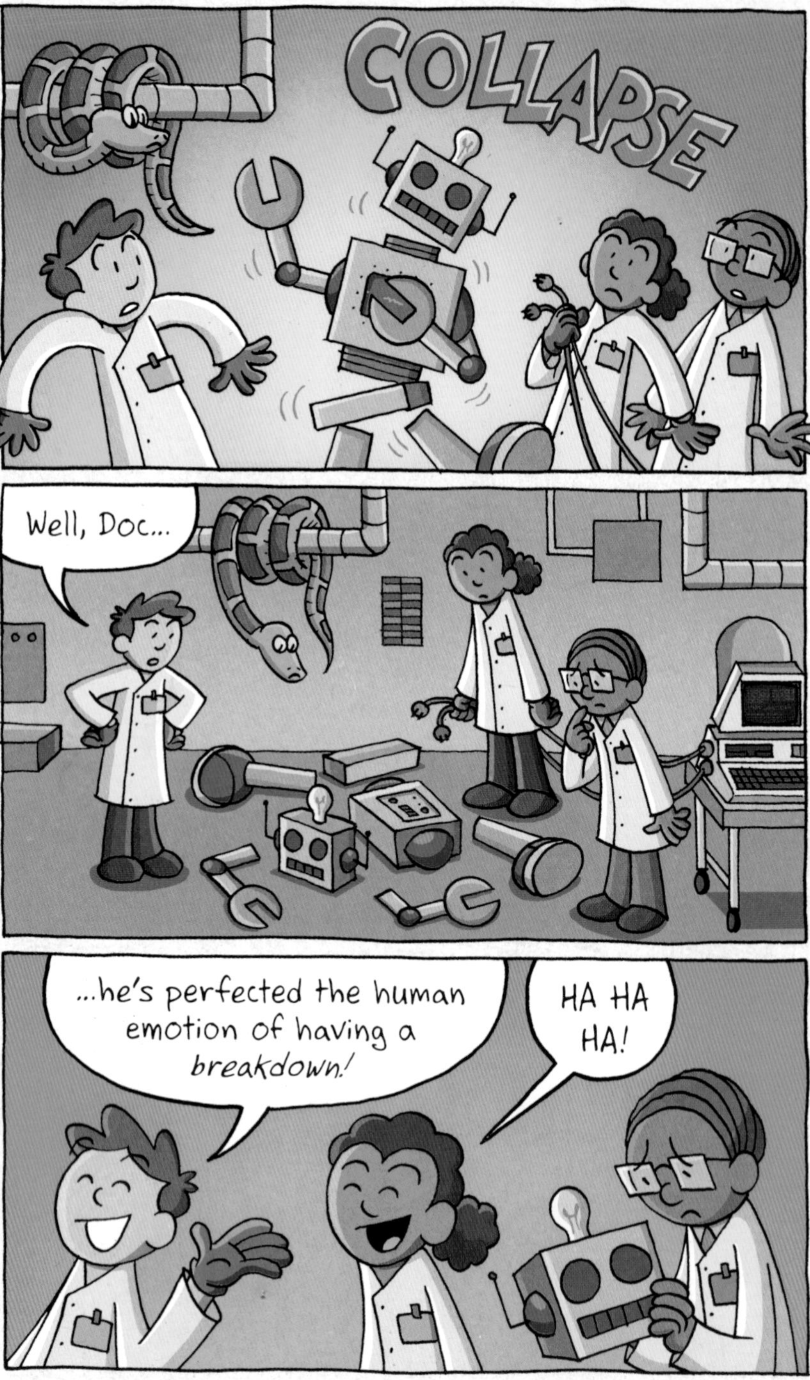
COLLAPSE
Well, Doc...
...he's perfected the human emotion of having a *breakdown!*
HA HA HA!

Chapter 5

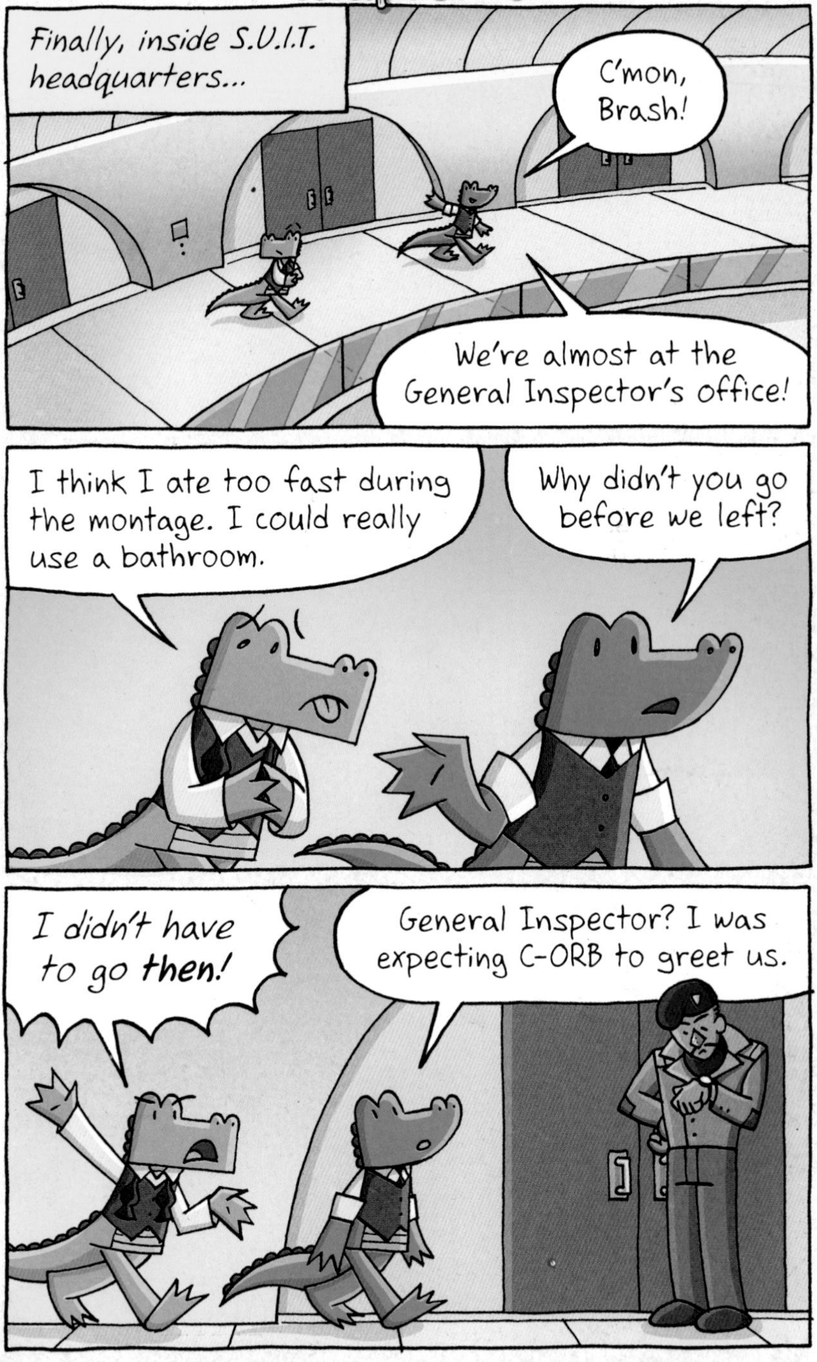
Finally, inside S.U.I.T. headquarters...
C'mon, Brash!
We're almost at the General Inspector's office!
I think I ate too fast during the montage. I could really use a bathroom.
Why didn't you go before we left?
I didn't have to go *then*!
General Inspector? I was expecting C-ORB to greet us.

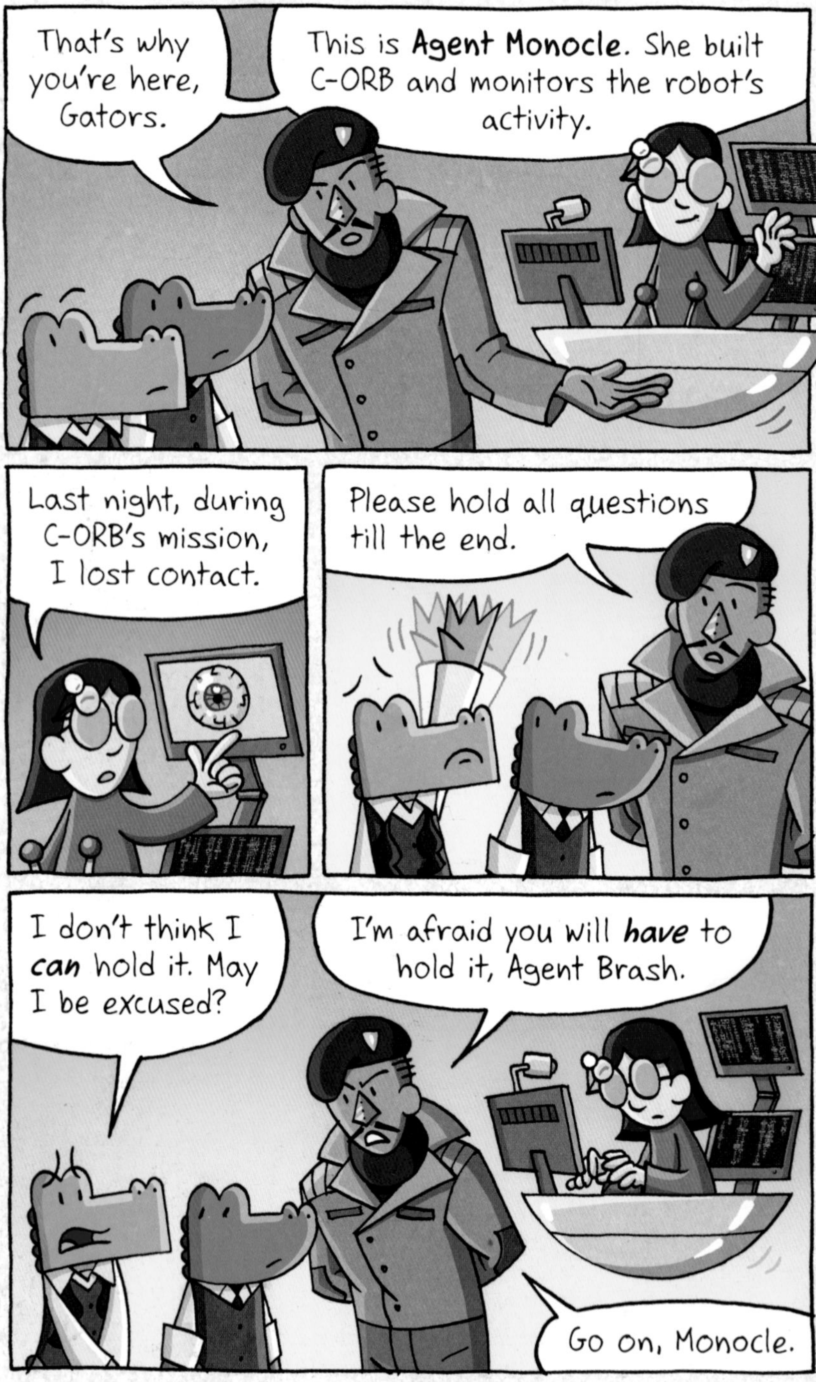
That's why you're here, Gators.
This is **Agent Monocle**. She built C-ORB and monitors the robot's activity.
Last night, during C-ORB's mission, I lost contact.
Please hold all questions till the end.
I don't think I ***can*** hold it. May I be excused?
I'm afraid you will ***have*** to hold it, Agent Brash.
Go on, Monocle.

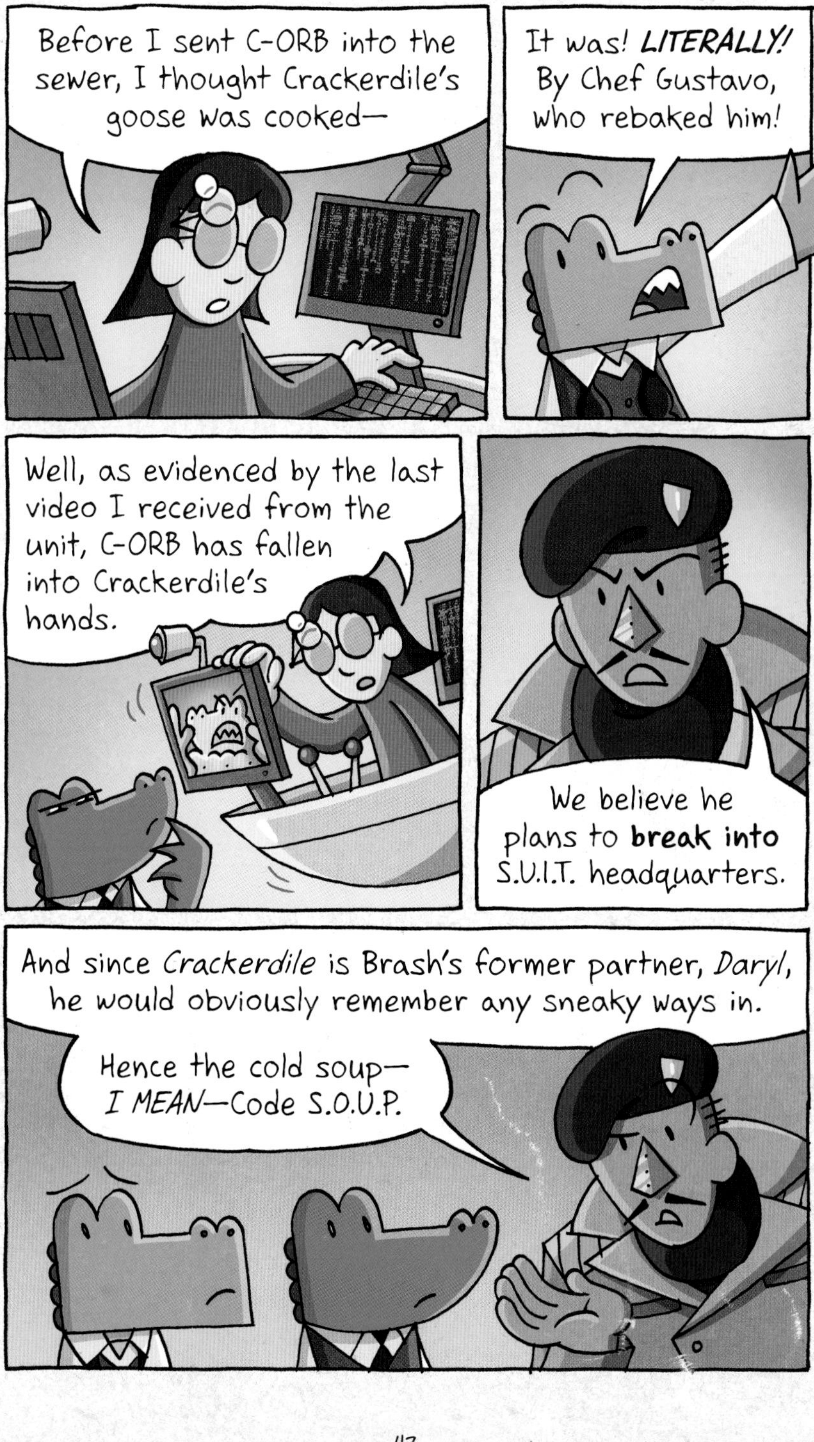
Before I sent C-ORB into the sewer, I thought Crackerdile's goose was cooked—
It was! **LITERALLY!** By Chef Gustavo, who rebaked him!
Well, as evidenced by the last video I received from the unit, C-ORB has fallen into Crackerdile's hands.
We believe he plans to **break into** S.U.I.T. headquarters.
And since *Crackerdile* is Brash's former partner, *Daryl*, he would obviously remember any sneaky ways in.
Hence the cold soup— *I MEAN*—Code S.O.U.P.

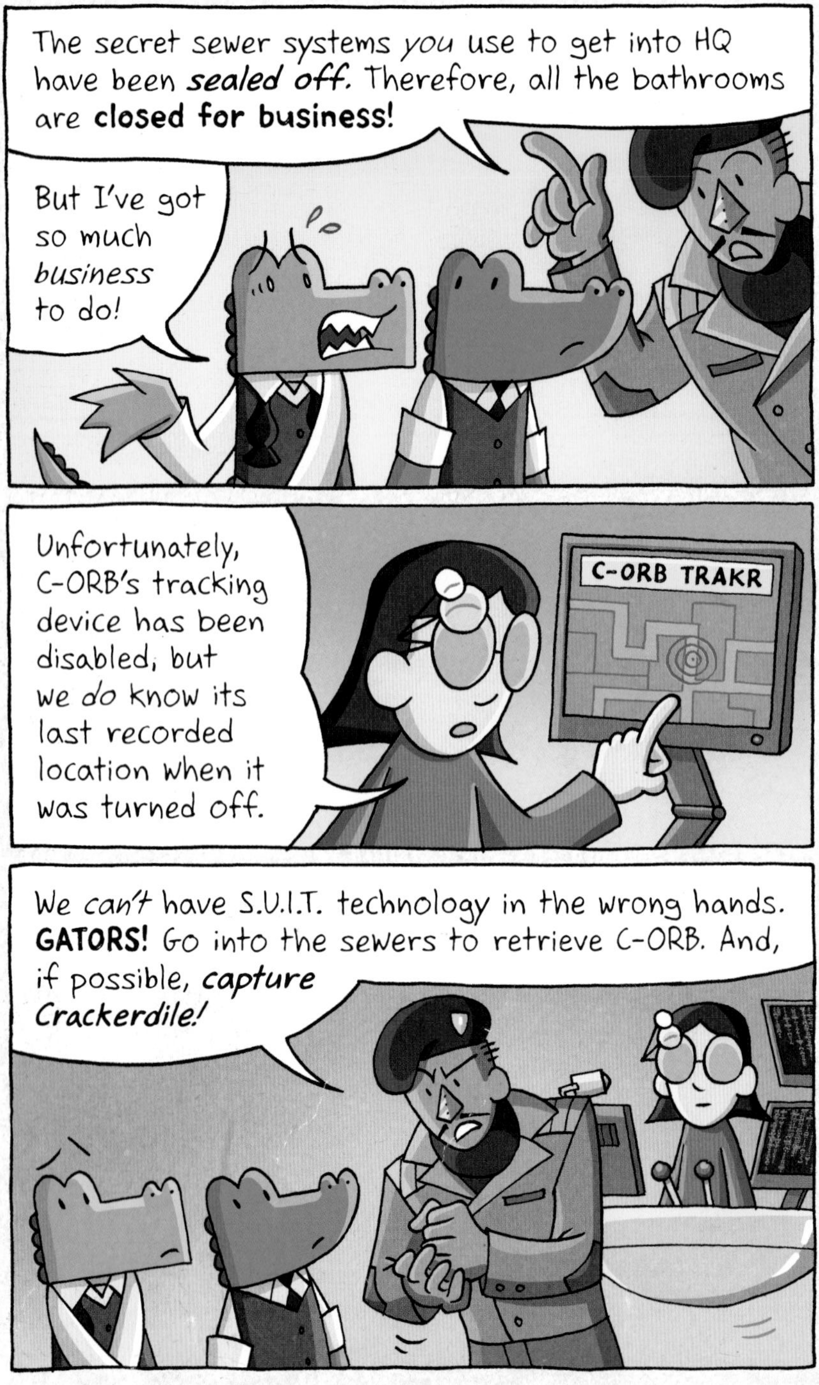
The secret sewer systems *you* use to get into HQ have been ***sealed off.*** Therefore, all the bathrooms are **closed for business!**
But I've got so much *business* to do!
Unfortunately, C-ORB's tracking device has been disabled, but we *do* know its last recorded location when it was turned off.
C-ORB TRAKR
We *can't* have S.U.I.T. technology in the wrong hands. **GATORS!** Go into the sewers to retrieve C-ORB. And, if possible, ***capture Crackerdile!***

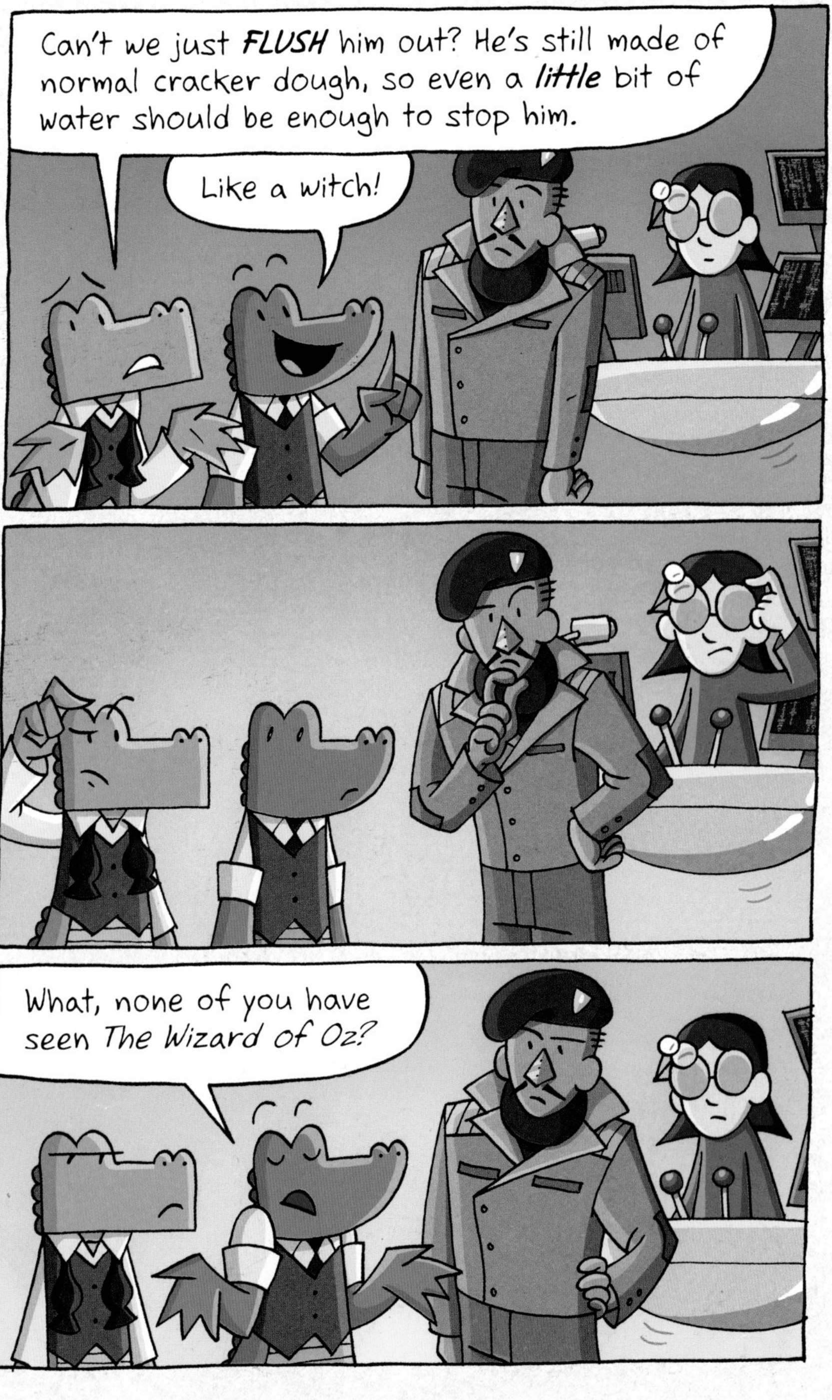
Can't we just FLUSH him out? He's still made of normal cracker dough, so even a little bit of water should be enough to stop him.
Like a witch!
What, none of you have seen The Wizard of Oz?

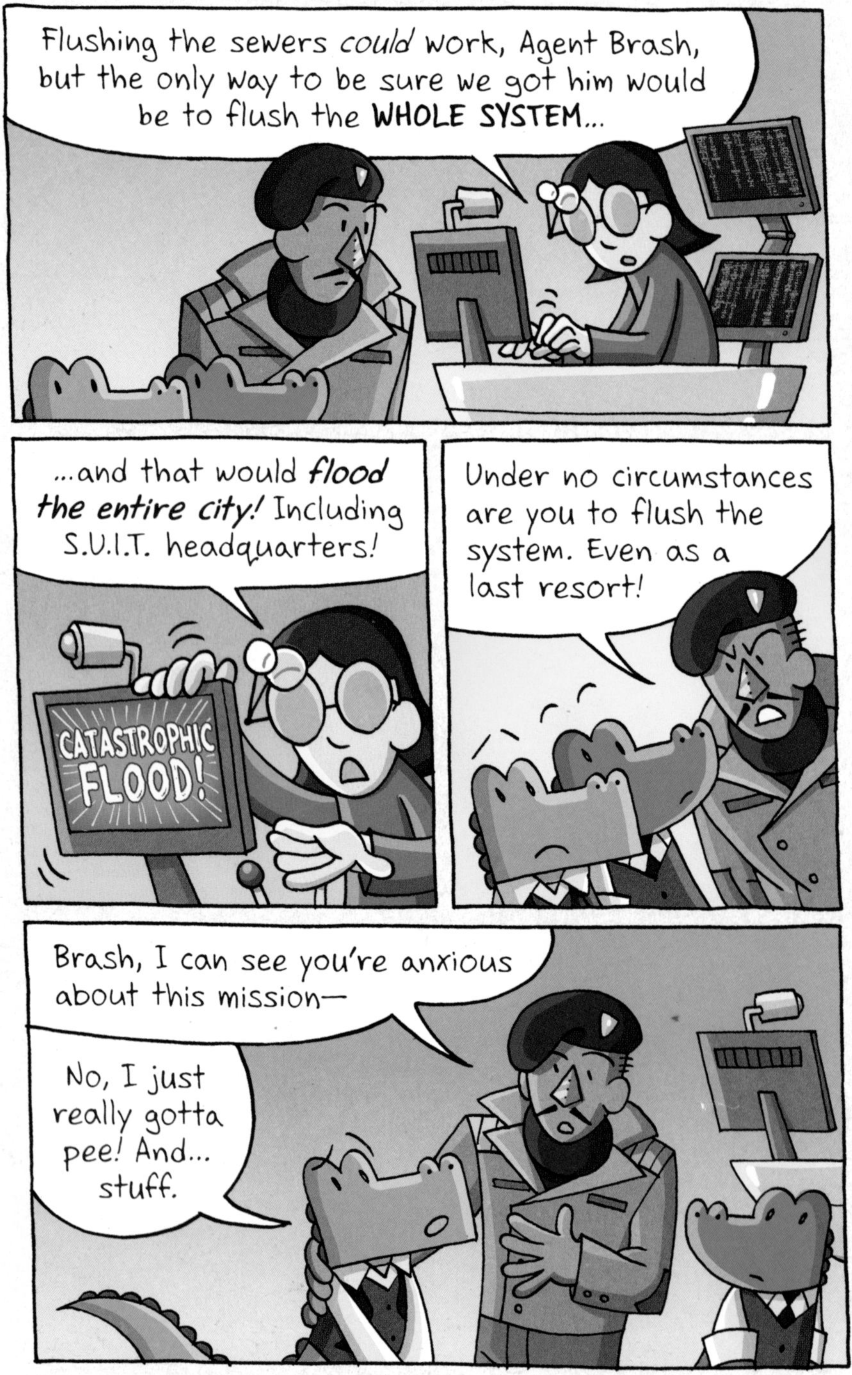

Flushing the sewers *could* work, Agent Brash, but the only way to be sure we got him would be to flush the **WHOLE SYSTEM**...
...and that would ***flood the entire city!*** Including S.U.I.T. headquarters!
CATASTROPHIC FLOOD!
Under no circumstances are you to flush the system. Even as a last resort!
Brash, I can see you're anxious about this mission—
No, I just really gotta pee! And... stuff.

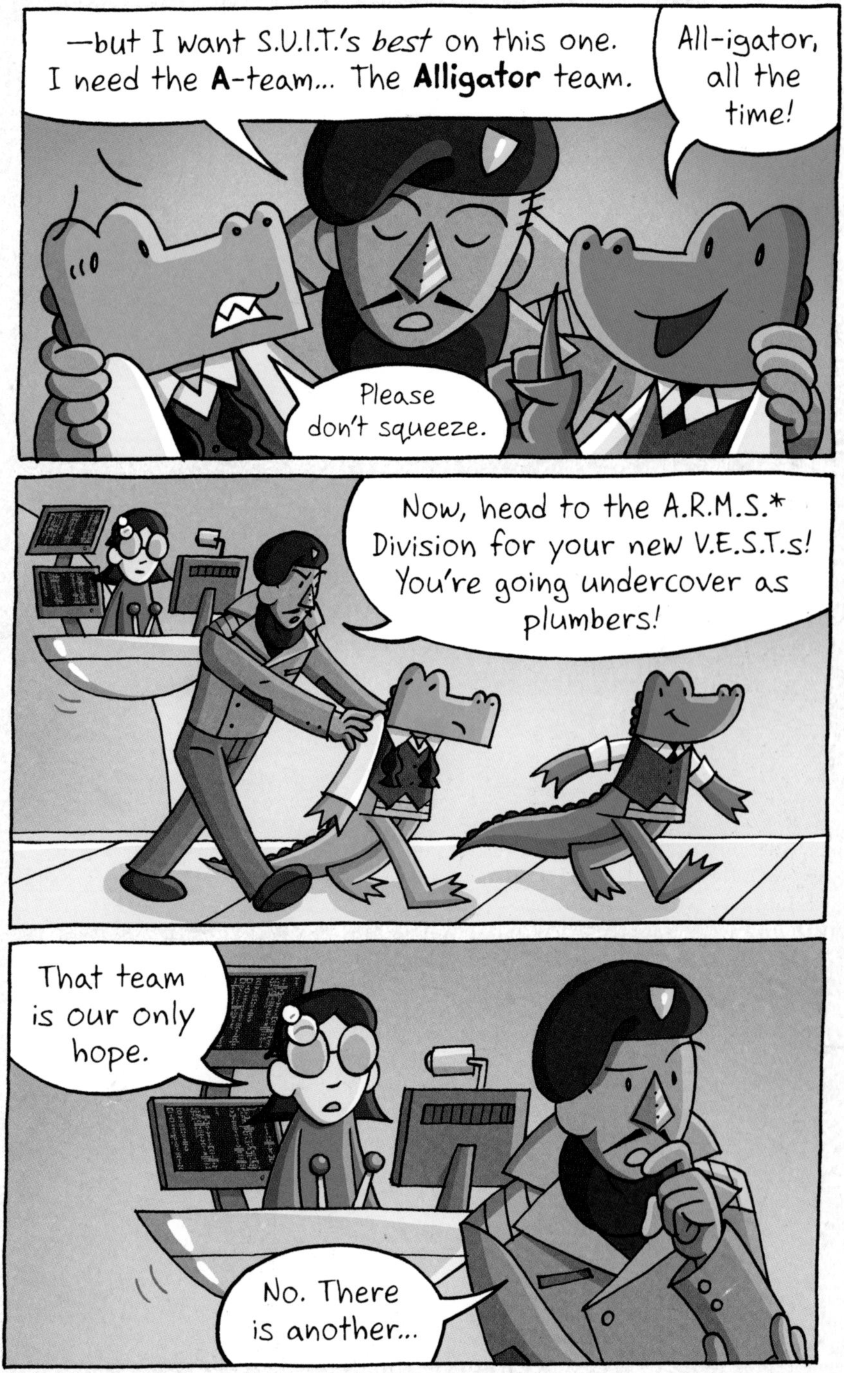
—but I want S.U.I.T.'s *best* on this one. I need the **A**-team... The **Alligator** team.
All-igator, all the time!
Please don't squeeze.
Now, head to the A.R.M.S.* Division for your new V.E.S.T.s! You're going undercover as plumbers!
That team is our only hope.
No. There is another...

*Apparel Research and Manufacturing... Something

Chapter 6

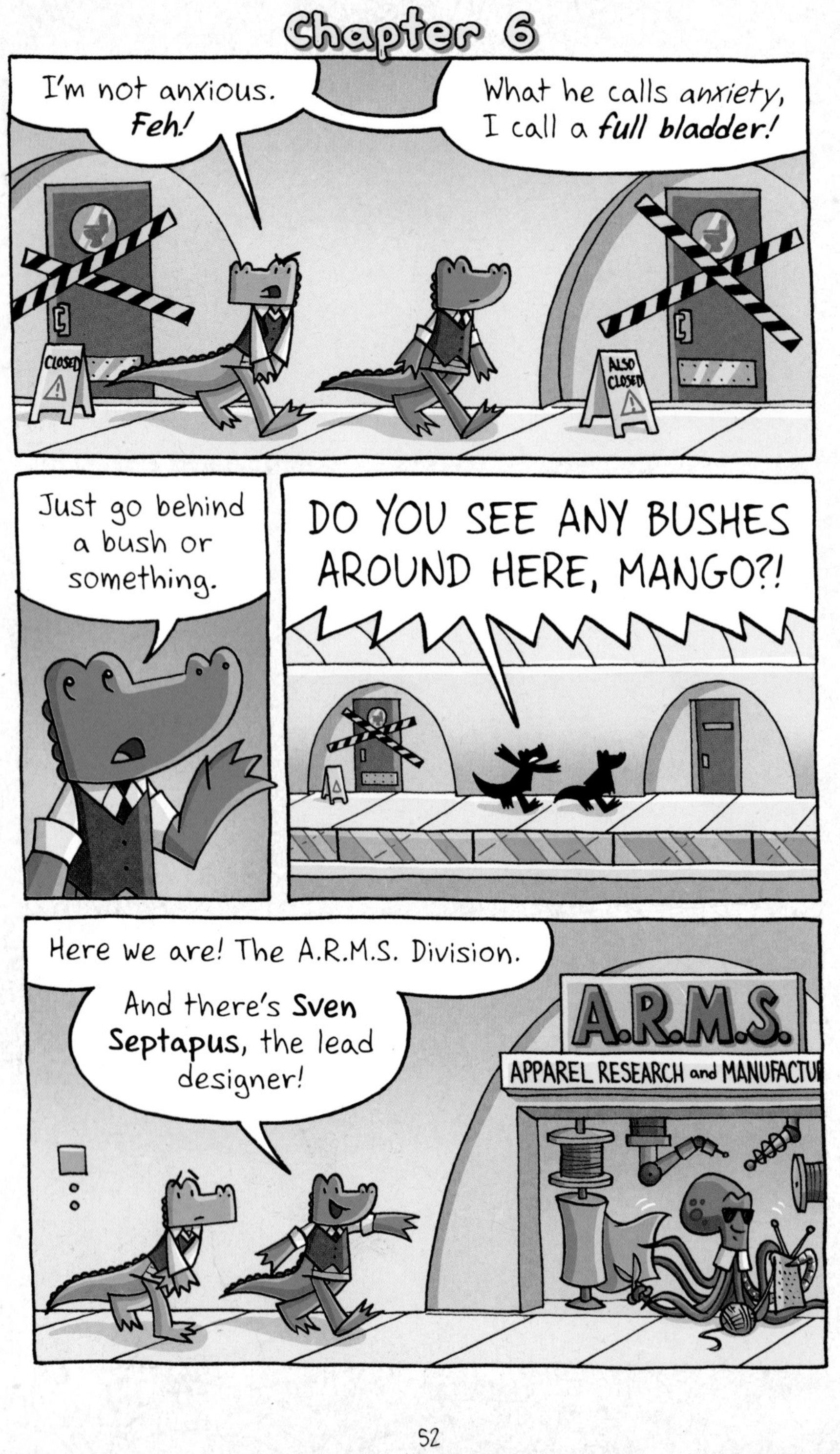
I'm not anxious. *Feh!*
What he calls *anxiety*, I call a ***full bladder!***
CLOSED
ALSO CLOSED
Just go behind a bush or something.
DO YOU SEE ANY BUSHES AROUND HERE, MANGO?!
Here we are! The A.R.M.S. Division.
And there's **Sven Septapus**, the lead designer!
A.R.M.S.
APPAREL RESEARCH and MANUFACTU

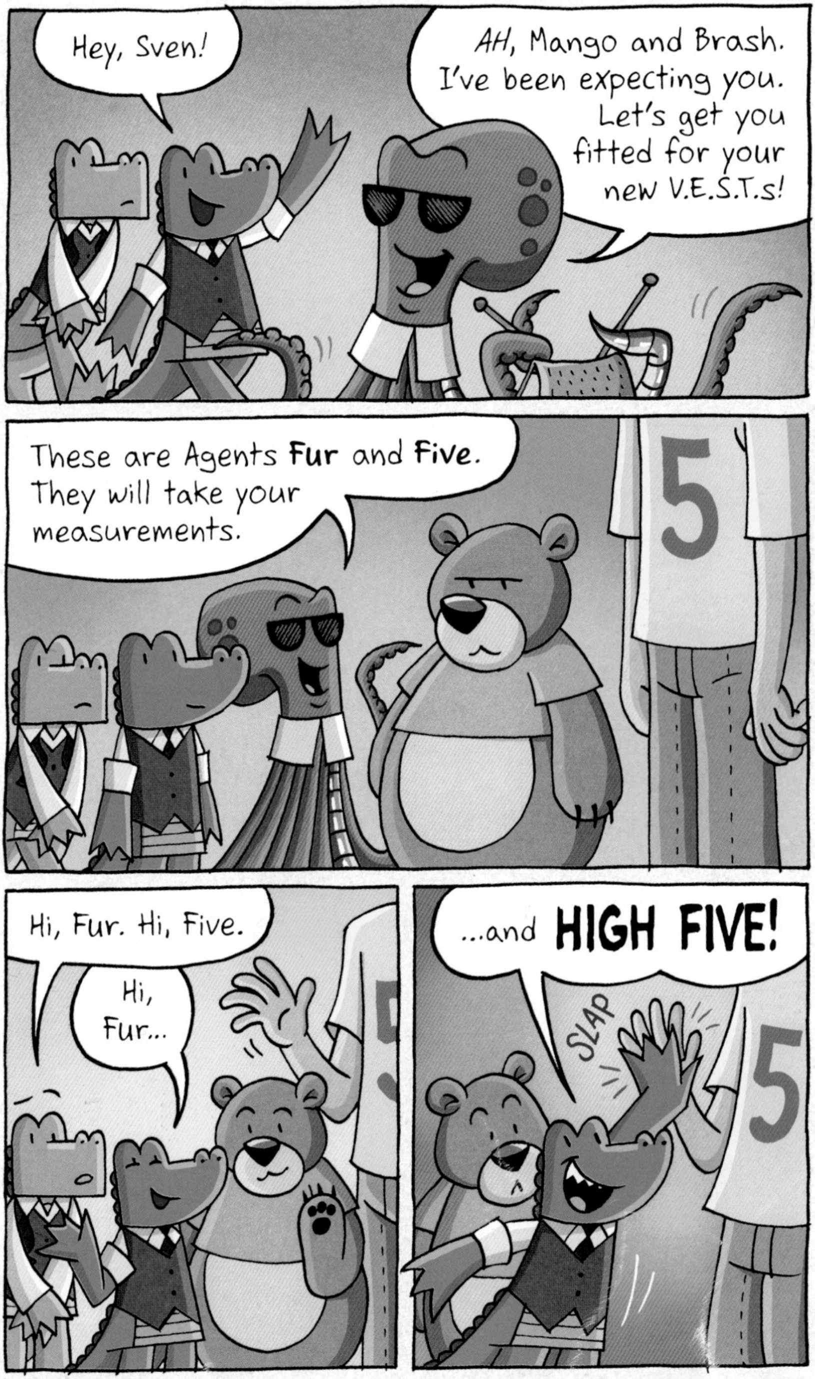
Hey, Sven!
AH, Mango and Brash. I've been expecting you. Let's get you fitted for your new V.E.S.T.s!
These are Agents **Fur** and **Five**. They will take your measurements.
Hi, Fur. Hi, Five.
Hi, Fur...
...and **HIGH FIVE!**
SLAP

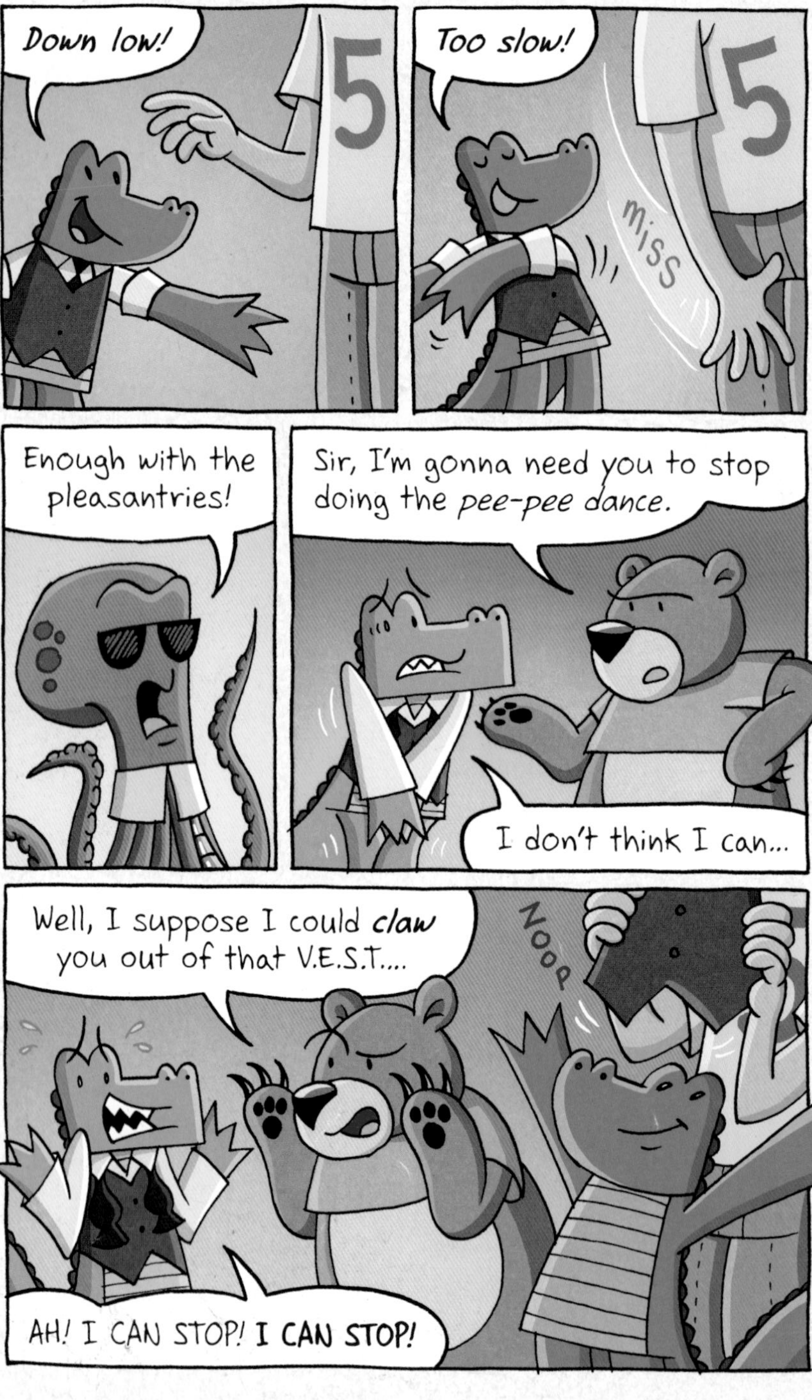
Down low!
Too slow!
MISS
Enough with the pleasantries!
Sir, I'm gonna need you to stop doing the *pee-pee dance.*
I don't think I can...
Well, I suppose I could *claw* you out of that V.E.S.T....
NOOP
AH! I CAN STOP! **I CAN STOP!**

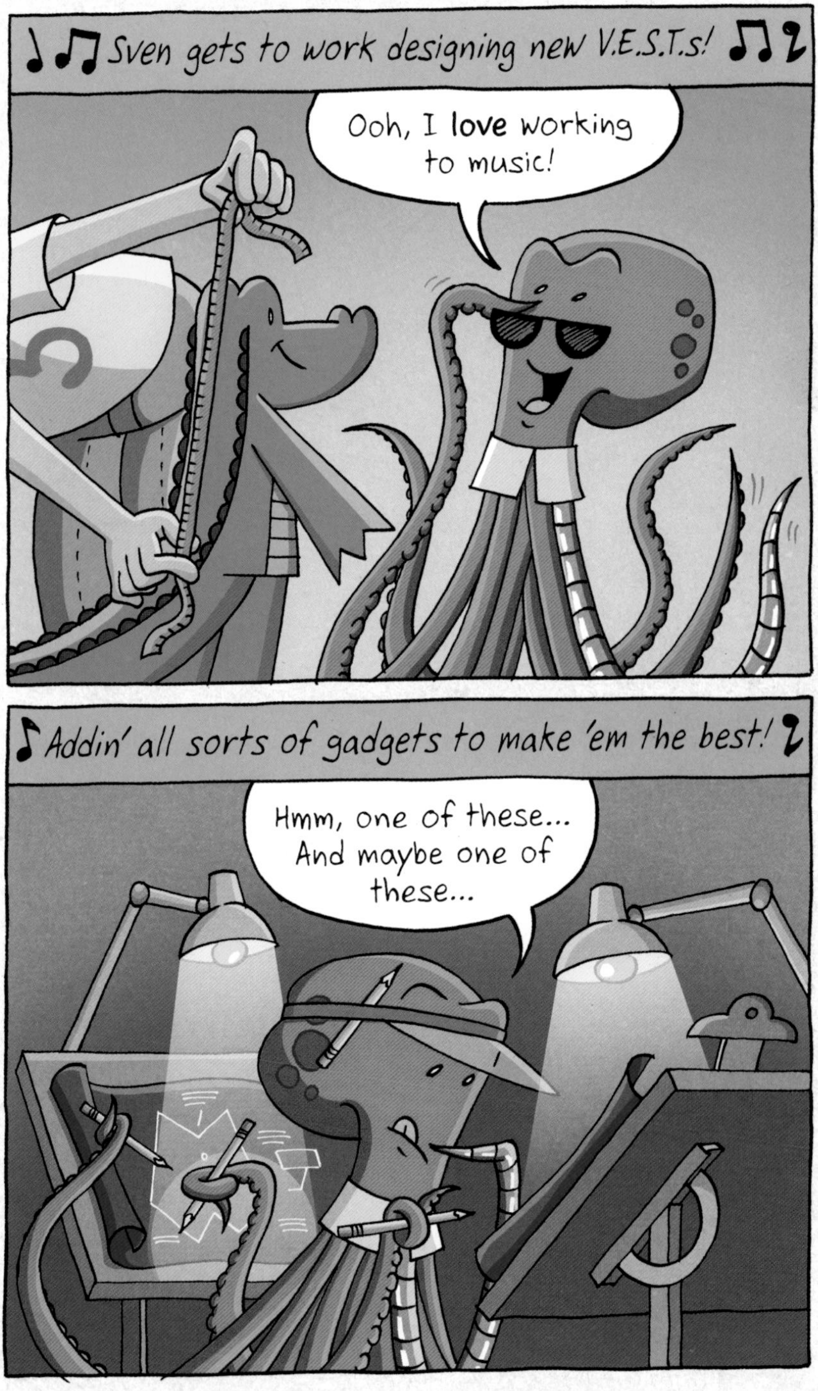
Sven gets to work designing new V.E.S.T.s!
Ooh, I **love** working to music!
Addin' all sorts of gadgets to make 'em the best!
Hmm, one of these... And maybe one of these...

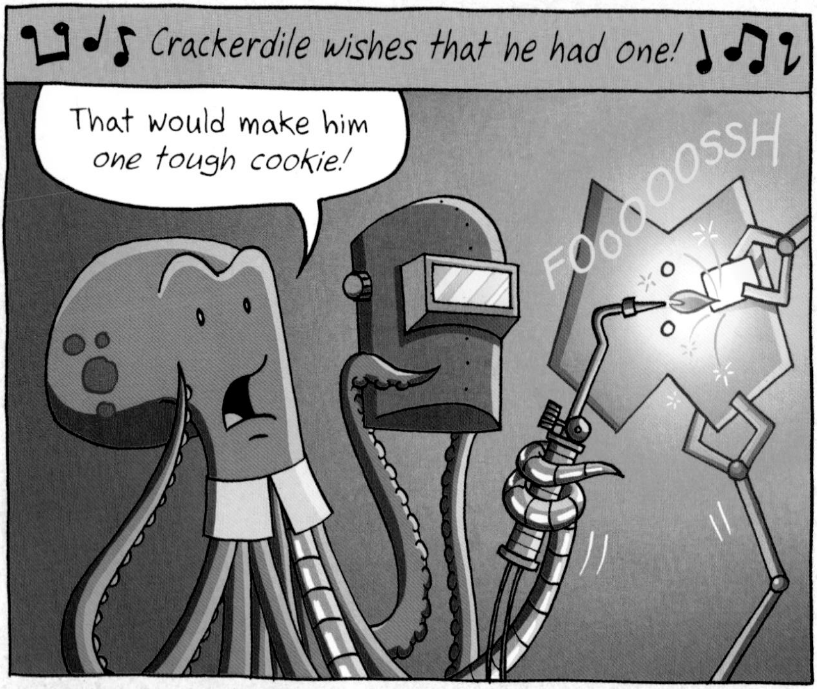
Crackerdile wishes that he had one!
That would make him one tough cookie!
FOOOOOOSSH

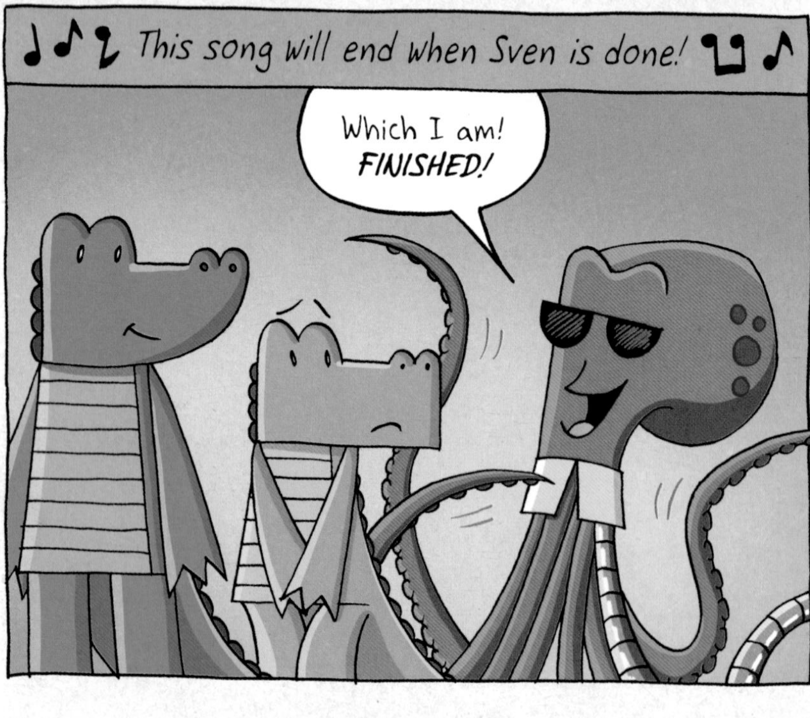
This song will end when Sven is done!
Which I am! FINISHED!

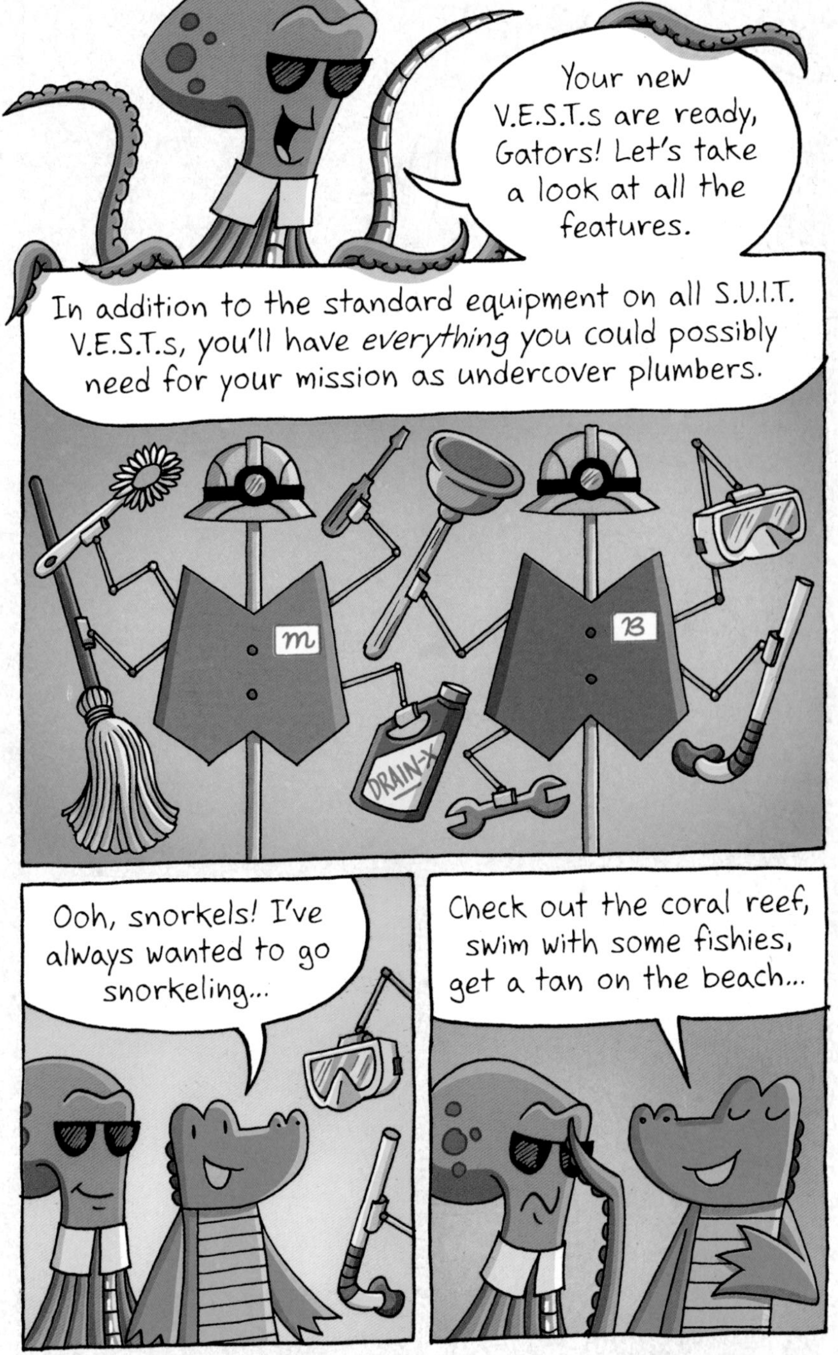
Your new V.E.S.T.s are ready, Gators! Let's take a look at all the features.
In addition to the standard equipment on all S.U.I.T. V.E.S.T.s, you'll have *everything* you could possibly need for your mission as undercover plumbers.
m
B
DRAIN-X
Ooh, snorkels! I've always wanted to go snorkeling...
Check out the coral reef, swim with some fishies, get a tan on the beach...

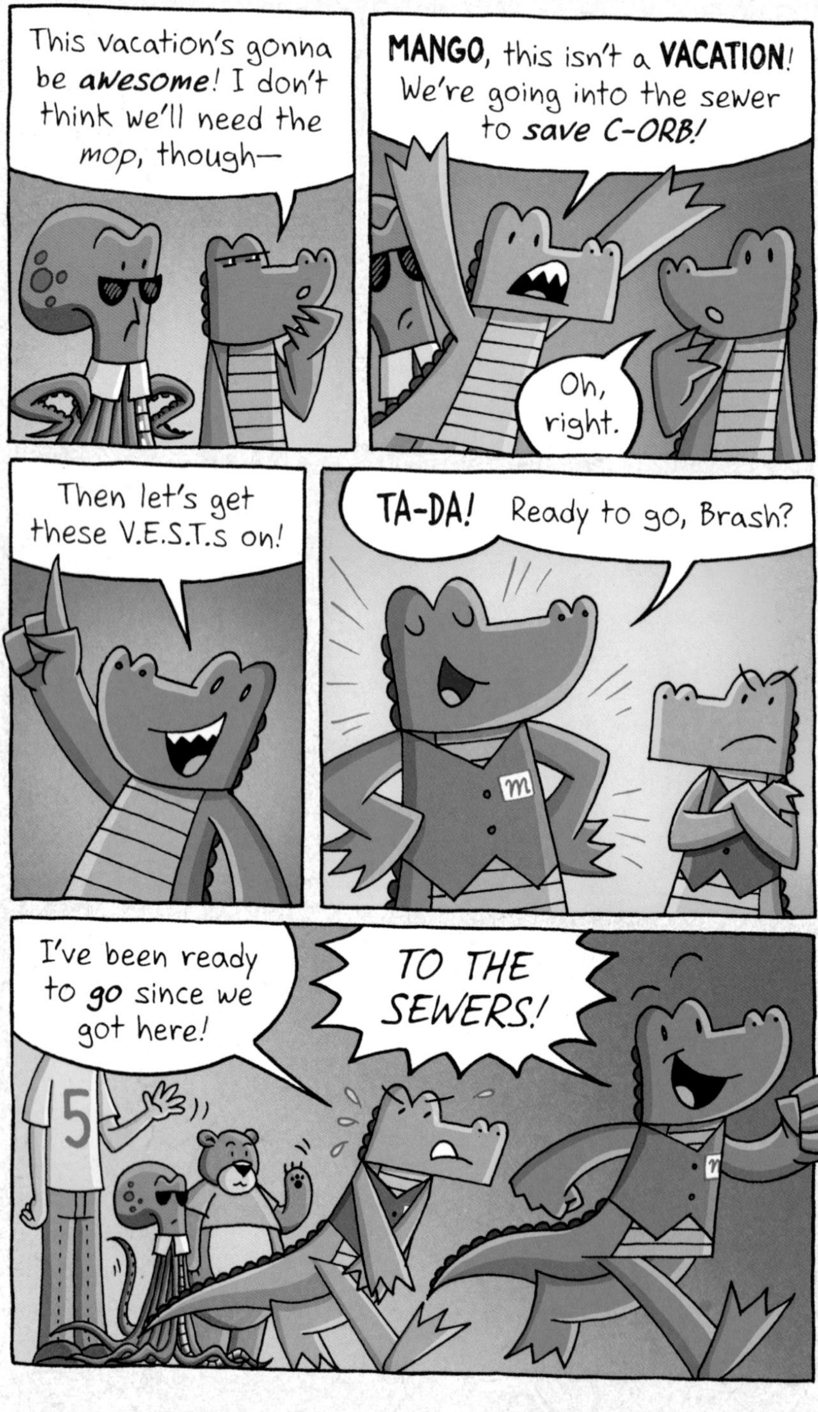
This vacation's gonna be *awesome*! I don't think we'll need the *mop*, though—
MANGO, this isn't a **VACATION**! We're going into the sewer to *save C-ORB!*
Oh, right.
Then let's get these V.E.S.T.s on!
TA-DA! Ready to go, Brash?
I've been ready to *go* since we got here!
TO THE SEWERS!
5

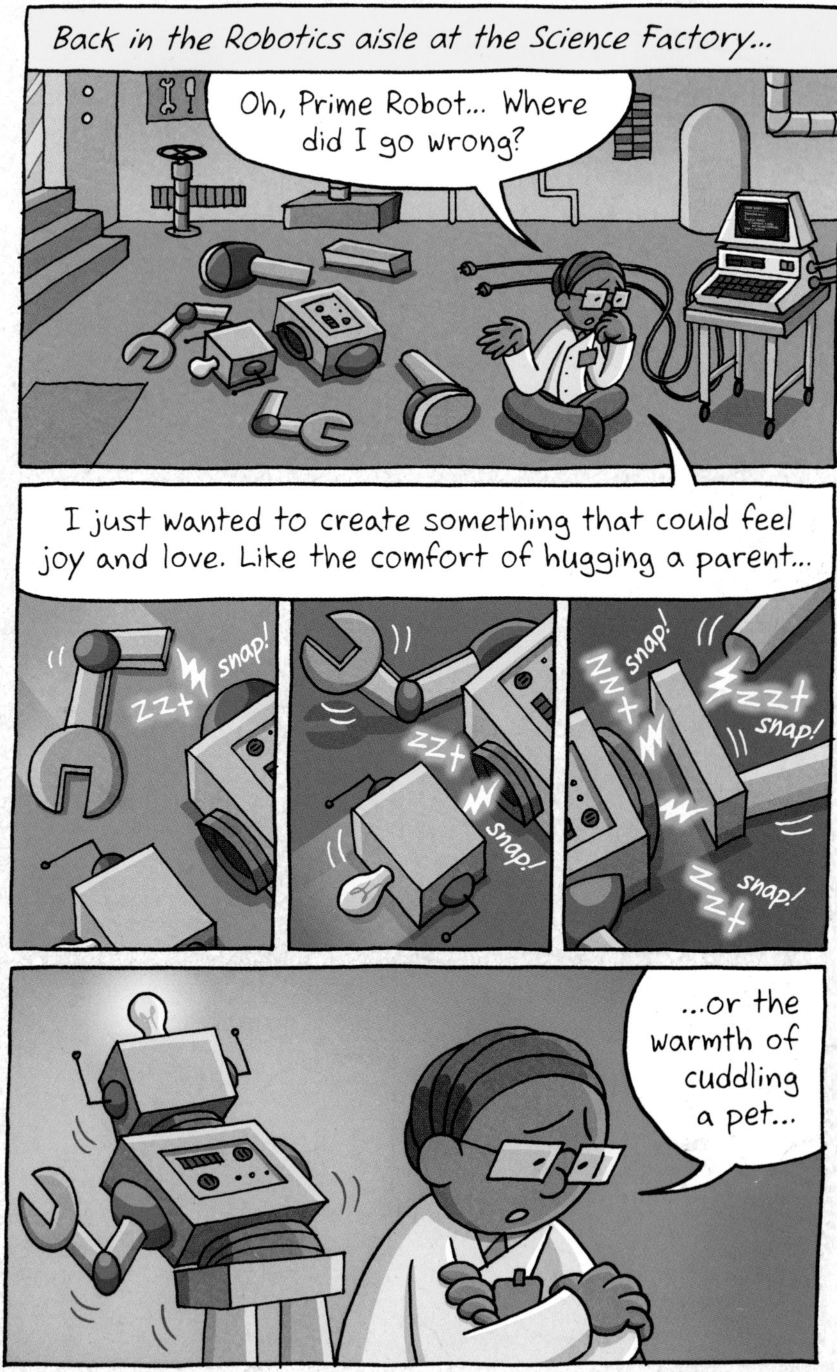
Back in the Robotics aisle at the Science Factory...
Oh, Prime Robot... Where did I go wrong?
I just wanted to create something that could feel joy and love. Like the comfort of hugging a parent...
zzt
snap!
zzt
snap!
zzt
snap!
zzt
snap!
zzt
snap!
...or the warmth of cuddling a pet...

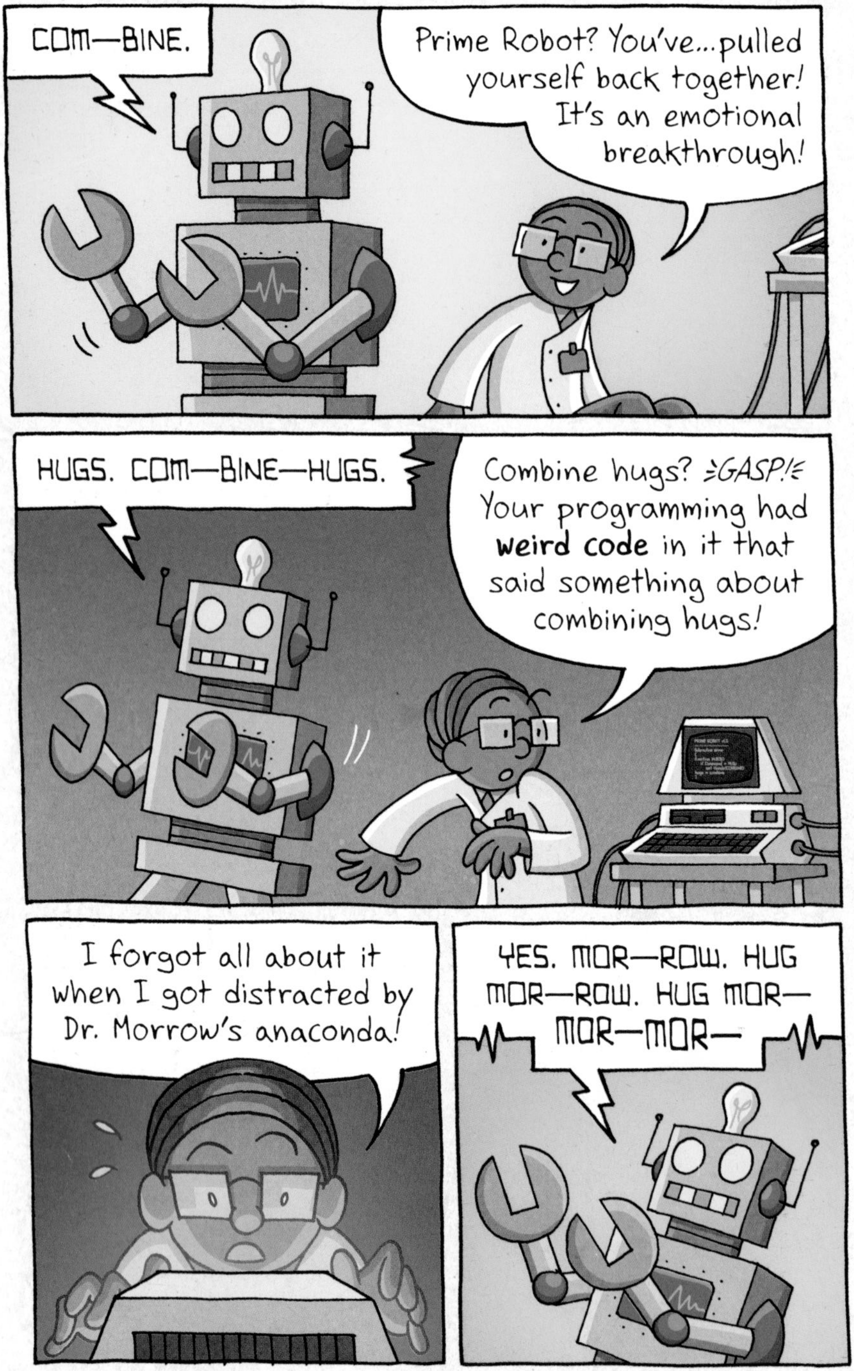
COM—BINE.
Prime Robot? You've...pulled yourself back together! It's an emotional breakthrough!
HUGS. COM—BINE—HUGS.
Combine hugs? *GASP!* Your programming had **weird code** in it that said something about combining hugs!
I forgot all about it when I got distracted by Dr. Morrow's anaconda!
YES. MOR—ROW. HUG MOR—ROW. HUG MOR—MOR—MOR—

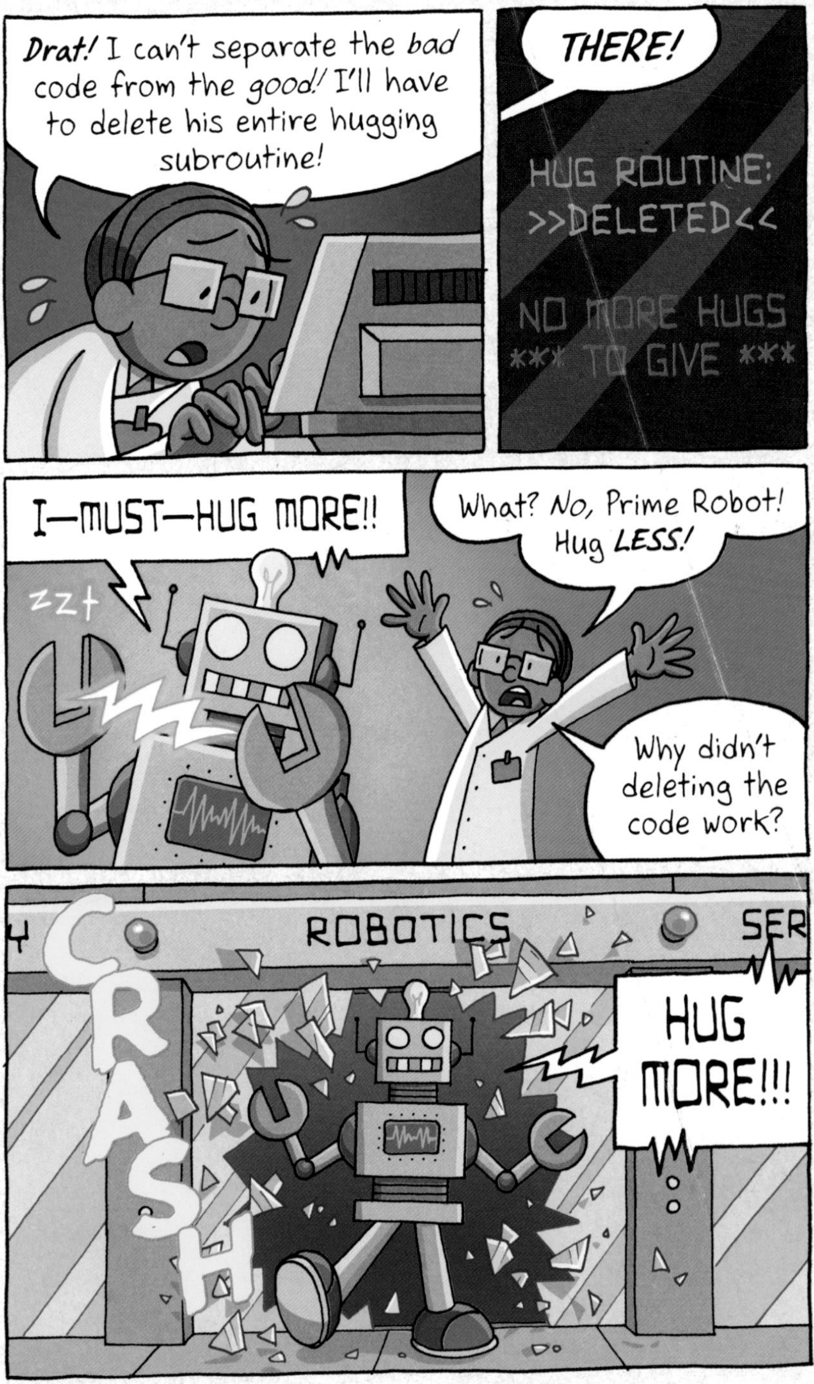
Drat! I can't separate the bad code from the good! I'll have to delete his entire hugging subroutine!
THERE!
HUG ROUTINE:
>>DELETED<<
NO MORE HUGS
*** TO GIVE ***
I—MUST—HUG MORE!!
ZZT
What? No, Prime Robot! Hug LESS!
Why didn't deleting the code work?
ROBOTICS
SER
CRASH
HUG MORE!!!

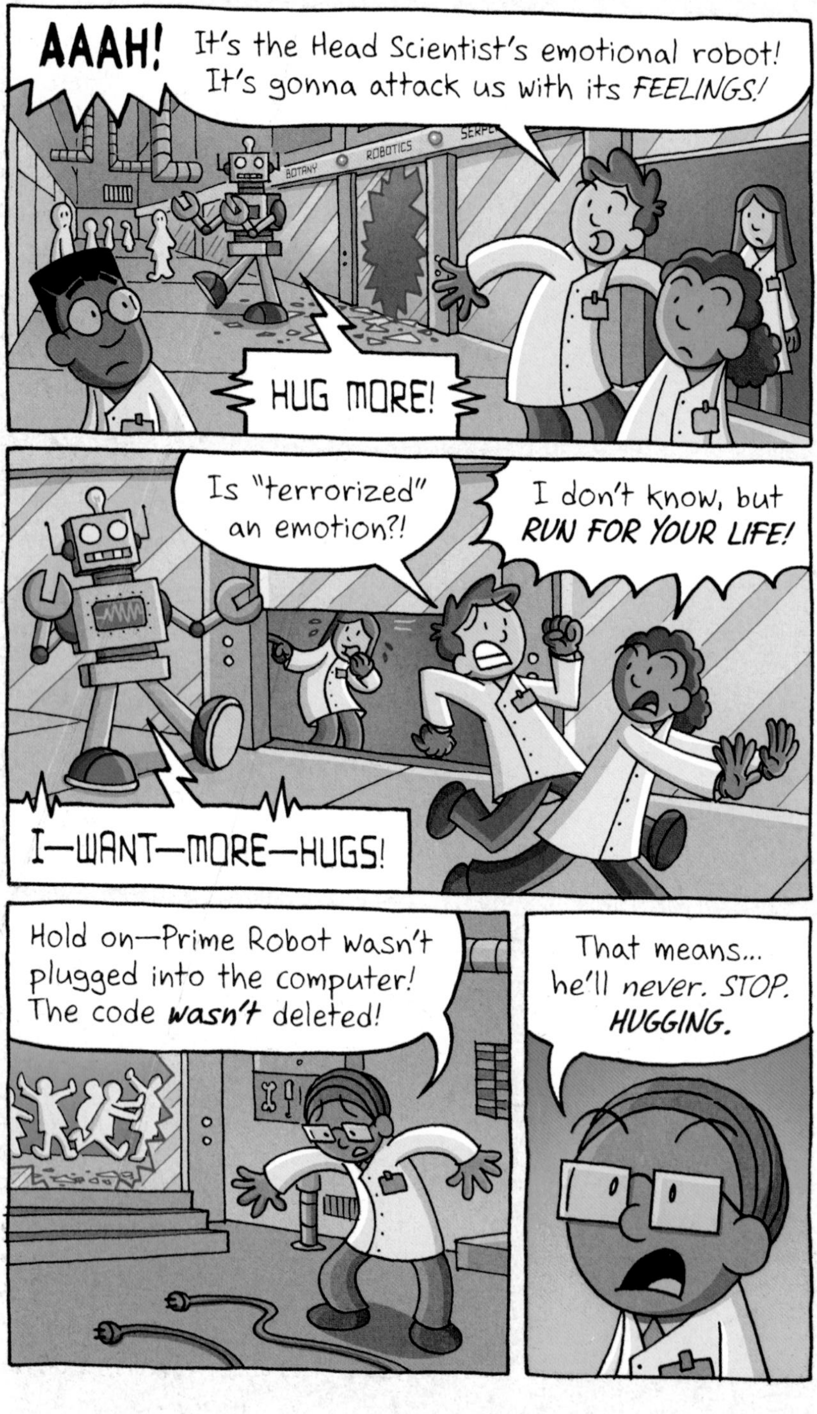
AAAH! It's the Head Scientist's emotional robot! It's gonna attack us with its FEELINGS!
BOTANY
ROBOTICS
HUG MORE!
Is "terrorized" an emotion?!
I don't know, but RUN FOR YOUR LIFE!
I—WANT—MORE—HUGS!
Hold on—Prime Robot wasn't plugged into the computer! The code **wasn't** deleted!
That means... he'll *never. STOP.* ***HUGGING.***

Chapter 7

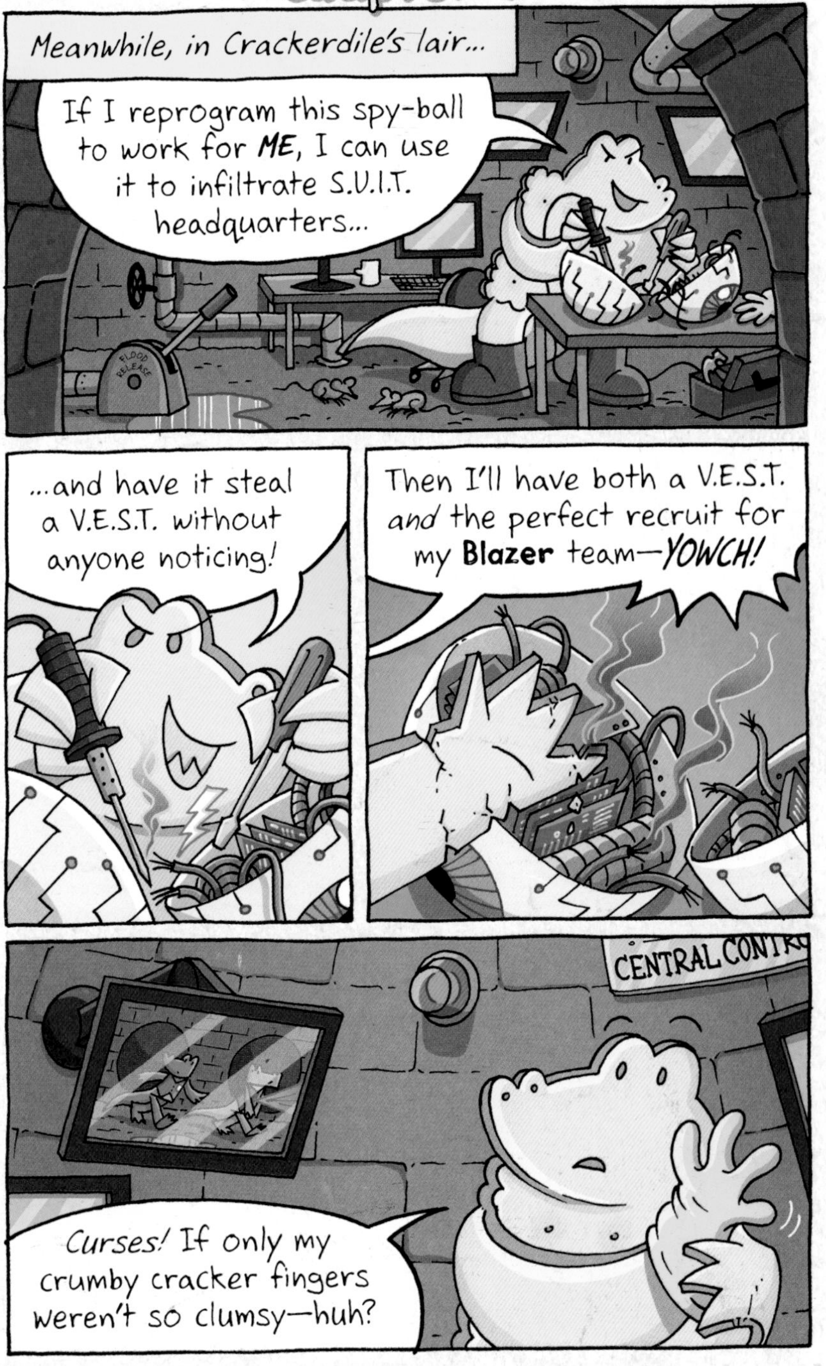

Meanwhile, in Crackerdile's lair...
If I reprogram this spy-ball to work for ME, I can use it to infiltrate S.U.I.T. headquarters...
FLOOD RELEASE
...and have it steal a V.E.S.T. without anyone noticing!
Then I'll have both a V.E.S.T. and the perfect recruit for my Blazer team—YOWCH!
CENTRAL CONTR
Curses! If only my crumby cracker fingers weren't so clumsy—huh?

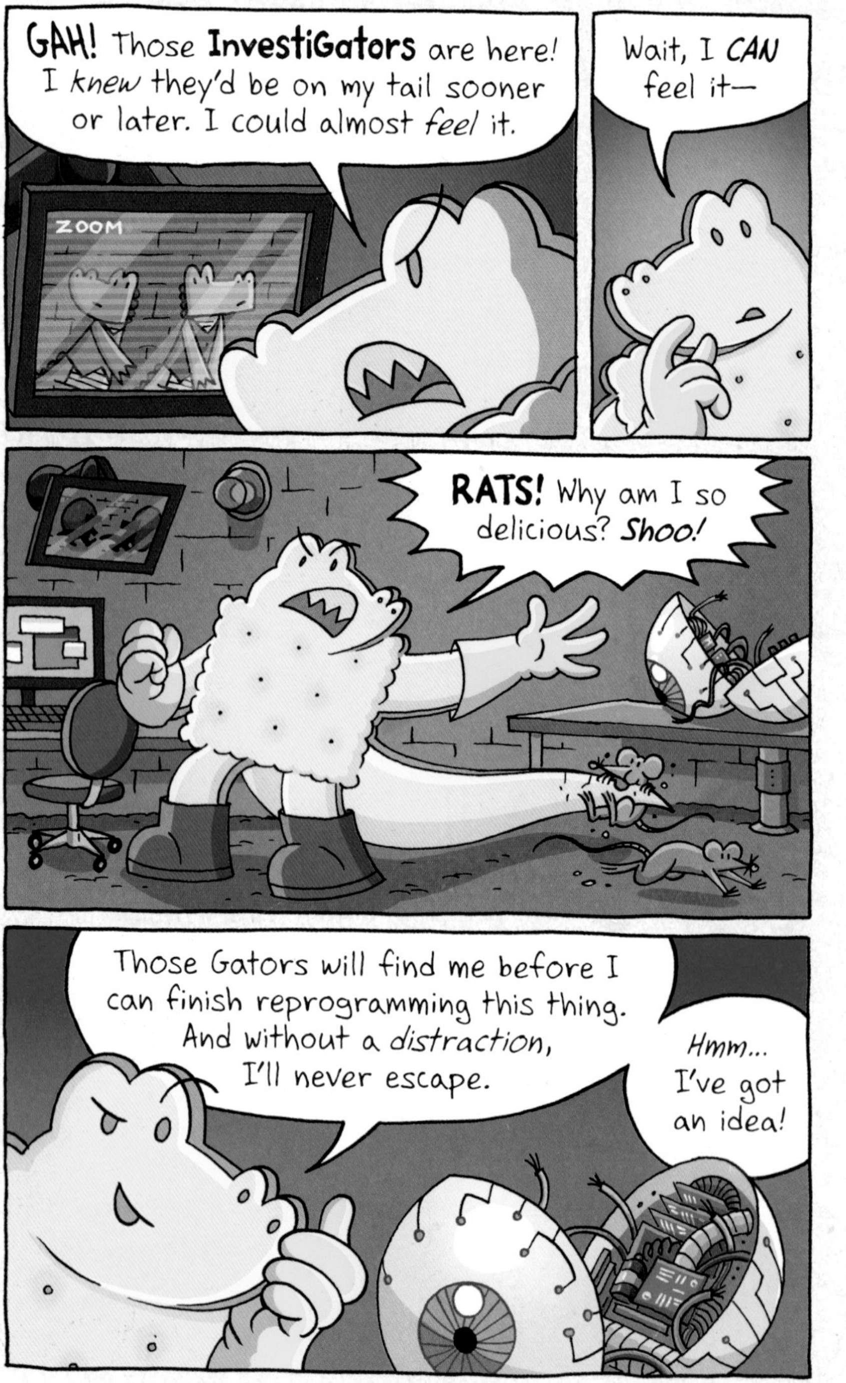
GAH! Those InvestiGators are here! I knew they'd be on my tail sooner or later. I could almost feel it.
ZOOM
Wait, I CAN feel it—
RATS! Why am I so delicious? Shoo!
Those Gators will find me before I can finish reprogramming this thing. And without a distraction, I'll never escape.
Hmm... I've got an idea!

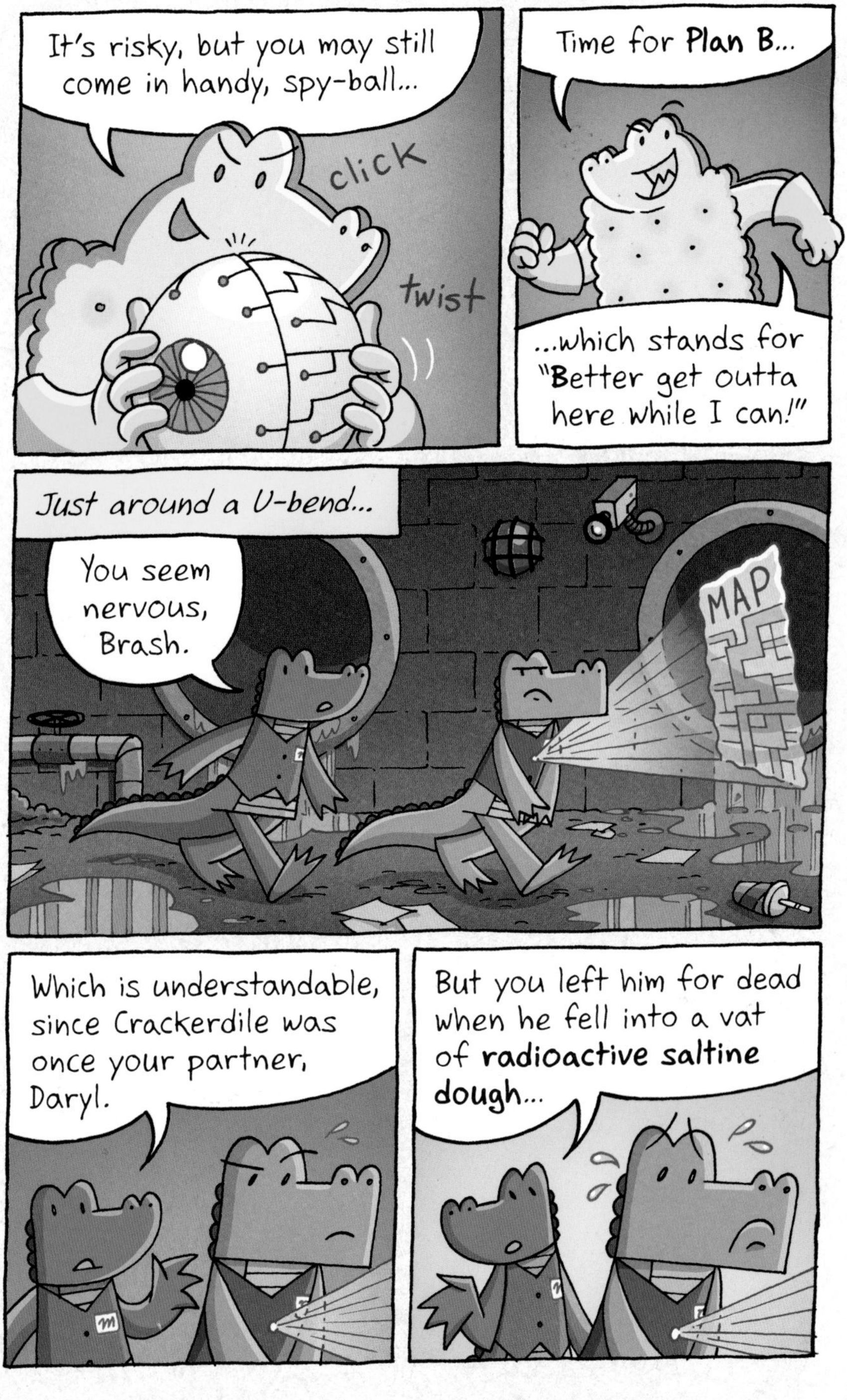
It's risky, but you may still come in handy, spy-ball...
click
twist
Time for **Plan B**...
...which stands for "**B**etter get outta here while I can!"
Just around a U-bend...
MAP
You seem nervous, Brash.
Which is understandable, since Crackerdile was once your partner, Daryl.
But you left him for dead when he fell into a vat of **radioactive saltine dough**...

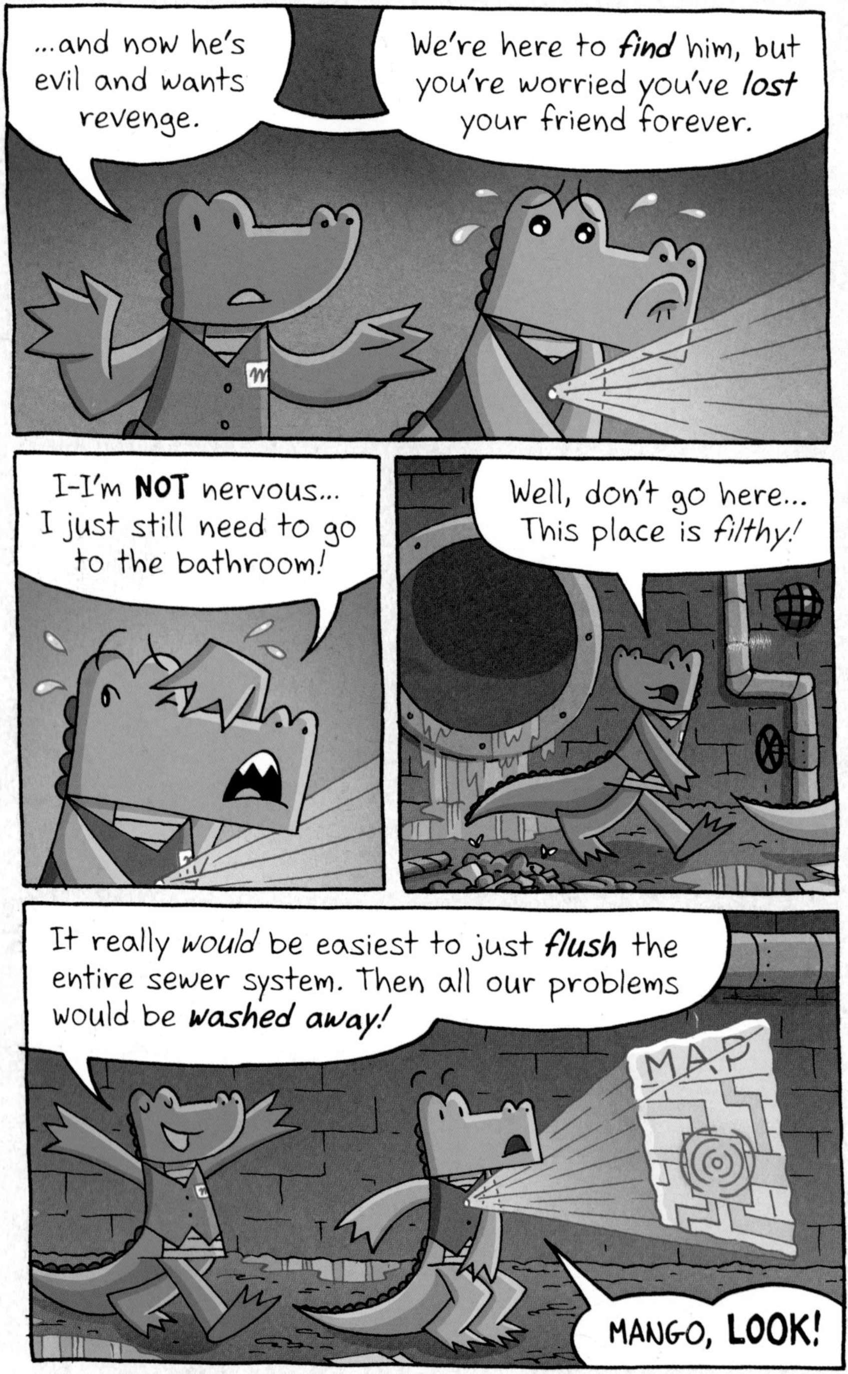
...and now he's evil and wants revenge.
We're here to *find* him, but you're worried you've *lost* your friend forever.
I-I'm **NOT** nervous... I just still need to go to the bathroom!
Well, don't go here... This place is *filthy*!
It really *would* be easiest to just **flush** the entire sewer system. Then all our problems would be **washed away**!
MAP
MANGO, **LOOK!**

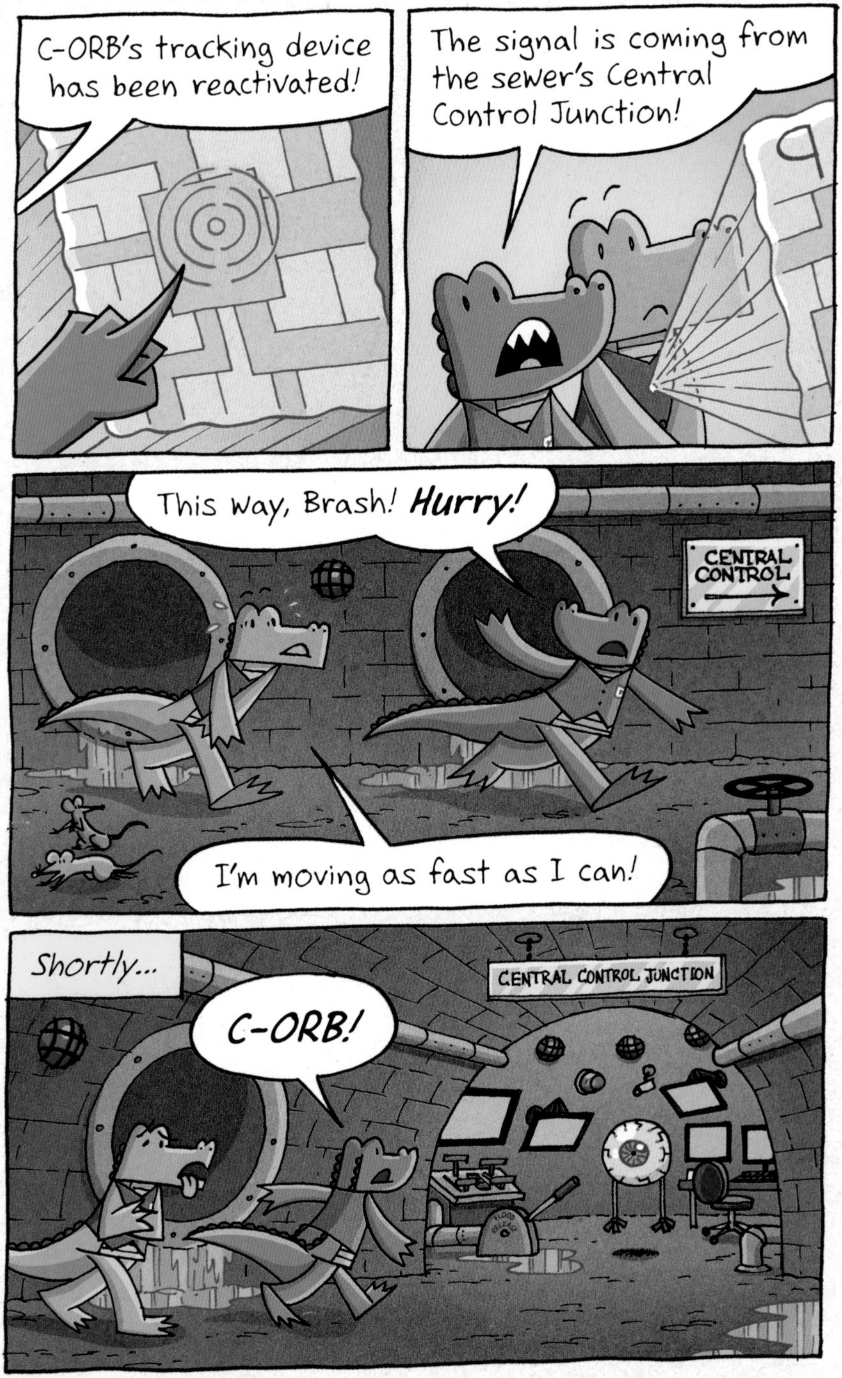
C-ORB's tracking device has been reactivated!
The signal is coming from the sewer's Central Control Junction!
This way, Brash! Hurry!
CENTRAL CONTROL
I'm moving as fast as I can!
Shortly...
CENTRAL CONTROL JUNCTION
C-ORB!

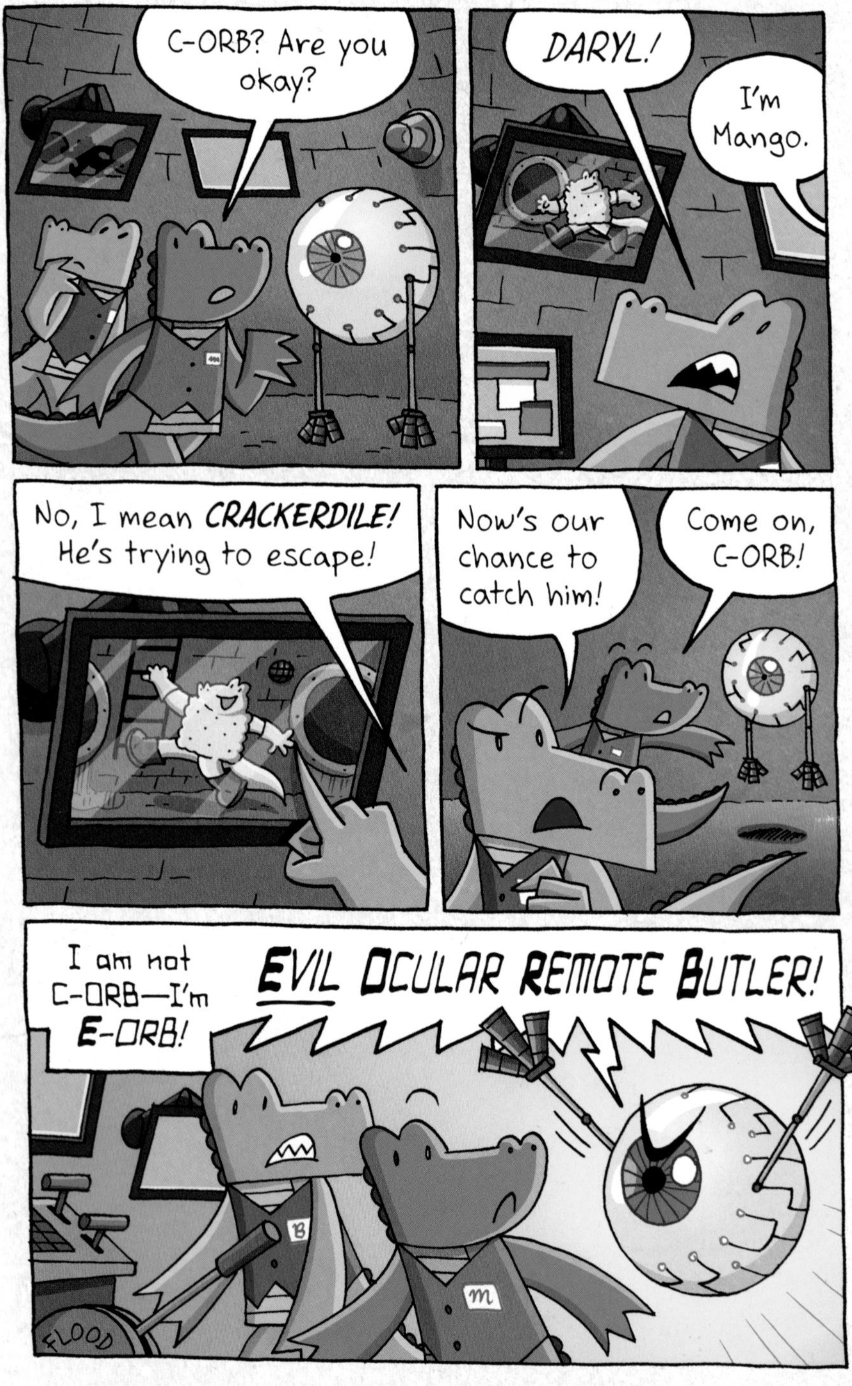
C-ORB? Are you okay?
DARYL!
I'm Mango.
No, I mean CRACKERDILE! He's trying to escape!
Now's our chance to catch him!
Come on, C-ORB!
I am not C-ORB—I'm E-ORB!
EVIL OCULAR REMOTE BUTLER!
FLOOD

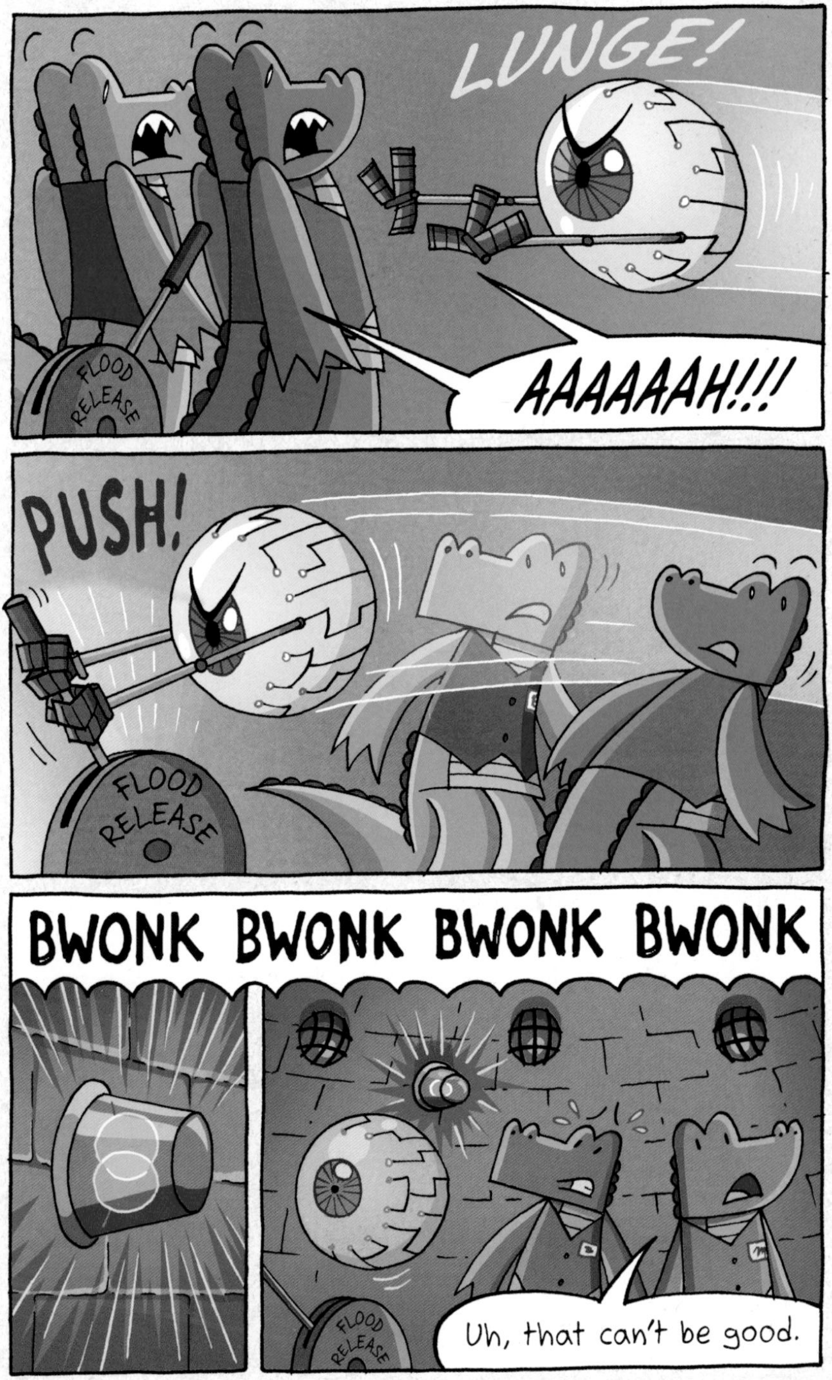
LUNGE!
AAAAAAH!!!
FLOOD RELEASE
PUSH!
FLOOD RELEASE
BWONK BWONK BWONK BWONK
FLOOD RELEASE
Uh, that can't be good.

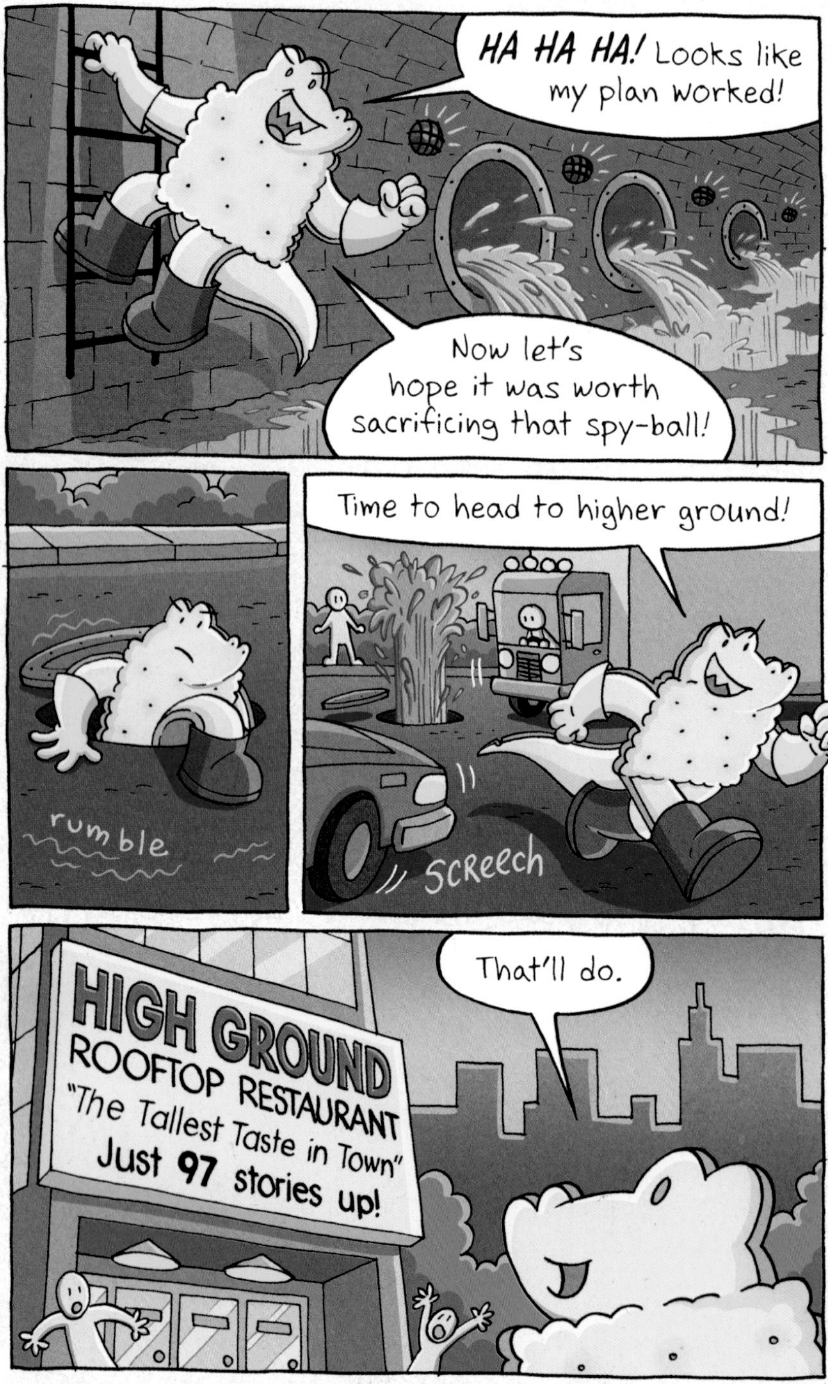
HA HA HA! Looks like my plan worked!
Now let's hope it was worth sacrificing that spy-ball!
rumble
Time to head to higher ground!
SCREECH
HIGH GROUND
ROOFTOP RESTAURANT
"The Tallest Taste in Town"
Just 97 stories up!
That'll do.

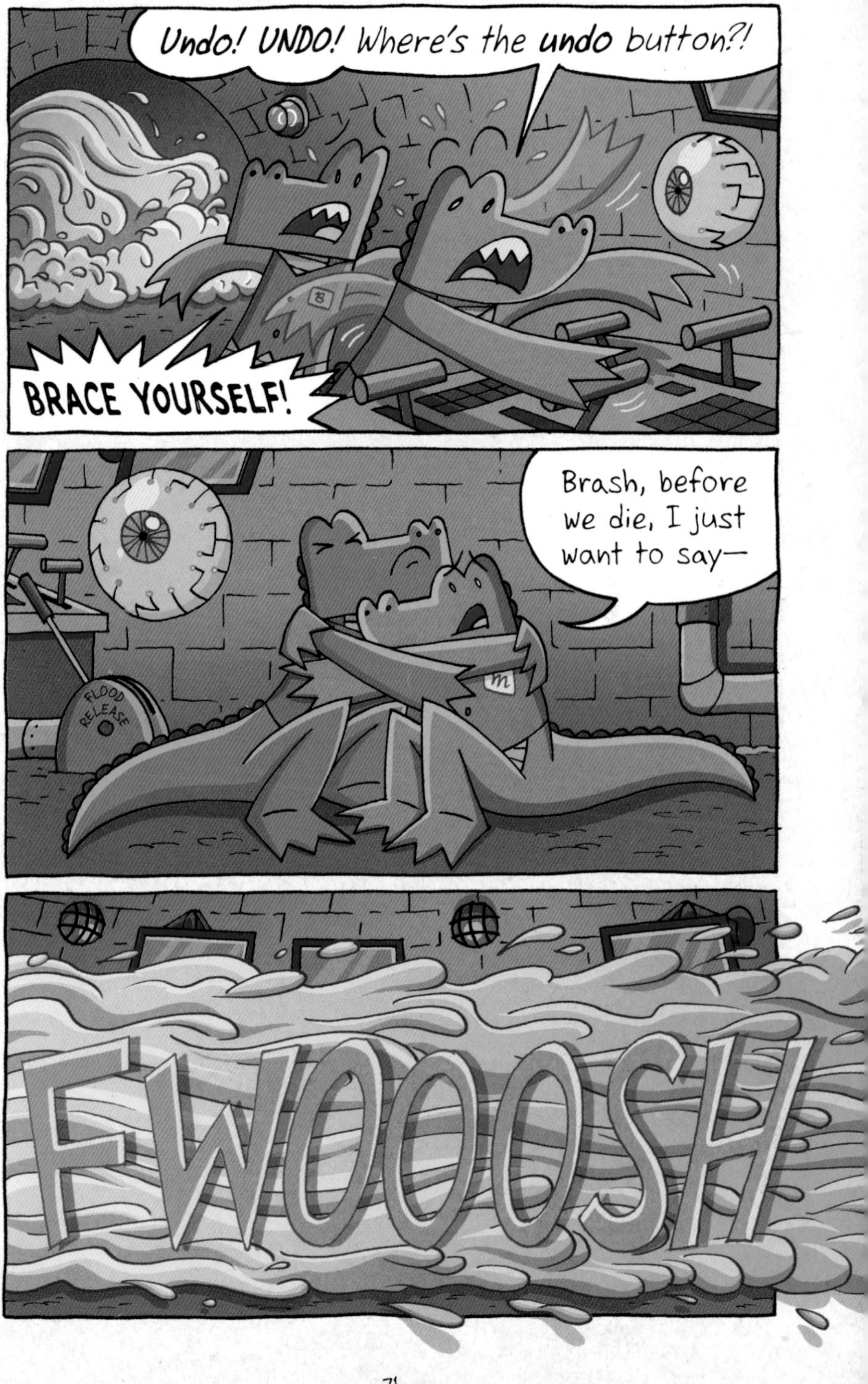
Undo! UNDO! Where's the undo button?!
BRACE YOURSELF!
Brash, before we die, I just want to say—
FLOOD RELEASE
FWOOOSH

Chapter 8

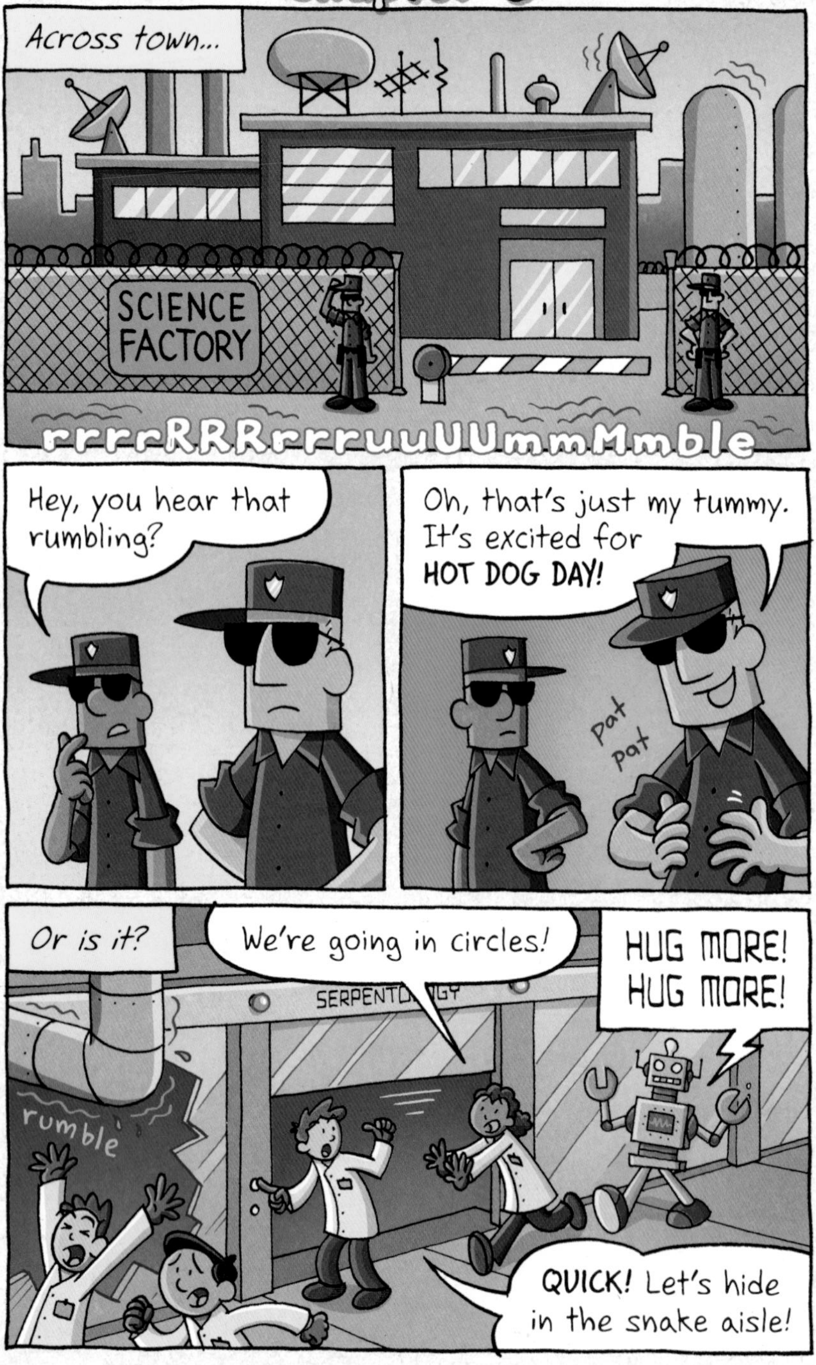
Across town...
SCIENCE FACTORY
rrrrRRRrrrruuUUmmMmble
Hey, you hear that rumbling?
Oh, that's just my tummy. It's excited for HOT DOG DAY!
pat pat
Or is it?
We're going in circles!
HUG MORE! HUG MORE!
rumble
QUICK! Let's hide in the snake aisle!

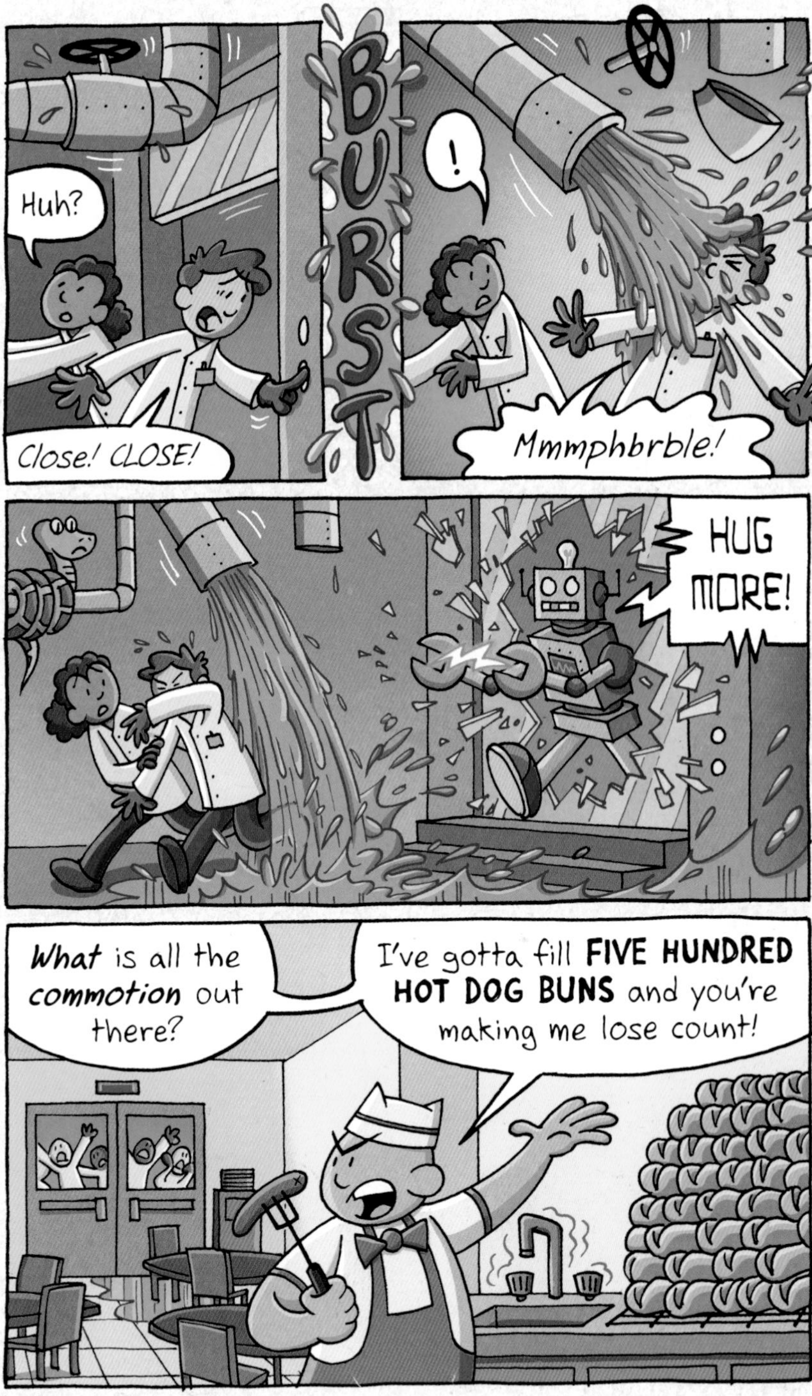
Huh?
Close! CLOSE!
BURST
!
Mmmphbrble!
HUG MORE!
What is all the commotion out there?
I've gotta fill FIVE HUNDRED HOT DOG BUNS and you're making me lose count!

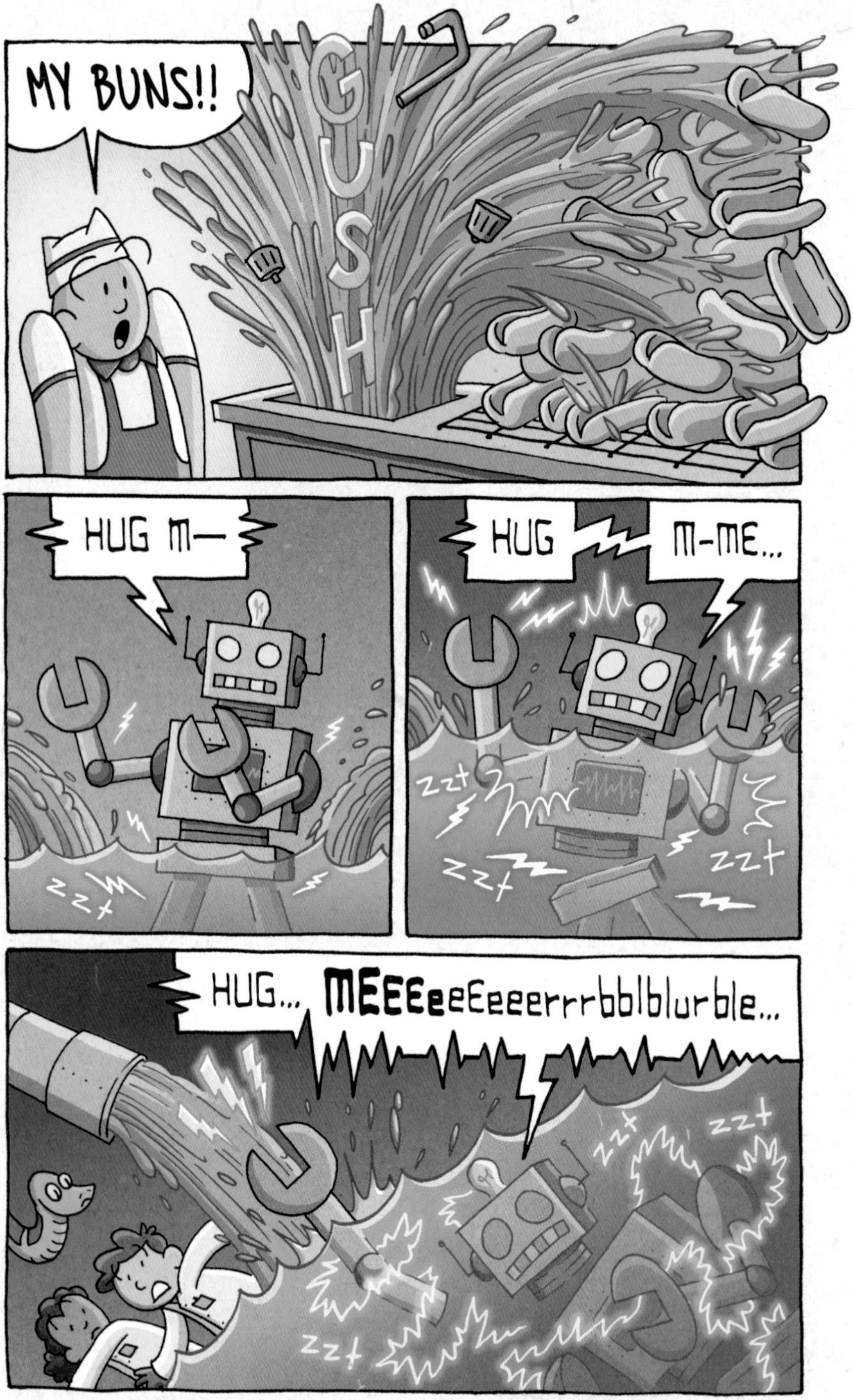
MY BUNS!!
GUSH
HUG M—
HUG
M-ME...
ZZT
ZZT
ZZT
HUG... MEEEeeEeeerrrbblblurble...
ZZT
ZZT
ZZT

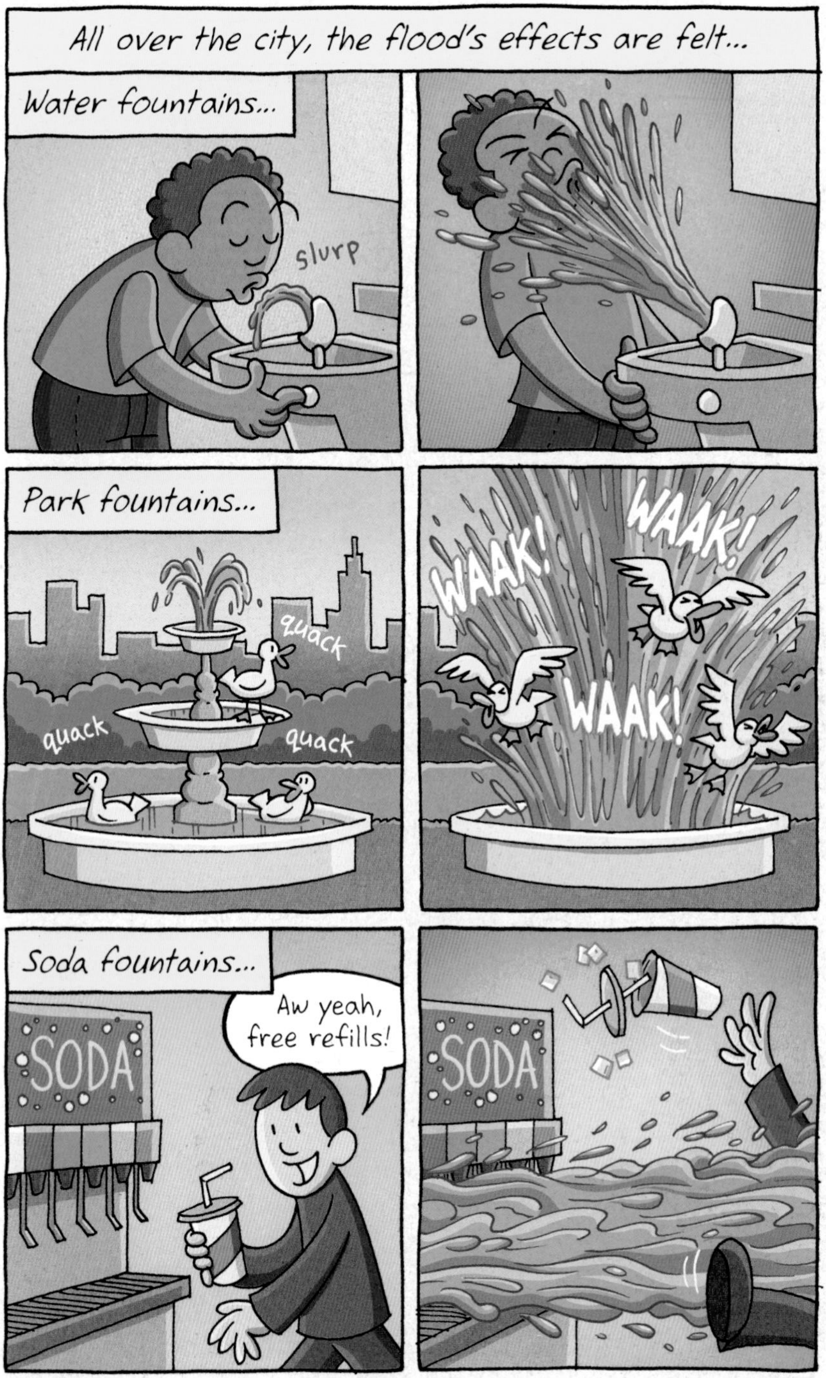
All over the city, the flood's effects are felt...
Water fountains...
slurp
Park fountains...
quack
quack
quack
WAAK!
WAAK!
WAAK!
Soda fountains...
SODA
Aw yeah, free refills!
SODA

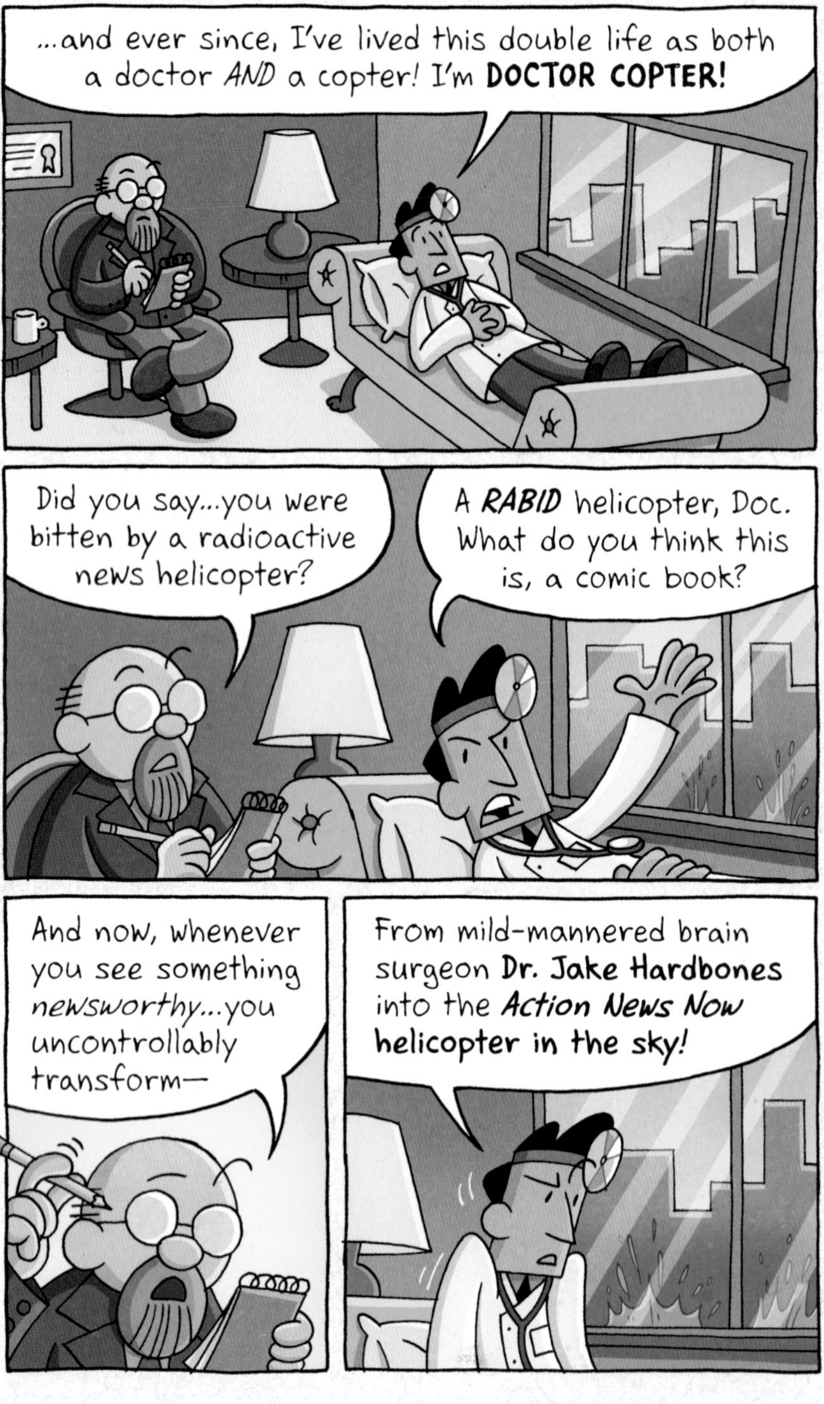
...and ever since, I've lived this double life as both a doctor *AND* a copter! I'm **DOCTOR COPTER!**
Did you say...you were bitten by a radioactive news helicopter?
A ***RABID*** helicopter, Doc. What do you think this is, a comic book?
And now, whenever you see something *newsworthy*...you uncontrollably transform—
From mild-mannered brain surgeon **Dr. Jake Hardbones** into the ***Action News Now*** **helicopter in the sky!**

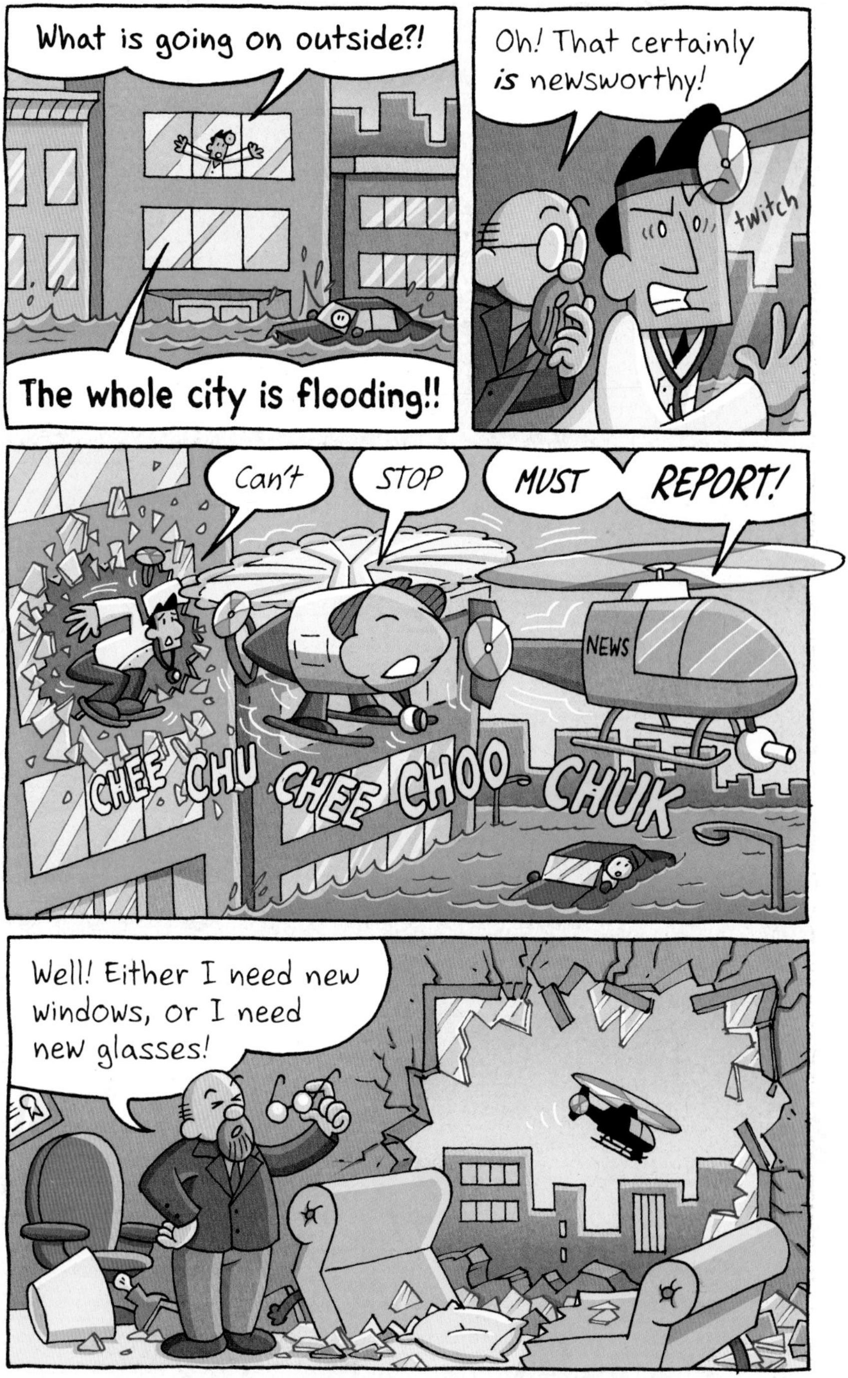

What is going on outside?!
The whole city is flooding!!
Oh! That certainly *is* newsworthy!
twitch
Can't
STOP
MUST
REPORT!
NEWS
CHEE CHU CHEE CHOO CHUK
Well! Either I need new windows, or I need new glasses!

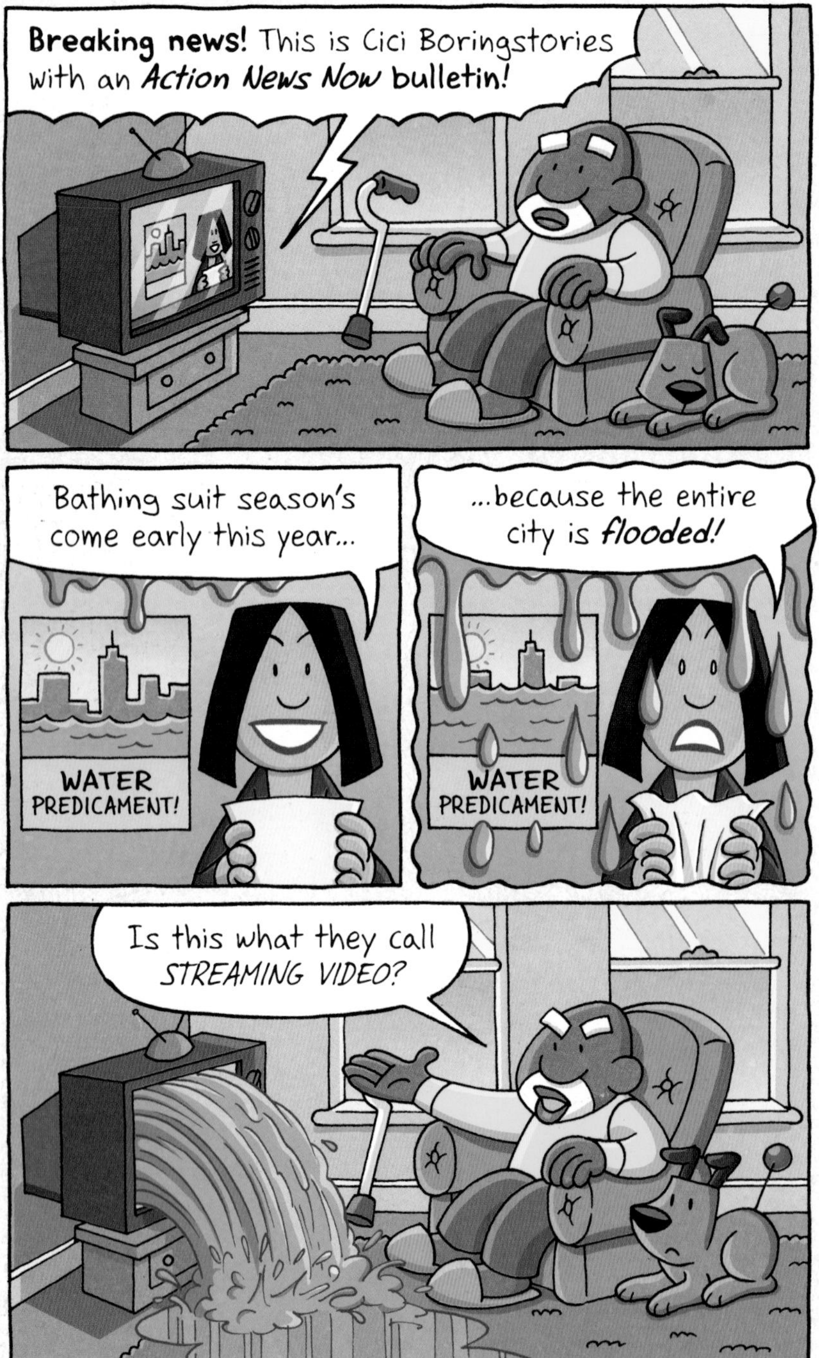
Breaking news! This is Cici Boringstories with an Action News Now bulletin!
Bathing suit season's come early this year...
WATER PREDICAMENT!
...because the entire city is flooded!
WATER PREDICAMENT!
Is this what they call STREAMING VIDEO?

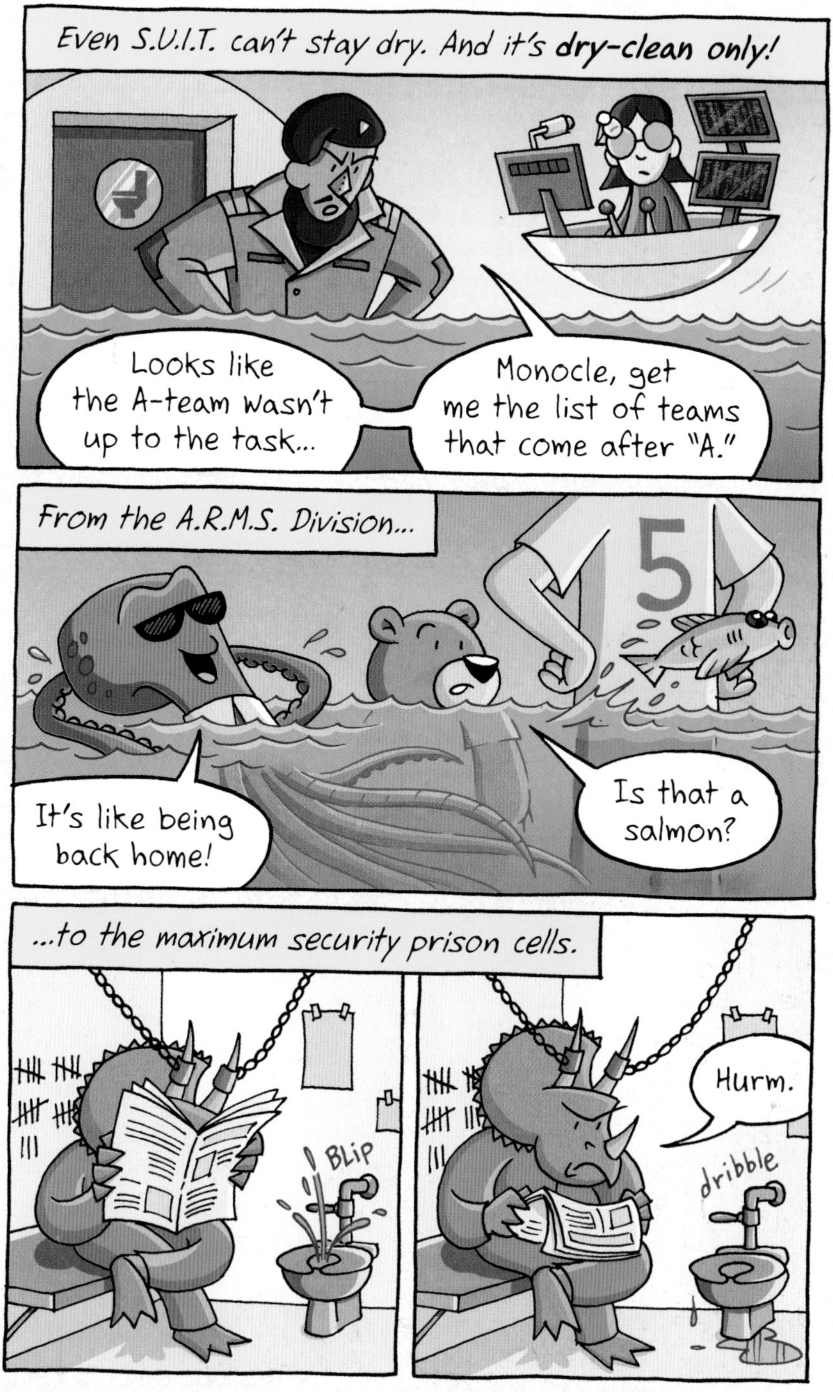

Even S.U.I.T. can't stay dry. And it's **dry-clean only!**
Looks like the A-team wasn't up to the task...
Monocle, get me the list of teams that come after "A."
From the A.R.M.S. Division...
It's like being back home!
Is that a salmon?
...to the maximum security prison cells.
BLIP
Hurm.
dribble

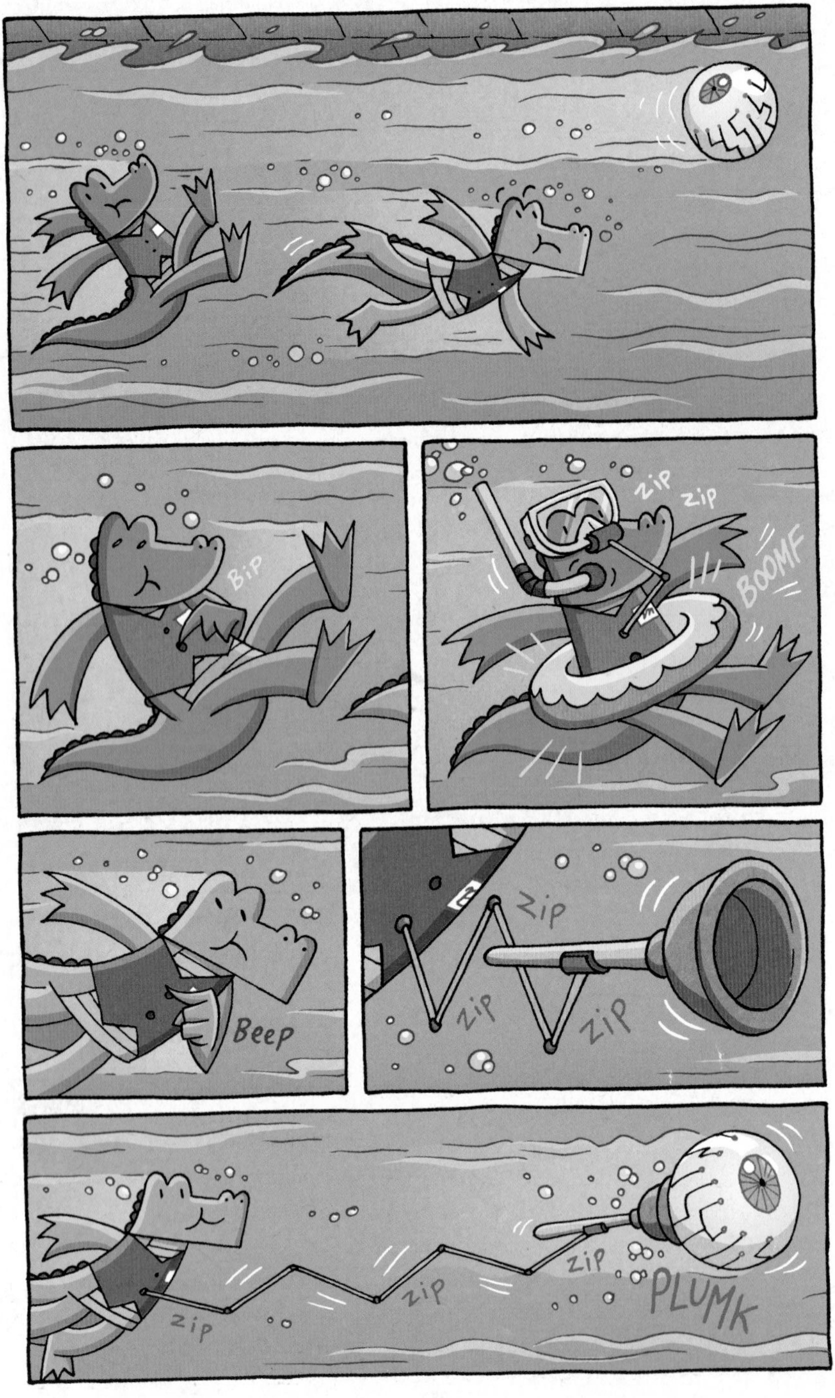
BIP
ZIP
ZIP
BOOMF
Beep
ZIP
ZIP
ZIP
ZIP
ZIP
ZIP
PLUMK

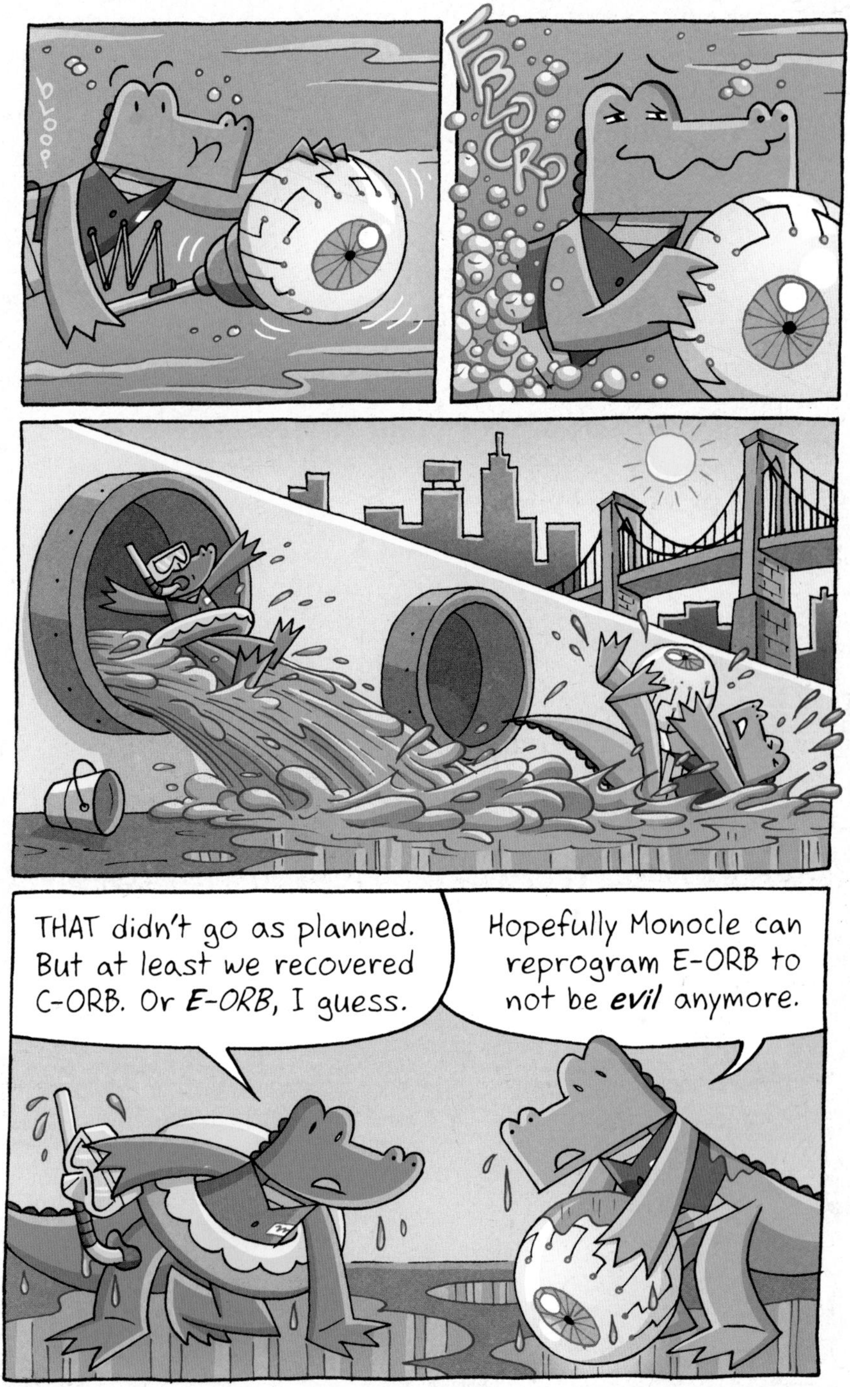
bLOOP
FBLOCRP
THAT didn't go as planned. But at least we recovered C-ORB. Or *E-ORB*, I guess.
Hopefully Monocle can reprogram E-ORB to not be *evil* anymore.

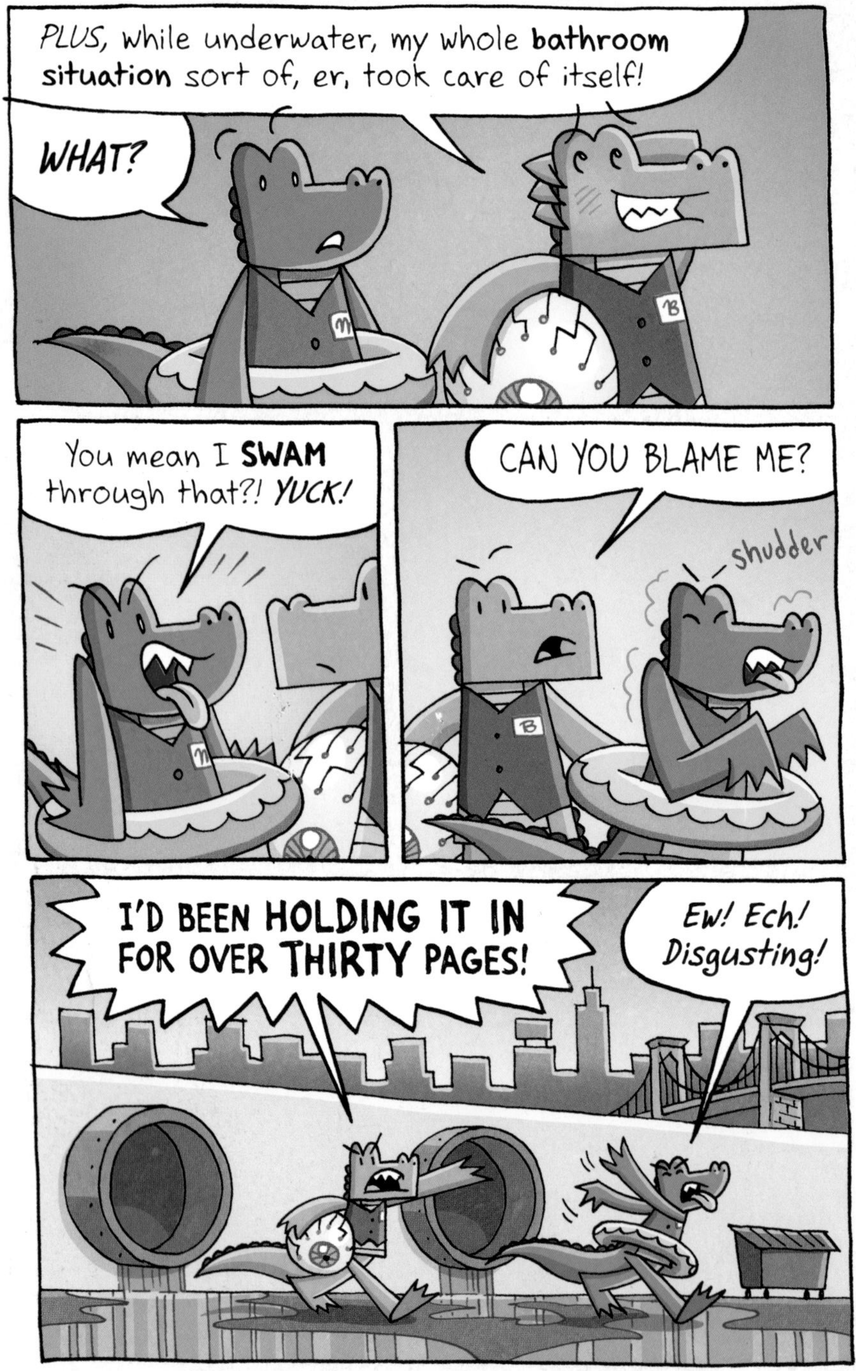
PLUS, while underwater, my whole bathroom situation sort of, er, took care of itself!
WHAT?
You mean I SWAM through that?! YUCK!
CAN YOU BLAME ME?
shudder
I'D BEEN HOLDING IT IN FOR OVER THIRTY PAGES!
Ew! Ech! Disgusting!

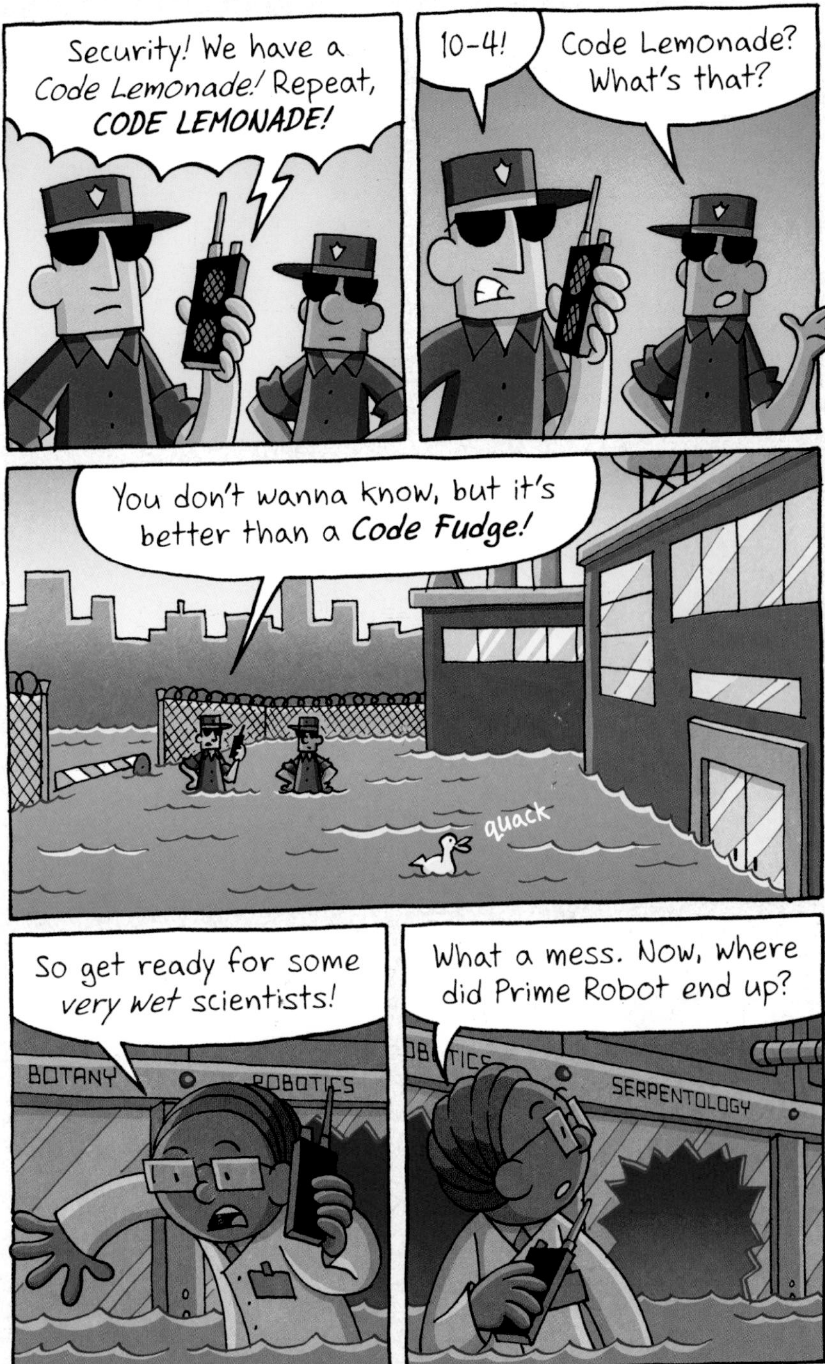
Security! We have a Code Lemonade! Repeat, CODE LEMONADE!
10-4!
Code Lemonade? What's that?
You don't wanna know, but it's better than a Code Fudge!
quack
So get ready for some very wet scientists!
BOTANY
ROBOTICS
What a mess. Now, where did Prime Robot end up?
SERPENTOLOGY

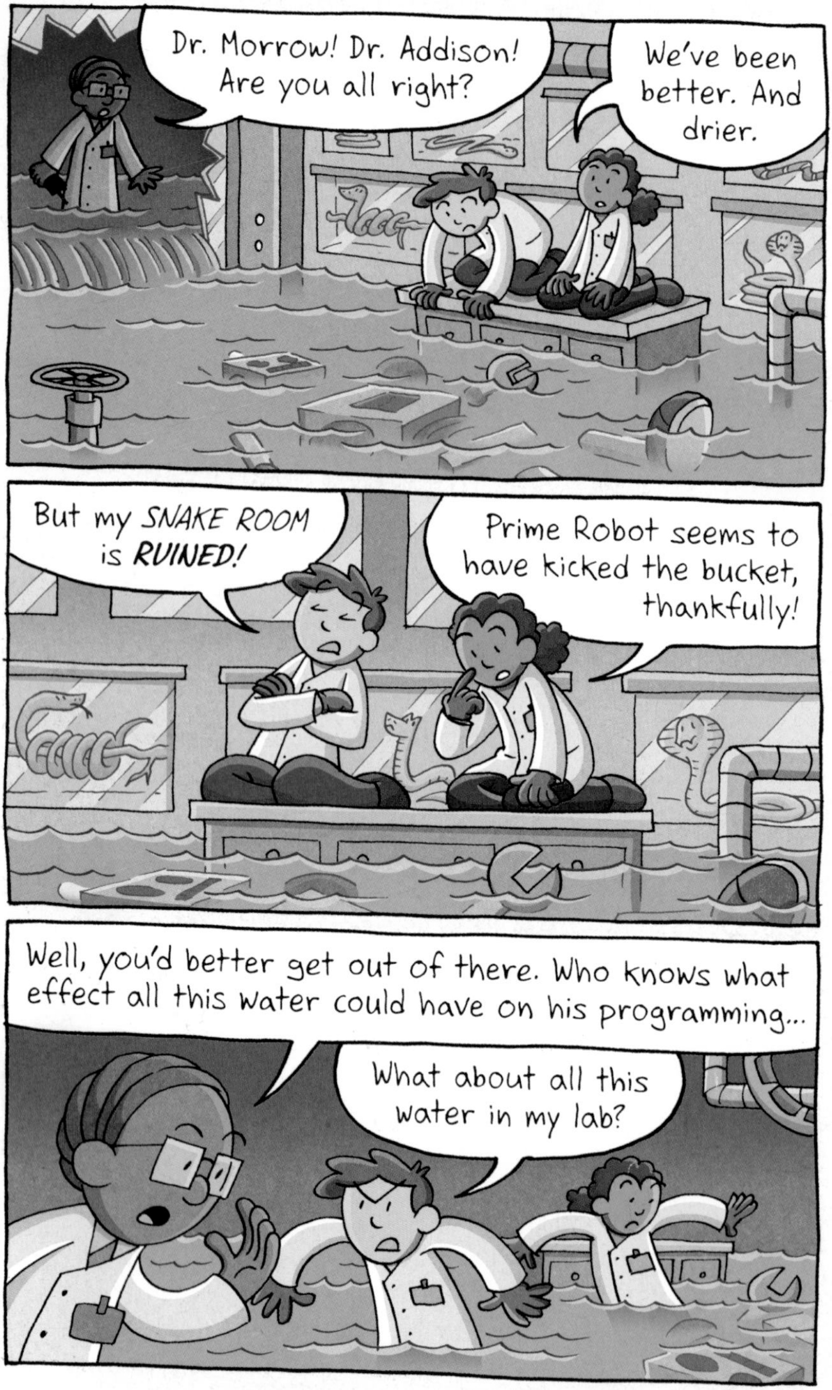

Dr. Morrow! Dr. Addison! Are you all right?
We've been better. And drier.
But my *SNAKE ROOM* is ***RUINED!***
Prime Robot seems to have kicked the bucket, thankfully!
Well, you'd better get out of there. Who knows what effect all this water could have on his programming...
What about all this water in my lab?

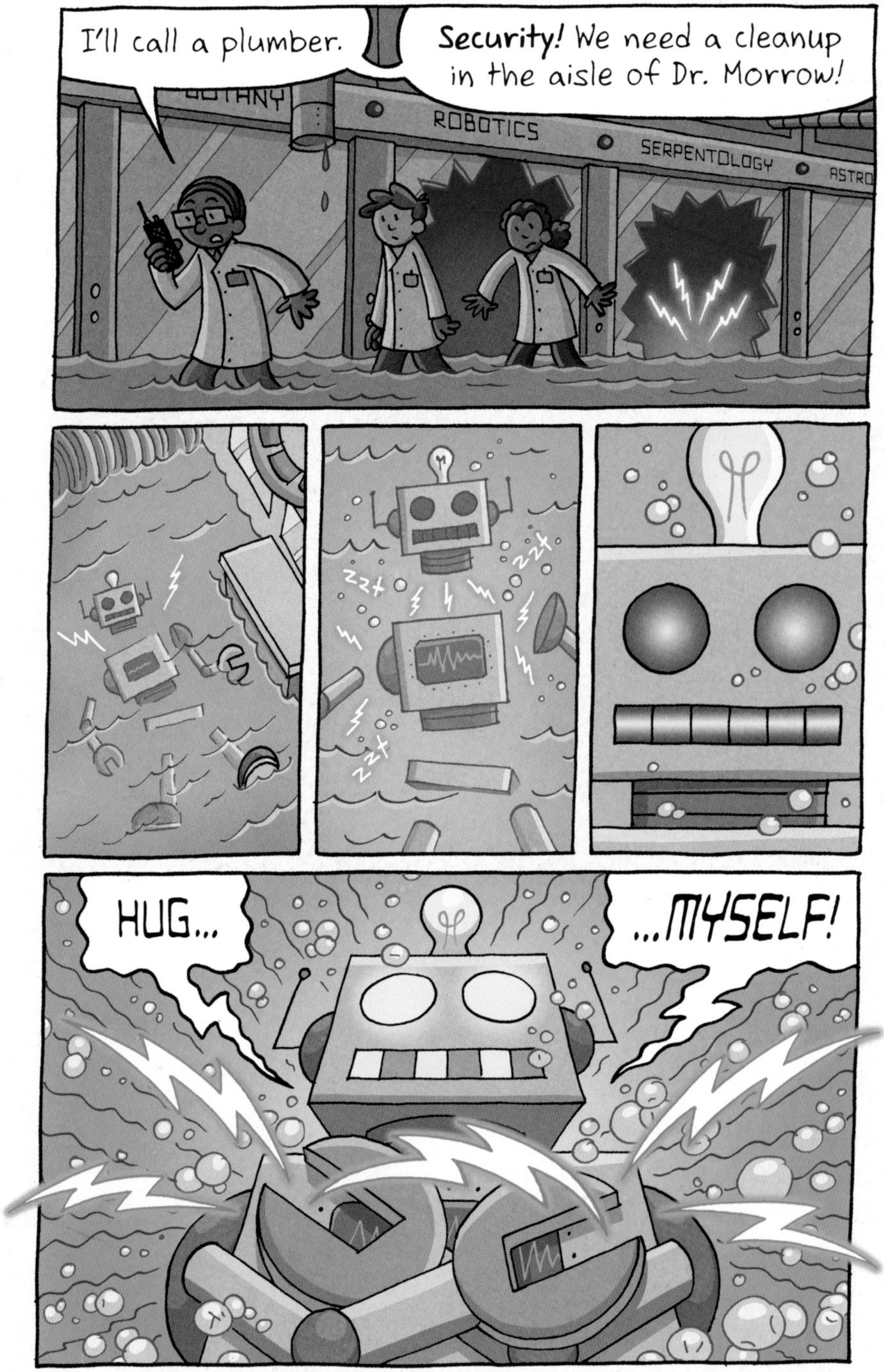
I'll call a plumber.
Security! We need a cleanup in the aisle of Dr. Morrow!
BOTANY
ROBOTICS
SERPENTOLOGY
ASTRO
ZZT
ZZT
ZZT
HUG...
...MYSELF!

Chapter 9

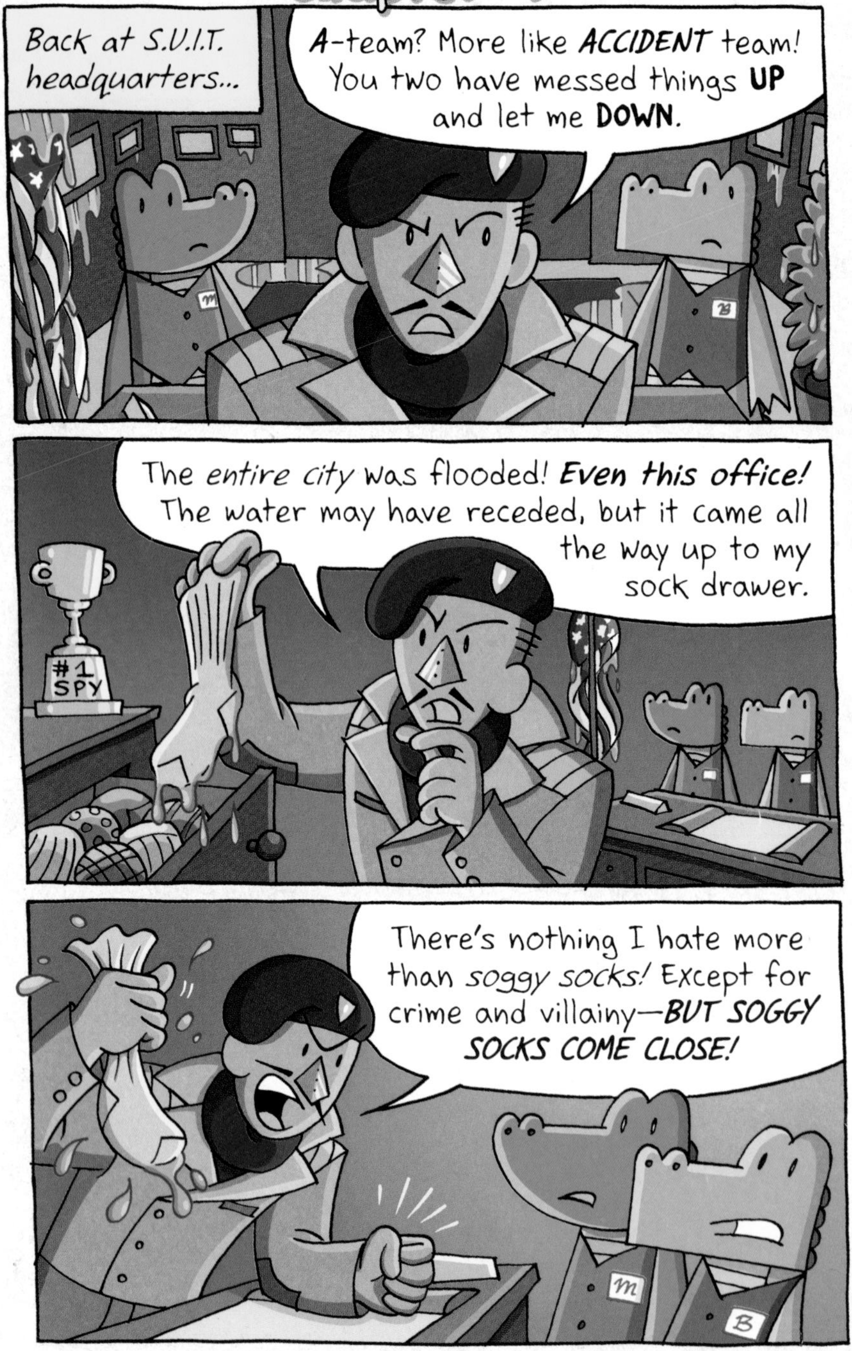

Back at S.U.I.T. headquarters...
A-team? More like ACCIDENT team! You two have messed things UP and let me DOWN.
The entire city was flooded! Even this office! The water may have receded, but it came all the way up to my sock drawer.
#1 SPY
There's nothing I hate more than soggy socks! Except for crime and villainy—BUT SOGGY SOCKS COME CLOSE!

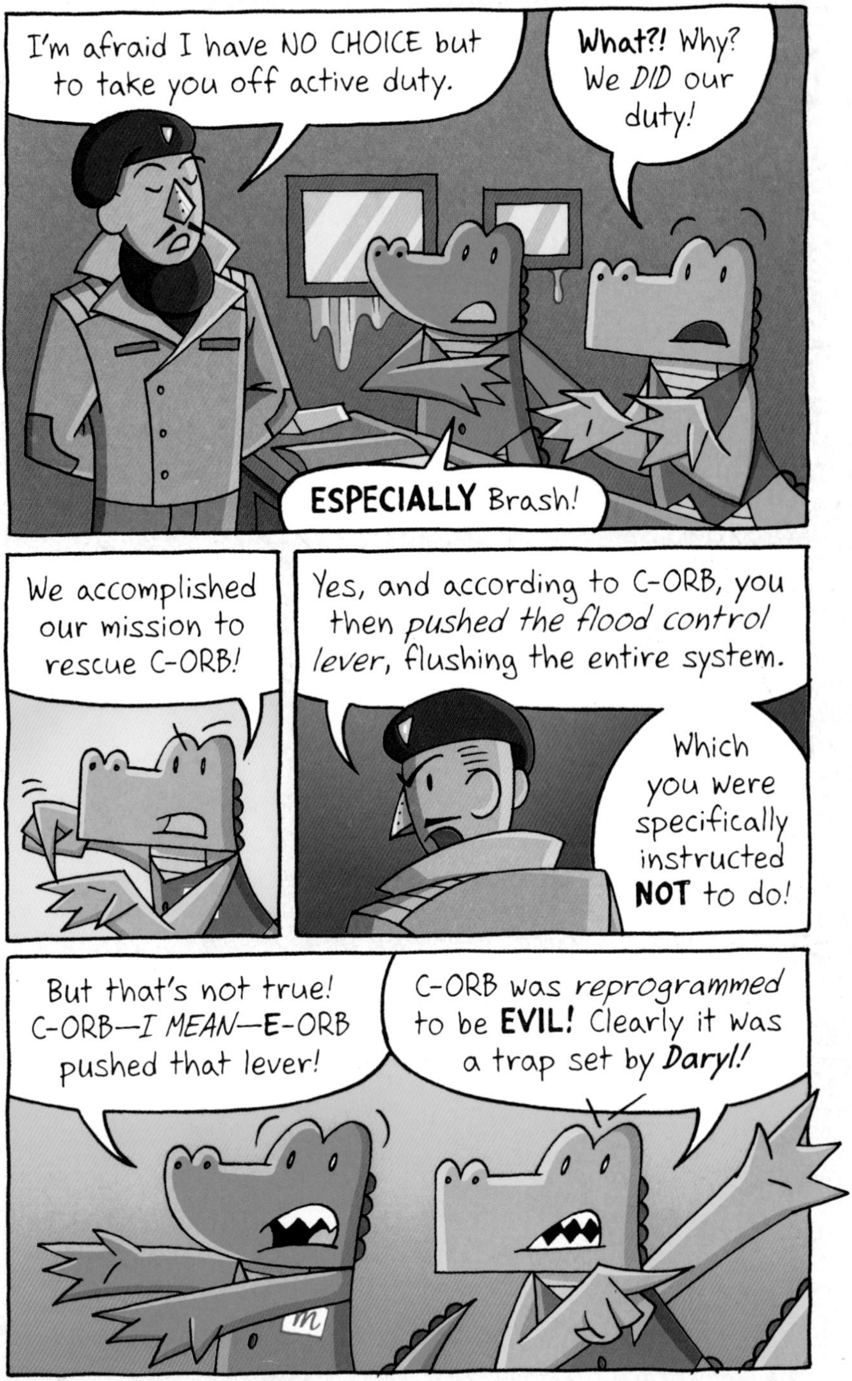
I'm afraid I have NO CHOICE but to take you off active duty.
What?! Why? We *DID* our duty!
ESPECIALLY Brash!
We accomplished our mission to rescue C-ORB!
Yes, and according to C-ORB, you then *pushed the flood control lever*, flushing the entire system.
Which you were specifically instructed **NOT** to do!
But that's not true! C-ORB—*I MEAN*—**E**-ORB pushed that lever!
C-ORB was *reprogrammed* to be **EVIL!** Clearly it was a trap set by ***Daryl!***

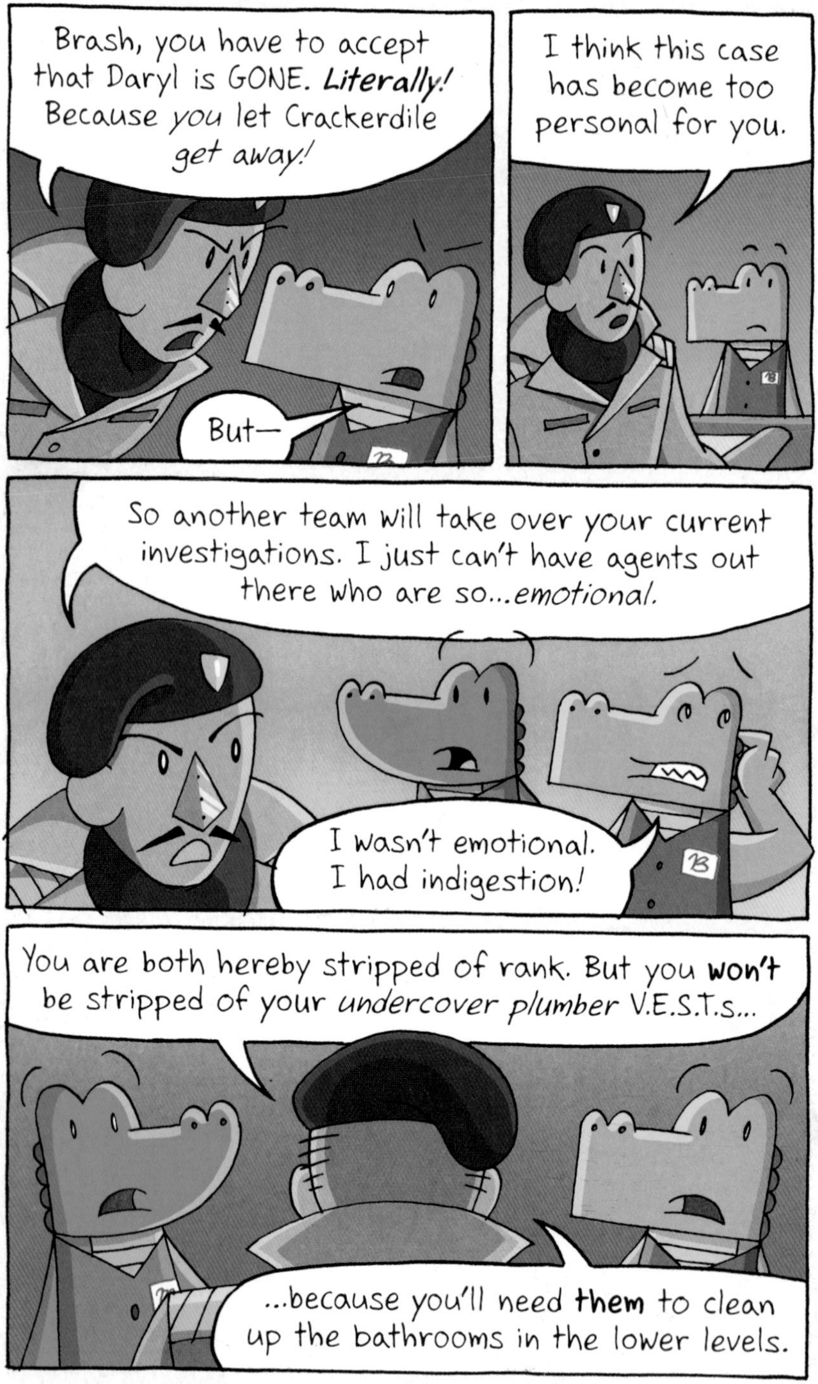
Brash, you have to accept that Daryl is GONE. ***Literally!*** Because *you* let Crackerdile *get away!*
But—
I think this case has become too personal for you.
So another team will take over your current investigations. I just can't have agents out there who are so...*emotional.*
I wasn't emotional. I had indigestion!
You are both hereby stripped of rank. But you **won't** be stripped of your *undercover plumber* V.E.S.T.s...
...because you'll need **them** to clean up the bathrooms in the lower levels.

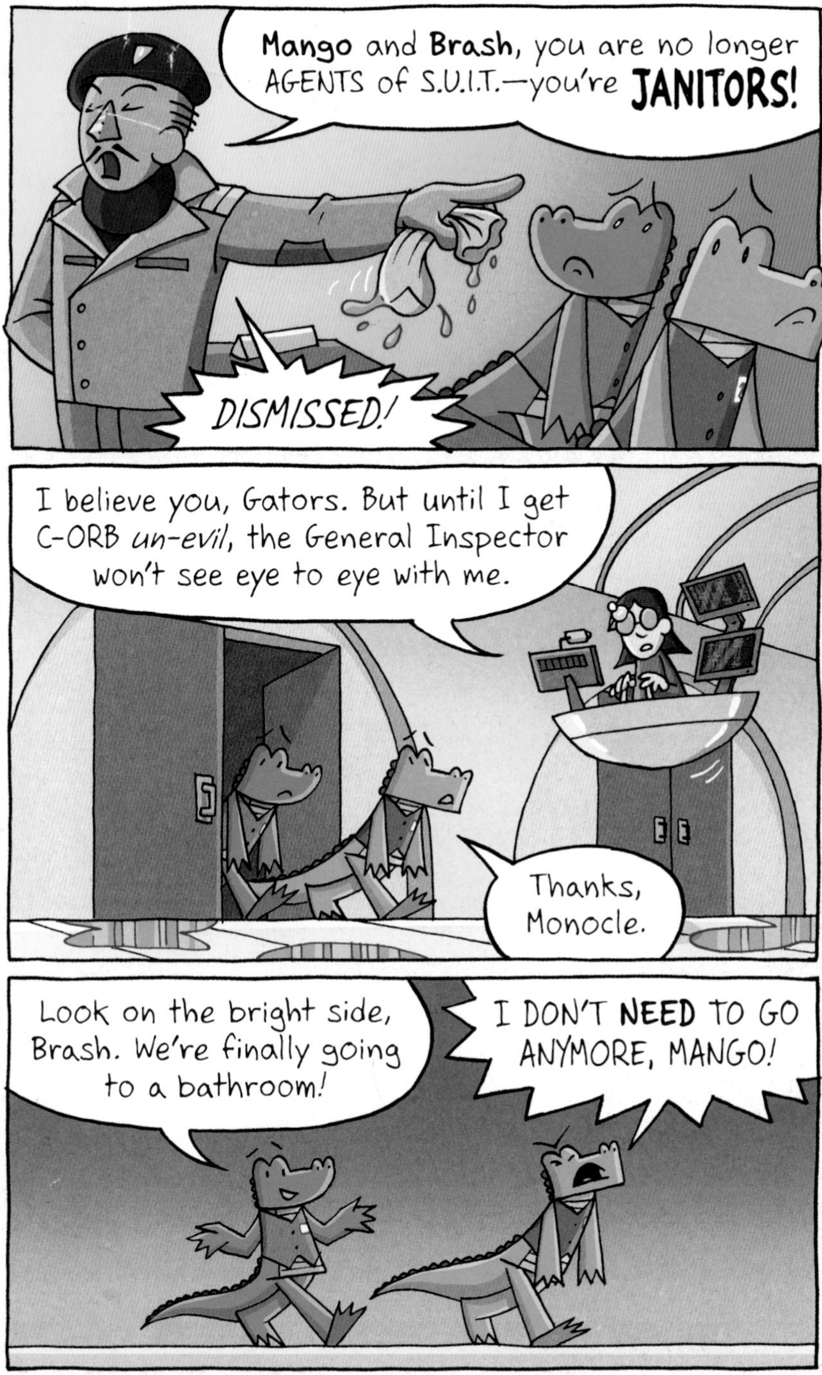
Mango and Brash, you are no longer AGENTS of S.U.I.T.—you're JANITORS!
DISMISSED!
I believe you, Gators. But until I get C-ORB un-evil, the General Inspector won't see eye to eye with me.
Thanks, Monocle.
Look on the bright side, Brash. We're finally going to a bathroom!
I DON'T NEED TO GO ANYMORE, MANGO!

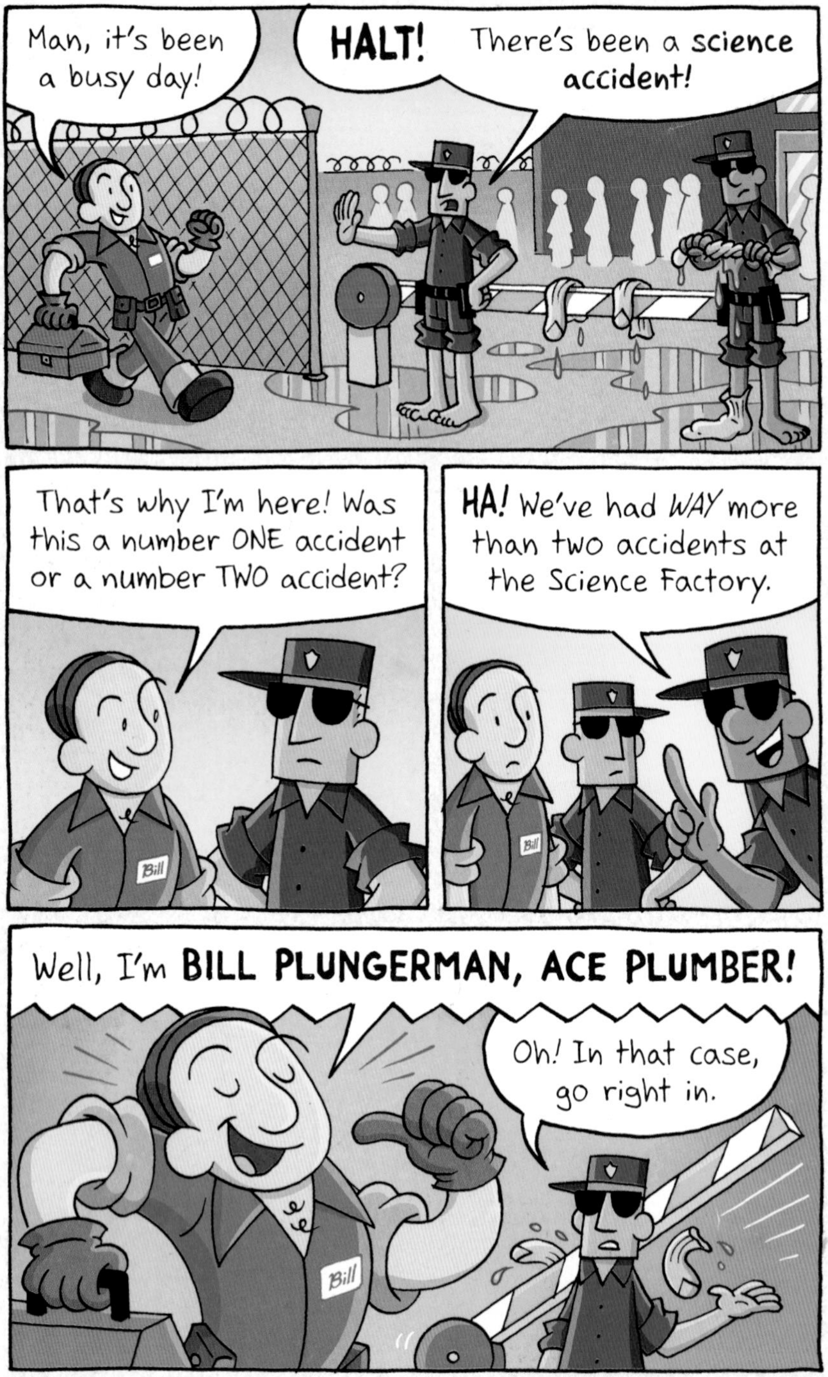
Man, it's been a busy day!
HALT! There's been a science accident!
That's why I'm here! Was this a number ONE accident or a number TWO accident?
Bill
HA! We've had WAY more than two accidents at the Science Factory.
Bill
Well, I'm BILL PLUNGERMAN, ACE PLUMBER!
Oh! In that case, go right in.
Bill

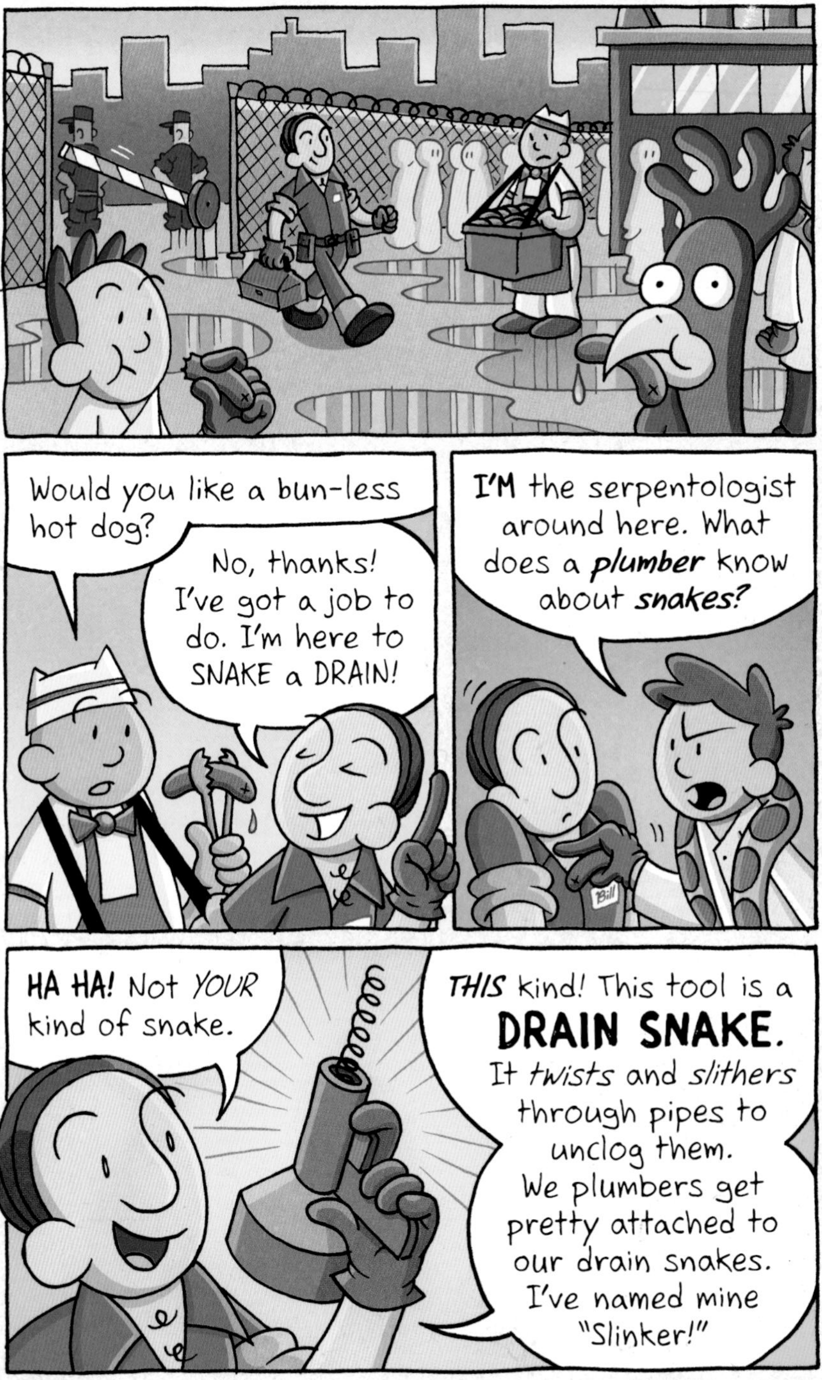
Would you like a bun-less hot dog?
No, thanks! I've got a job to do. I'm here to SNAKE a DRAIN!
I'M the serpentologist around here. What does a ***plumber*** know about ***snakes?***
Bill
HA HA! Not *YOUR* kind of snake.
THIS kind! This tool is a **DRAIN SNAKE.** It *twists* and *slithers* through pipes to unclog them. We plumbers get pretty attached to our drain snakes. I've named mine "Slinker!"

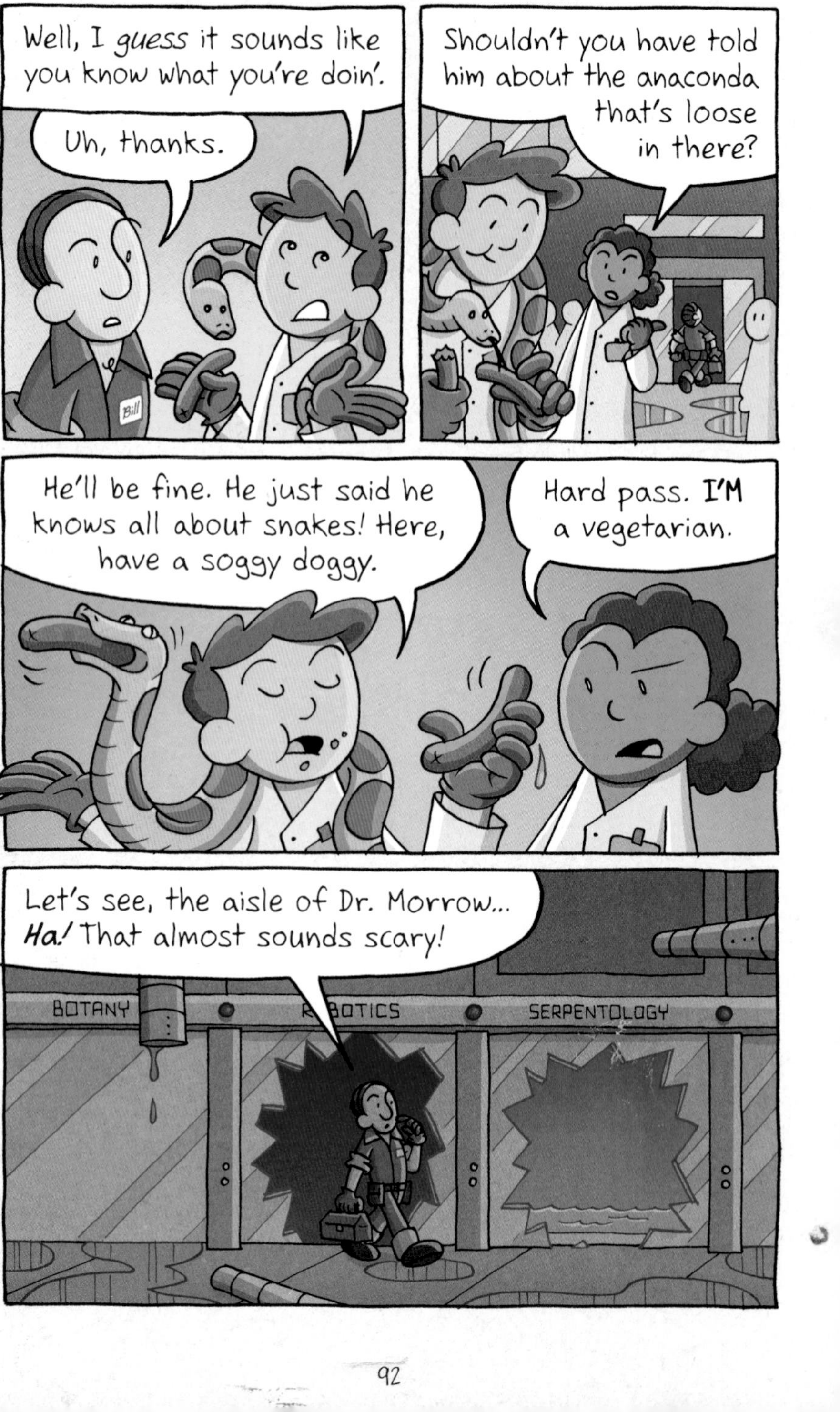

Well, I *guess* it sounds like you know what you're doin'.
Uh, thanks.
Shouldn't you have told him about the anaconda that's loose in there?
Bill
He'll be fine. He just said he knows all about snakes! Here, have a soggy doggy.
Hard pass. **I'M** a vegetarian.
Let's see, the aisle of Dr. Morrow... ***Ha!*** That almost sounds scary!
BOTANY
SERPENTOLOGY

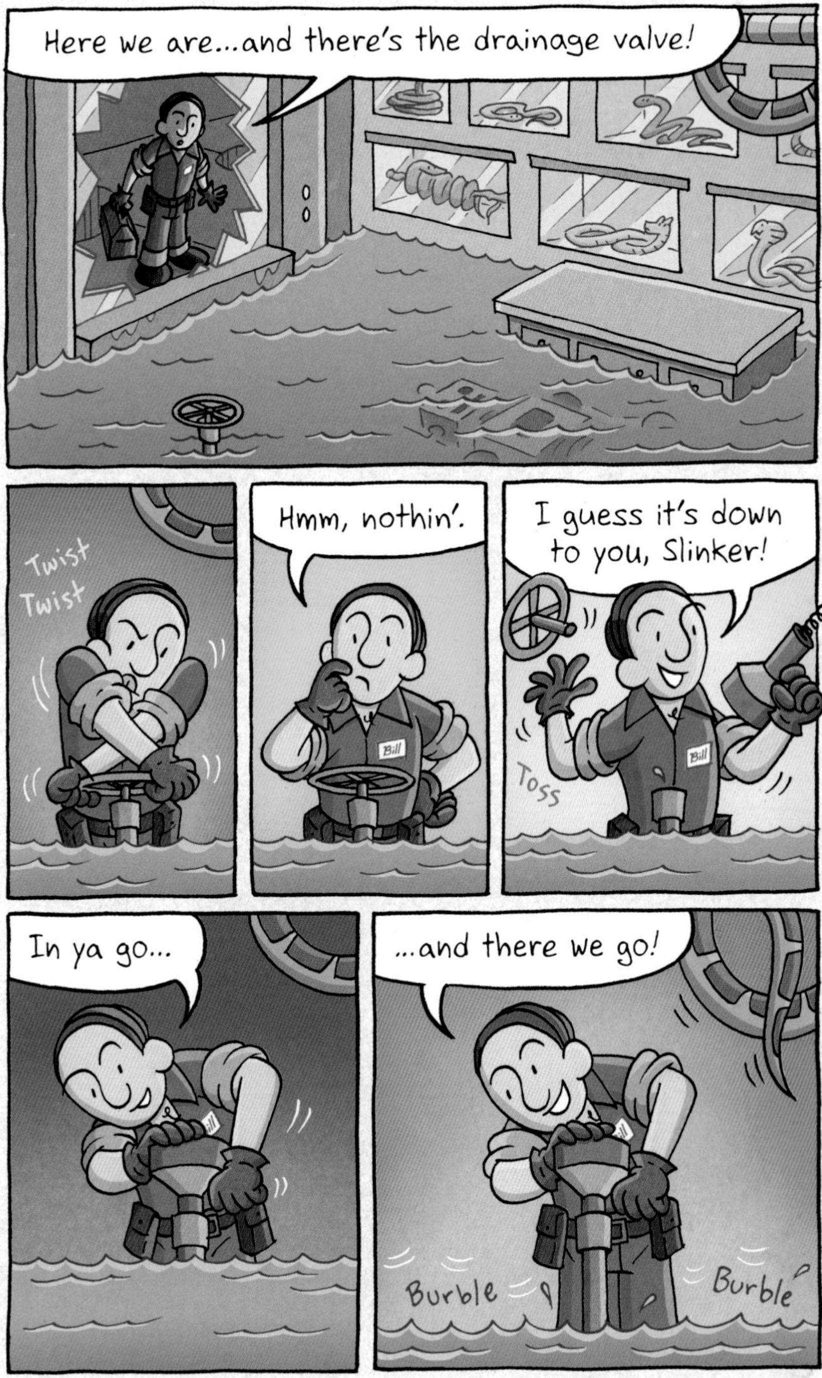
Here we are...and there's the drainage valve!
Twist
Twist
Hmm, nothin'.
I guess it's down to you, Slinker!
Bill
Bill
Toss
In ya go...
...and there we go!
Burble
Burble

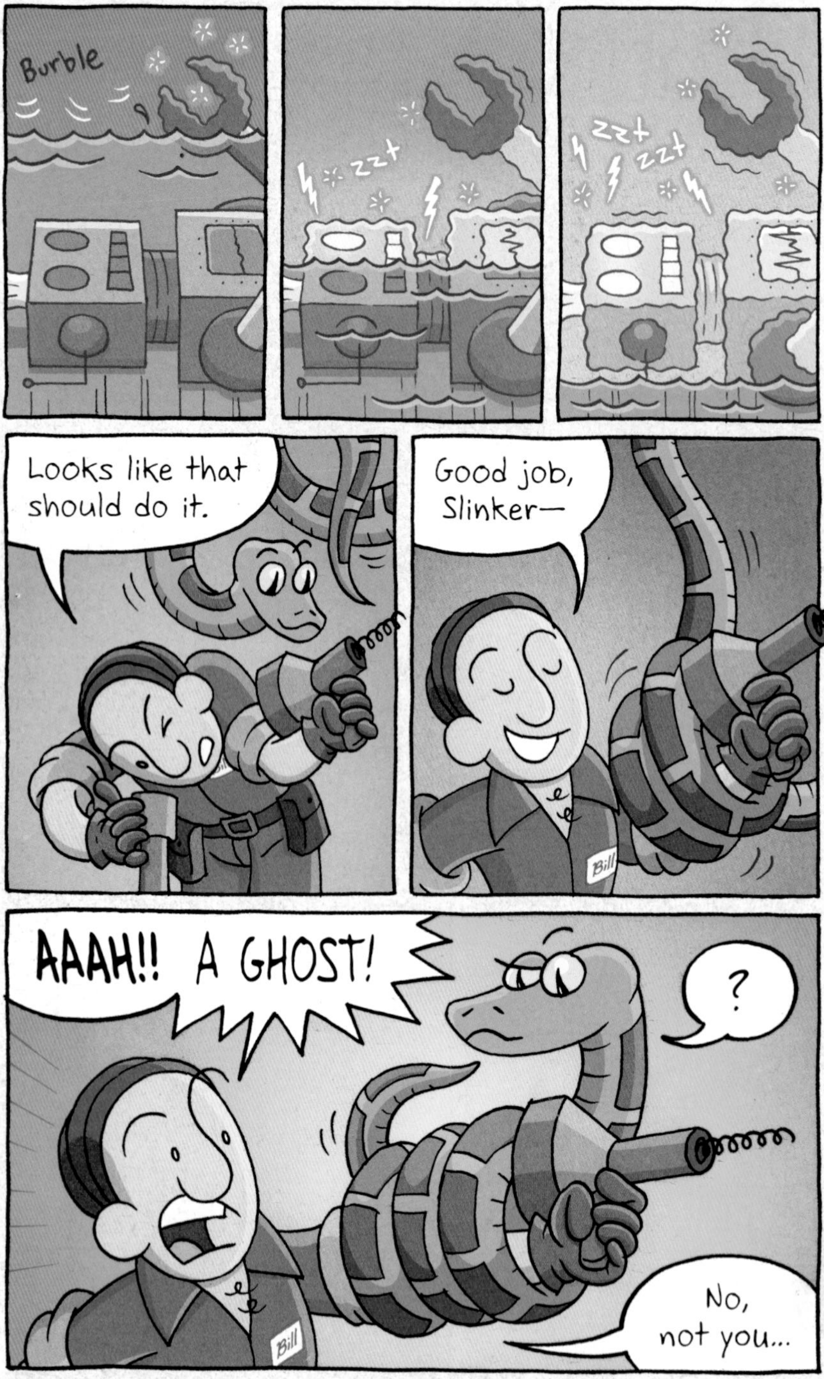
Burble
zzt
zzt
zzt
Looks like that should do it.
Good job, Slinker—
Bill
AAAH!! A GHOST!
?
No, not you...
Bill

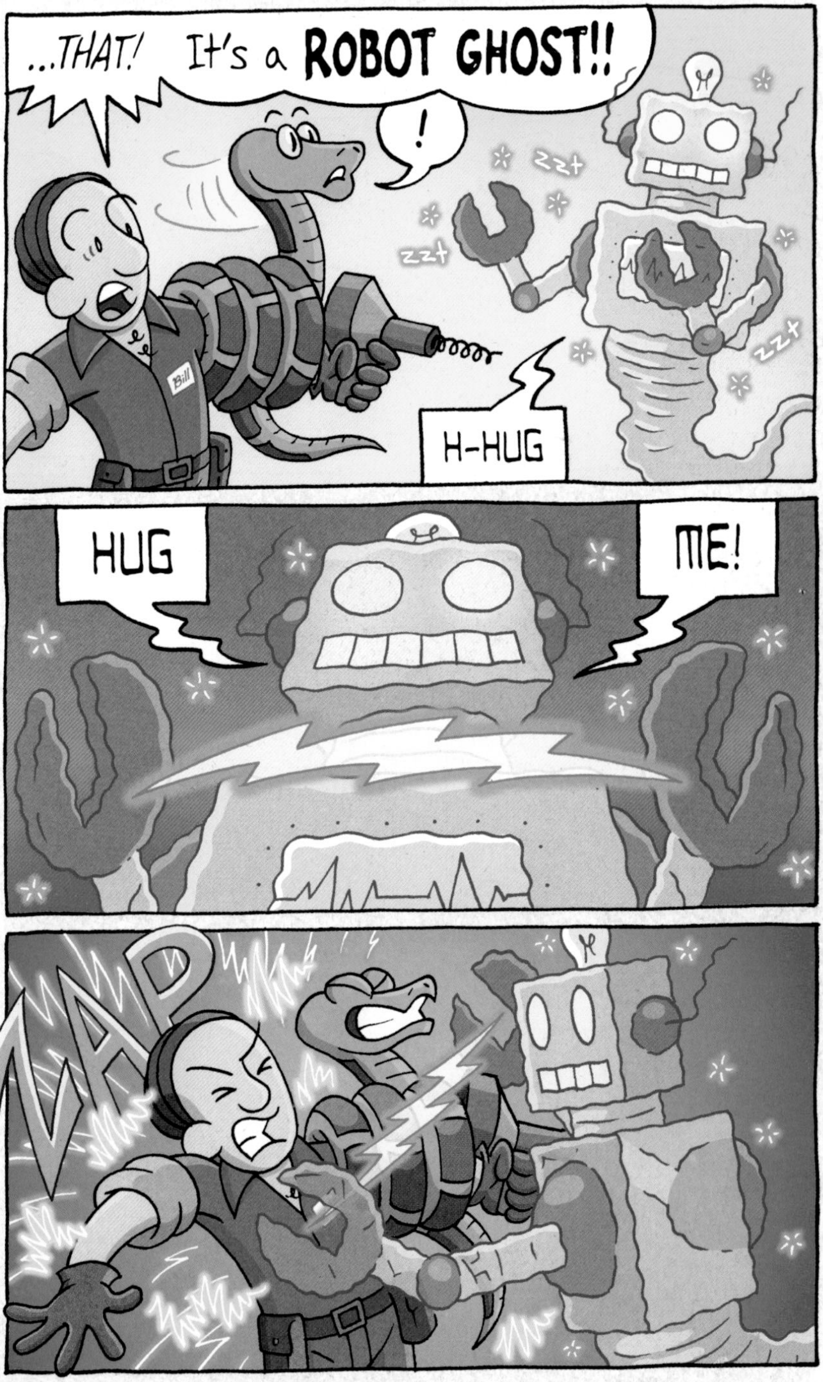
...THAT! It's a ROBOT GHOST!!
!
ZZT
ZZT
ZZT
H-HUG
HUG
ME!
ZAP

Chapter 10

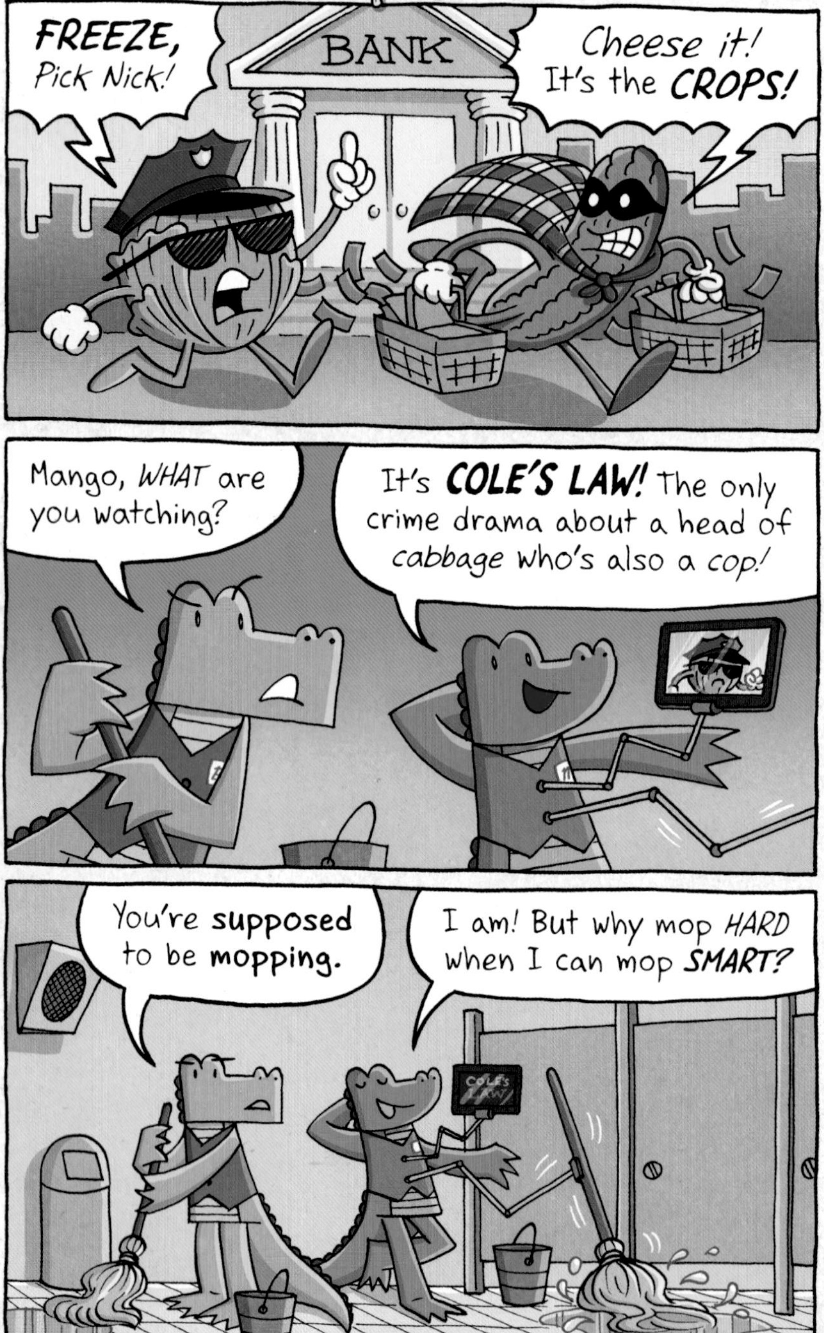

FREEZE, Pick Nick!
BANK
Cheese it! It's the CROPS!
Mango, WHAT are you watching?
It's COLE'S LAW! The only crime drama about a head of cabbage who's also a cop!
You're supposed to be mopping.
I am! But why mop HARD when I can mop SMART?
COLE'S LAW

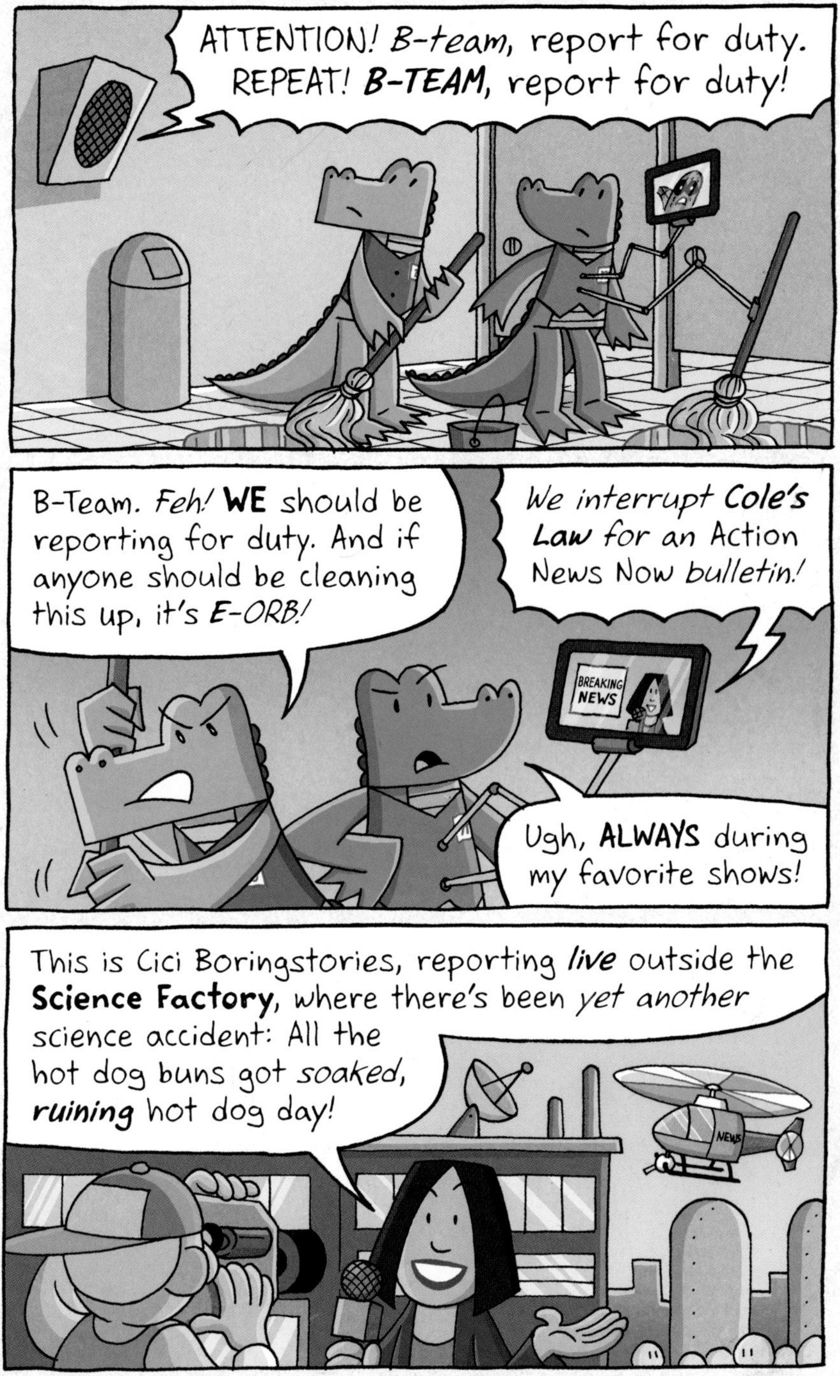
ATTENTION! *B-team*, report for duty. REPEAT! ***B-TEAM***, report for duty!
B-Team. *Feh!* **WE** should be reporting for duty. And if anyone should be cleaning this up, it's ***E-ORB!***
We interrupt ***Cole's Law*** *for an* Action News Now *bulletin!*
BREAKING NEWS
Ugh, **ALWAYS** during my favorite shows!
This is Cici Boringstories, reporting *live* outside the **Science Factory**, where there's been *yet another* science accident: All the hot dog buns got *soaked*, ***ruining*** hot dog day!
NEWS

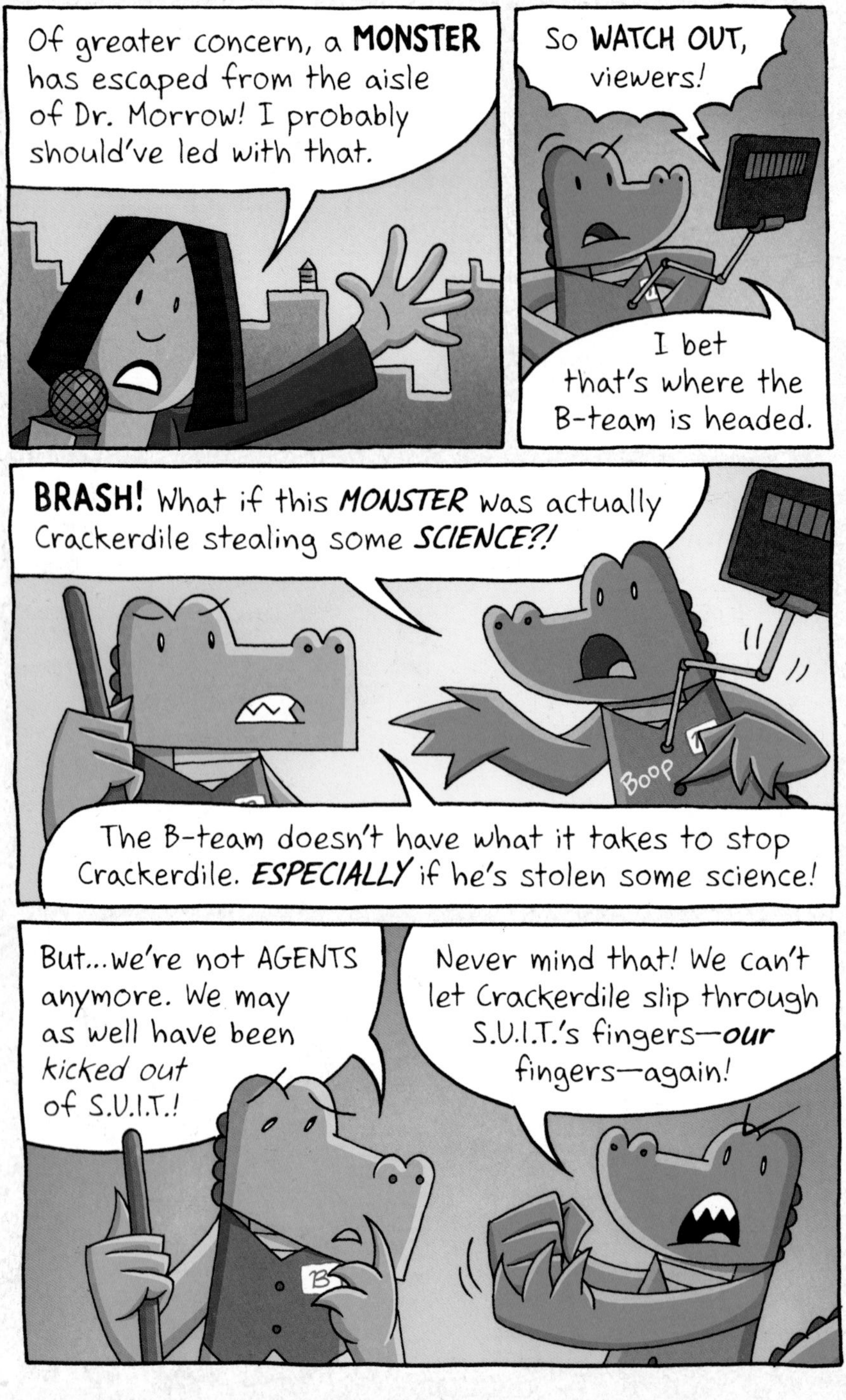
Of greater concern, a **MONSTER** has escaped from the aisle of Dr. Morrow! I probably should've led with that.
So **WATCH OUT,** viewers!
I bet that's where the B-team is headed.
BRASH! What if this ***MONSTER*** was actually Crackerdile stealing some ***SCIENCE?!***
BOOP
The B-team doesn't have what it takes to stop Crackerdile. ***ESPECIALLY*** if he's stolen some science!
But...we're not AGENTS anymore. We may as well have been *kicked out* of S.U.I.T.!
Never mind that! We can't let Crackerdile slip through S.U.I.T.'s fingers—***our*** fingers—again!

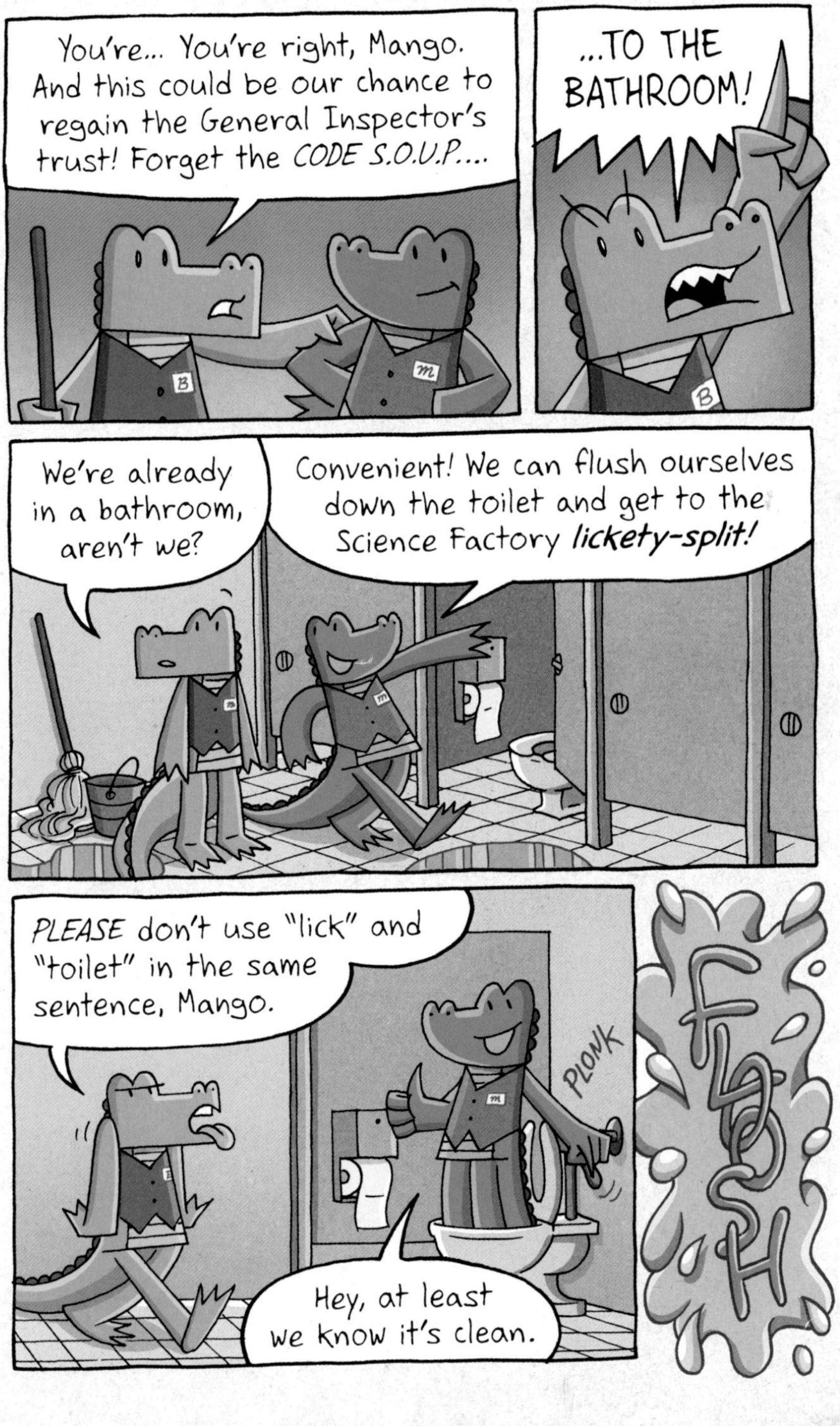
You're... You're right, Mango. And this could be our chance to regain the General Inspector's trust! Forget the *CODE S.O.U.P.*....
...TO THE BATHROOM!
We're already in a bathroom, aren't we?
Convenient! We can flush ourselves down the toilet and get to the Science Factory ***lickety-split!***
PLEASE don't use "lick" and "toilet" in the same sentence, Mango.
PLONK
Hey, at least we know it's clean.
FLUSH

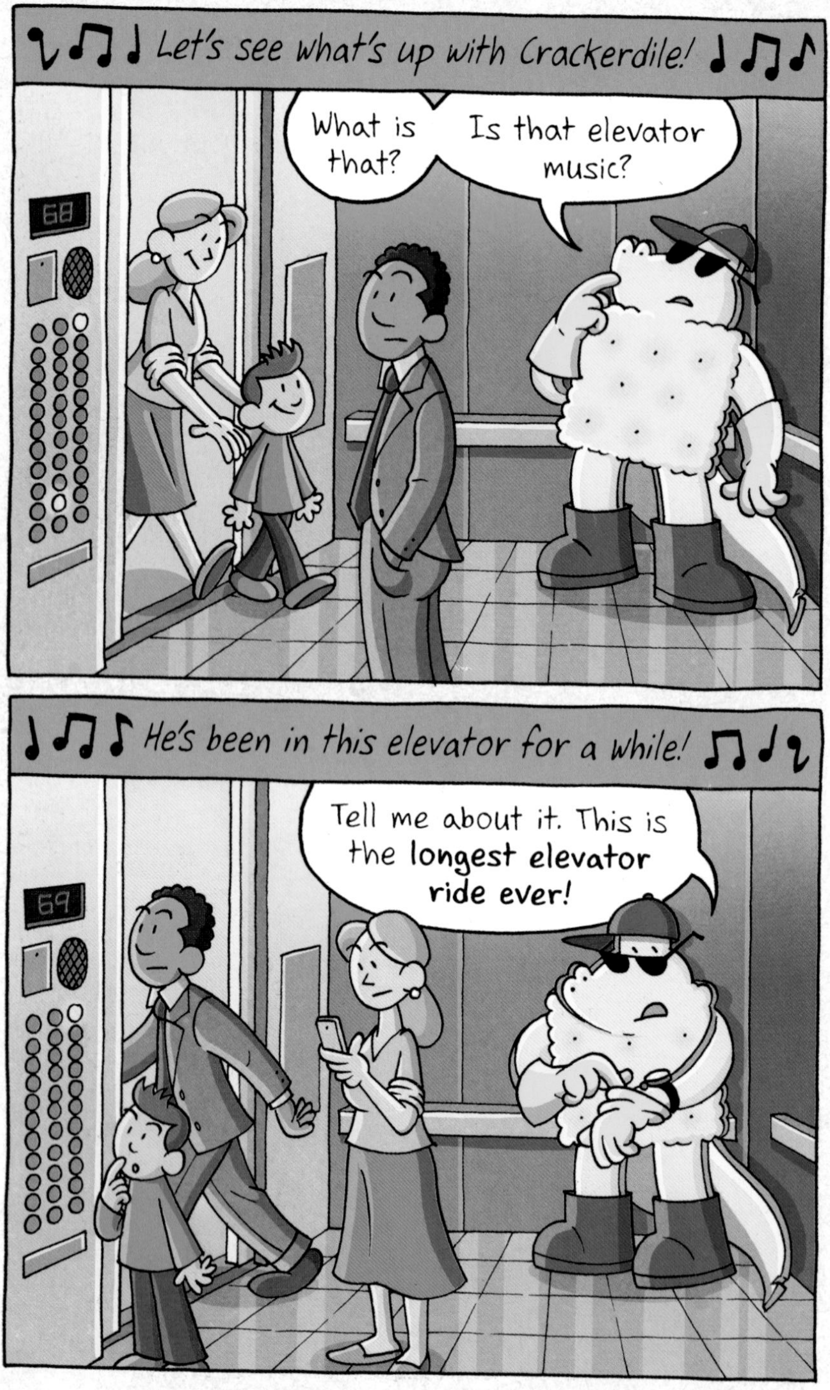
Let's see what's up with Crackerdile!
What is that?
Is that elevator music?
He's been in this elevator for a while!
Tell me about it. This is the **longest elevator ride ever!**

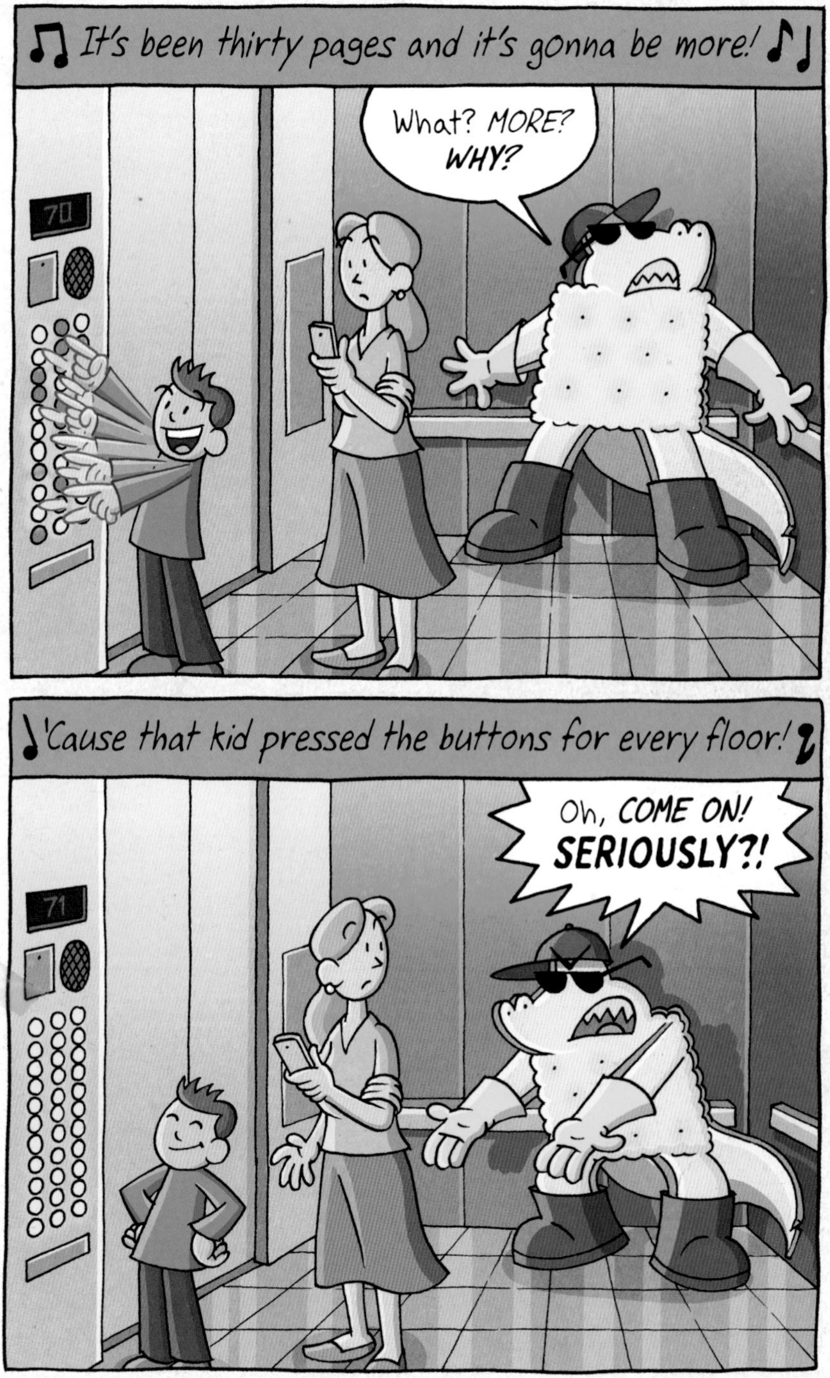
It's been thirty pages and it's gonna be more!
What? MORE? WHY?
70
'Cause that kid pressed the buttons for every floor!
Oh, COME ON! SERIOUSLY?!
71

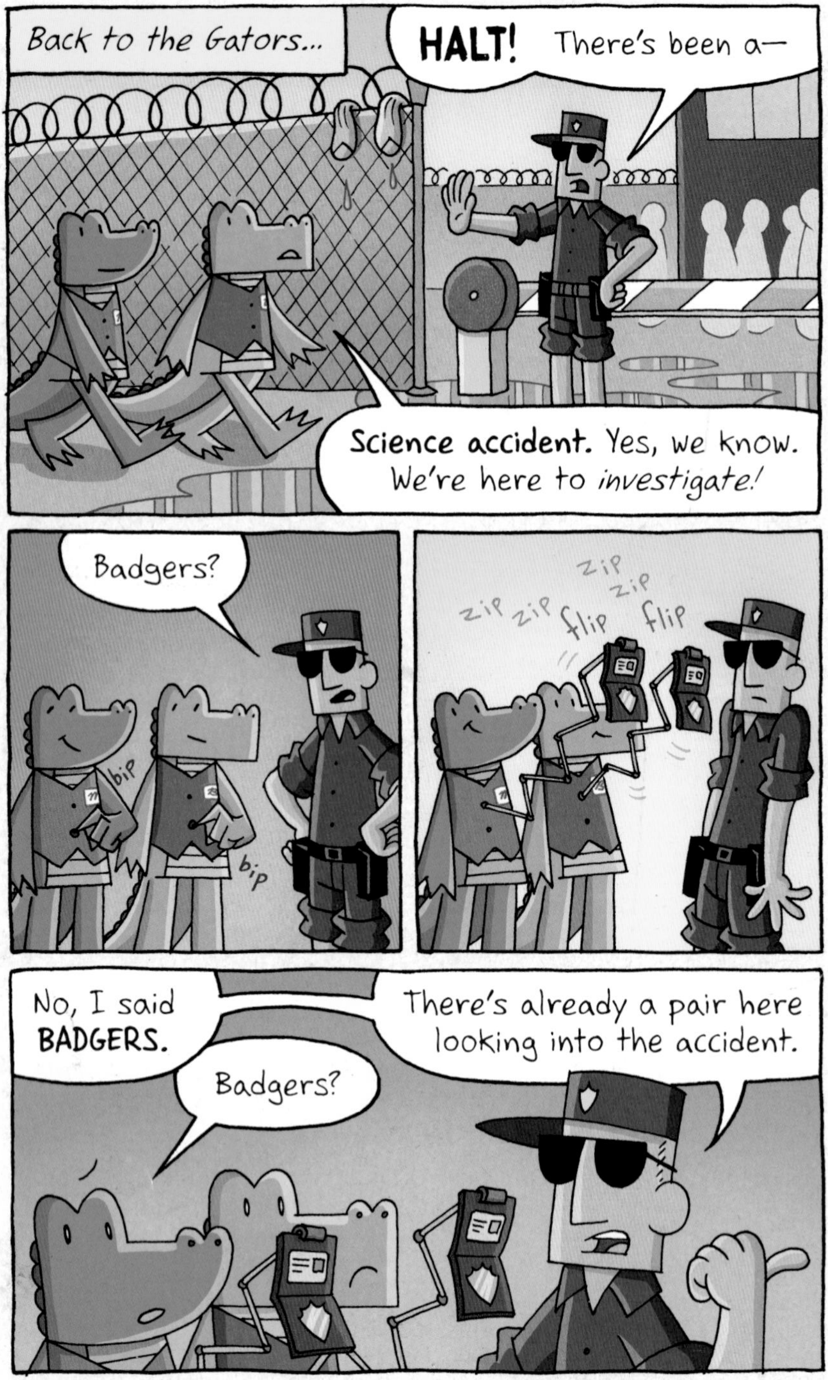
Back to the Gators...
HALT! There's been a—
Science accident. Yes, we know. We're here to investigate!
Badgers?
bip
bip
zip zip zip zip
flip flip
No, I said BADGERS.
Badgers?
There's already a pair here looking into the accident.

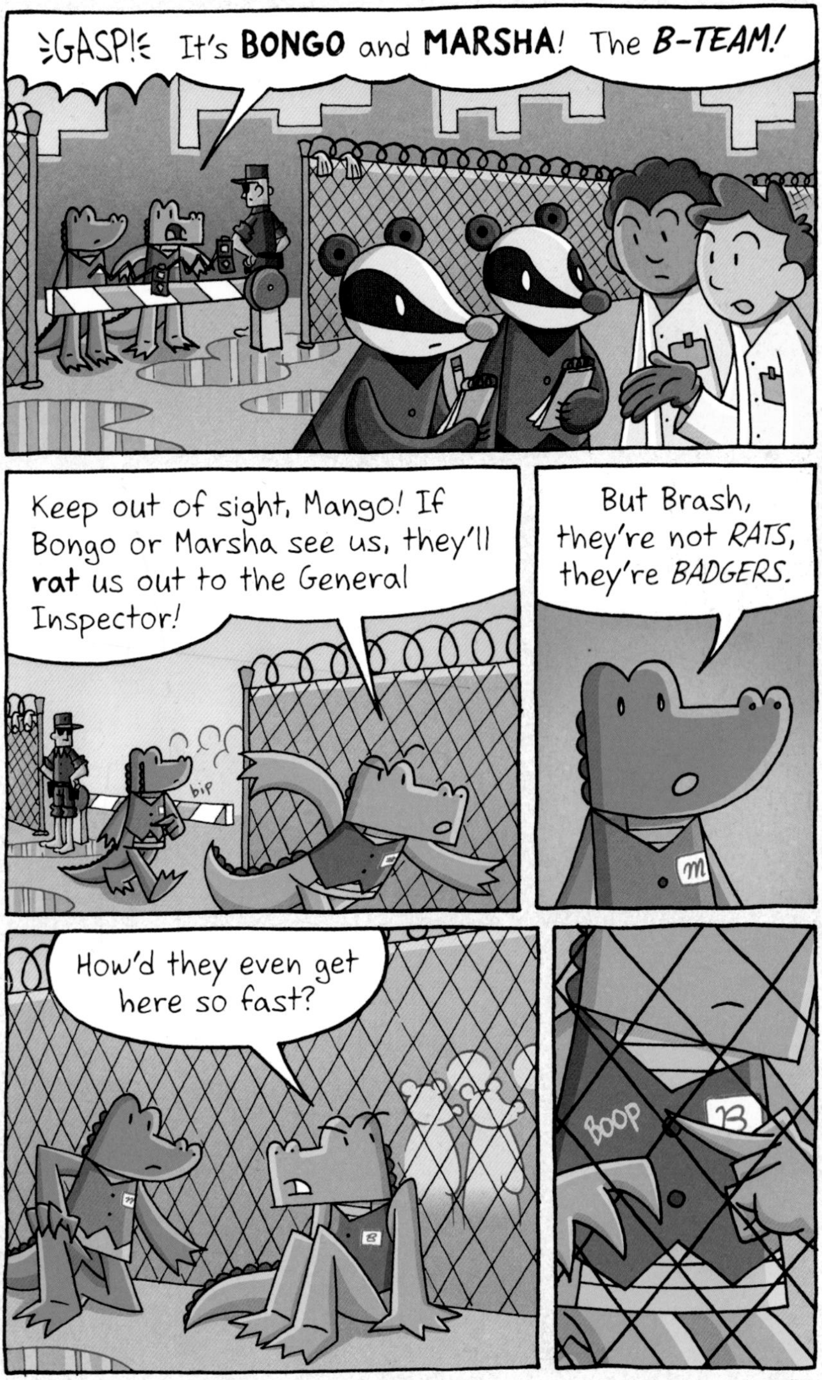

GASP! It's **BONGO** and **MARSHA**! The *B-TEAM!*
Keep out of sight, Mango! If Bongo or Marsha see us, they'll **rat** us out to the General Inspector!
bip
But Brash, they're not *RATS*, they're *BADGERS*.
How'd they even get here so fast?
BOOP

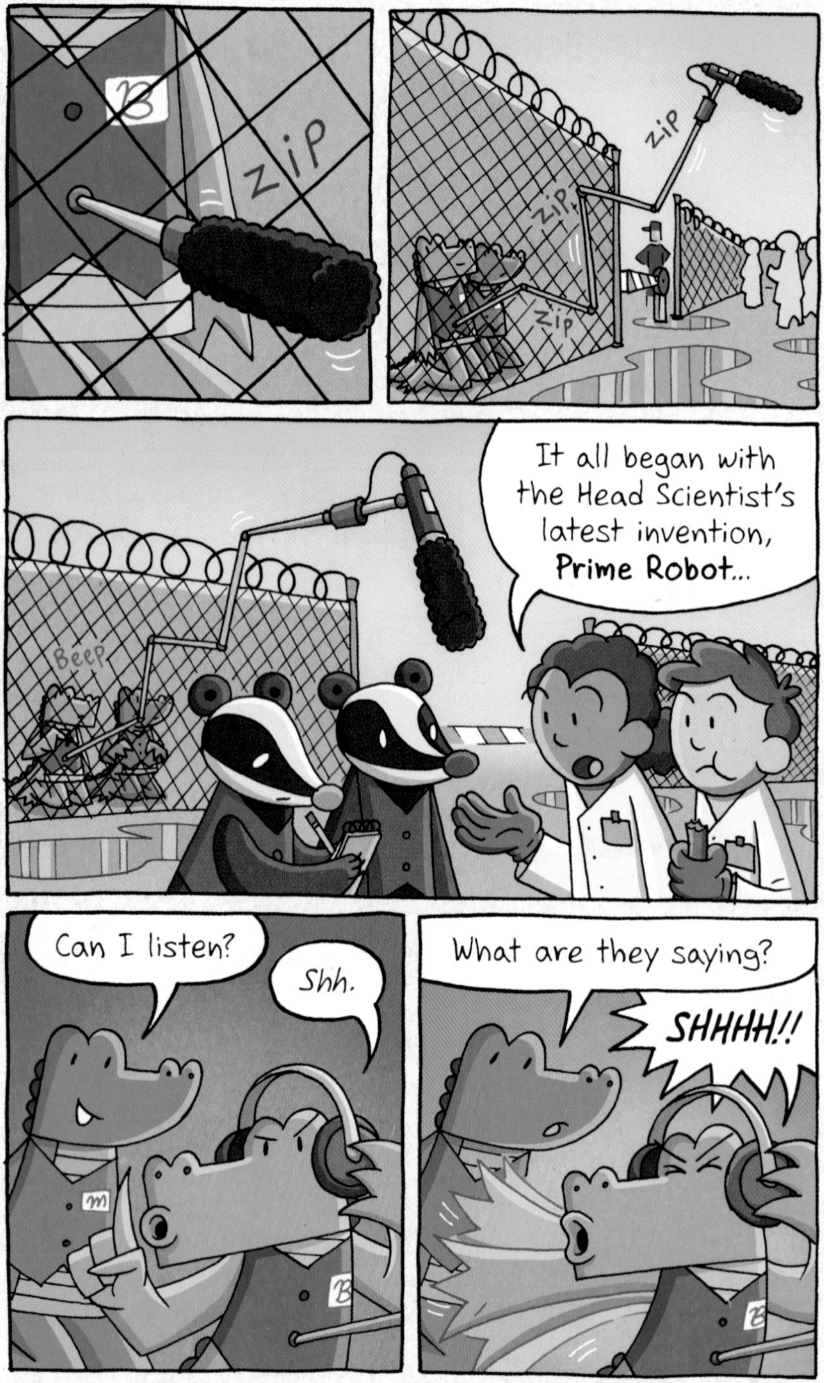
zip
zip
zip
zip
It all began with the Head Scientist's latest invention, **Prime Robot**...
Beep
Can I listen?
Shh.
What are they saying?
SHHHH!!

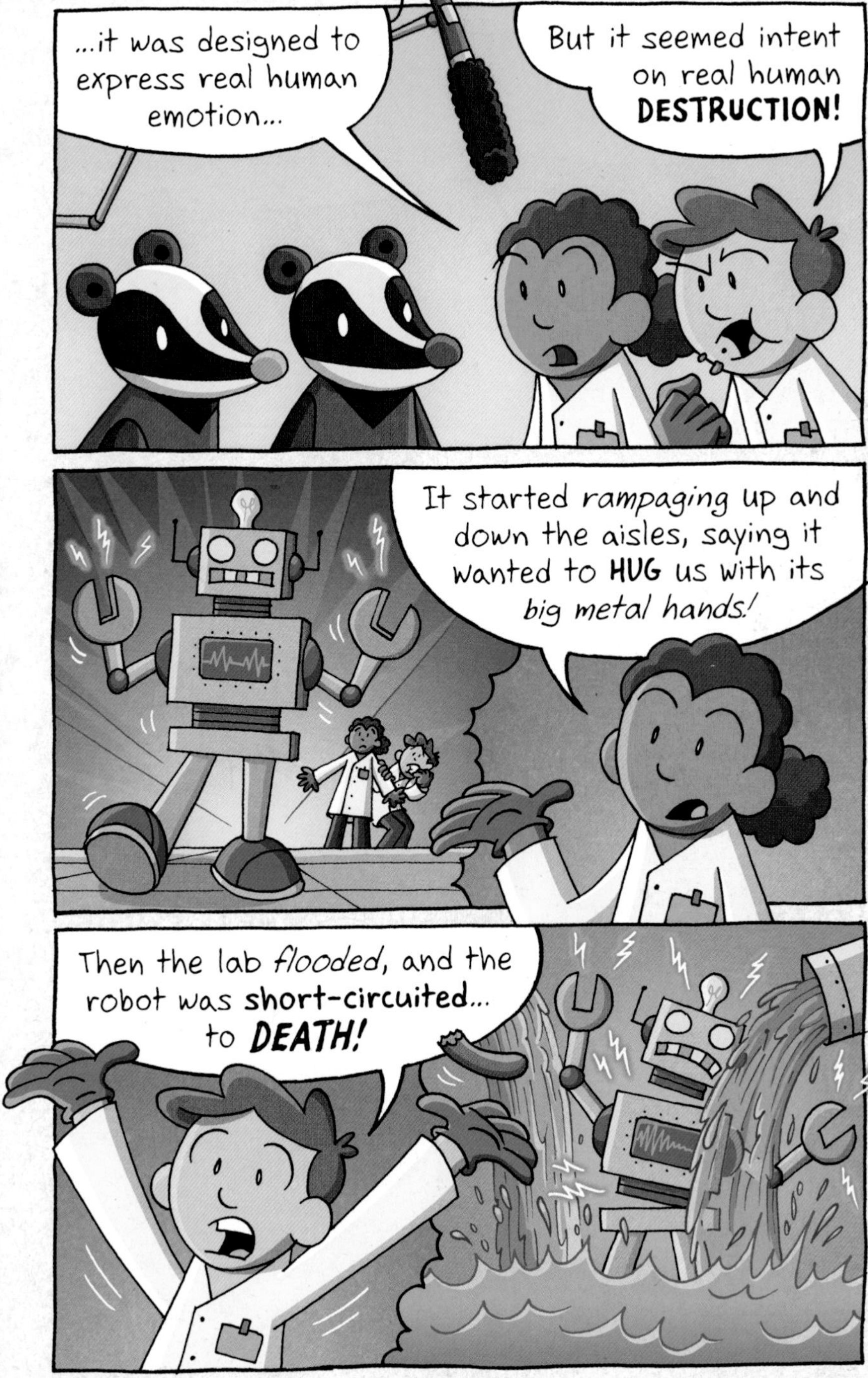
...it was designed to express real human emotion...
But it seemed intent on real human **DESTRUCTION!**
It started *rampaging* up and down the aisles, saying it wanted to **HUG** us with its *big metal hands!*
Then the lab *flooded*, and the robot was **short-circuited...** to ***DEATH!***

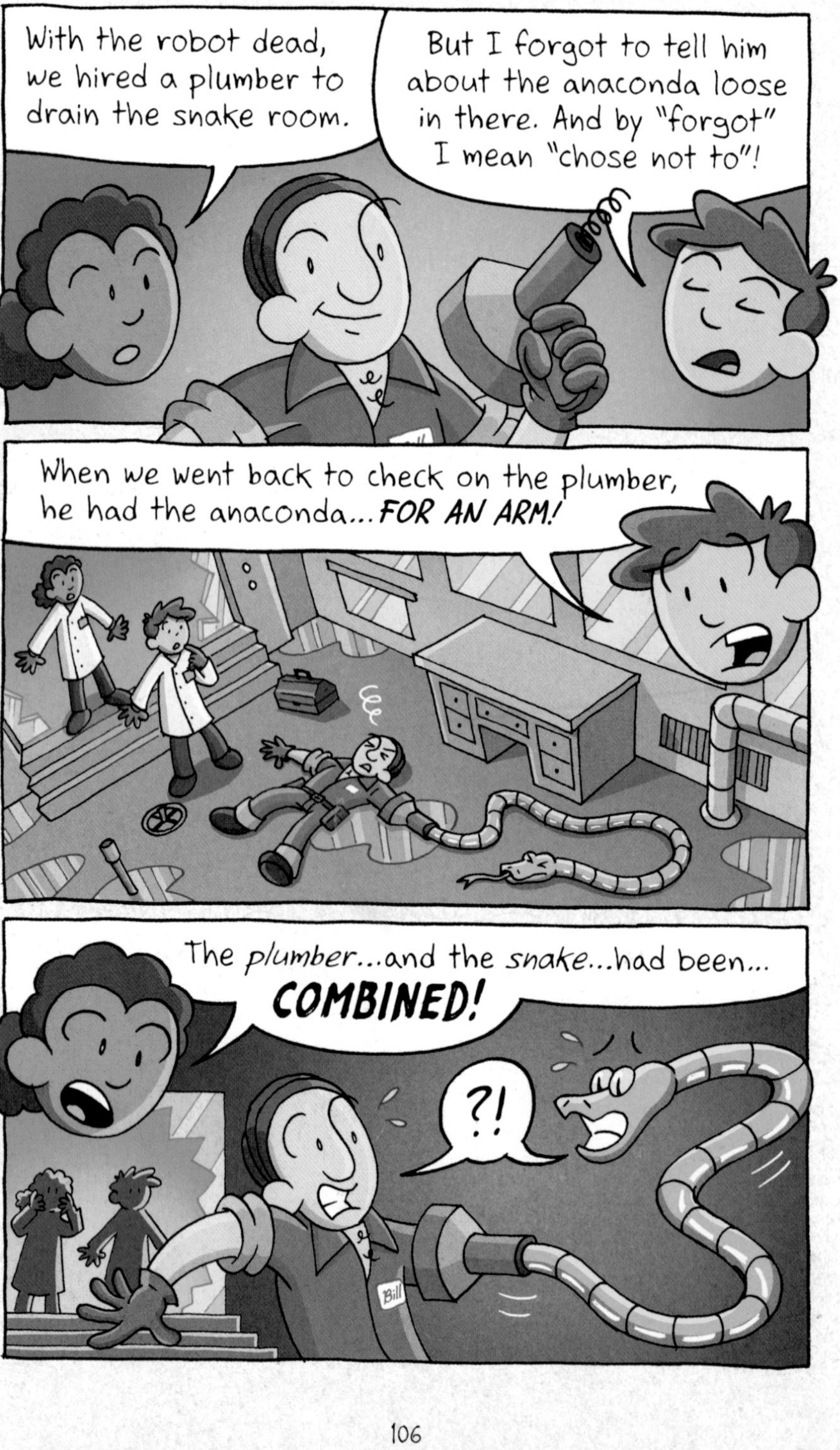
With the robot dead, we hired a plumber to drain the snake room.
But I forgot to tell him about the anaconda loose in there. And by "forgot" I mean "chose not to"!
Bill
When we went back to check on the plumber, he had the anaconda...FOR AN ARM!
The plumber...and the snake...had been... COMBINED!
?!
Bill

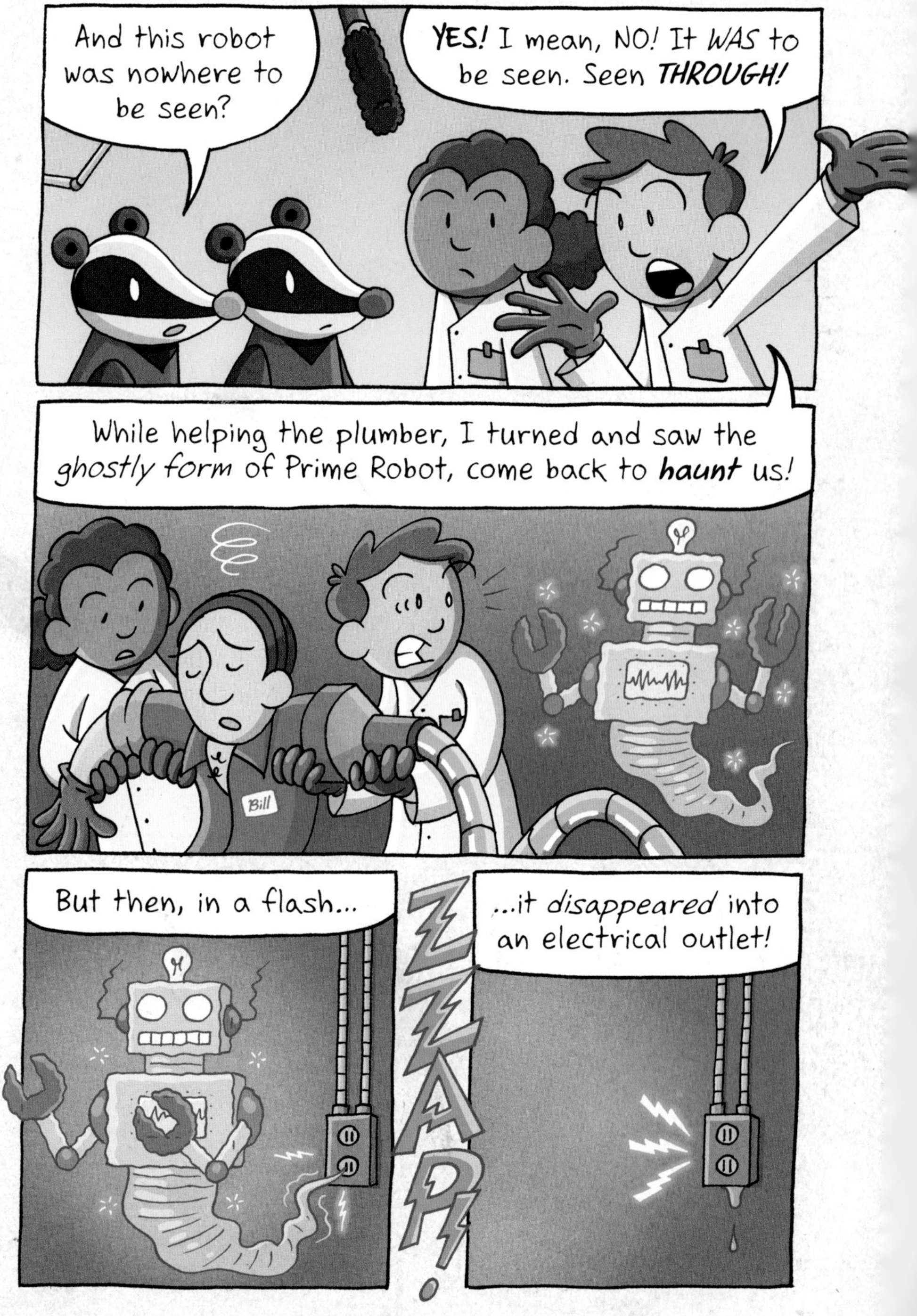
And this robot was nowhere to be seen?
YES! I mean, NO! It WAS to be seen. Seen THROUGH!
While helping the plumber, I turned and saw the ghostly form of Prime Robot, come back to haunt us!
Bill
But then, in a flash...
ZZZAP!
...it disappeared into an electrical outlet!

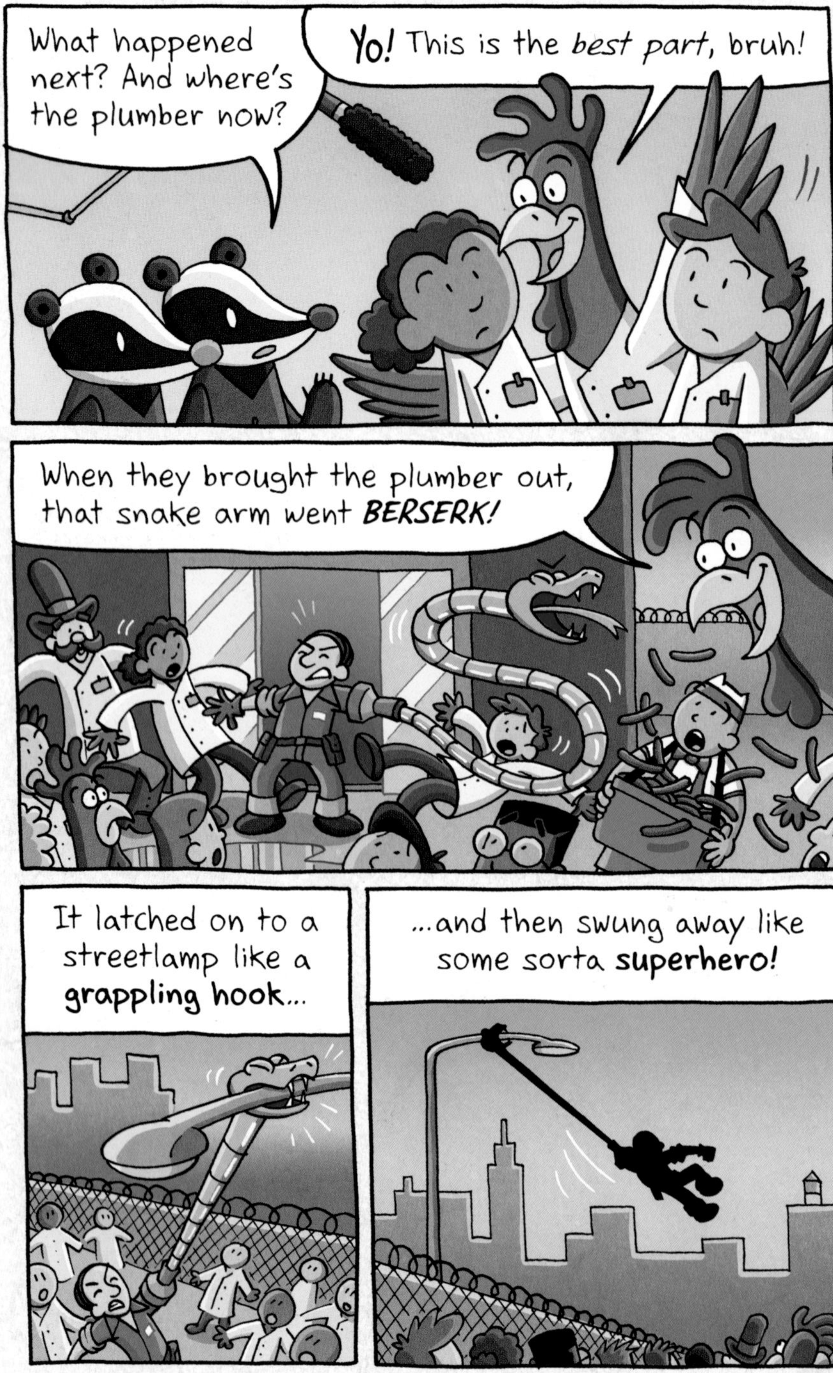
What happened next? And where's the plumber now?
Yo! This is the *best part*, bruh!
When they brought the plumber out, that snake arm went **BERSERK!**
It latched on to a streetlamp like a **grappling hook**...
...and then swung away like some sorta **superhero!**

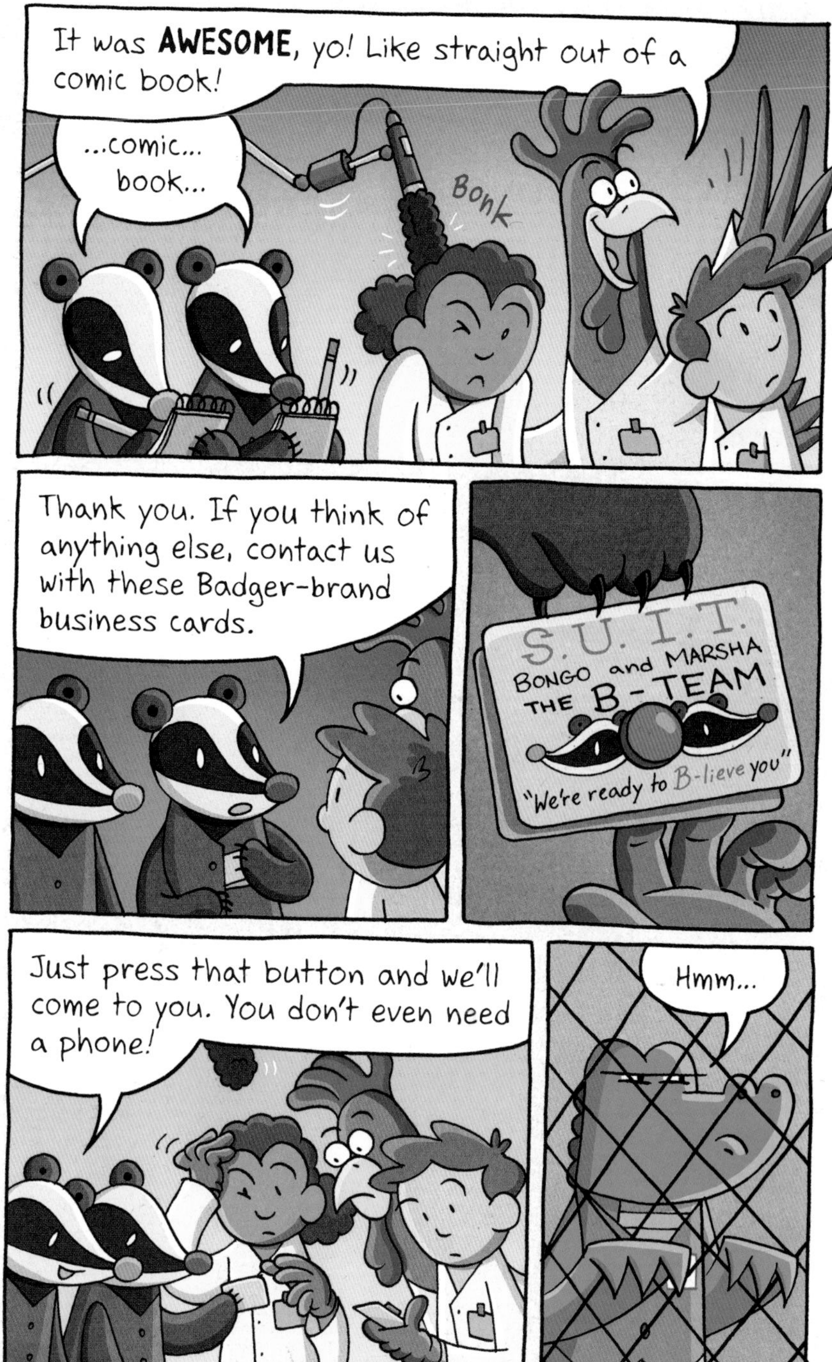
It was **AWESOME**, yo! Like straight out of a comic book!
...comic... book...
Bonk
Thank you. If you think of anything else, contact us with these Badger-brand business cards.
S.U.I.T.
BONGO and MARSHA
THE B-TEAM
"We're ready to B-lieve you"
Just press that button and we'll come to you. You don't even need a phone!
Hmm...

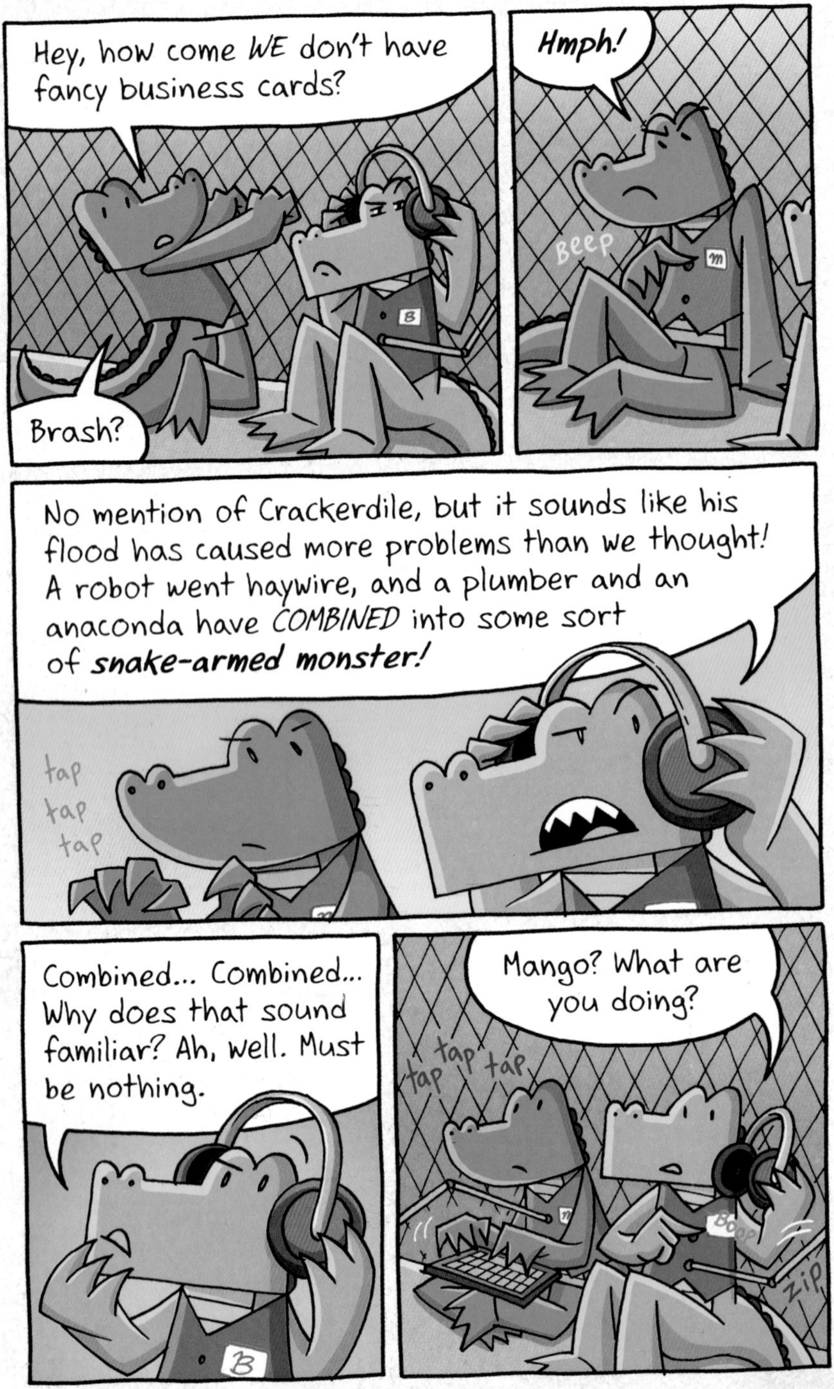
Hey, how come WE don't have fancy business cards?
Brash?
Hmph!
BEEP
No mention of Crackerdile, but it sounds like his flood has caused more problems than we thought! A robot went haywire, and a plumber and an anaconda have COMBINED into some sort of **snake-armed monster!**
tap tap tap
Combined... Combined... Why does that sound familiar? Ah, well. Must be nothing.
Mango? What are you doing?
tap tap tap
Boop
zip

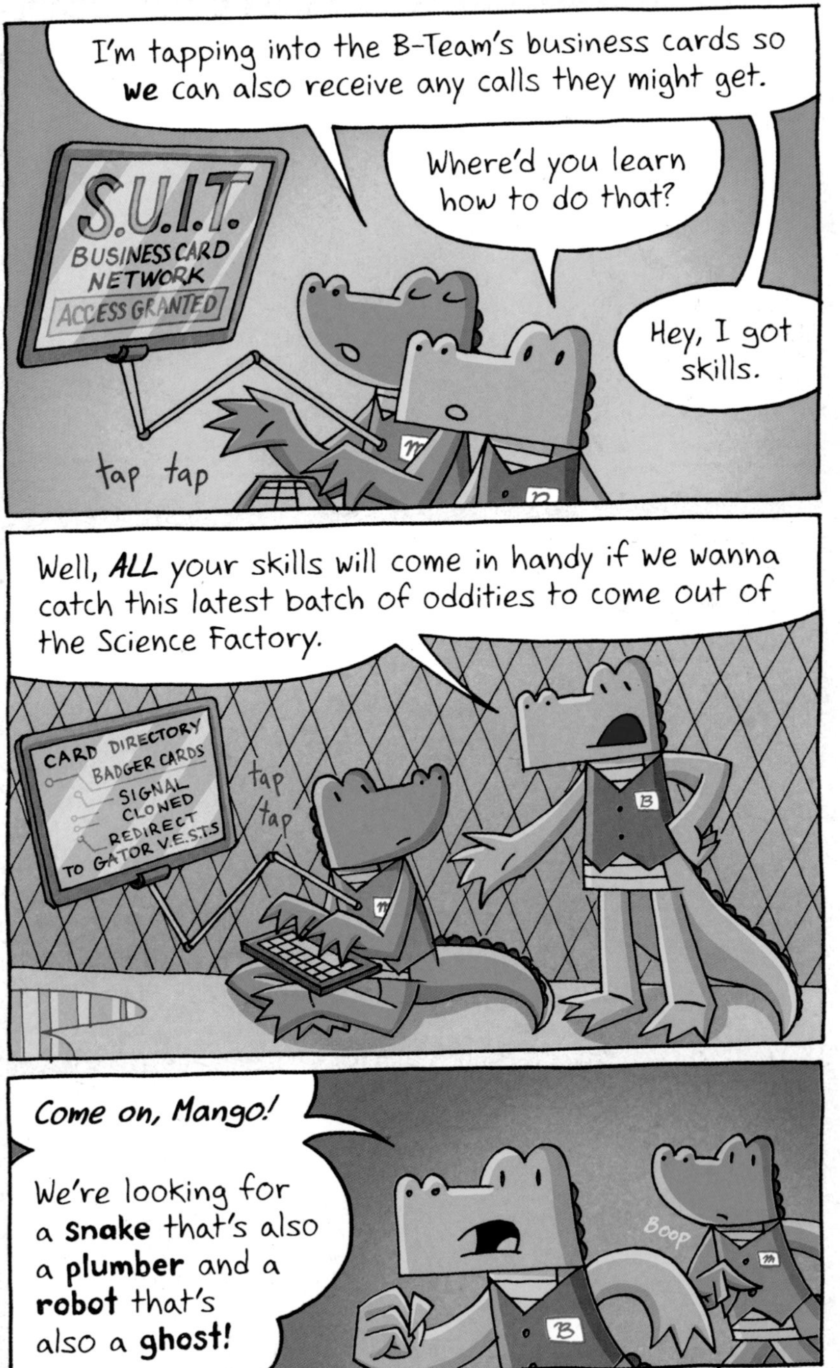
I'm tapping into the B-Team's business cards so **we** can also receive any calls they might get.
S.U.I.T. BUSINESS CARD NETWORK ACCESS GRANTED
Where'd you learn how to do that?
Hey, I got skills.
tap tap
Well, ***ALL*** your skills will come in handy if we wanna catch this latest batch of oddities to come out of the Science Factory.
CARD DIRECTORY BADGER CARDS SIGNAL CLONED REDIRECT TO GATOR V.E.S.T.S
tap tap
Come on, Mango!
We're looking for a **snake** that's also a **plumber** and a **robot** that's also a **ghost!**
Boop

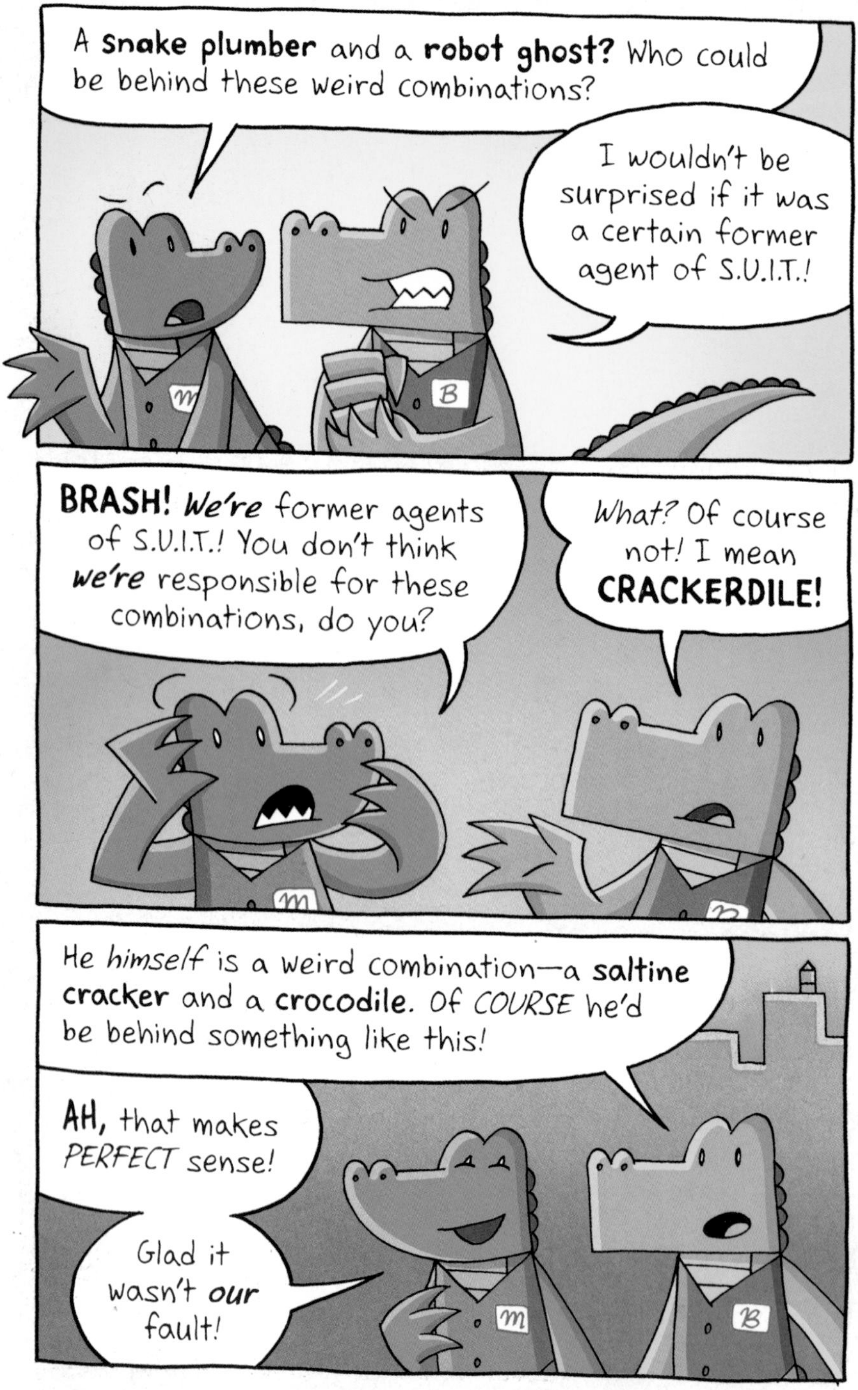
A **snake plumber** and a **robot ghost?** Who could be behind these weird combinations?
I wouldn't be surprised if it was a certain former agent of S.U.I.T.!
BRASH! ***We're*** former agents of S.U.I.T.! You don't think ***we're*** responsible for these combinations, do you?
What? Of course not! I mean **CRACKERDILE!**
He *himself* is a weird combination—a **saltine cracker** and a **crocodile.** Of *COURSE* he'd be behind something like this!
AH, that makes *PERFECT* sense!
Glad it wasn't ***our*** fault!

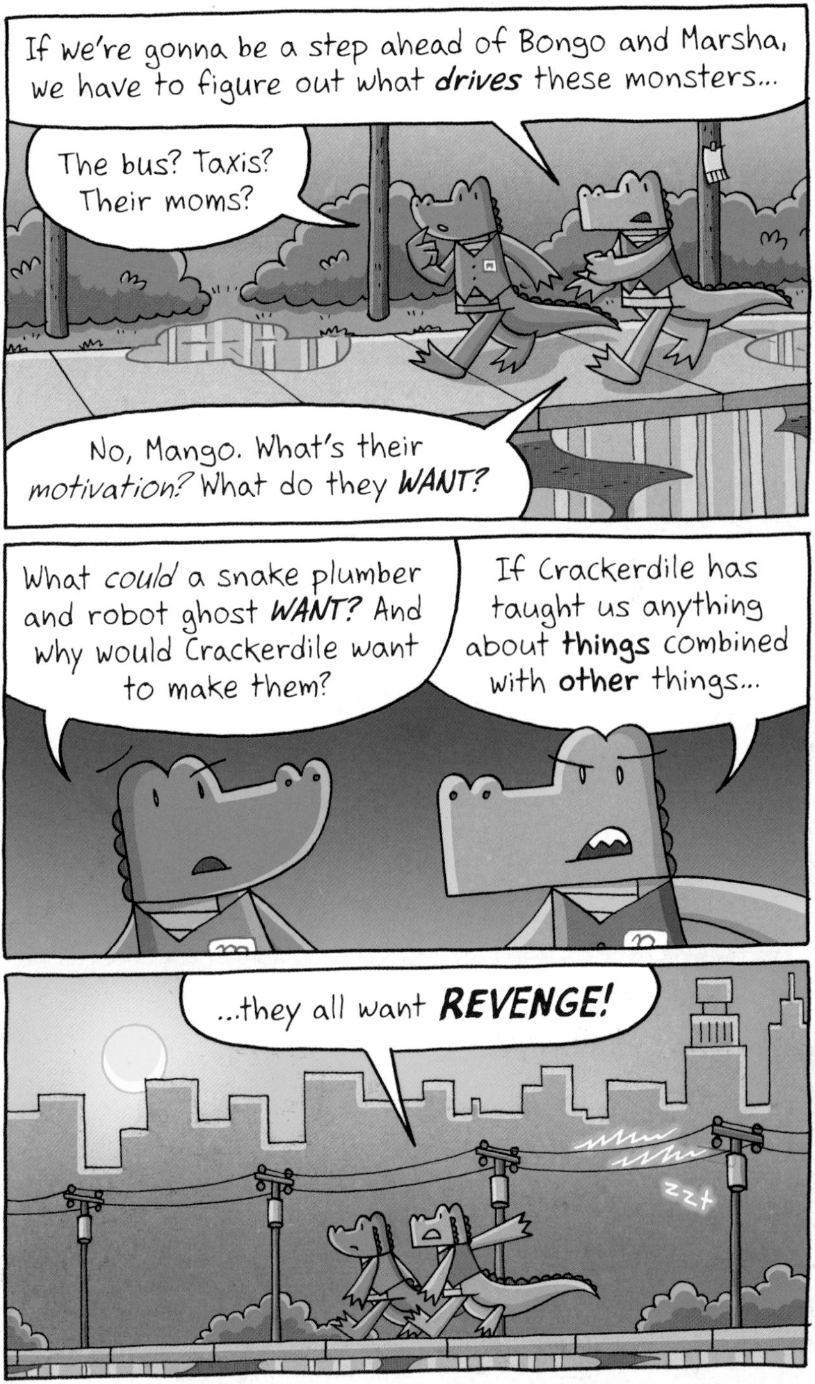
If we're gonna be a step ahead of Bongo and Marsha, we have to figure out what **drives** these monsters...
The bus? Taxis? Their moms?
No, Mango. What's their *motivation?* What do they ***WANT?***
What *could* a snake plumber and robot ghost ***WANT?*** And why would Crackerdile want to make them?
If Crackerdile has taught us anything about **things** combined with **other** things...
...they all want **REVENGE!**
zzt

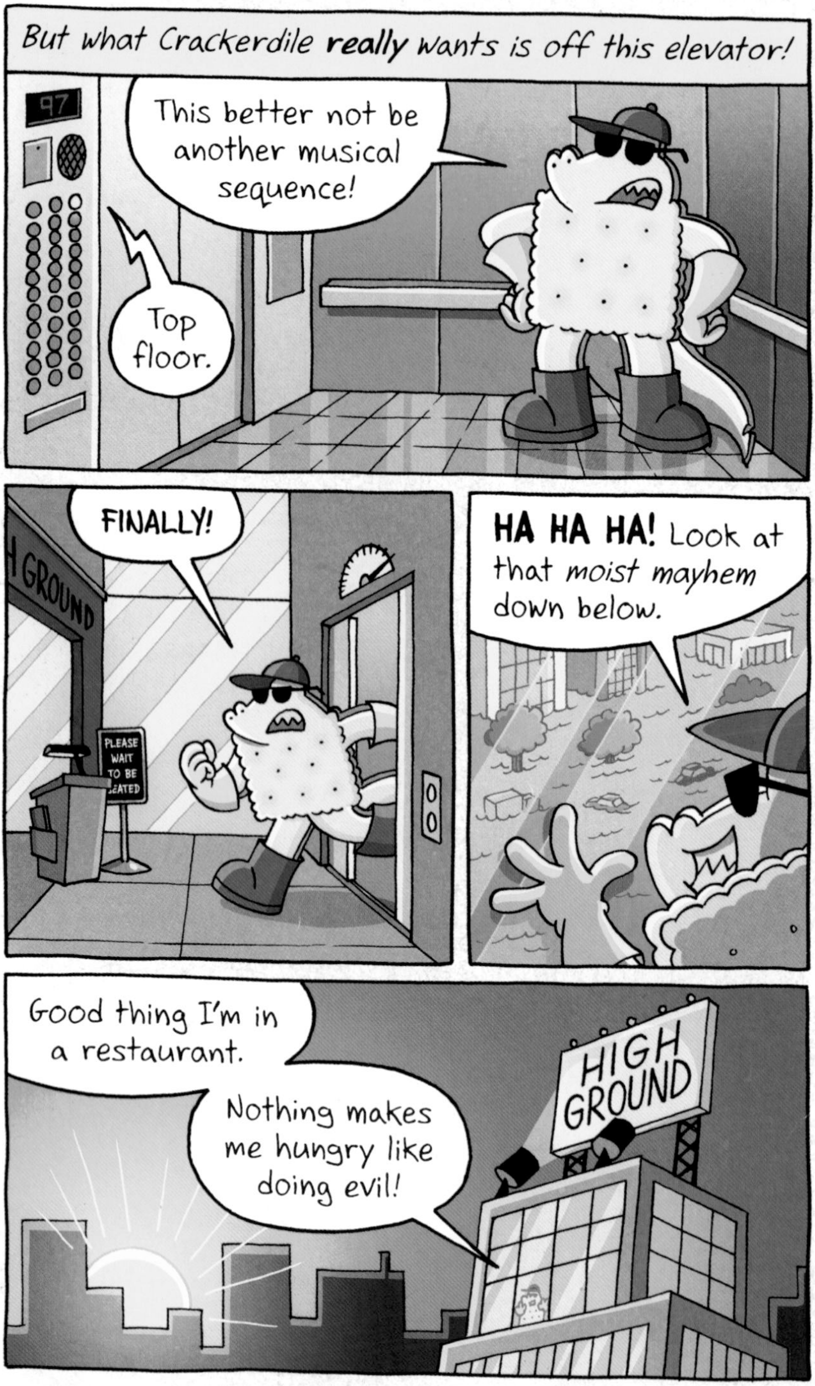
But what Crackerdile **really** wants is off this elevator!
97
This better not be another musical sequence!
Top floor.
FINALLY!
GROUND
PLEASE WAIT TO BE SEATED
HA HA HA! Look at that *moist mayhem* down below.
Good thing I'm in a restaurant.
Nothing makes me hungry like doing evil!
HIGH GROUND

Chapter 11-ish

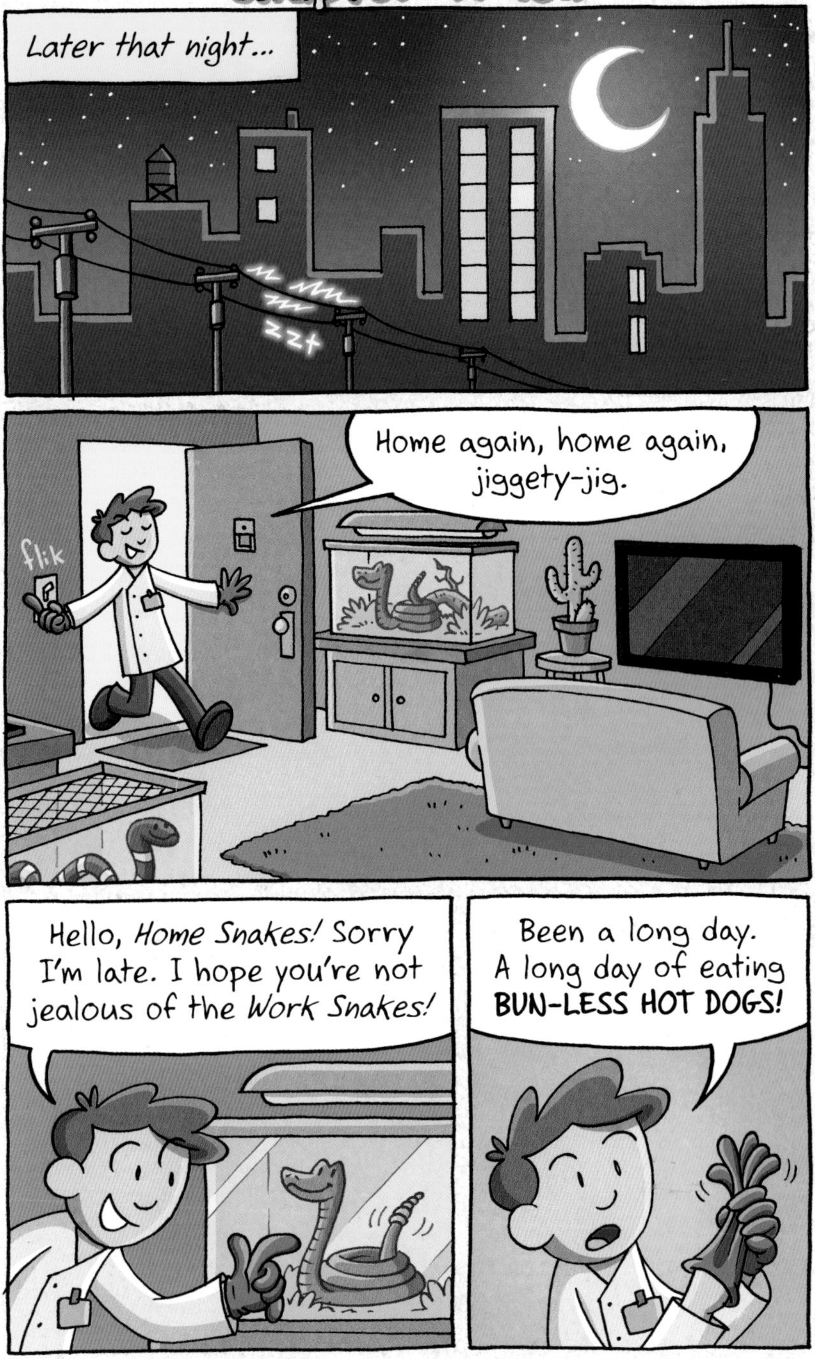
Later that night...
zzt
flik
Home again, home again, jiggety-jig.
Hello, *Home Snakes!* Sorry I'm late. I hope you're not jealous of the *Work Snakes!*
Been a long day. A long day of eating **BUN-LESS HOT DOGS!**

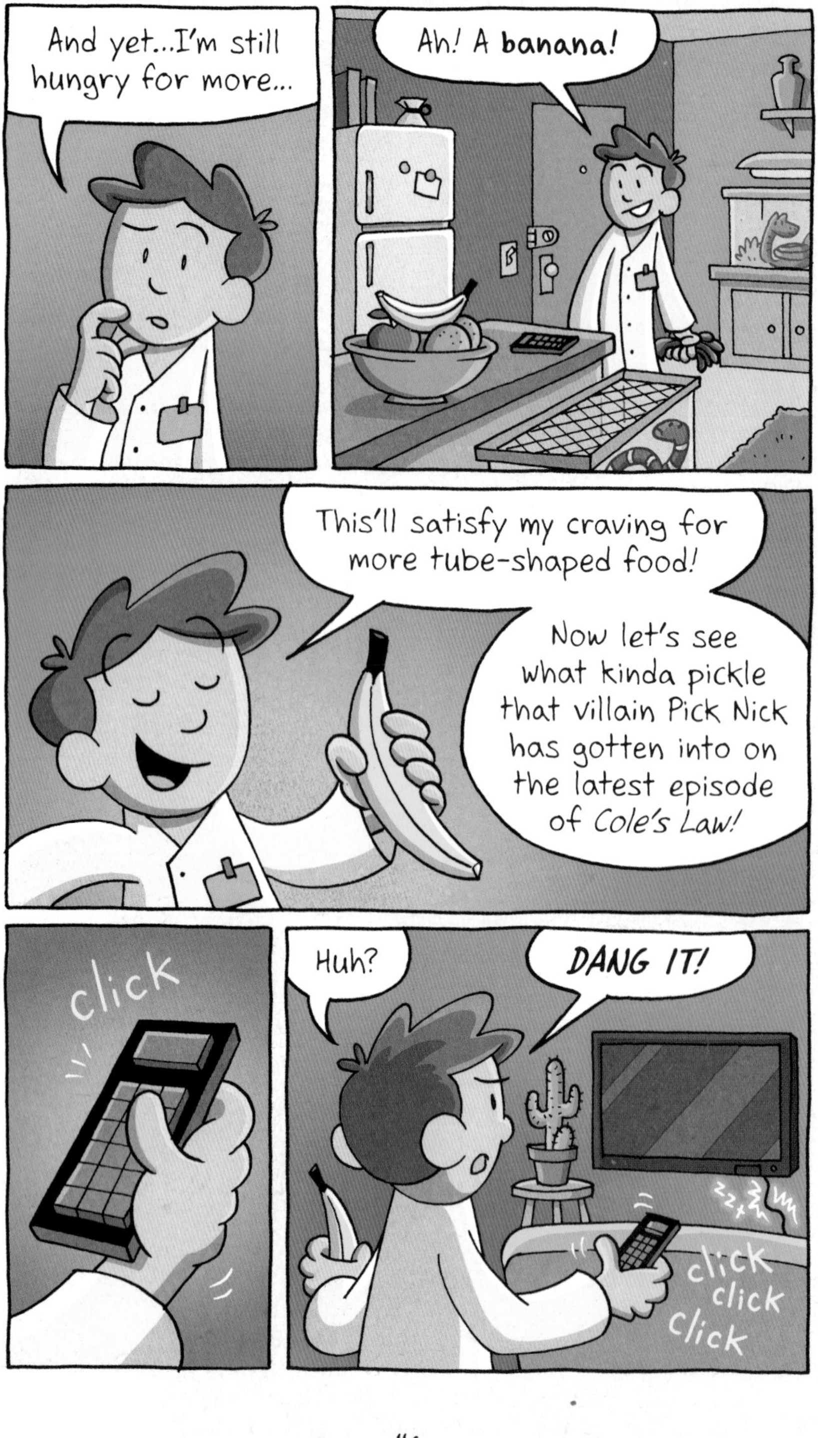
And yet...I'm still hungry for more...
Ah! A **banana!**
This'll satisfy my craving for more tube-shaped food!
Now let's see what kinda pickle that villain Pick Nick has gotten into on the latest episode of *Cole's Law!*
click
Huh?
DANG IT!
click click click

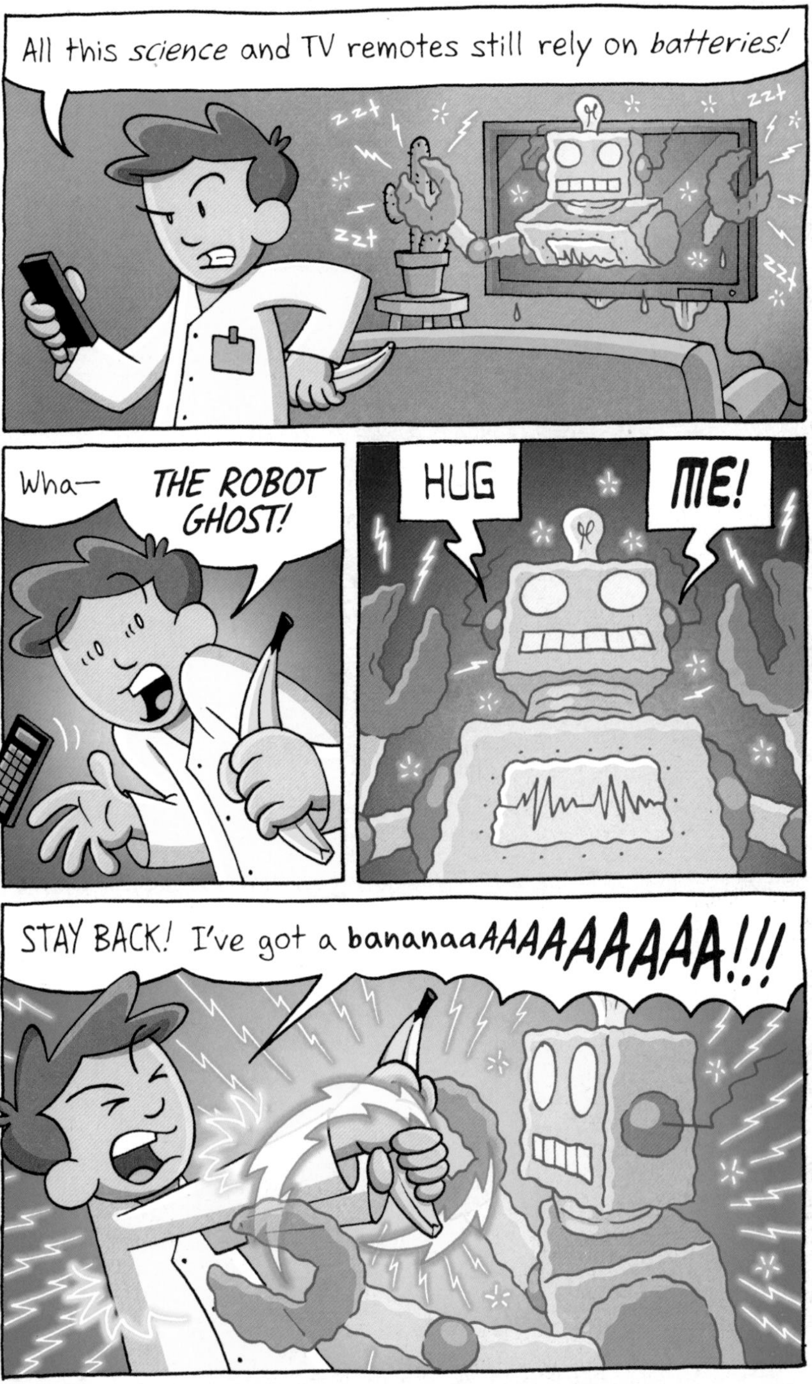
All this science and TV remotes still rely on batteries!
zzt
zzt
zzt
zzt
Wha—
THE ROBOT GHOST!
HUG
ME!
STAY BACK! I've got a bananaaAAAAAAAAA!!!

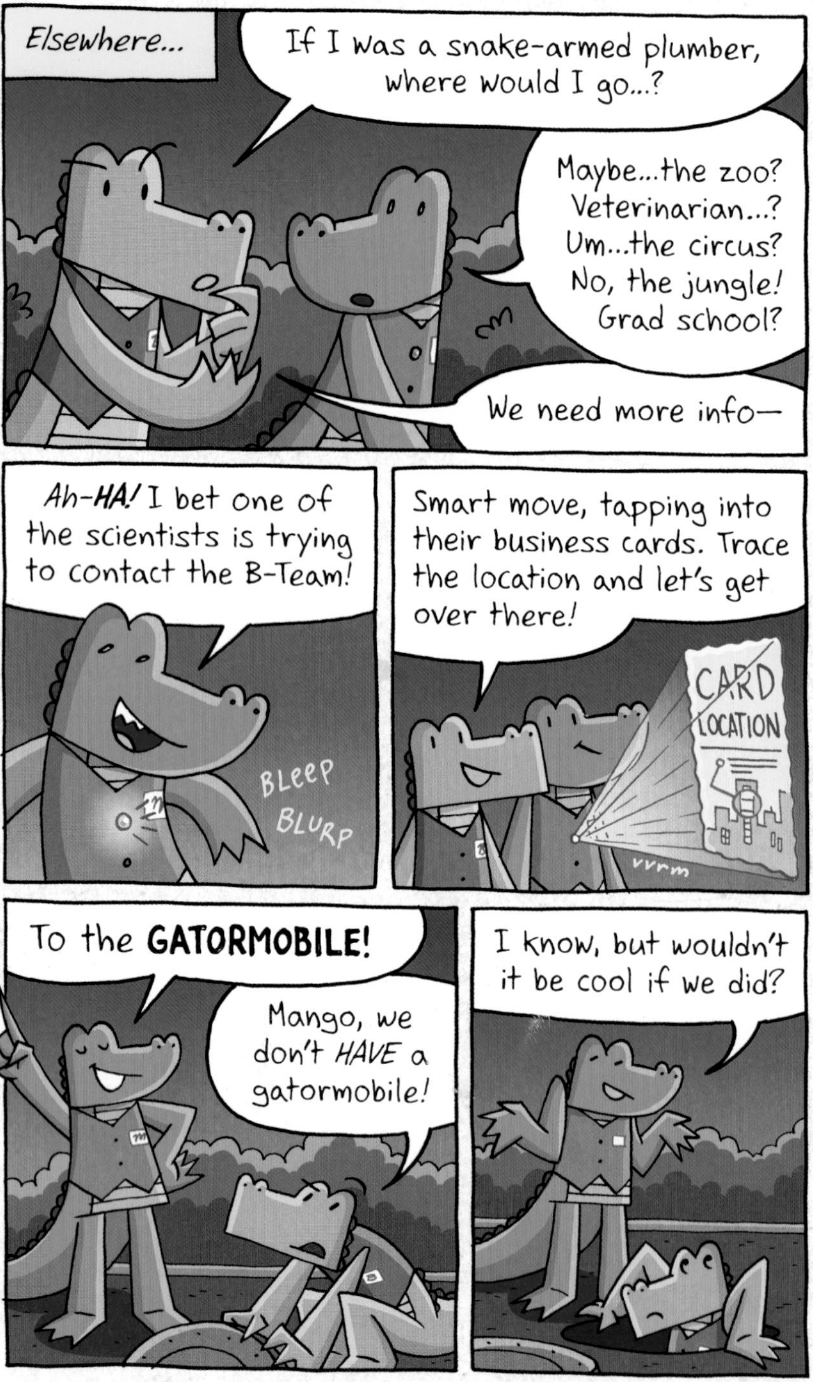
Elsewhere...
If I was a snake-armed plumber, where would I go...?
Maybe...the zoo? Veterinarian...? Um...the circus? No, the jungle! Grad school?
We need more info—
Ah-HA! I bet one of the scientists is trying to contact the B-Team!
BLEEP
BLURP
Smart move, tapping into their business cards. Trace the location and let's get over there!
CARD LOCATION
vvrm
To the GATORMOBILE!
Mango, we don't HAVE a gatormobile!
I know, but wouldn't it be cool if we did?

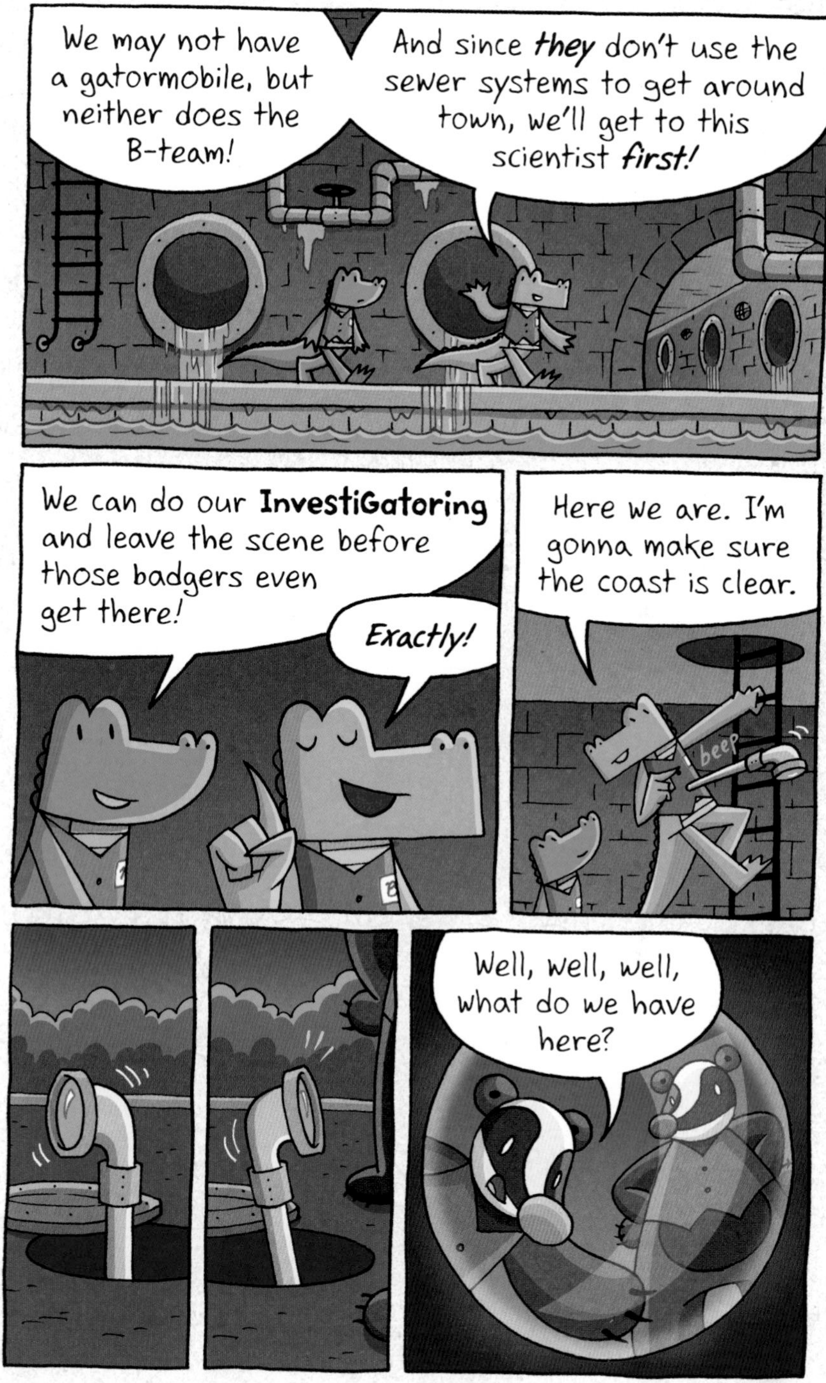

We may not have a gatormobile, but neither does the B-team!
And since they don't use the sewer systems to get around town, we'll get to this scientist first!
We can do our InvestiGatoring and leave the scene before those badgers even get there!
Exactly!
Here we are. I'm gonna make sure the coast is clear.
beep
Well, well, well, what do we have here?

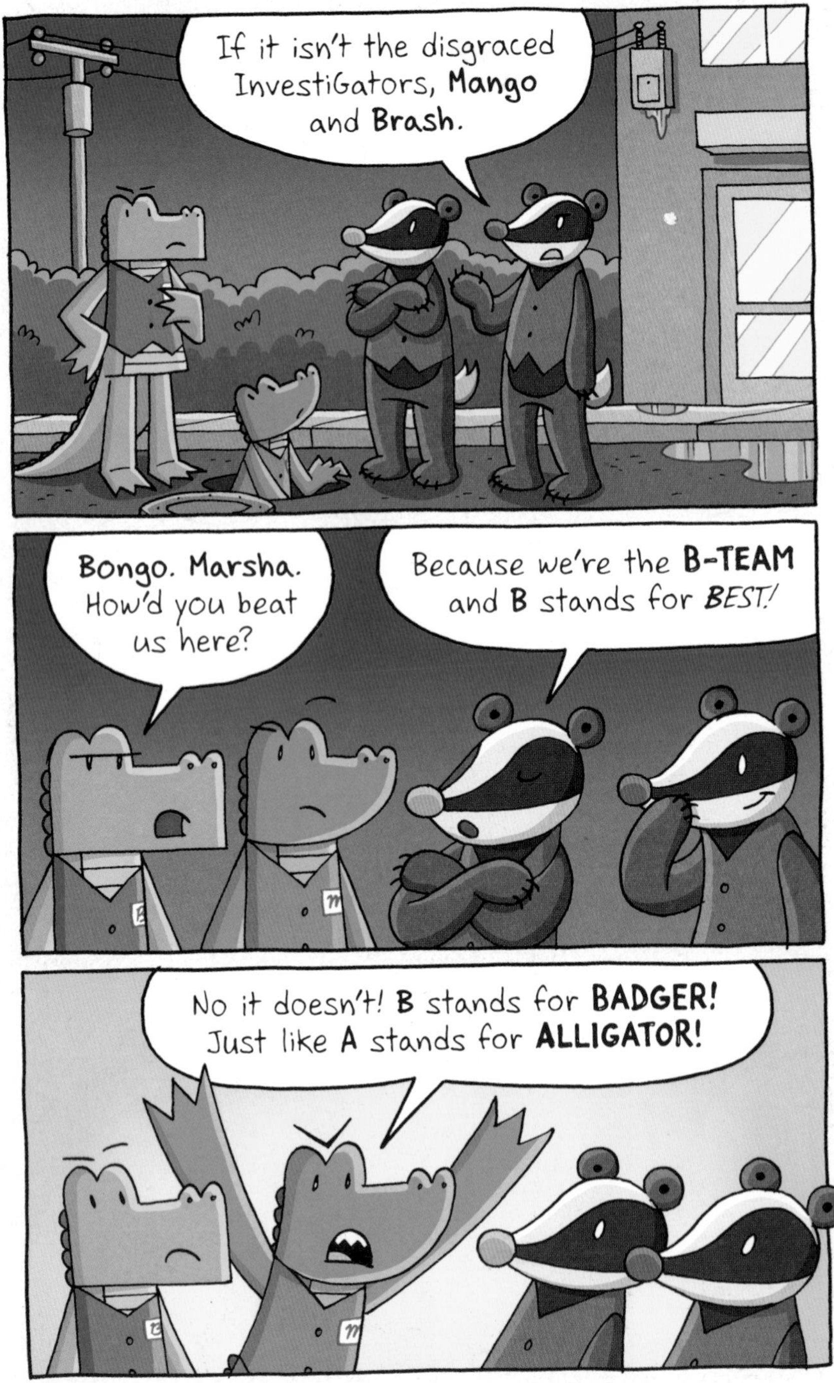
If it isn't the disgraced InvestiGators, **Mango** and **Brash**.
Bongo. Marsha. How'd you beat us here?
Because we're the **B-TEAM** and **B** stands for ***BEST!***
No it doesn't! **B** stands for **BADGER!** Just like **A** stands for **ALLIGATOR!**

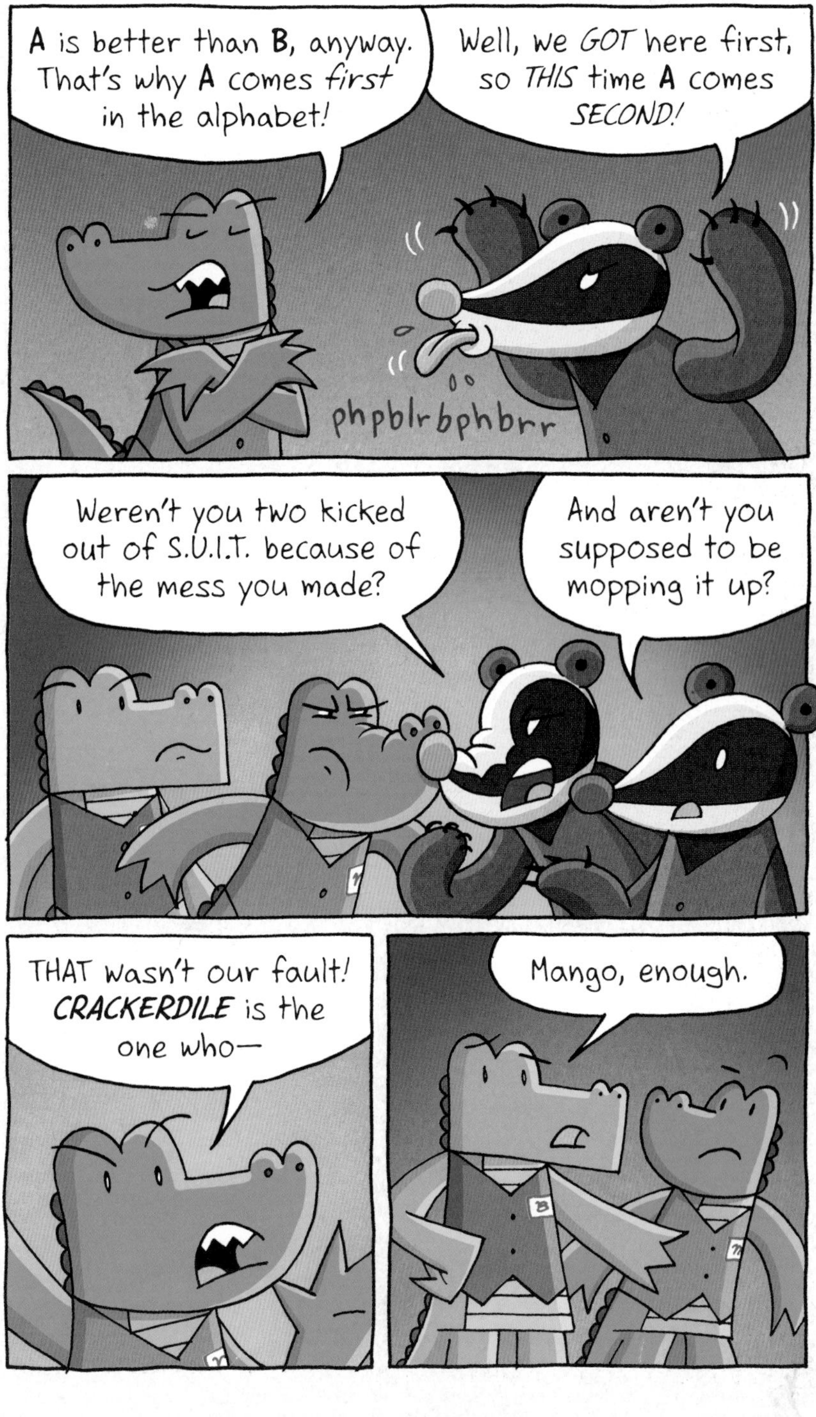
A is better than B, anyway. That's why A comes first in the alphabet!
Well, we GOT here first, so THIS time A comes SECOND!
phpblrbphbrr
Weren't you two kicked out of S.U.I.T. because of the mess you made?
And aren't you supposed to be mopping it up?
THAT wasn't our fault! CRACKERDILE is the one who—
Mango, enough.

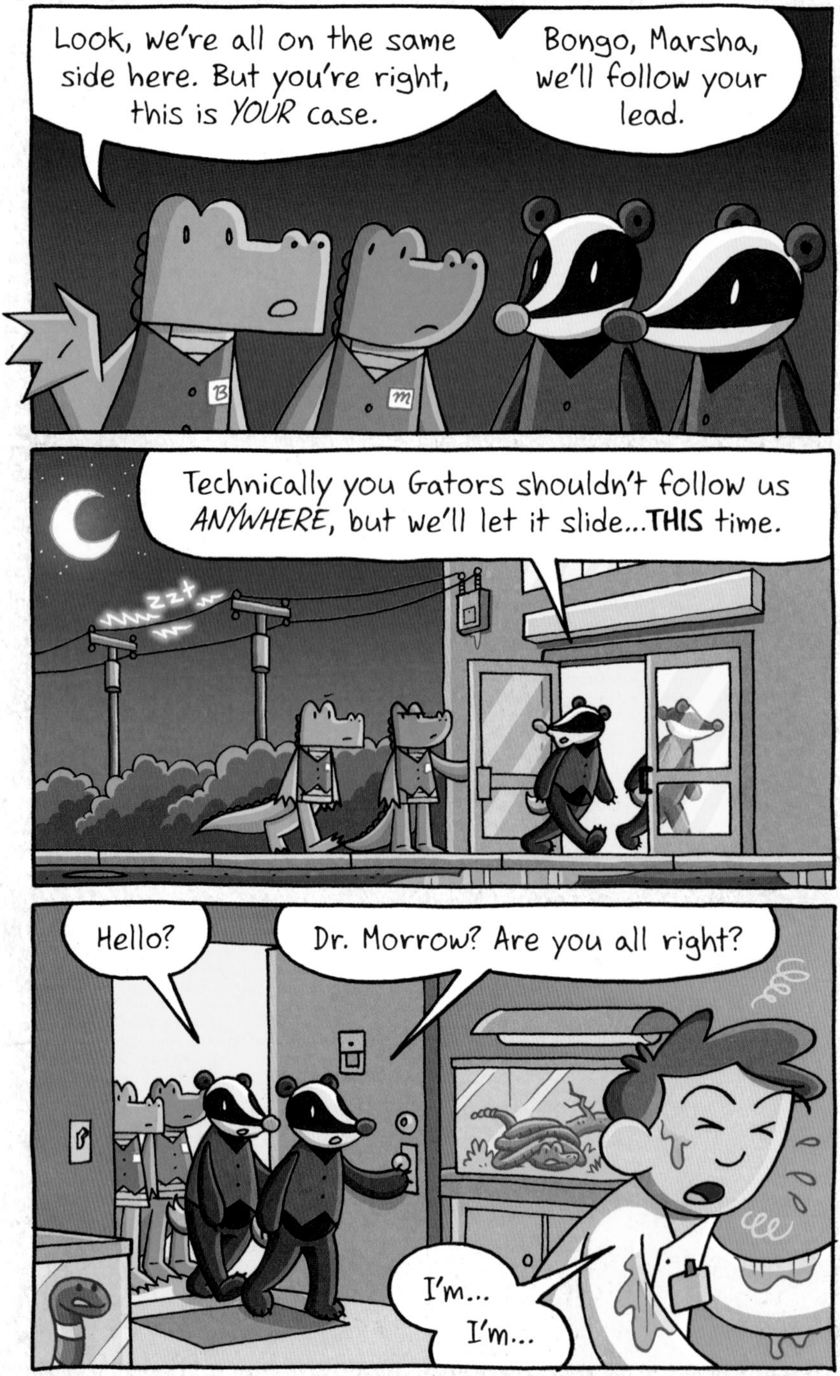

Look, we're all on the same side here. But you're right, this is *YOUR* case.
Bongo, Marsha, we'll follow your lead.
Technically you Gators shouldn't follow us *ANYWHERE*, but we'll let it slide...**THIS** time.
Hello?
Dr. Morrow? Are you all right?
I'm...
I'm...

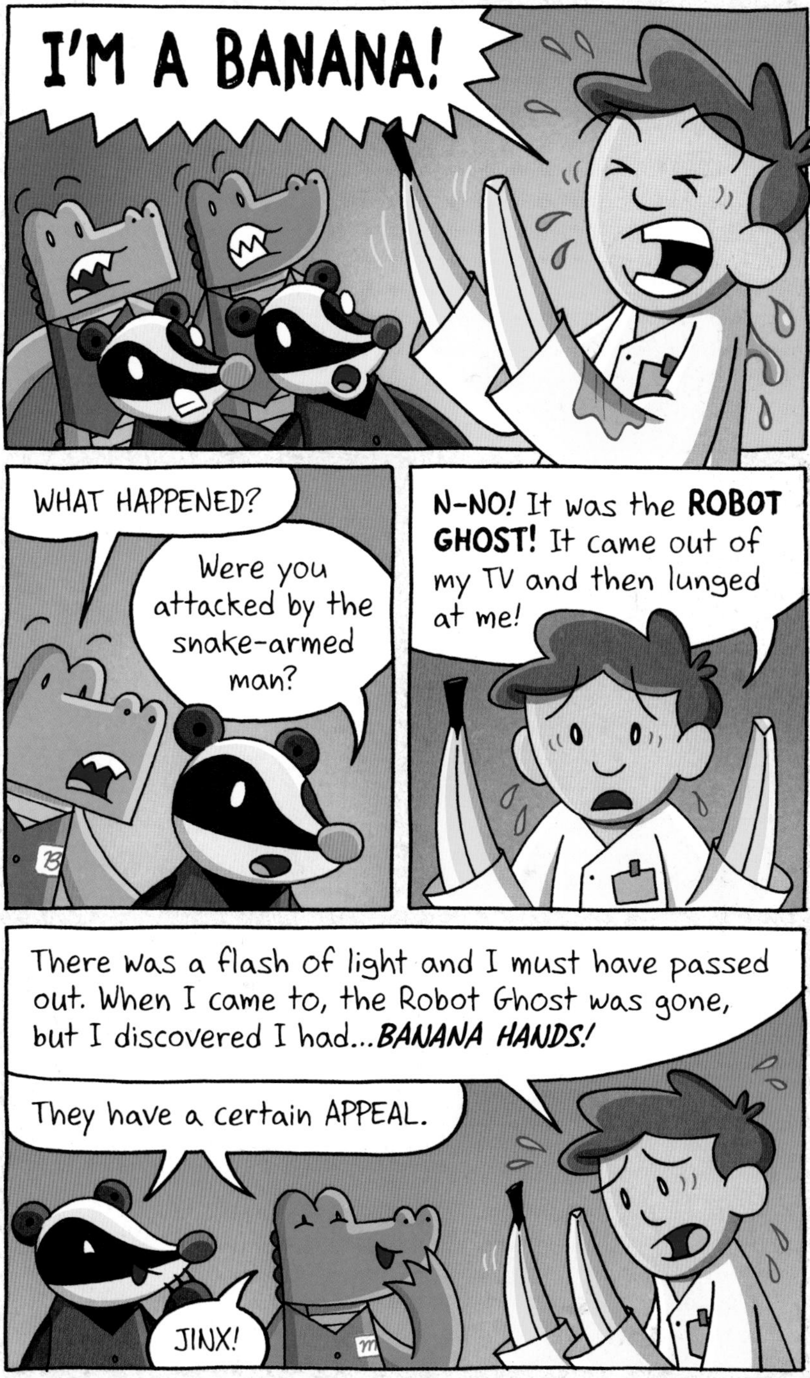
I'M A BANANA!
WHAT HAPPENED?
Were you attacked by the snake-armed man?
N-NO! It was the ROBOT GHOST! It came out of my TV and then lunged at me!
There was a flash of light and I must have passed out. When I came to, the Robot Ghost was gone, but I discovered I had...BANANA HANDS!
They have a certain APPEAL.
JINX!

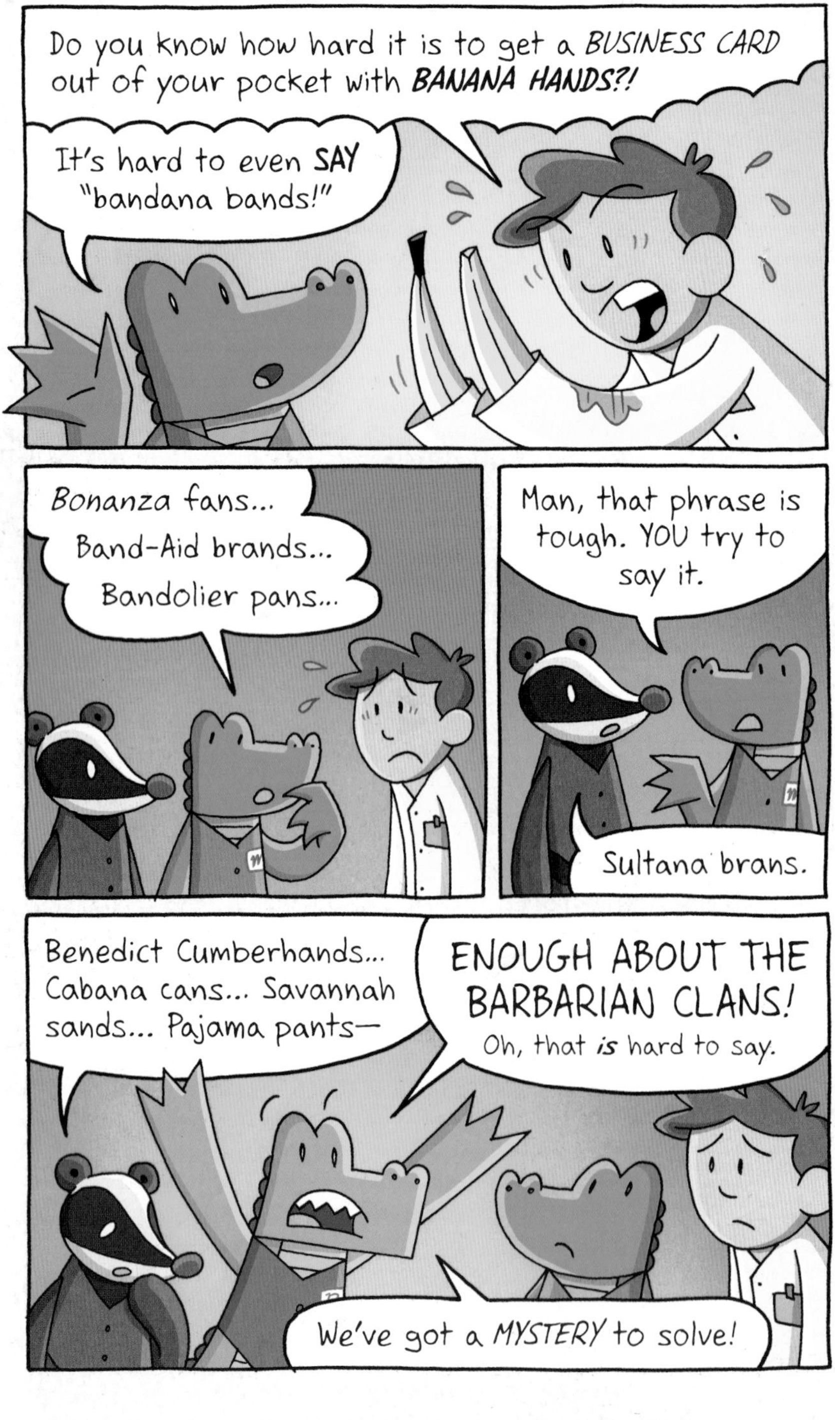
Do you know how hard it is to get a BUSINESS CARD out of your pocket with BANANA HANDS?!
It's hard to even SAY "bandana bands!"
Bonanza fans... Band-Aid brands... Bandolier pans...
Man, that phrase is tough. YOU try to say it.
Sultana brans.
Benedict Cumberhands... Cabana cans... Savannah sands... Pajama pants—
ENOUGH ABOUT THE BARBARIAN CLANS! Oh, that is hard to say.
We've got a MYSTERY to solve!

Dr. Morrow, you say the Robot Ghost attacked you. Then when you awoke, you were drenched in sweat and had...barbecue...barometer...blueberry—

Banana hands.

Thank you.

And yeah, now that you mention it, I guess I *am* all sweaty. Huh.

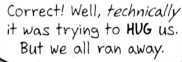

And this same robot tried to attack you and the other scientists *BEFORE* it became a ghost?

Correct! Well, *technically* it was trying to **HUG** us. But we all ran away.

And now it's come back to taunt you—

"Haunt."

—by giving you...

...fruity fists?

Banana hands.

Hey, I said it!

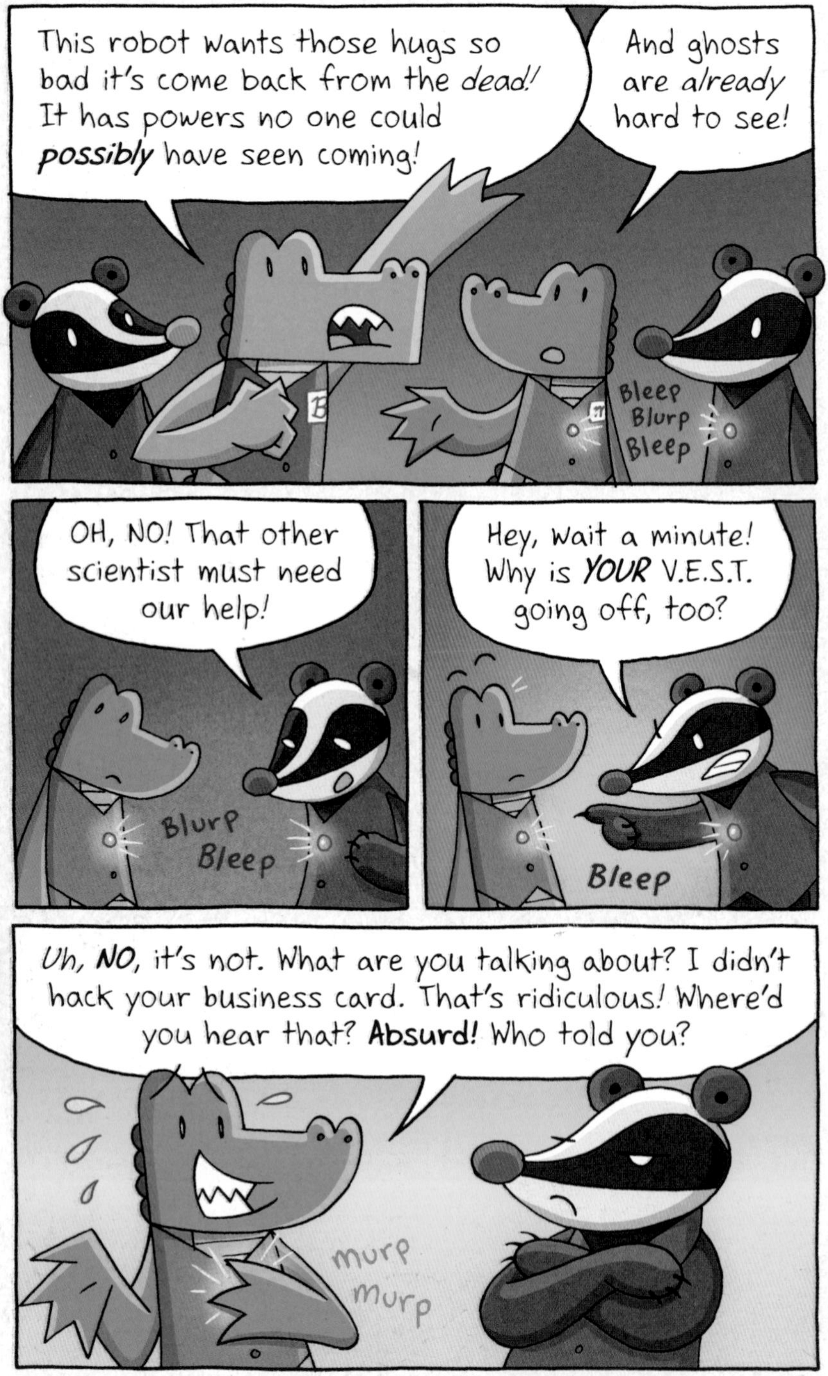
This robot wants those hugs so bad it's come back from the *dead!* It has powers no one could ***possibly*** have seen coming!
And ghosts are *already* hard to see!
Bleep Blurp Bleep
OH, NO! That other scientist must need our help!
Blurp Bleep
Hey, wait a minute! Why is ***YOUR*** V.E.S.T. going off, too?
Bleep
Uh, ***NO,*** it's not. What are you talking about? I didn't hack your business card. That's ridiculous! Where'd you hear that? **Absurd!** Who told you?
murp murp

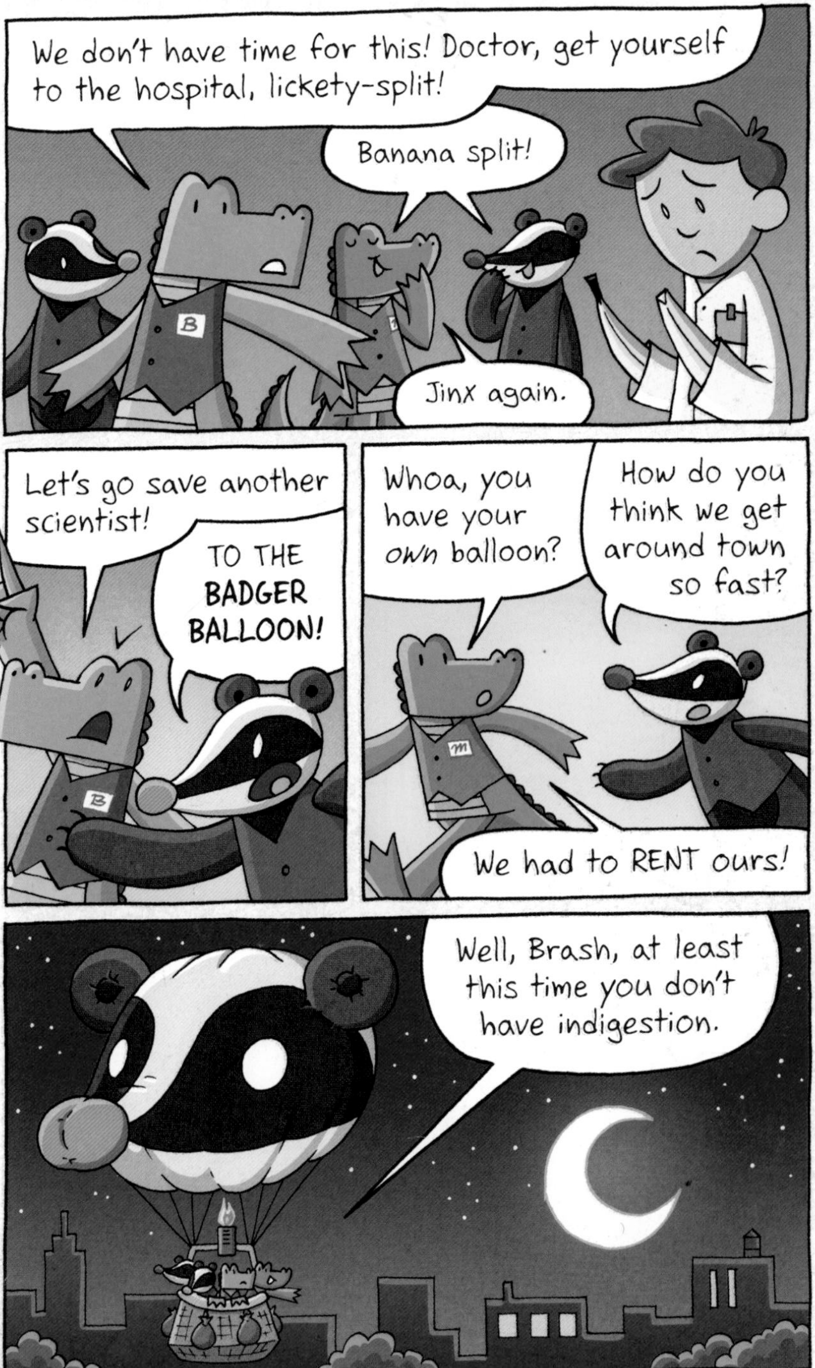
We don't have time for this! Doctor, get yourself to the hospital, lickety-split!
Banana split!
Jinx again.
Let's go save another scientist!
TO THE **BADGER BALLOON!**
Whoa, you have your *own* balloon?
How do you think we get around town so fast?
We had to RENT ours!
Well, Brash, at least this time you don't have indigestion.

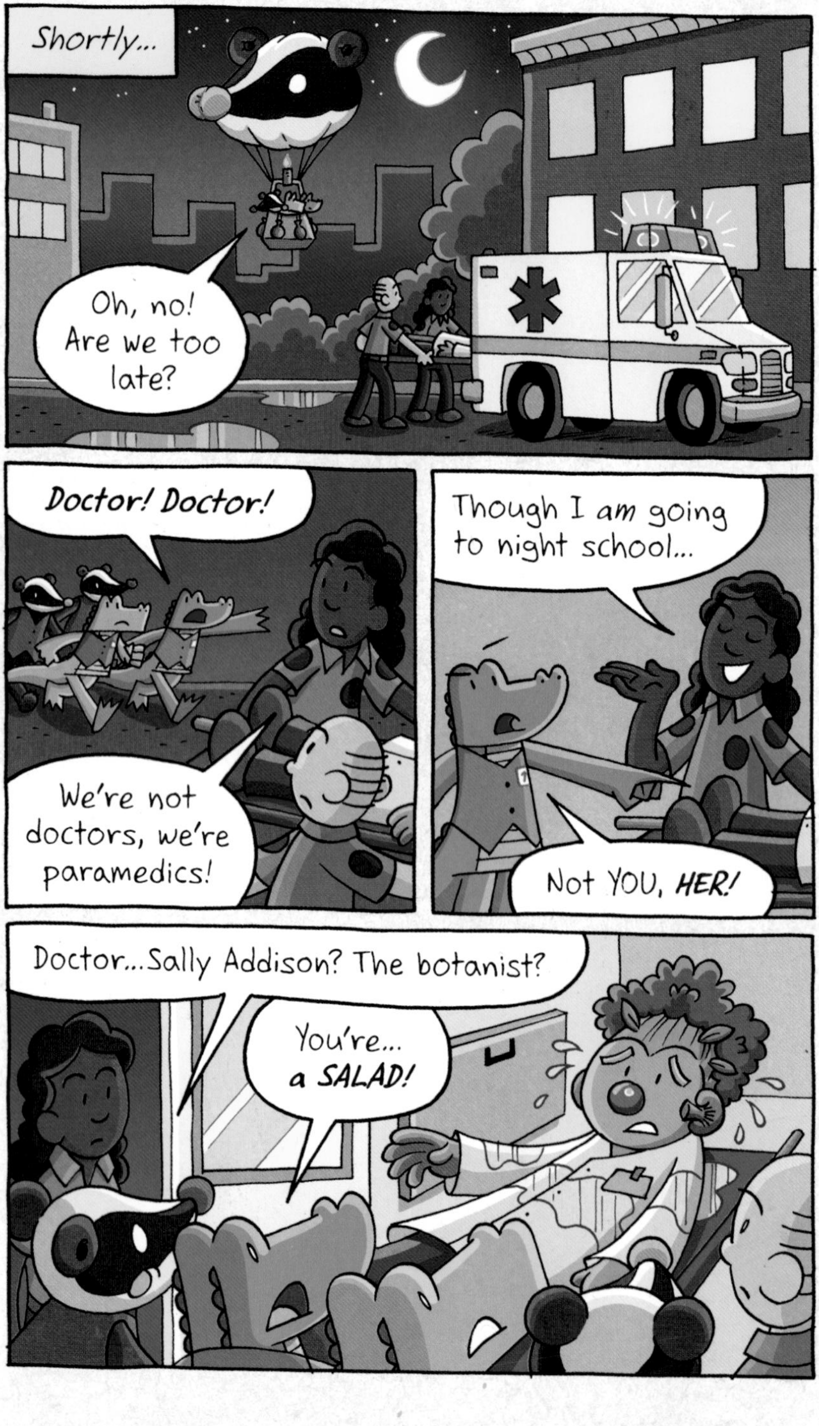
Shortly...
Oh, no! Are we too late?
Doctor! Doctor!
We're not doctors, we're paramedics!
Though I am going to night school...
Not YOU, HER!
Doctor...Sally Addison? The botanist?
You're... a SALAD!

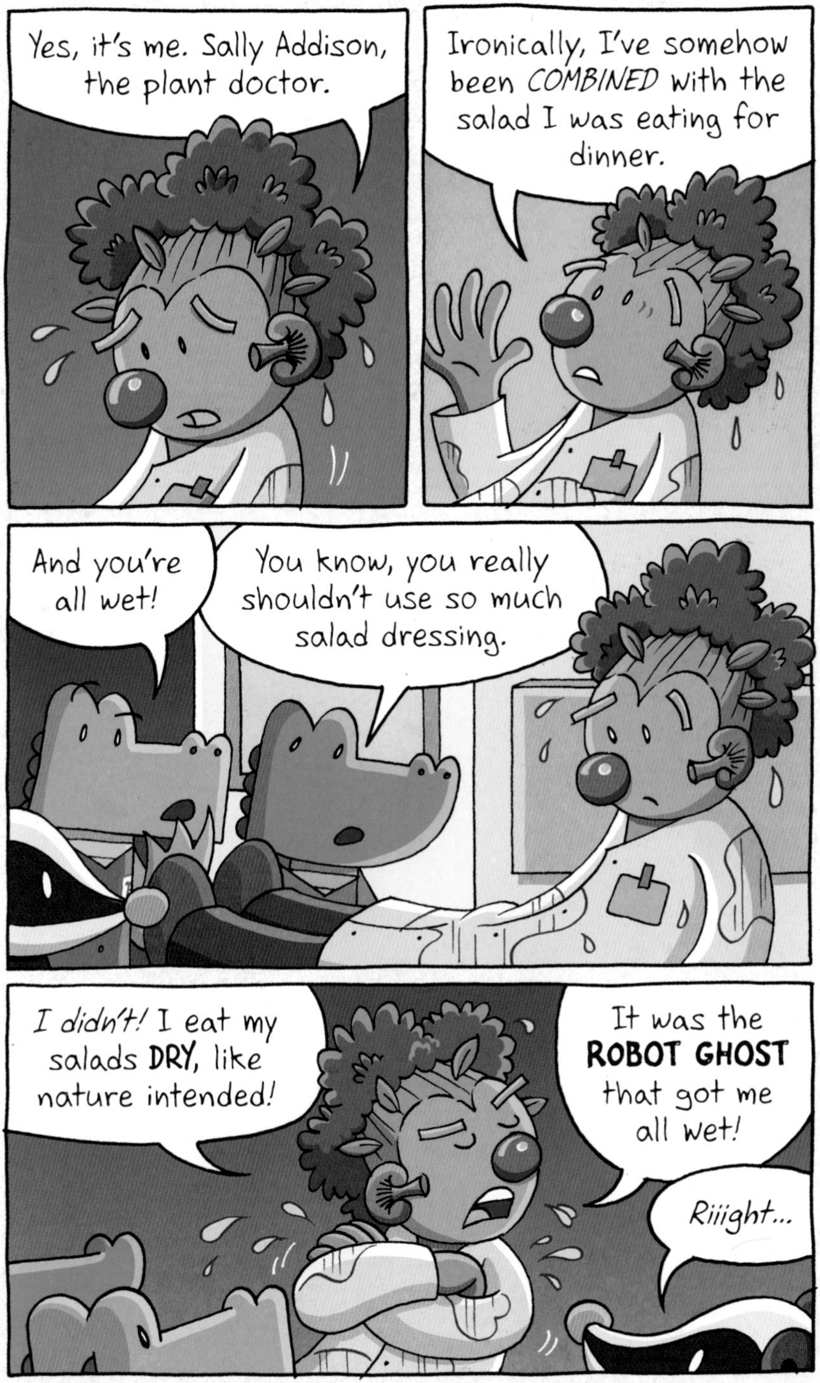
Yes, it's me. Sally Addison, the plant doctor.
Ironically, I've somehow been *COMBINED* with the salad I was eating for dinner.
And you're all wet!
You know, you really shouldn't use so much salad dressing.
I didn't! I eat my salads **DRY**, like nature intended!
It was the **ROBOT GHOST** that got me all wet!
Riiight...

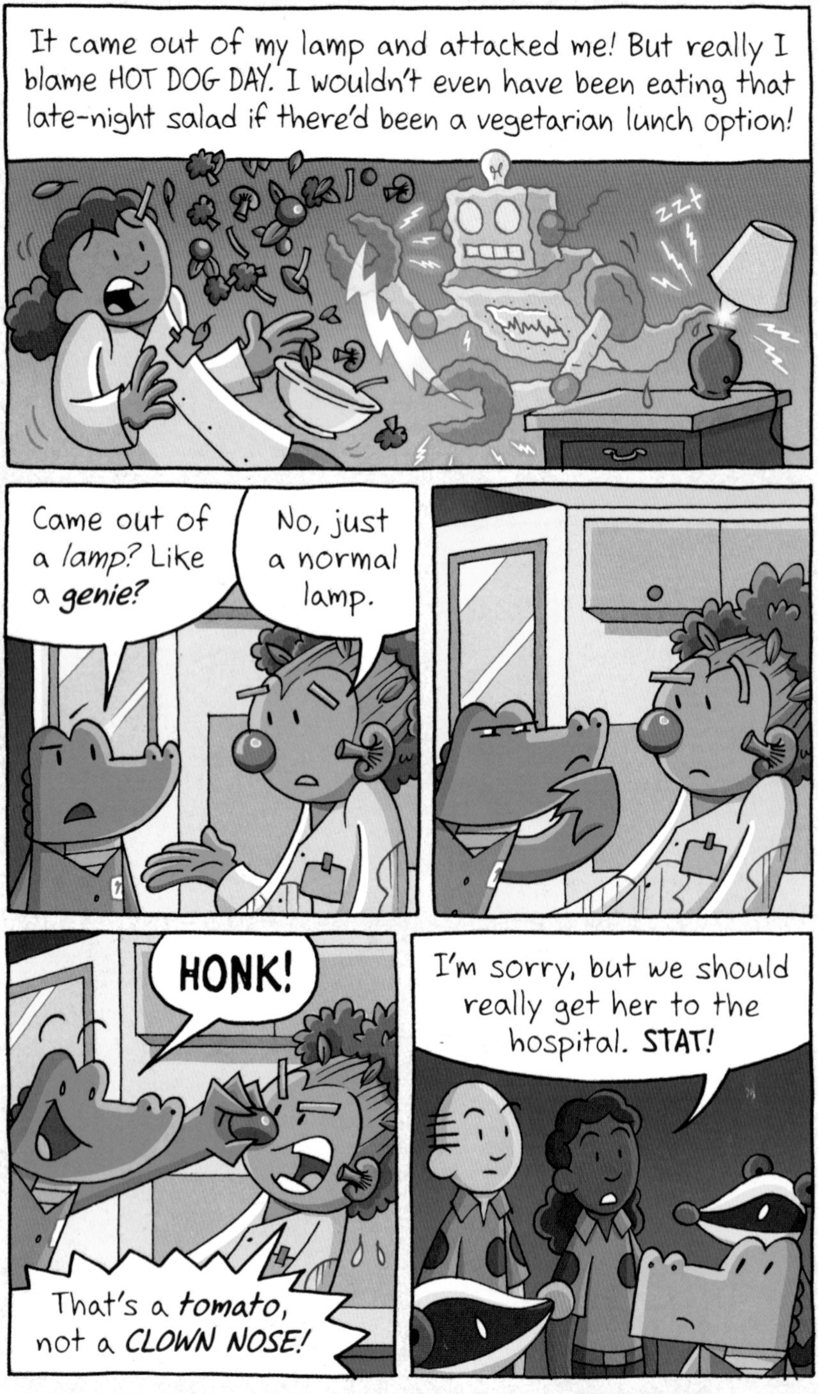
It came out of my lamp and attacked me! But really I blame HOT DOG DAY. I wouldn't even have been eating that late-night salad if there'd been a vegetarian lunch option!
ZZZ
Came out of a *lamp?* Like a ***genie?***
No, just a normal lamp.
HONK!
That's a *tomato,* not a *CLOWN NOSE!*
I'm sorry, but we should really get her to the hospital. **STAT!**

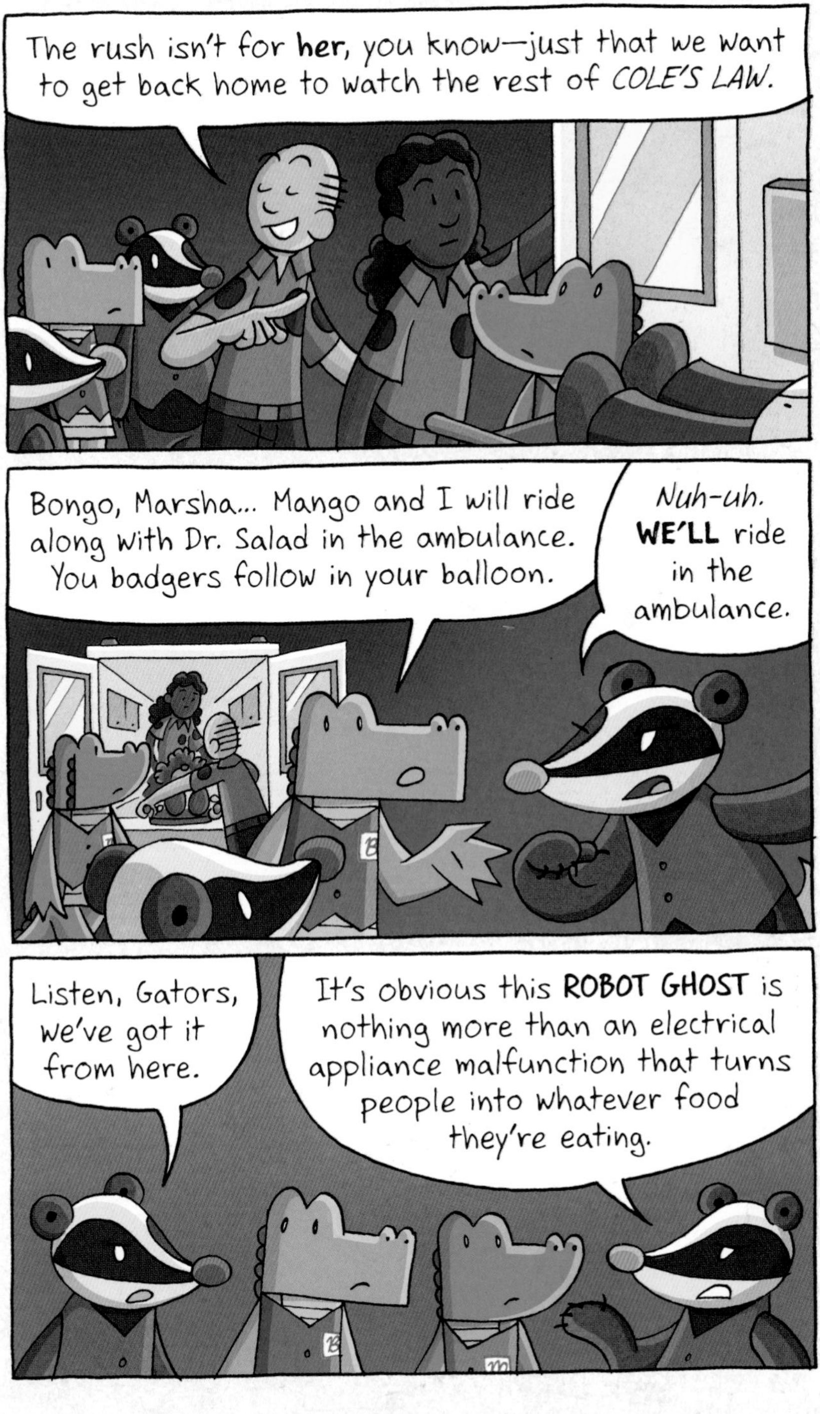
The rush isn't for **her**, you know—just that we want to get back home to watch the rest of *COLE'S LAW.*
Bongo, Marsha... Mango and I will ride along with Dr. Salad in the ambulance. You badgers follow in your balloon.
Nuh-uh. **WE'LL** ride in the ambulance.
Listen, Gators, we've got it from here.
It's obvious this **ROBOT GHOST** is nothing more than an electrical appliance malfunction that turns people into whatever food they're eating.

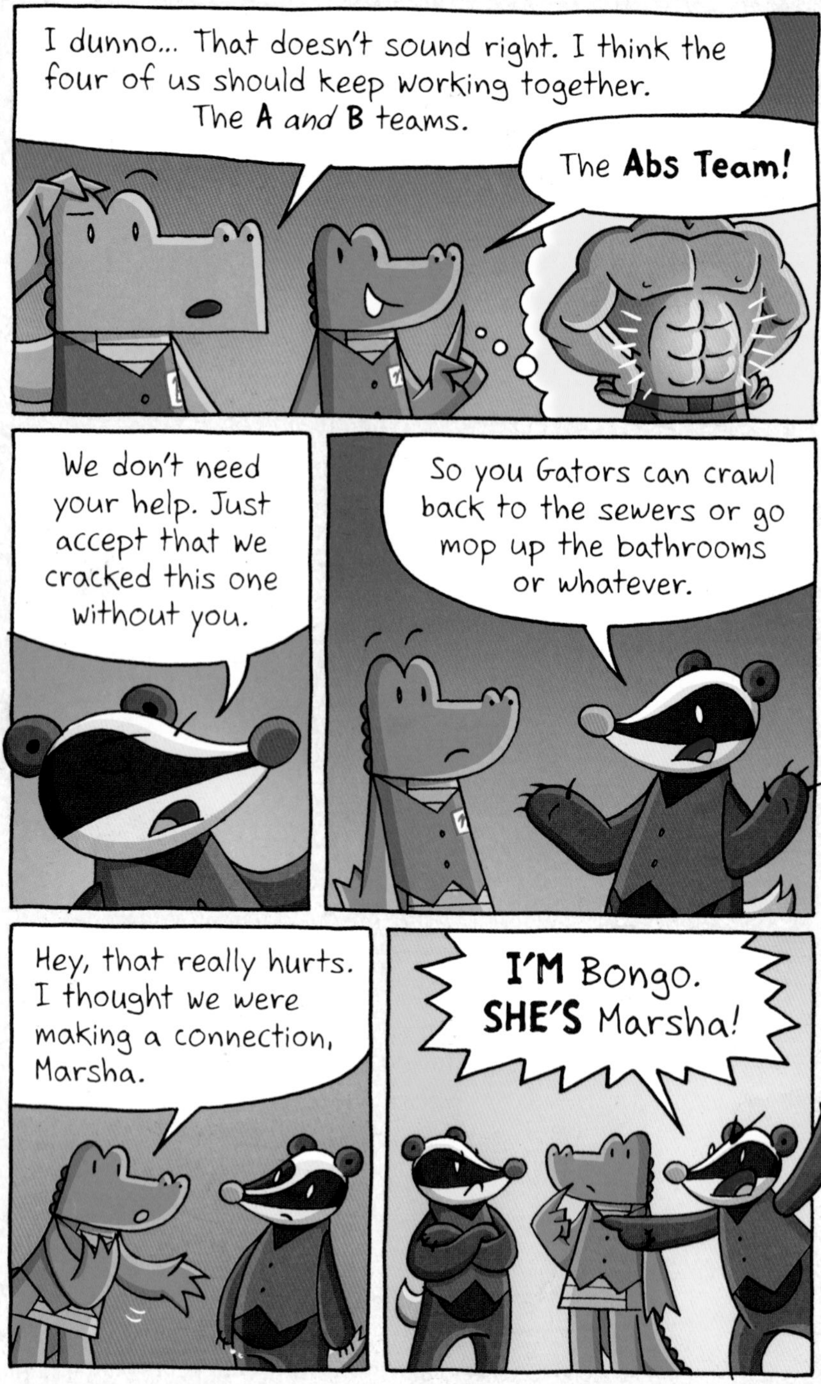
I dunno... That doesn't sound right. I think the four of us should keep working together. The A and B teams.
The Abs Team!
We don't need your help. Just accept that we cracked this one without you.
So you Gators can crawl back to the sewers or go mop up the bathrooms or whatever.
Hey, that really hurts. I thought we were making a connection, Marsha.
I'M Bongo. SHE'S Marsha!

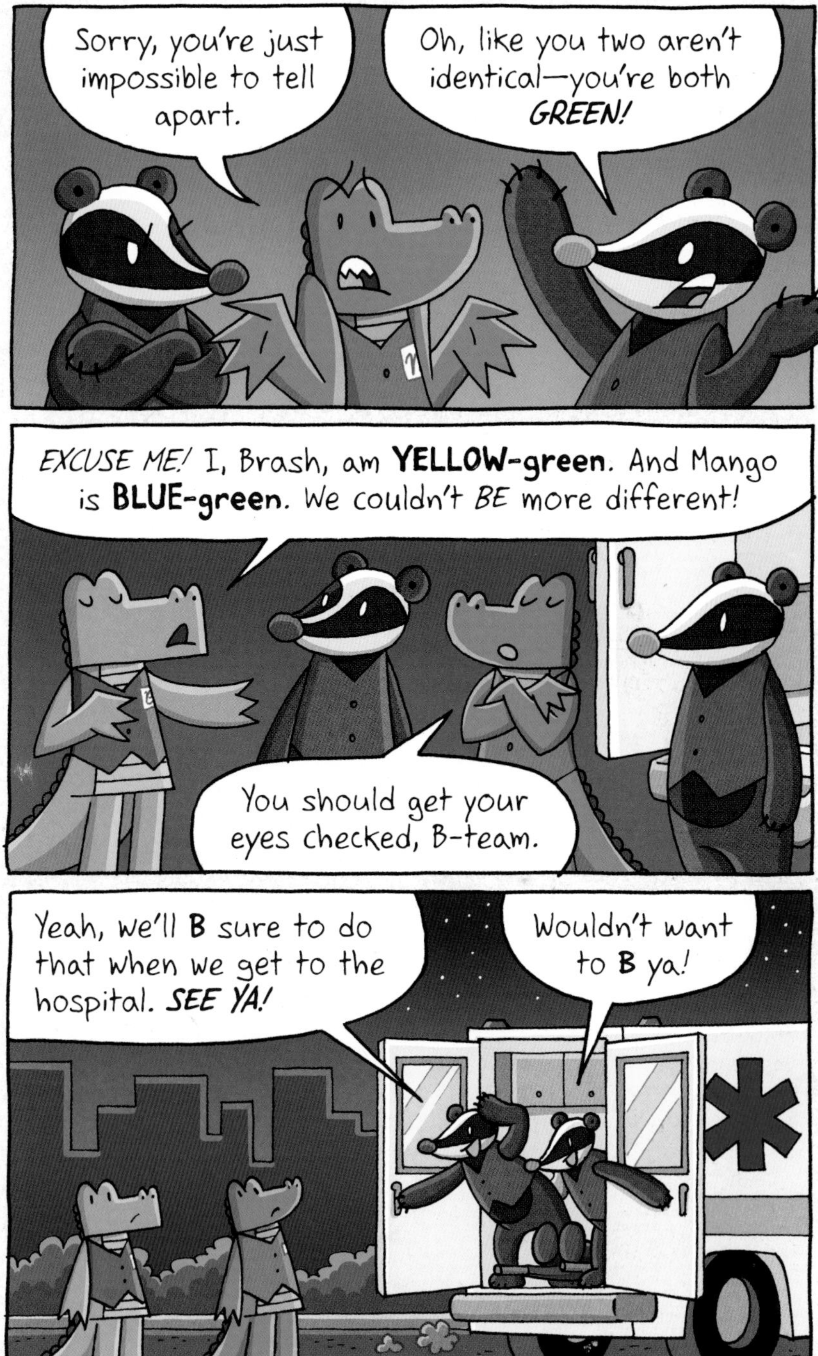

Sorry, you're just impossible to tell apart.
Oh, like you two aren't identical—you're both GREEN!
EXCUSE ME! I, Brash, am YELLOW-green. And Mango is BLUE-green. We couldn't BE more different!
You should get your eyes checked, B-team.
Yeah, we'll B sure to do that when we get to the hospital. SEE YA!
Wouldn't want to B ya!

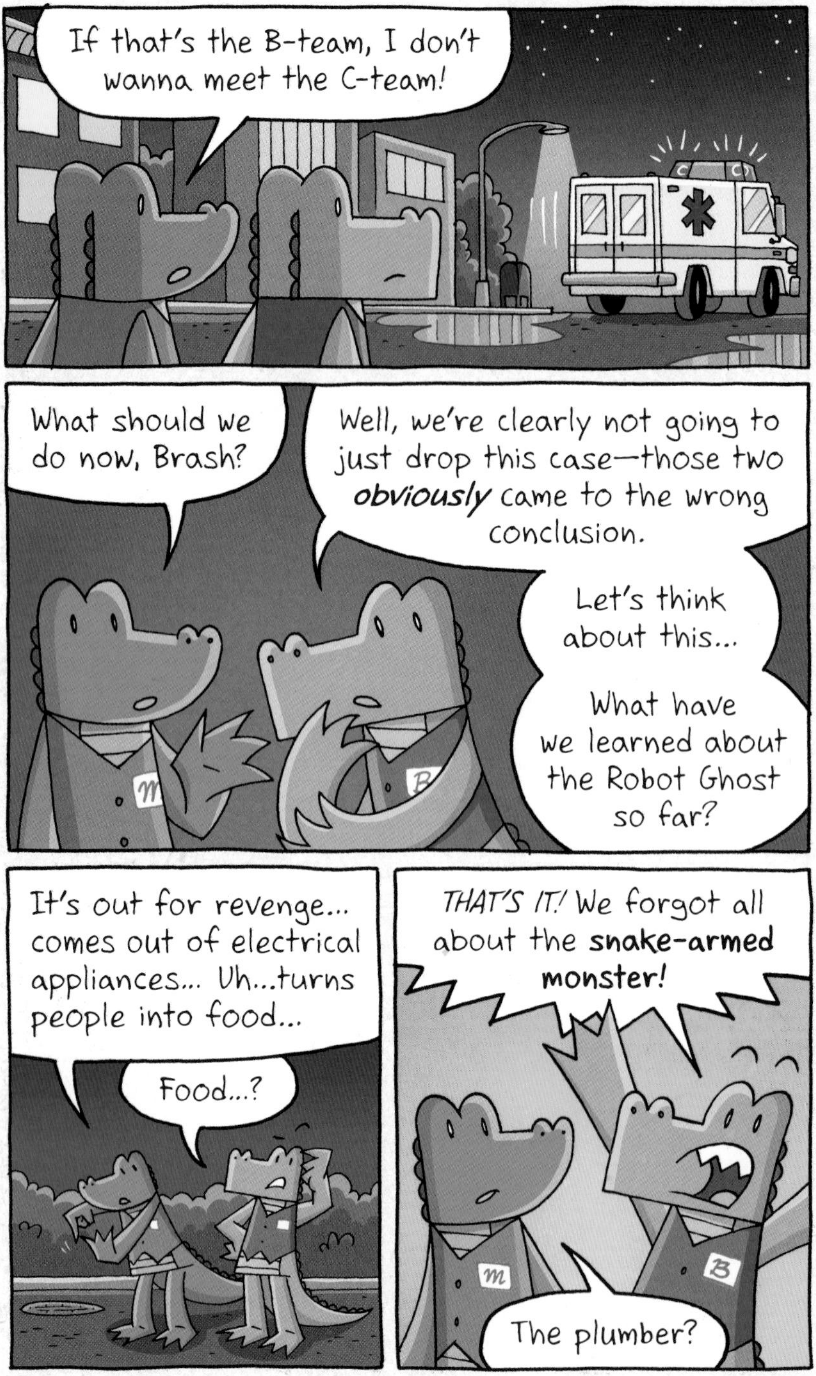

If that's the B-team, I don't wanna meet the C-team!
What should we do now, Brash?
Well, we're clearly not going to just drop this case—those two *obviously* came to the wrong conclusion.
Let's think about this...
What have we learned about the Robot Ghost so far?
It's out for revenge... comes out of electrical appliances... Uh...turns people into food...
Food...?
THAT'S IT! We forgot all about the **snake-armed monster!**
The plumber?

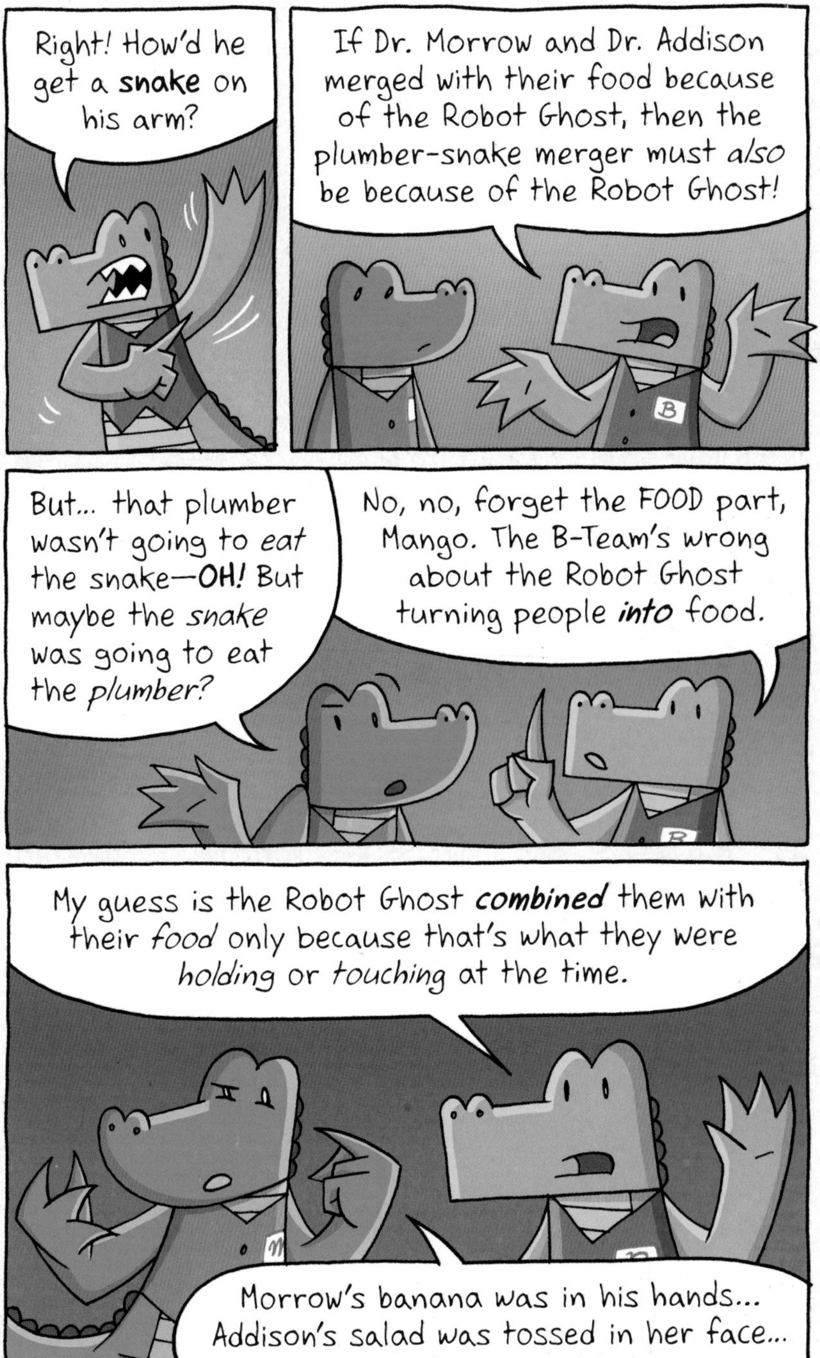
Right! How'd he get a **snake** on his arm?
If Dr. Morrow and Dr. Addison merged with their food because of the Robot Ghost, then the plumber-snake merger must *also* be because of the Robot Ghost!
But... that plumber wasn't going to *eat* the snake—**OH!** But maybe the *snake* was going to eat the *plumber?*
No, no, forget the FOOD part, Mango. The B-Team's wrong about the Robot Ghost turning people ***into*** food.
My guess is the Robot Ghost ***combined*** them with their *food* only because that's what they were *holding* or *touching* at the time.
Morrow's banana was in his hands... Addison's salad was tossed in her face...

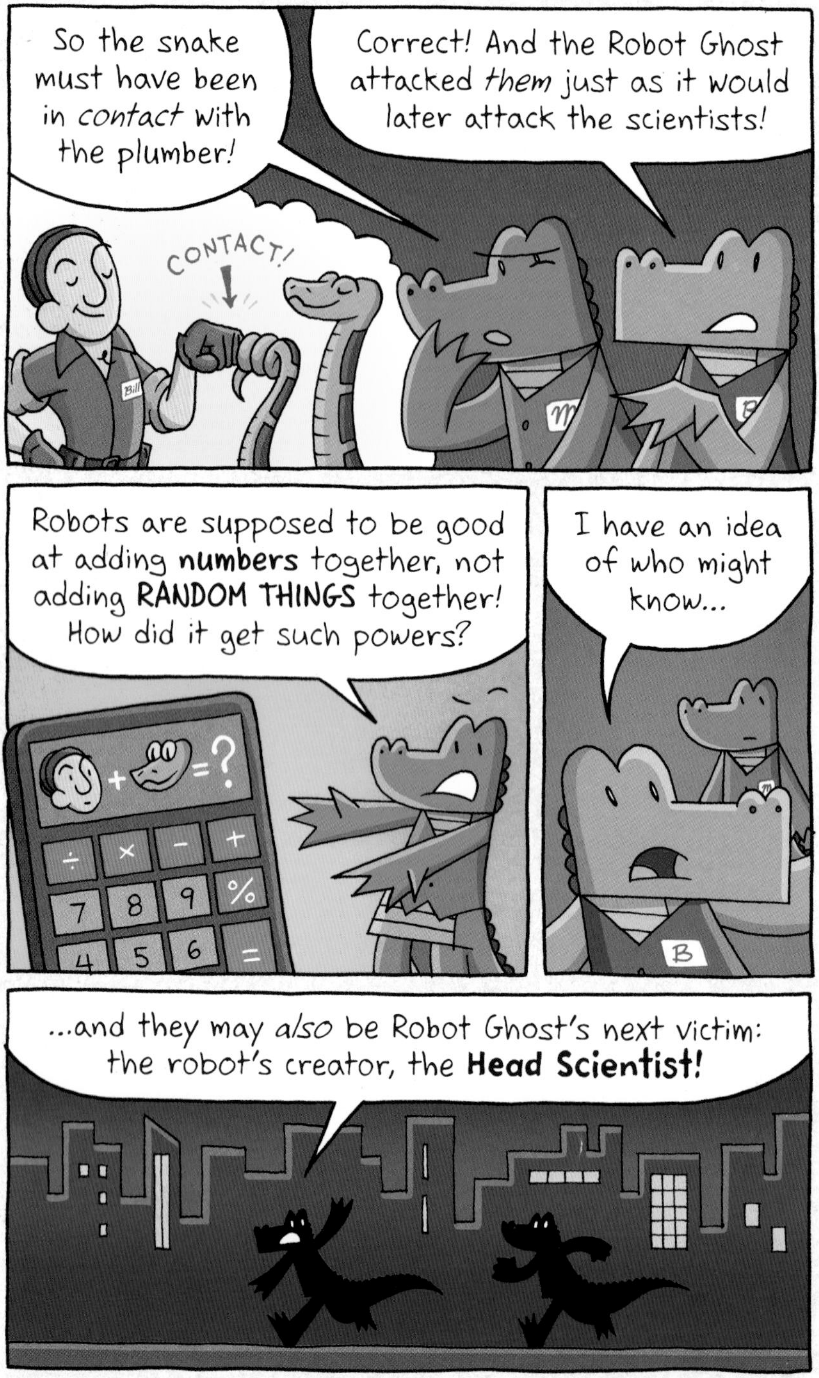
So the snake must have been in *contact* with the plumber!
Correct! And the Robot Ghost attacked *them* just as it would later attack the scientists!
CONTACT!
Bill
Robots are supposed to be good at adding **numbers** together, not adding **RANDOM THINGS** together! How did it get such powers?
I have an idea of who might know...
...and they may *also* be Robot Ghost's next victim: the robot's creator, the **Head Scientist!**

Chapter 12, probably

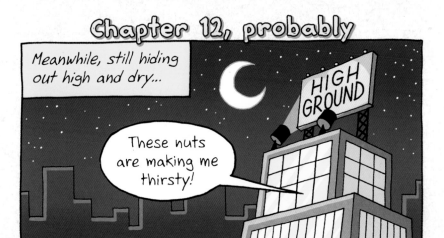

Meanwhile, still hiding out high and dry...

HIGH GROUND

These nuts are making me thirsty!

But I just ≥munch≤ keep ≥scarf≤ eating them!

MY CABBAGES!

Would you like some water?

NO! Water's the *LAST* thing I need!

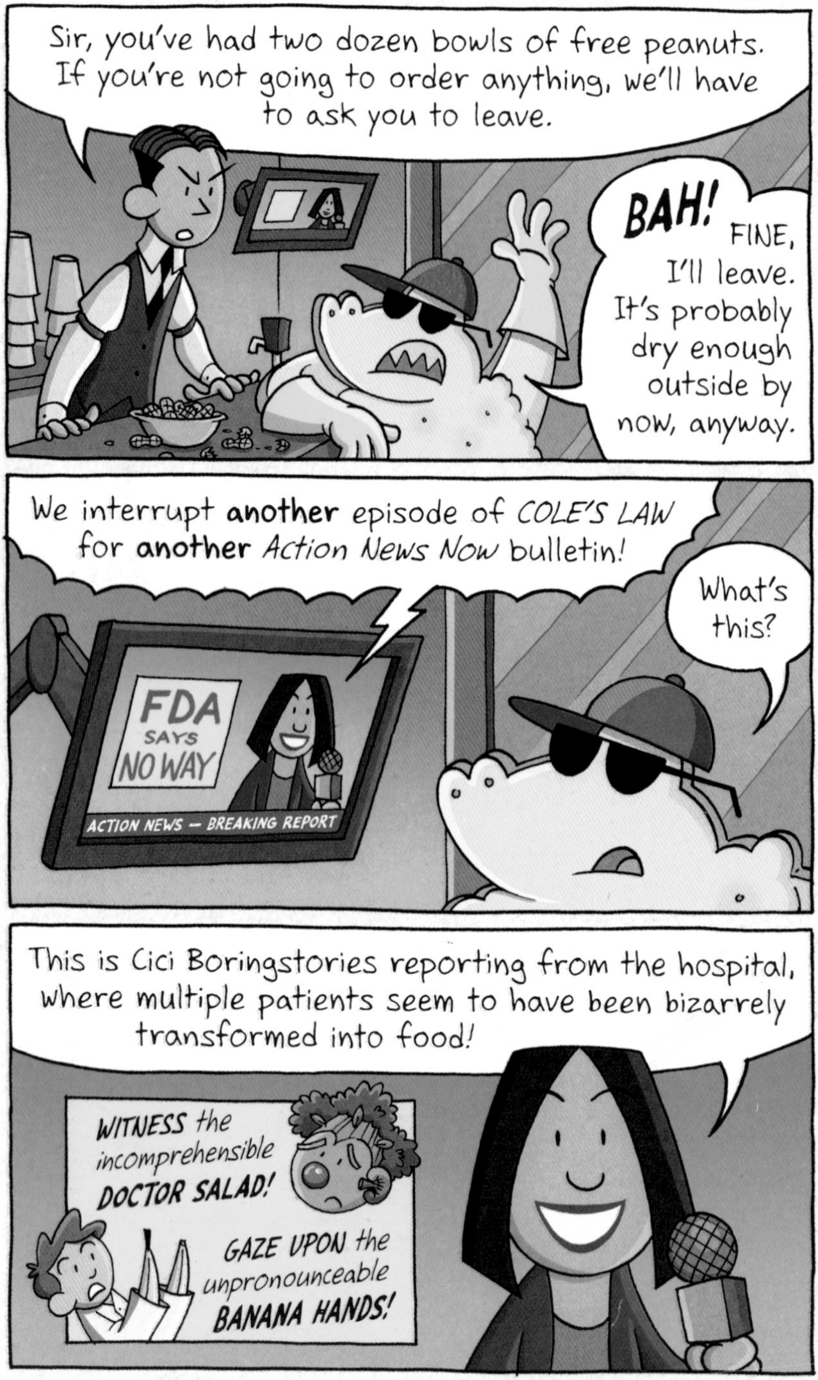
Sir, you've had two dozen bowls of free peanuts. If you're not going to order anything, we'll have to ask you to leave.
BAH! FINE, I'll leave. It's probably dry enough outside by now, anyway.
We interrupt **another** episode of *COLE'S LAW* for **another** *Action News Now* bulletin!
FDA SAYS NO WAY
ACTION NEWS — BREAKING REPORT
What's this?
This is Cici Boringstories reporting from the hospital, where multiple patients seem to have been bizarrely transformed into food!
WITNESS the incomprehensible DOCTOR SALAD!
GAZE UPON the unpronounceable BANANA HANDS!

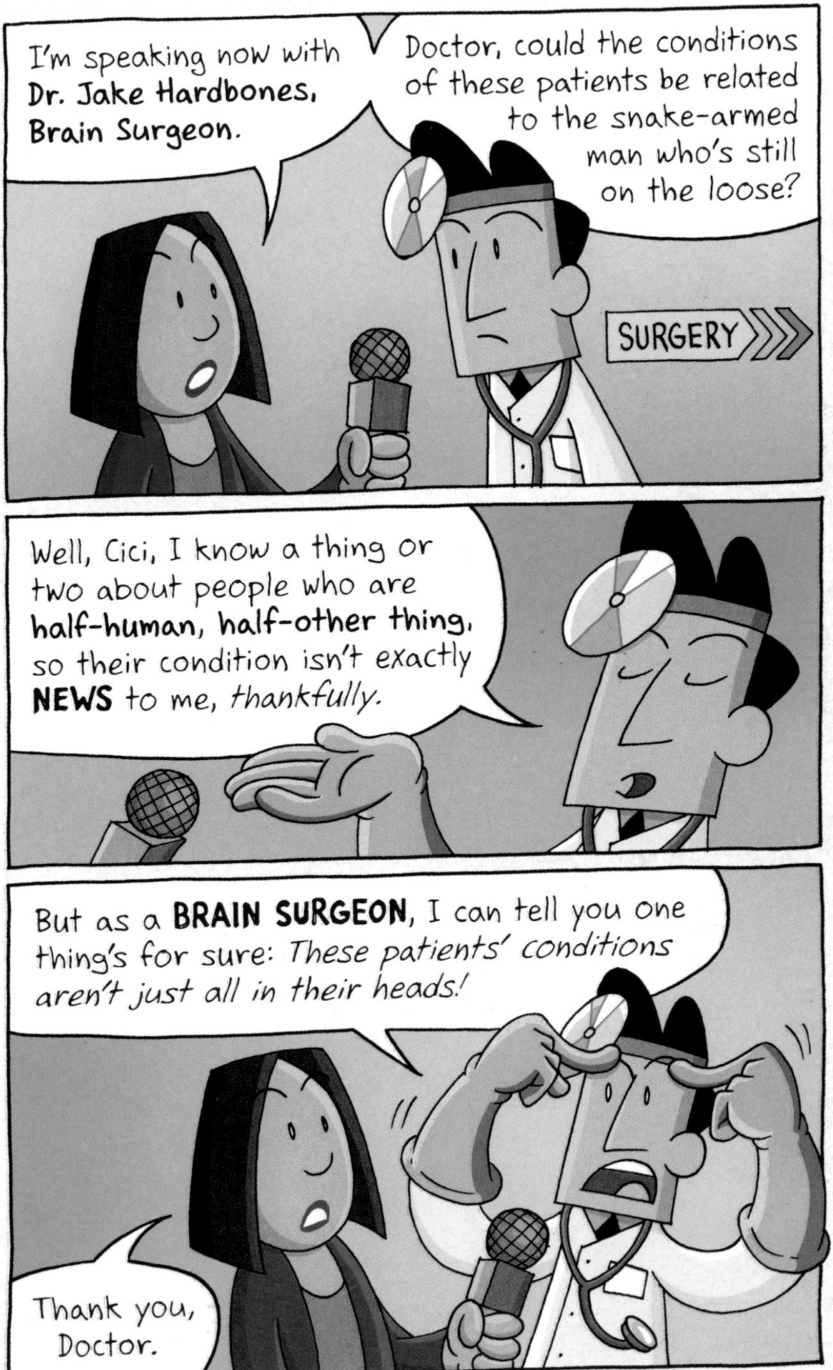
I'm speaking now with **Dr. Jake Hardbones, Brain Surgeon.**
Doctor, could the conditions of these patients be related to the snake-armed man who's still on the loose?
SURGERY
Well, Cici, I know a thing or two about people who are **half-human, half-other thing,** so their condition isn't exactly **NEWS** to me, *thankfully.*
But as a **BRAIN SURGEON**, I can tell you one thing's for sure: *These patients' conditions aren't just all in their heads!*
Thank you, Doctor.

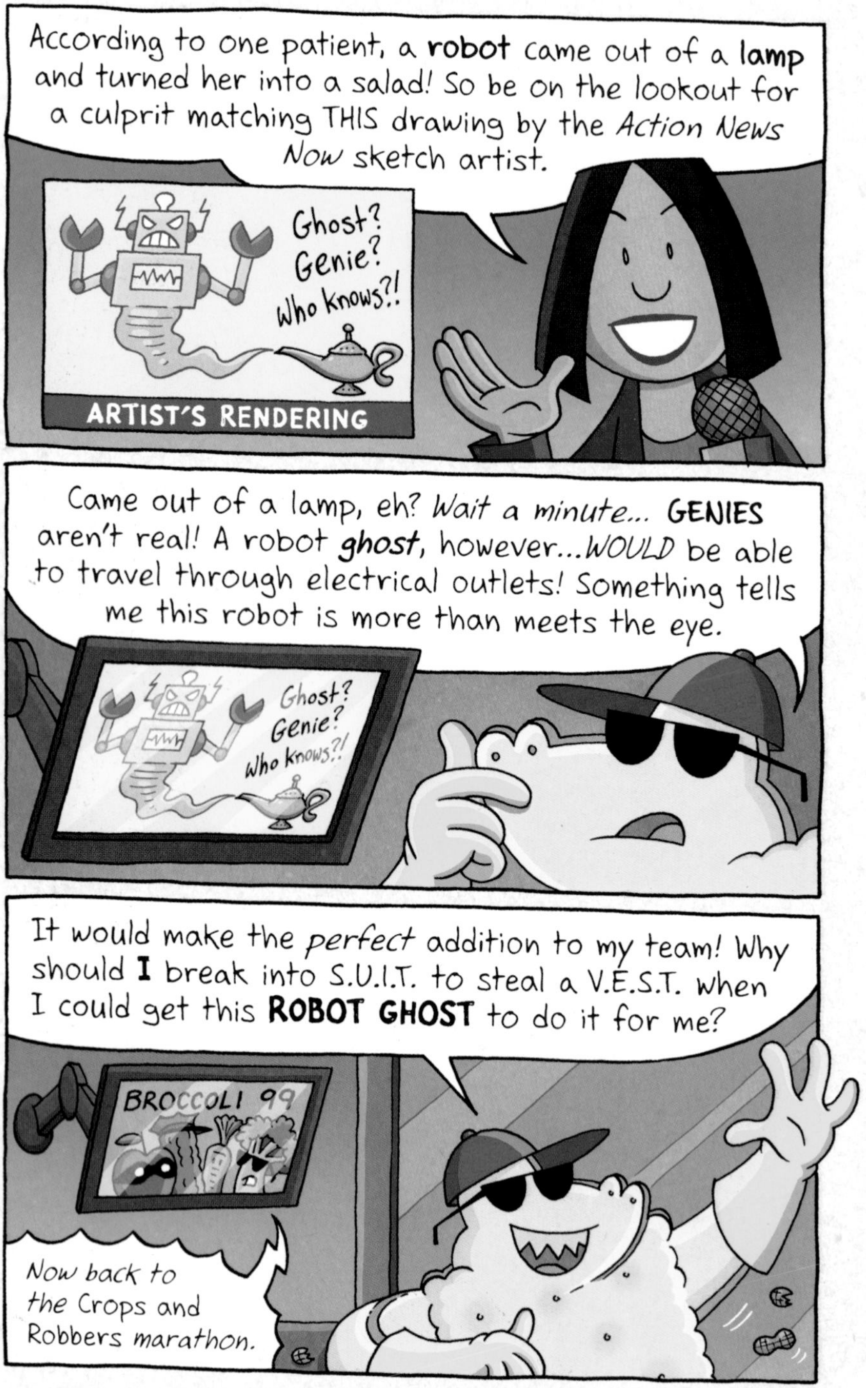
According to one patient, a **robot** came out of a **lamp** and turned her into a salad! So be on the lookout for a culprit matching THIS drawing by the *Action News Now* sketch artist.
Ghost? Genie? Who knows?!
ARTIST'S RENDERING
Came out of a lamp, eh? *Wait a minute...* **GENIES** aren't real! A robot ***ghost***, however...*WOULD* be able to travel through electrical outlets! Something tells me this robot is more than meets the eye.
Ghost? Genie? Who knows?!
It would make the *perfect* addition to my team! Why should **I** break into S.U.I.T. to steal a V.E.S.T. when I could get this **ROBOT GHOST** to do it for me?
BROCCOLI 99
Now back to the Crops and Robbers marathon.

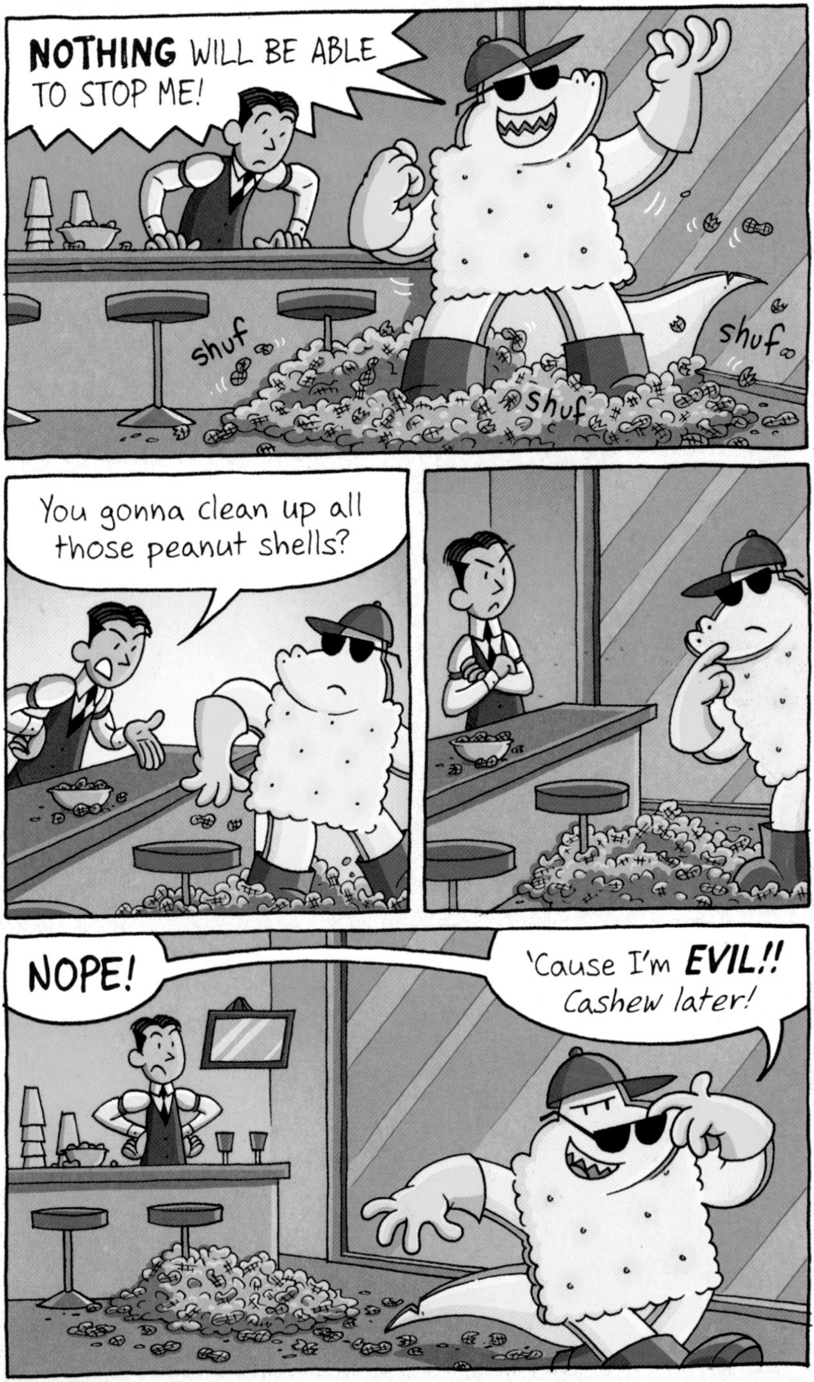
NOTHING WILL BE ABLE TO STOP ME!
shuf
shuf
shuf
You gonna clean up all those peanut shells?
NOPE!
'Cause I'm EVIL!! Cashew later!

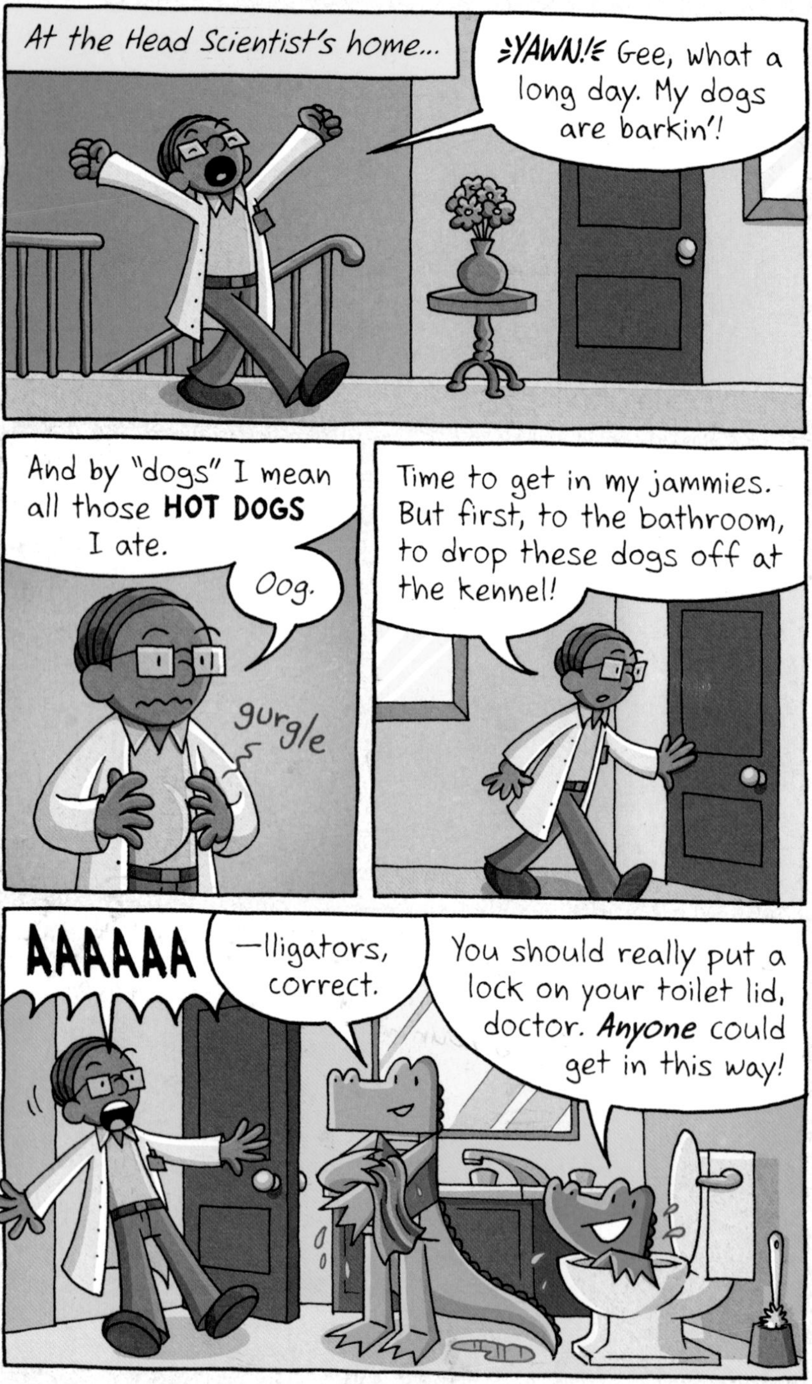
At the Head Scientist's home...
YAWN! Gee, what a long day. My dogs are barkin'!
And by "dogs" I mean all those HOT DOGS I ate.
Oog.
gurgle
Time to get in my jammies. But first, to the bathroom, to drop these dogs off at the kennel!
AAAAAA
—lligators, correct.
You should really put a lock on your toilet lid, doctor. Anyone could get in this way!

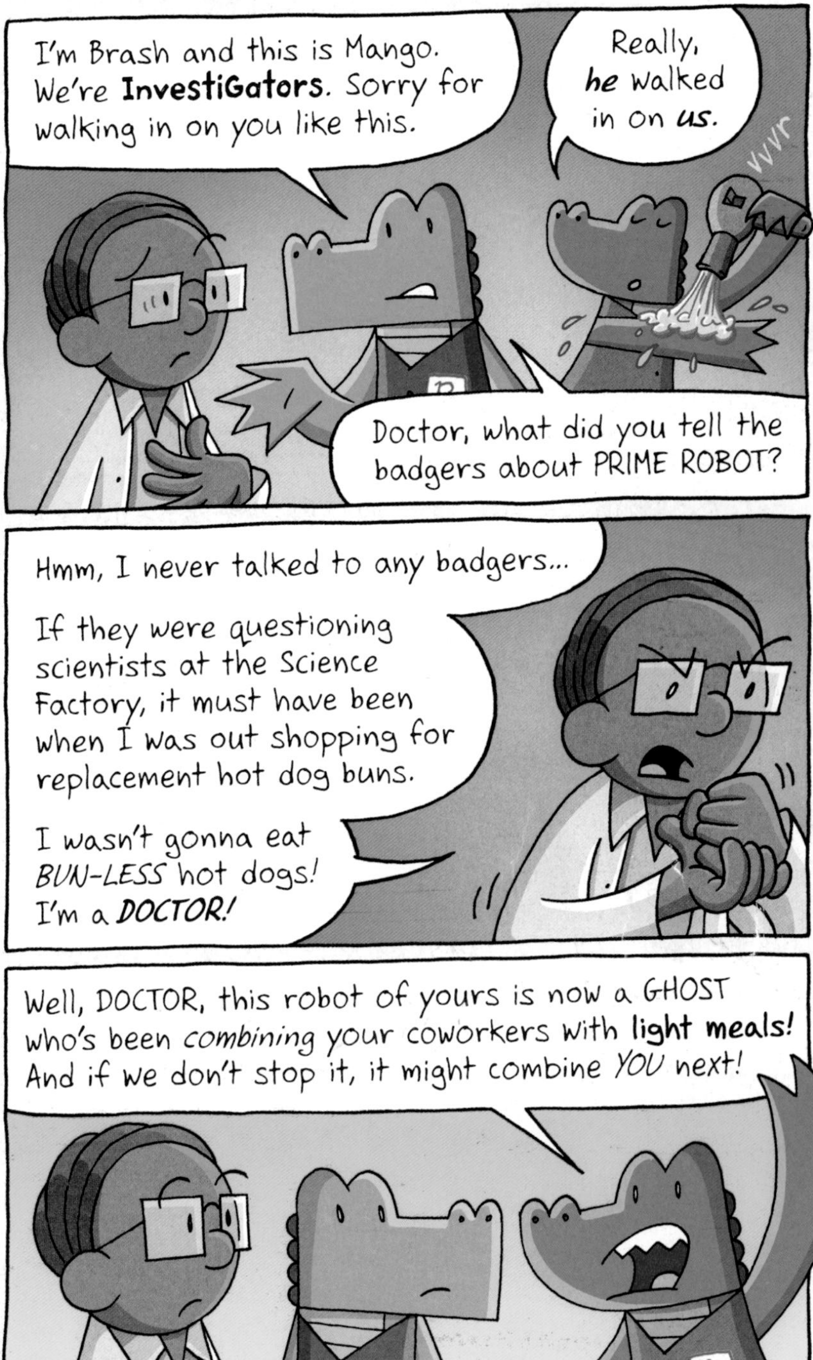
I'm Brash and this is Mango. We're **InvestiGators**. Sorry for walking in on you like this.
Really, ***he*** walked in on ***us***.
VVVr
Doctor, what did you tell the badgers about PRIME ROBOT?
Hmm, I never talked to any badgers...
If they were questioning scientists at the Science Factory, it must have been when I was out shopping for replacement hot dog buns.
I wasn't gonna eat *BUN-LESS* hot dogs! I'm a ***DOCTOR!***
Well, DOCTOR, this robot of yours is now a GHOST who's been *combining* your coworkers with **light meals!** And if we don't stop it, it might combine *YOU* next!

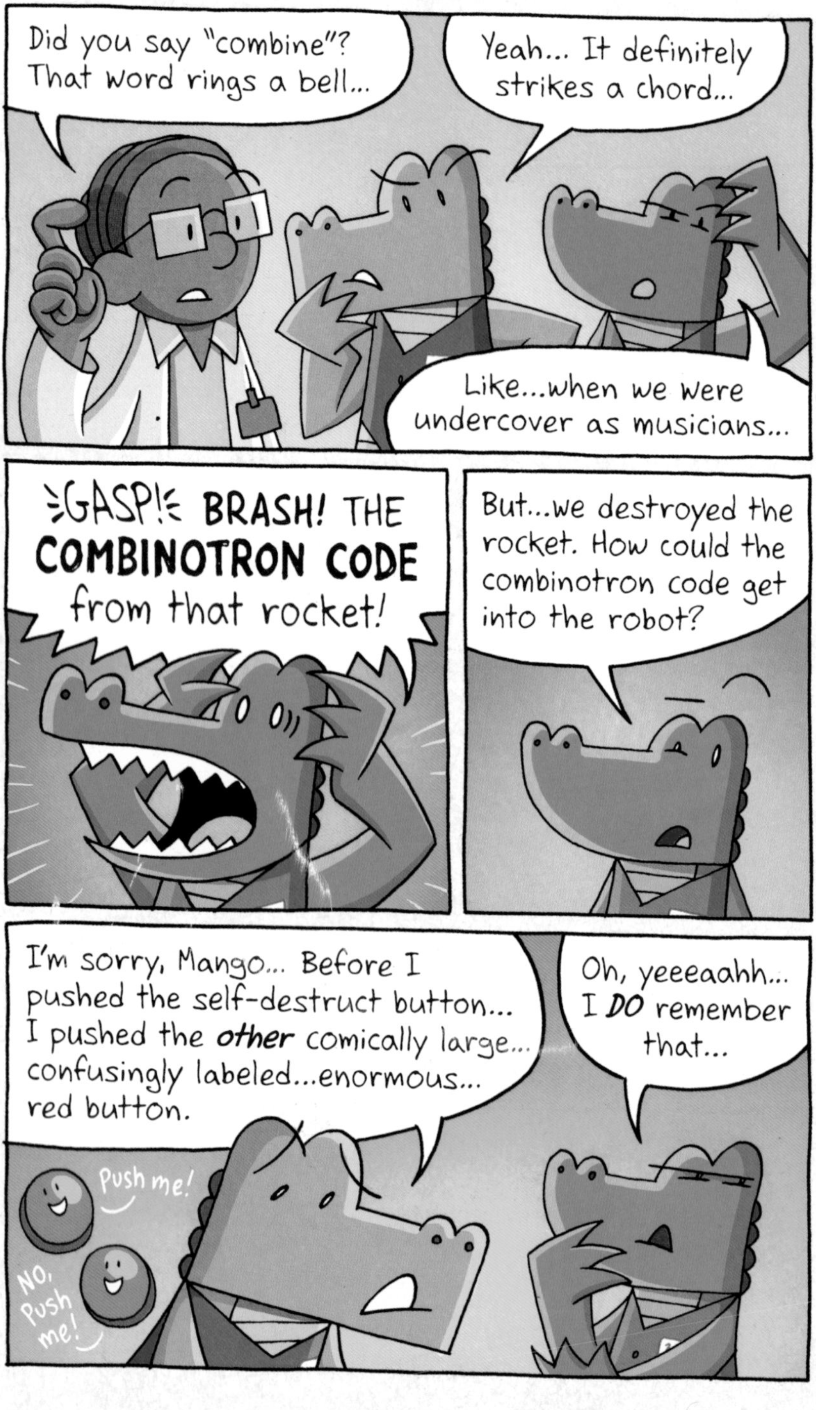
Did you say "combine"? That word rings a bell...
Yeah... It definitely strikes a chord...
Like...when we were undercover as musicians...
GASP! BRASH! THE COMBINOTRON CODE from that rocket!
But...we destroyed the rocket. How could the combinotron code get into the robot?
I'm sorry, Mango... Before I pushed the self-destruct button... I pushed the *other* comically large... confusingly labeled...enormous... red button.
Push me!
No, Push me!
Oh, yeeeaahh... I ***DO*** remember that...

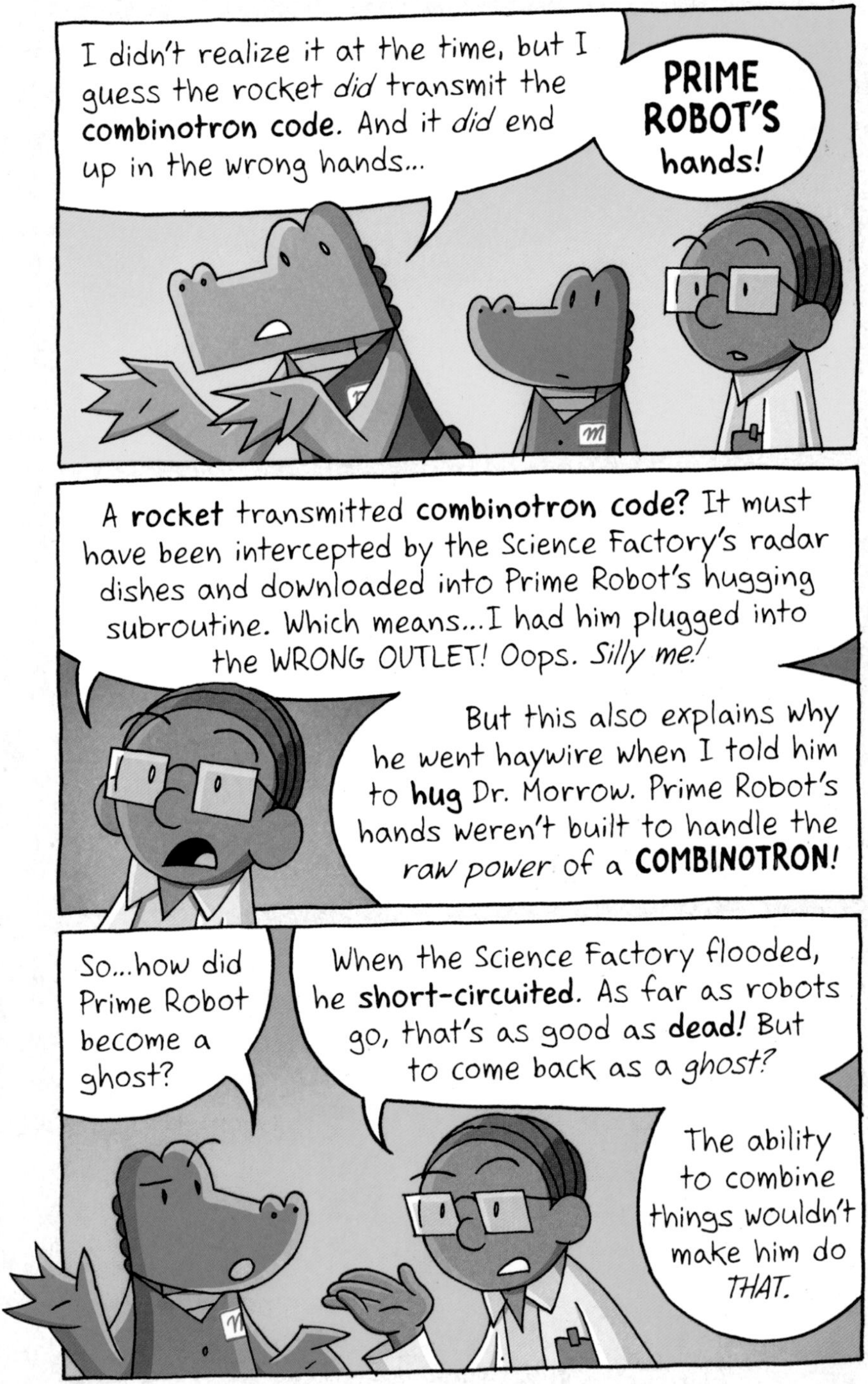
I didn't realize it at the time, but I guess the rocket did transmit the combinotron code. And it did end up in the wrong hands...
PRIME ROBOT'S hands!
A rocket transmitted combinotron code? It must have been intercepted by the Science Factory's radar dishes and downloaded into Prime Robot's hugging subroutine. Which means...I had him plugged into the WRONG OUTLET! Oops. Silly me!
But this also explains why he went haywire when I told him to hug Dr. Morrow. Prime Robot's hands weren't built to handle the raw power of a COMBINOTRON!
So...how did Prime Robot become a ghost?
When the Science Factory flooded, he short-circuited. As far as robots go, that's as good as dead! But to come back as a ghost?
The ability to combine things wouldn't make him do THAT.

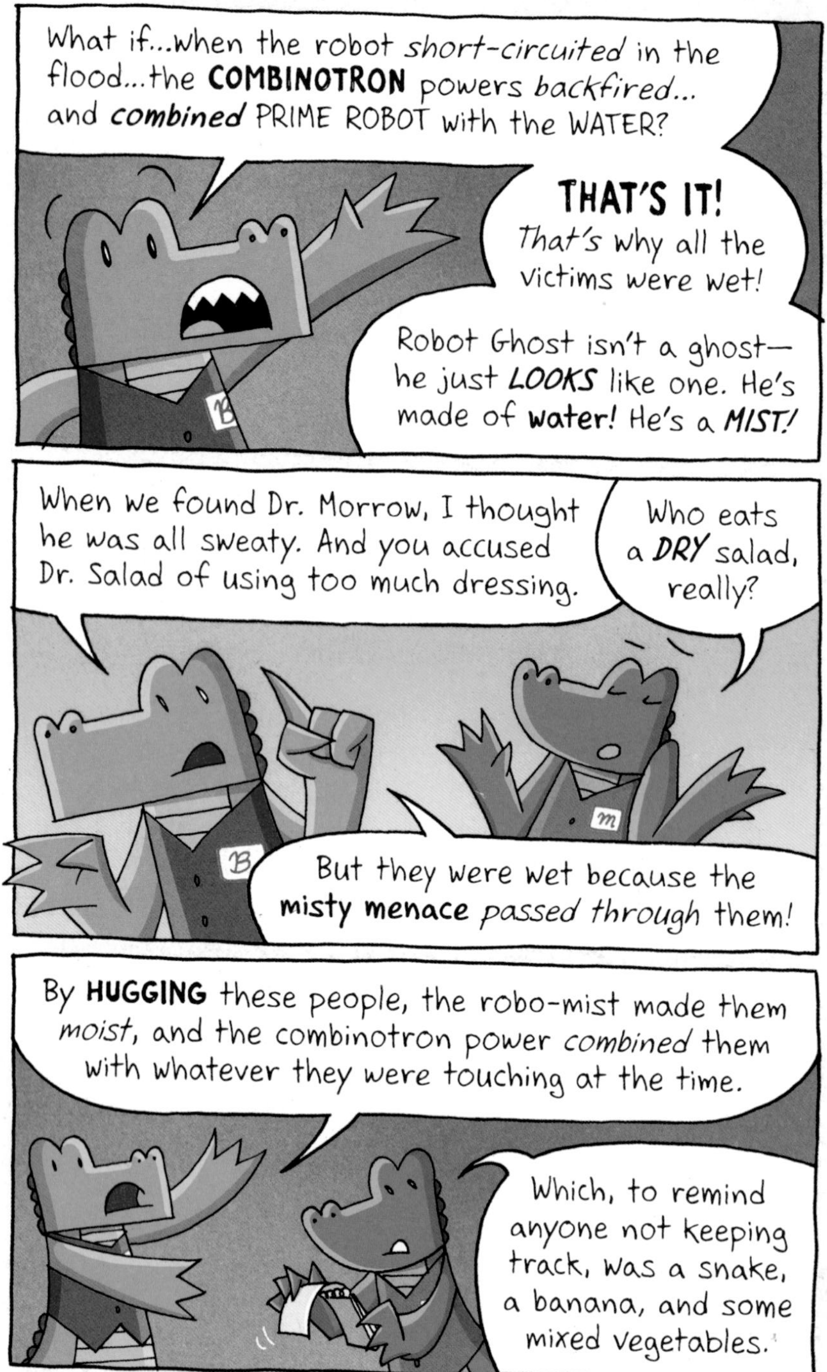

What if...when the robot *short-circuited* in the flood...the **COMBINOTRON** powers *backfired*... and ***combined*** PRIME ROBOT with the WATER?
THAT'S IT! *That's* why all the victims were wet!
Robot Ghost isn't a ghost—he just ***LOOKS*** like one. He's made of **water!** He's a ***MIST!***
When we found Dr. Morrow, I thought he was all sweaty. And you accused Dr. Salad of using too much dressing.
Who eats a ***DRY*** salad, really?
But they were wet because the **misty menace** *passed through* them!
By **HUGGING** these people, the robo-mist made them *moist*, and the combinotron power *combined* them with whatever they were touching at the time.
Which, to remind anyone not keeping track, was a snake, a banana, and some mixed vegetables.

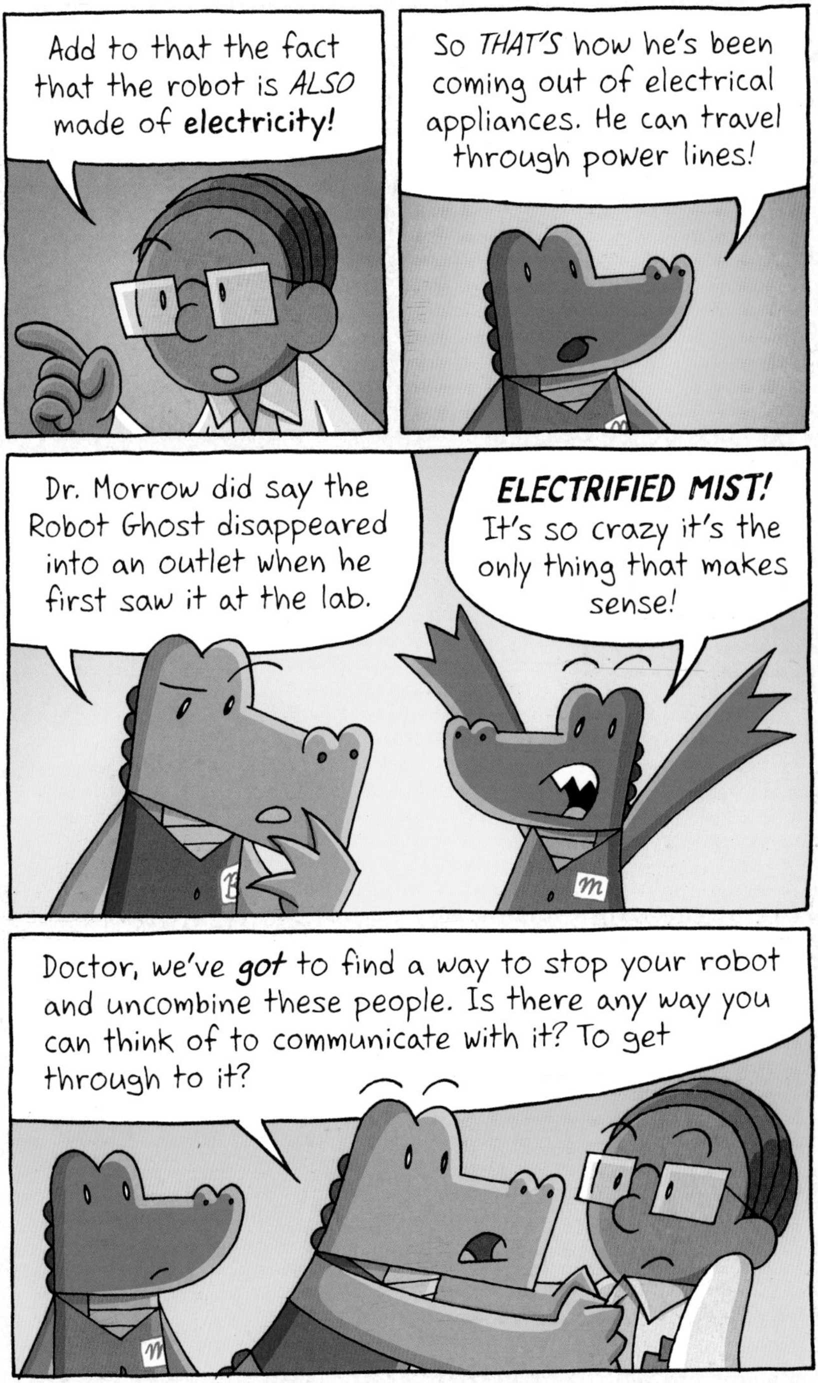
Add to that the fact that the robot is *ALSO* made of **electricity**!
So *THAT'S* how he's been coming out of electrical appliances. He can travel through power lines!
Dr. Morrow did say the Robot Ghost disappeared into an outlet when he first saw it at the lab.
ELECTRIFIED MIST! It's so crazy it's the only thing that makes sense!
Doctor, we've ***got*** to find a way to stop your robot and uncombine these people. Is there any way you can think of to communicate with it? To get through to it?

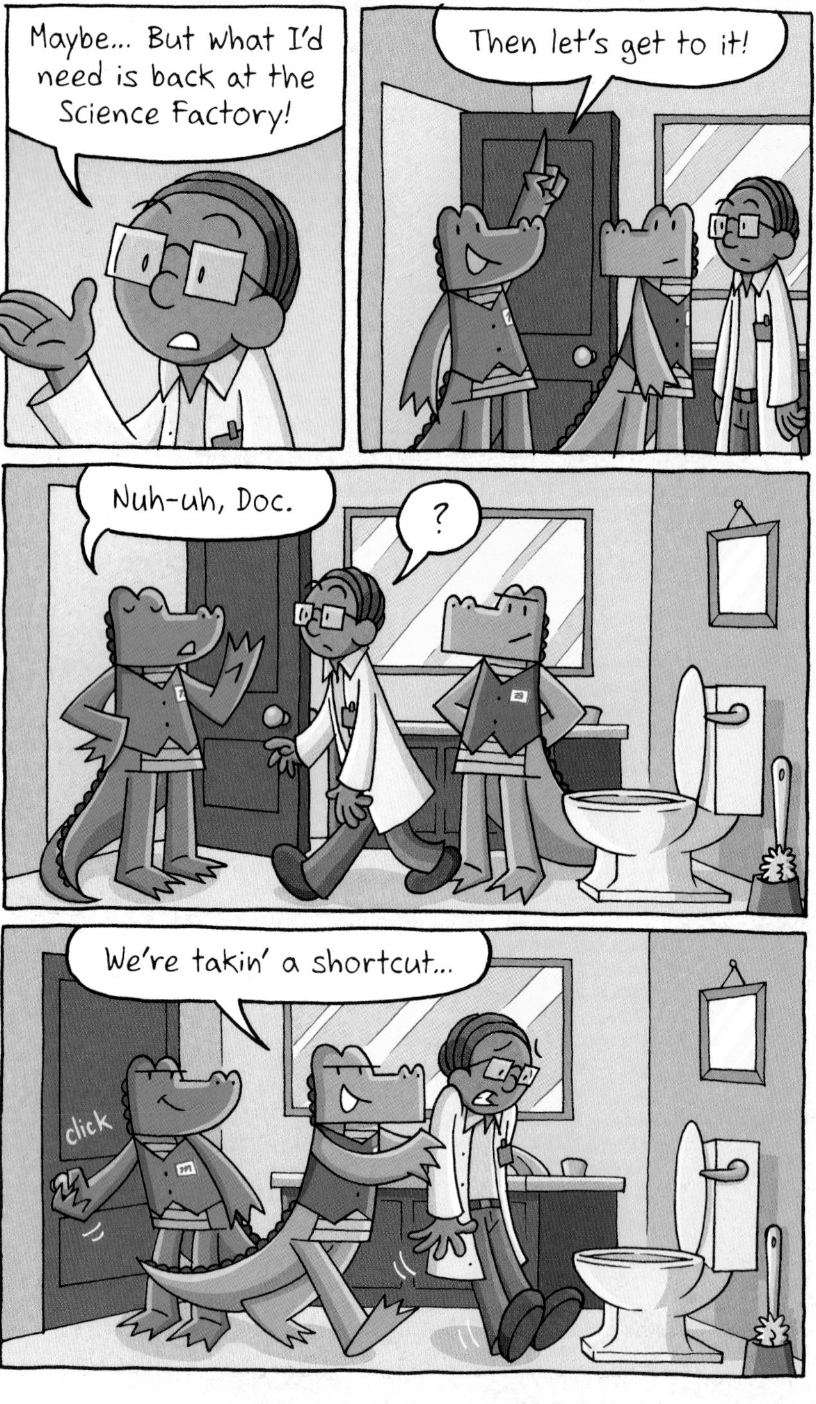
Maybe... But what I'd need is back at the Science Factory!
Then let's get to it!
Nuh-uh, Doc.
?
We're takin' a shortcut...
click

Chapter I've lost count

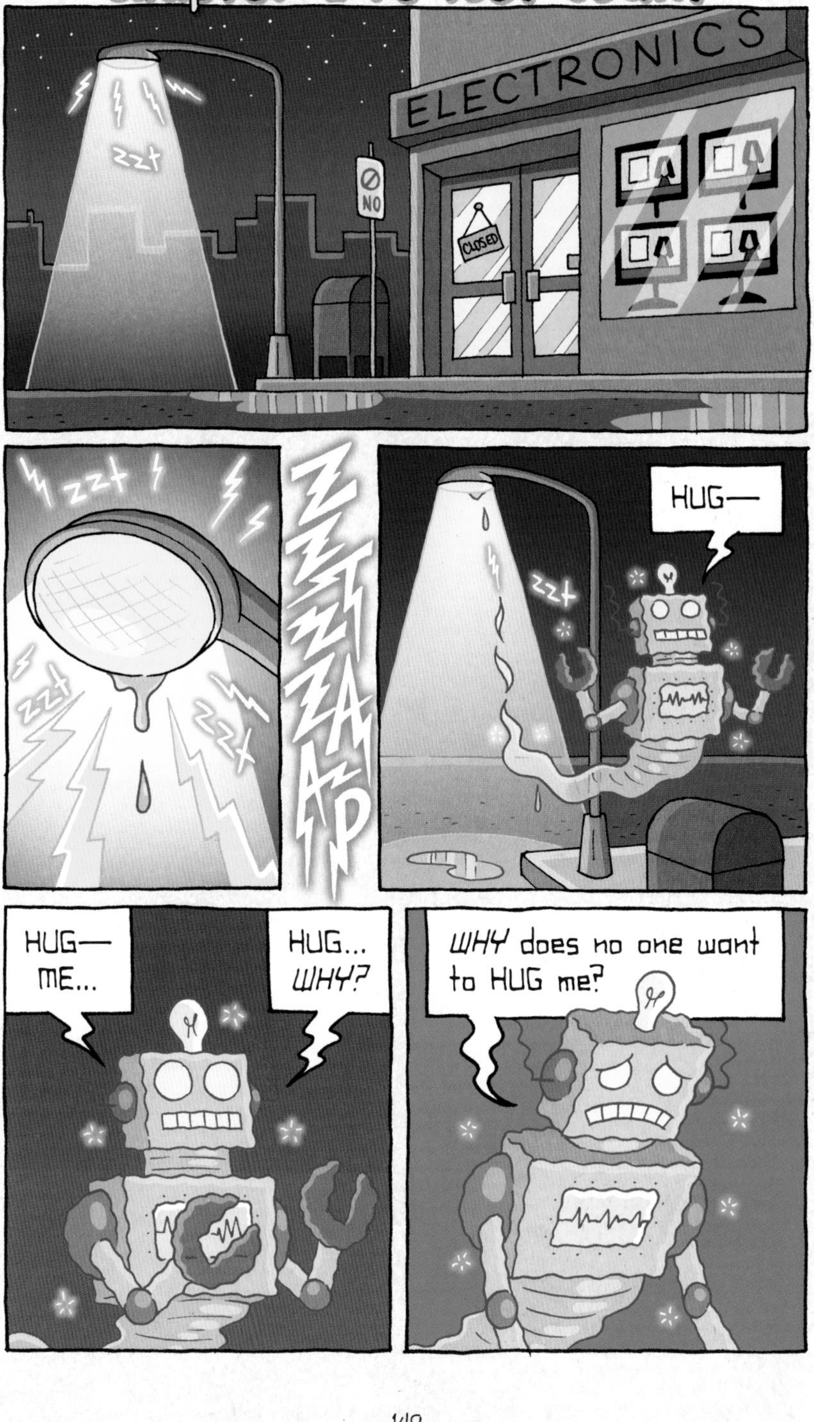
ELECTRONICS
ZZT
NO
CLOSED
ZZT
ZZT
ZZT
ZZZZZAAP
ZZT
HUG—
HUG—
ME...
HUG...
WHY?
WHY does no one want
to HUG me?

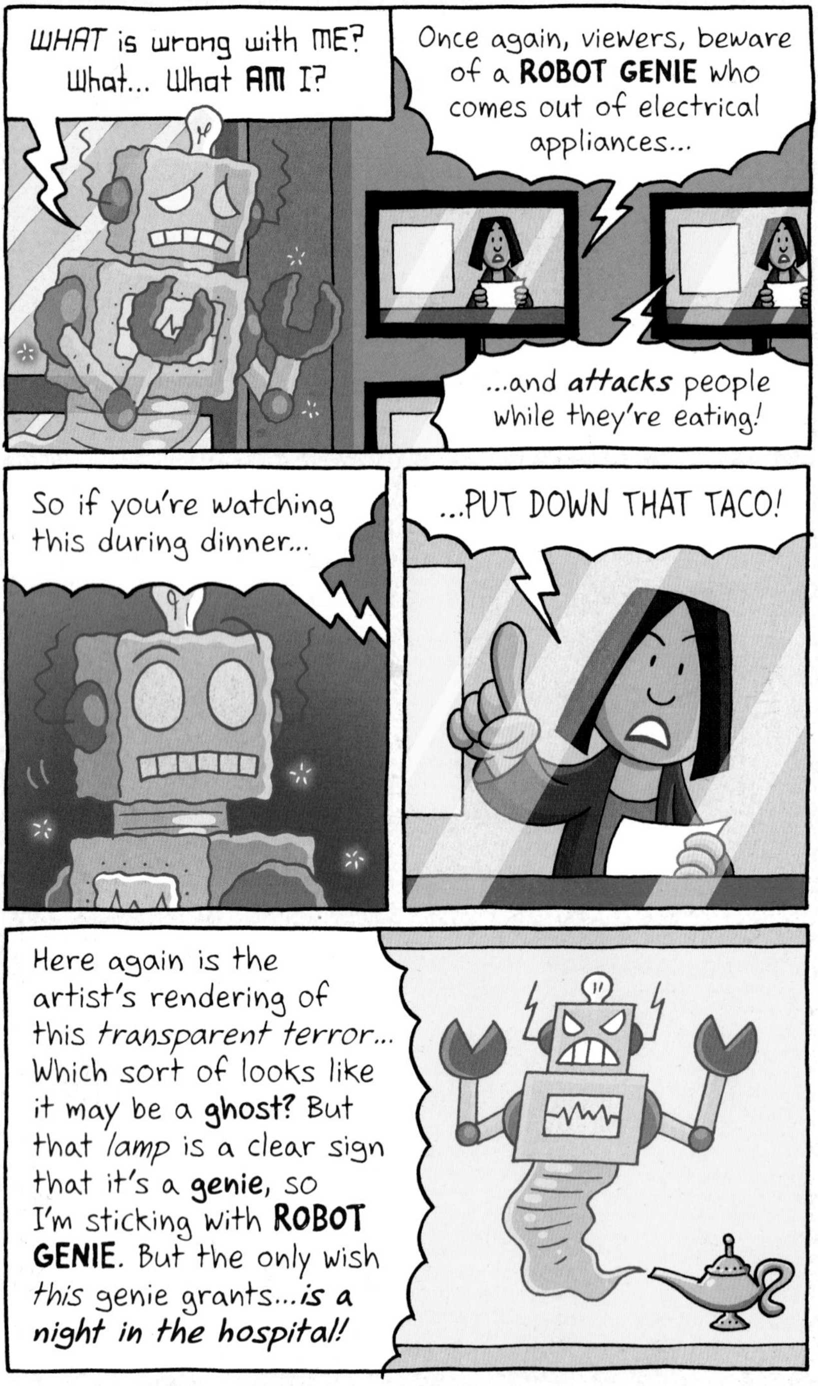
WHAT is wrong with ME? What... What AM I?
Once again, viewers, beware of a ROBOT GENIE who comes out of electrical appliances...
...and attacks people while they're eating!
So if you're watching this during dinner...
...PUT DOWN THAT TACO!
Here again is the artist's rendering of this transparent terror... Which sort of looks like it may be a ghost? But that lamp is a clear sign that it's a genie, so I'm sticking with ROBOT GENIE. But the only wish this genie grants... is a night in the hospital!

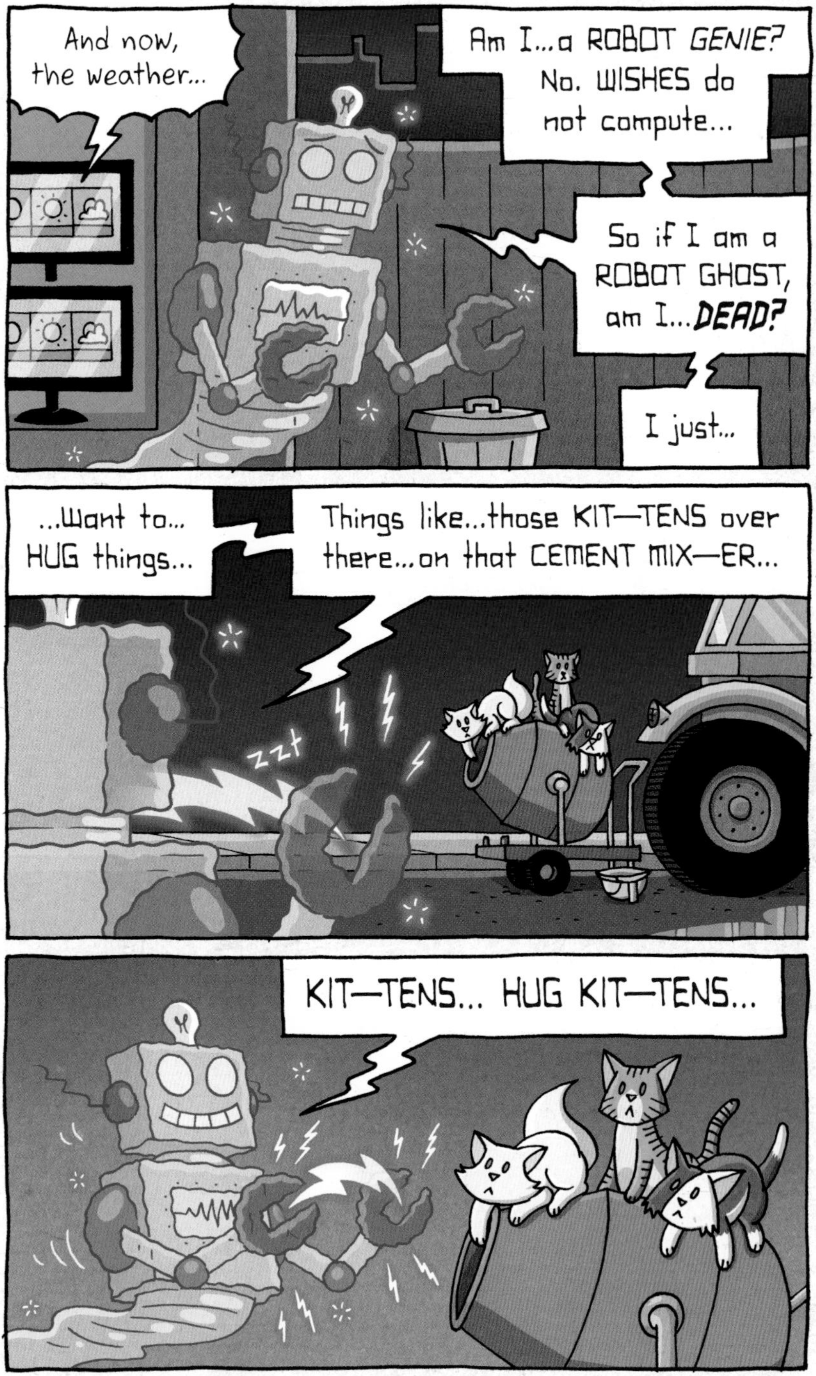
And now, the weather...
Am I...a ROBOT GENIE? No. WISHES do not compute...
So if I am a ROBOT GHOST, am I...DEAD?
I just...
...Want to... HUG things...
Things like...those KIT—TENS over there...on that CEMENT MIX—ER...
zzt
KIT—TENS... HUG KIT—TENS...

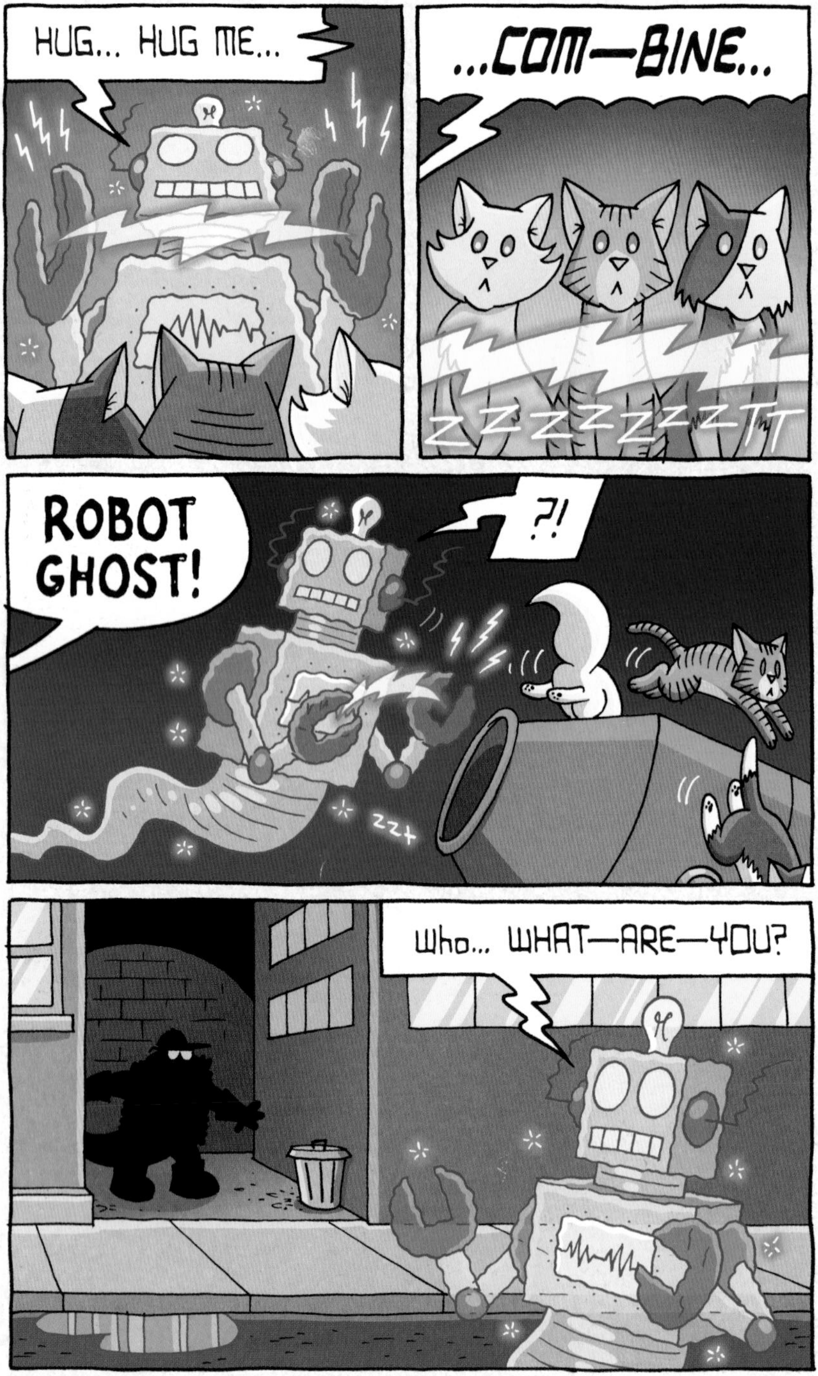
HUG... HUG ME...
...COM—BINE...
ZZZZZZZZZTT
ROBOT GHOST!
?!
ZZT
Who... WHAT—ARE—YOU?

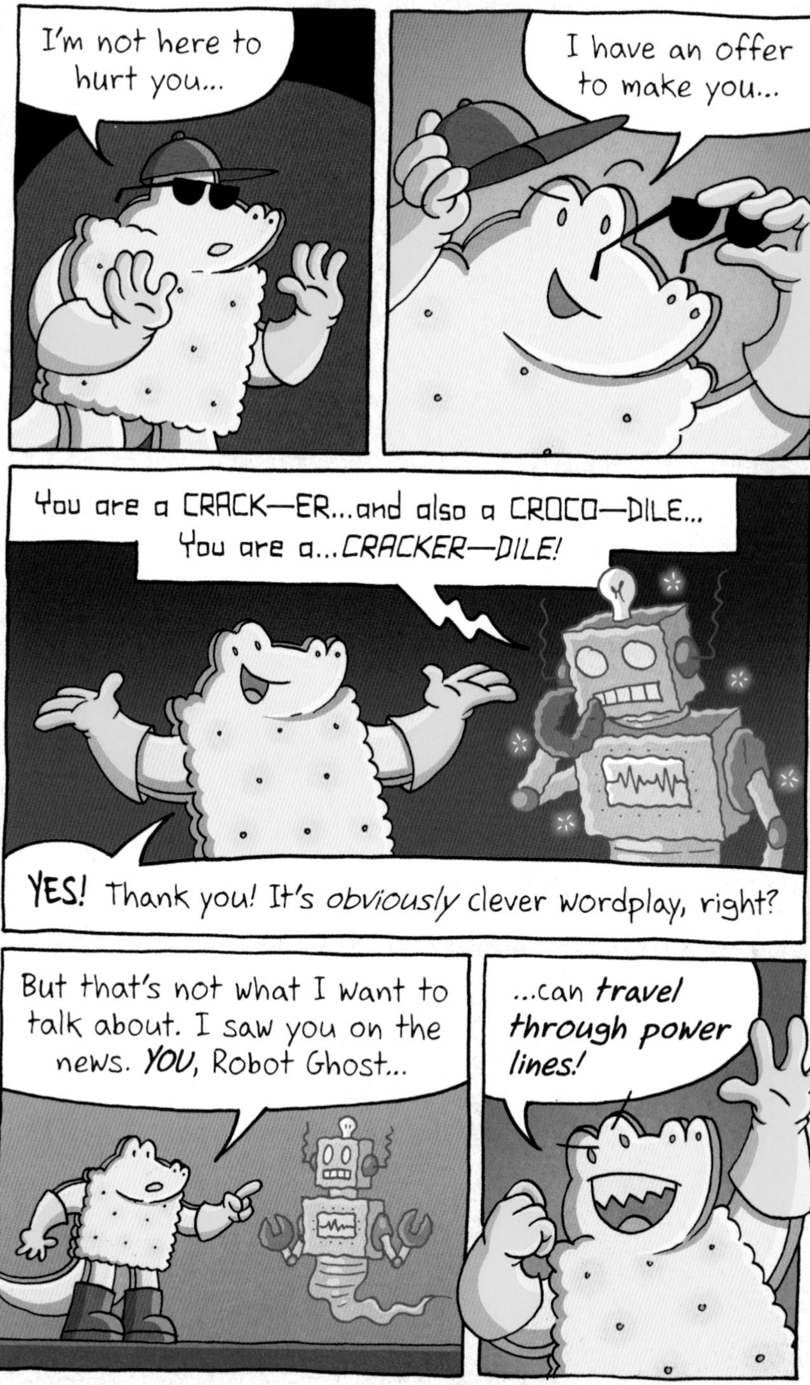
I'm not here to hurt you...
I have an offer to make you...
You are a CRACK—ER...and also a CROCO—DILE... You are a...CRACKER—DILE!
YES! Thank you! It's obviously clever wordplay, right?
But that's not what I want to talk about. I saw you on the news. YOU, Robot Ghost...
...can travel through power lines!

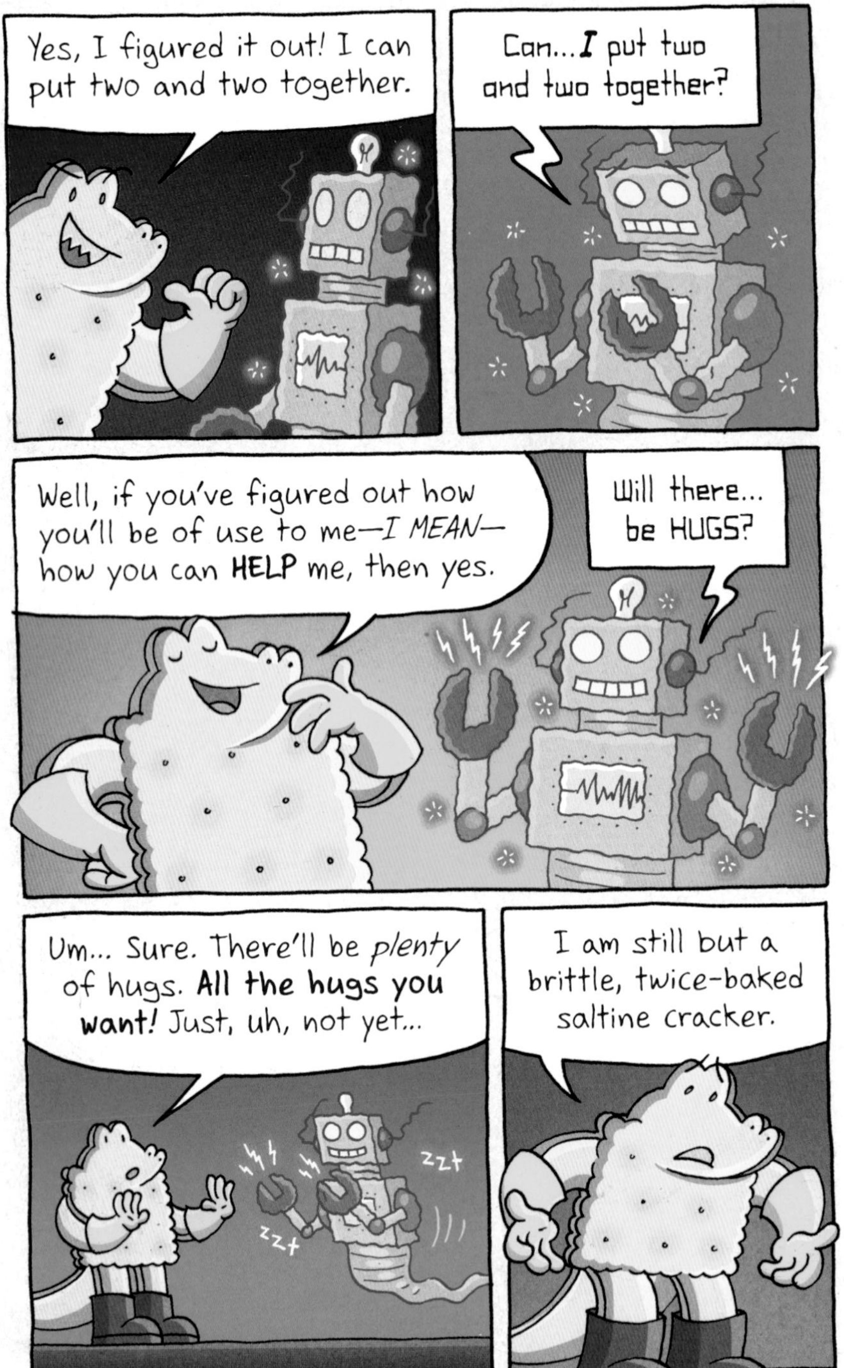
Yes, I figured it out! I can put two and two together.
Can... *I* put two and two together?
Well, if you've figured out how you'll be of use to me—*I MEAN*— how you can **HELP** me, then yes.
Will there... be HUGS?
Um... Sure. There'll be *plenty* of hugs. **All the hugs you want!** Just, uh, not yet...
ZZT
ZZT
I am still but a brittle, twice-baked saltine cracker.

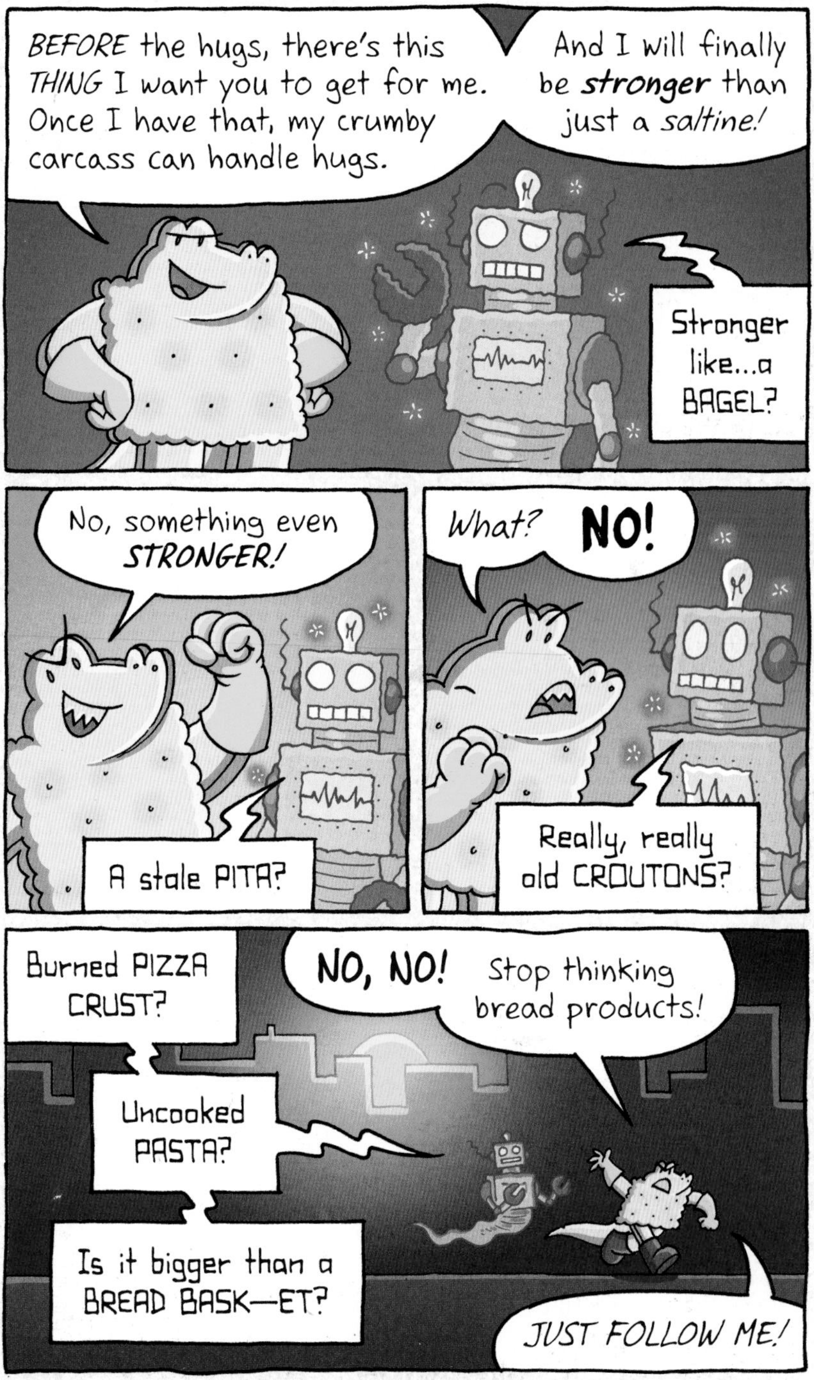
BEFORE the hugs, there's this *THING* I want you to get for me. Once I have that, my crumby carcass can handle hugs.
And I will finally be ***stronger*** than just a *saltine!*
Stronger like...a BAGEL?
No, something even ***STRONGER!***
A stale PITA?
What? **NO!**
Really, really old CROUTONS?
Burned PIZZA CRUST?
NO, NO! Stop thinking bread products!
Uncooked PASTA?
Is it bigger than a BREAD BASK—ET?
JUST FOLLOW ME!

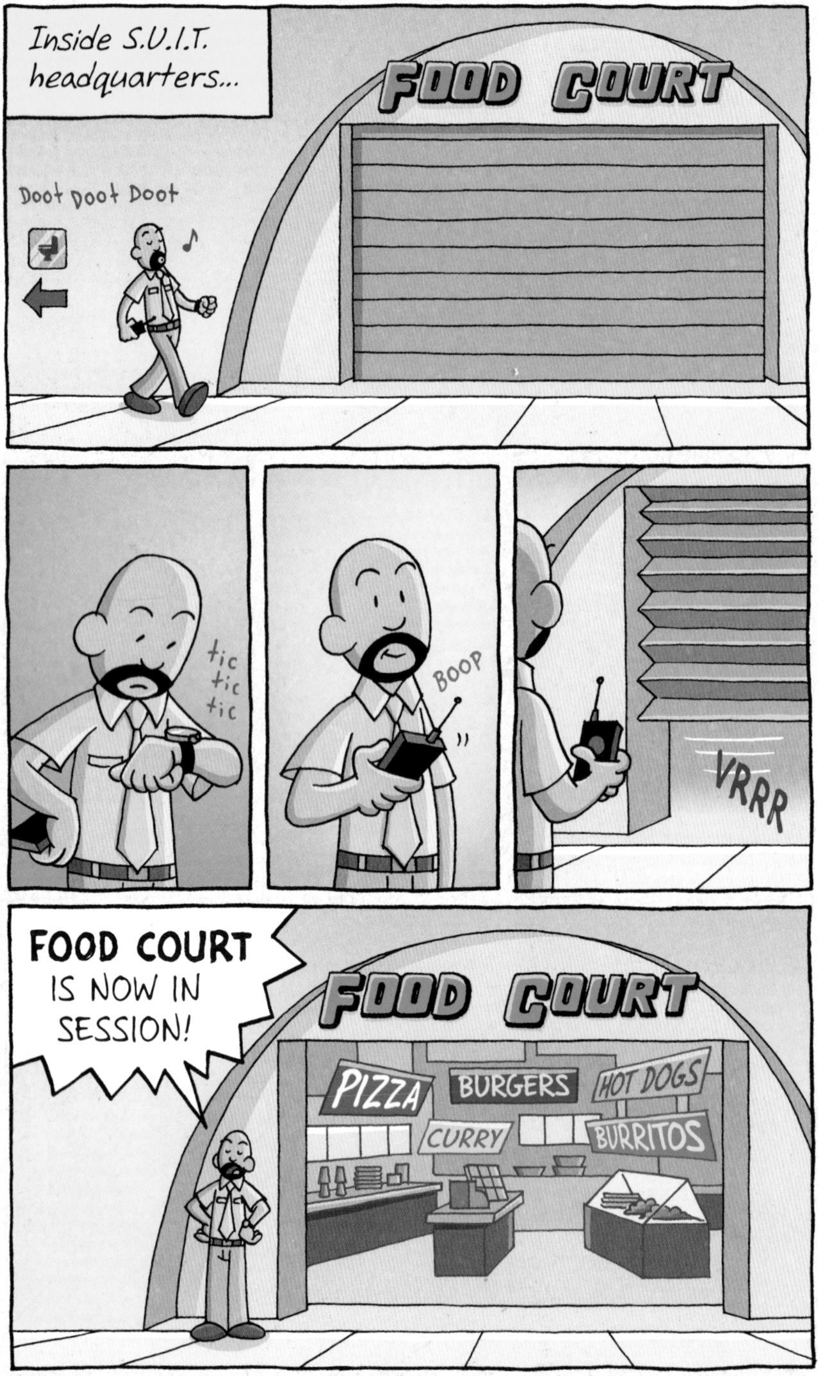

Inside S.U.I.T. headquarters...
FOOD COURT
Doot Doot Doot
tic tic tic
BOOP
VRRR
FOOD COURT IS NOW IN SESSION!
FOOD COURT
PIZZA
BURGERS
HOT DOGS
CURRY
BURRITOS

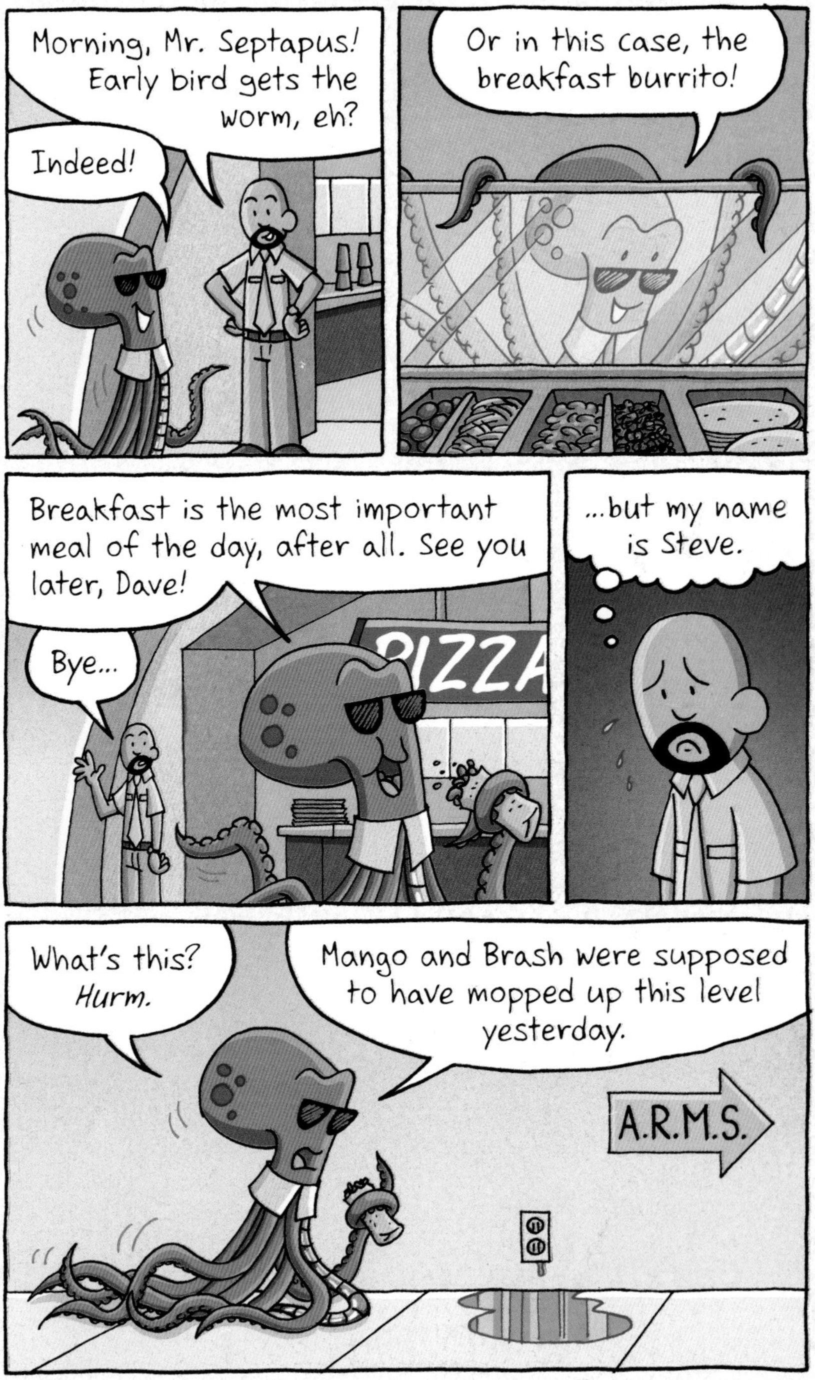
Morning, Mr. Septapus! Early bird gets the worm, eh?
Indeed!
Or in this case, the breakfast burrito!
Breakfast is the most important meal of the day, after all. See you later, Dave!
Bye...
PIZZA
...but my name is Steve.
What's this? *Hurm.*
Mango and Brash were supposed to have mopped up this level yesterday.
A.R.M.S.

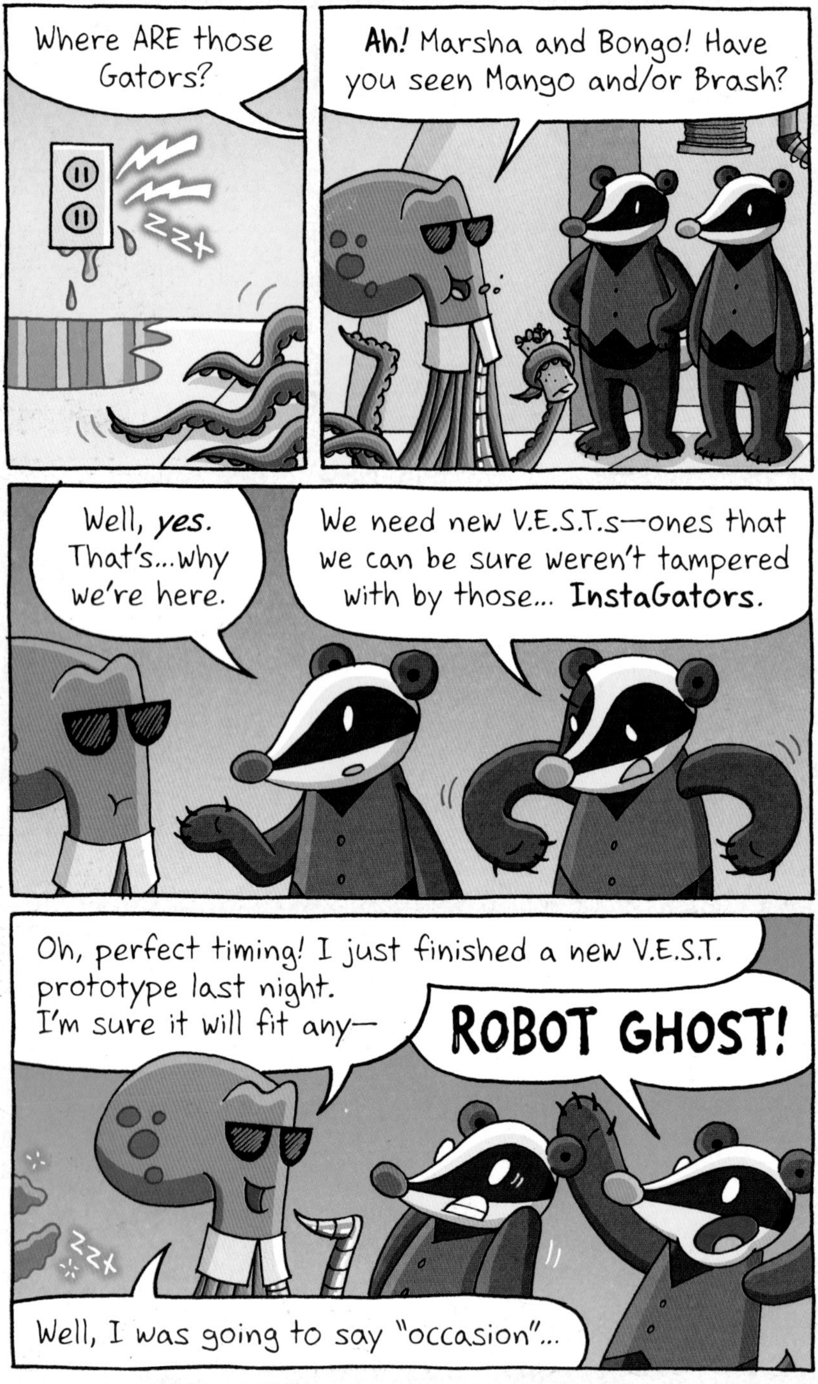
Where ARE those Gators?
ZZT
Ah! Marsha and Bongo! Have you seen Mango and/or Brash?
Well, yes. That's...why we're here.
We need new V.E.S.T.s—ones that we can be sure weren't tampered with by those... InstaGators.
Oh, perfect timing! I just finished a new V.E.S.T. prototype last night. I'm sure it will fit any—
ROBOT GHOST!
ZZT
Well, I was going to say "occasion"...

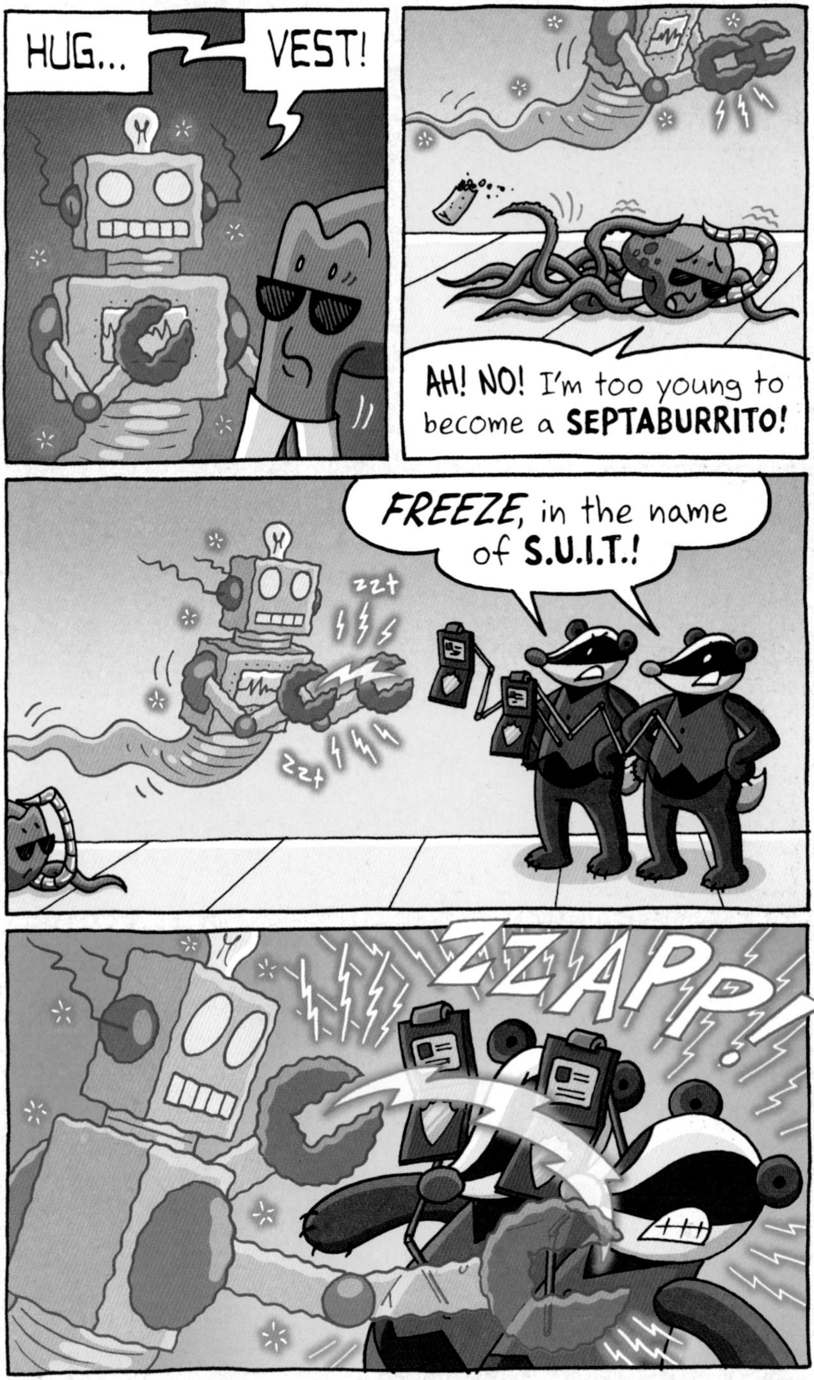
HUG...
VEST!
AH! NO! I'm too young to become a SEPTABURRITO!
FREEZE, in the name of S.U.I.T.!
ZZT
ZZT
ZZAPP!

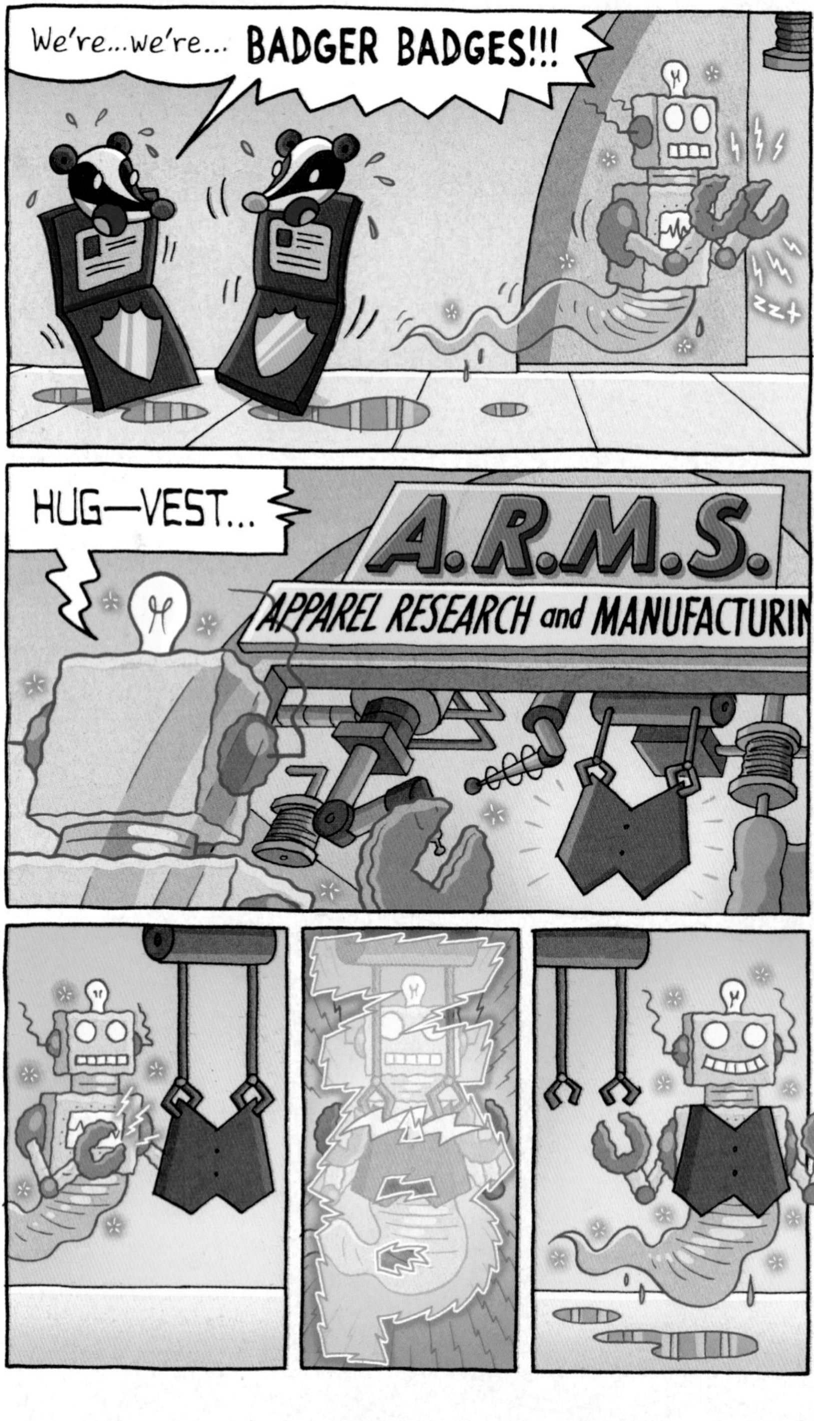
We're...we're... BADGER BADGES!!!
ZZT
HUG—VEST...
A.R.M.S.
APPAREL RESEARCH and MANUFACTURIN

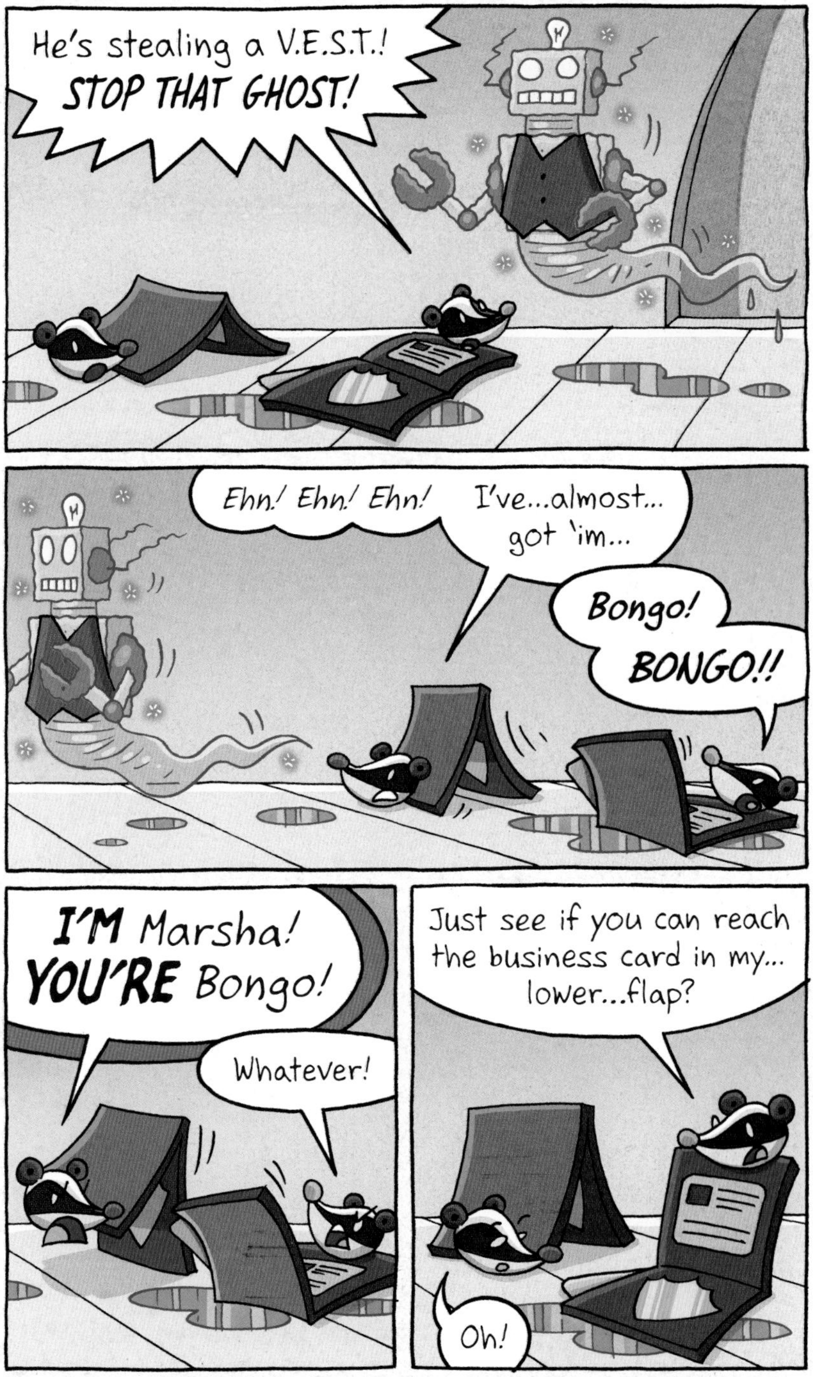
He's stealing a V.E.S.T.! STOP THAT GHOST!
Ehn! Ehn! Ehn!
I've...almost... got 'im...
Bongo! BONGO!!
I'M Marsha! YOU'RE Bongo!
Whatever!
Just see if you can reach the business card in my... lower...flap?
Oh!

Chapter something or other

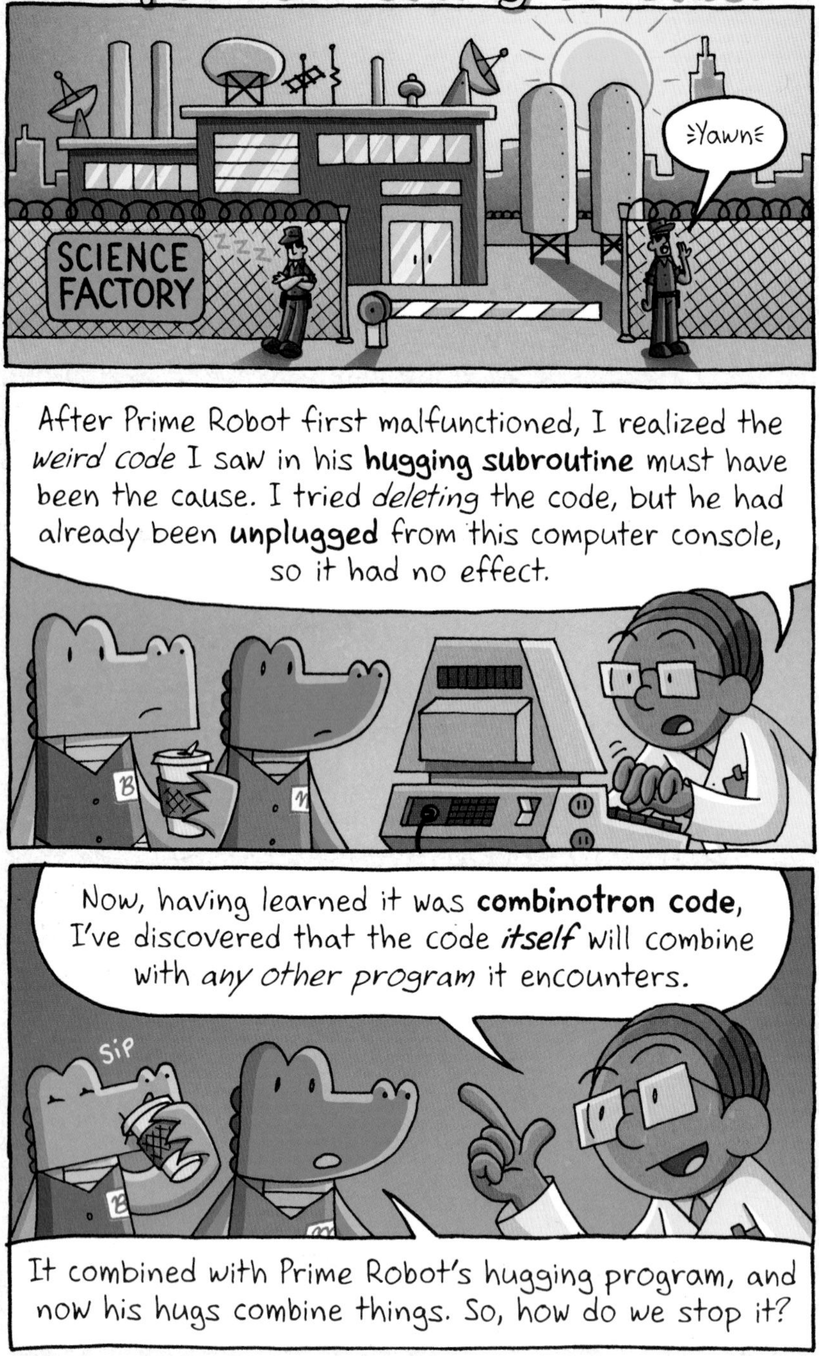
SCIENCE FACTORY
Z Z Z
Yawn
After Prime Robot first malfunctioned, I realized the *weird code* I saw in his **hugging subroutine** must have been the cause. I tried *deleting* the code, but he had already been **unplugged** from this computer console, so it had no effect.
Now, having learned it was **combinotron code**, I've discovered that the code *itself* will combine with *any other program* it encounters.
SIP
It combined with Prime Robot's hugging program, and now his hugs combine things. So, how do we stop it?

Now that I know what code I'm looking at, I can rewrite Prime Robot's main program so that it **separates** the combinotron code from his hugging subroutine.

That will take the combinotron powers **out** of his hands, and he'll no longer combine things by hugging them.

The trick will be finding a way to get him to download this new data. In his gaseous form, we can't just plug him into a computer.

He's a *mist.* Can't we just...upload to the cloud?

Hmm... If *hugs* caused **HIM** to combine with **WATER**... Can you invent a way for him to *hug* the **DATA?**

We heard you designed him with true human emotions. Maybe if we appeal to—

bleep blurp

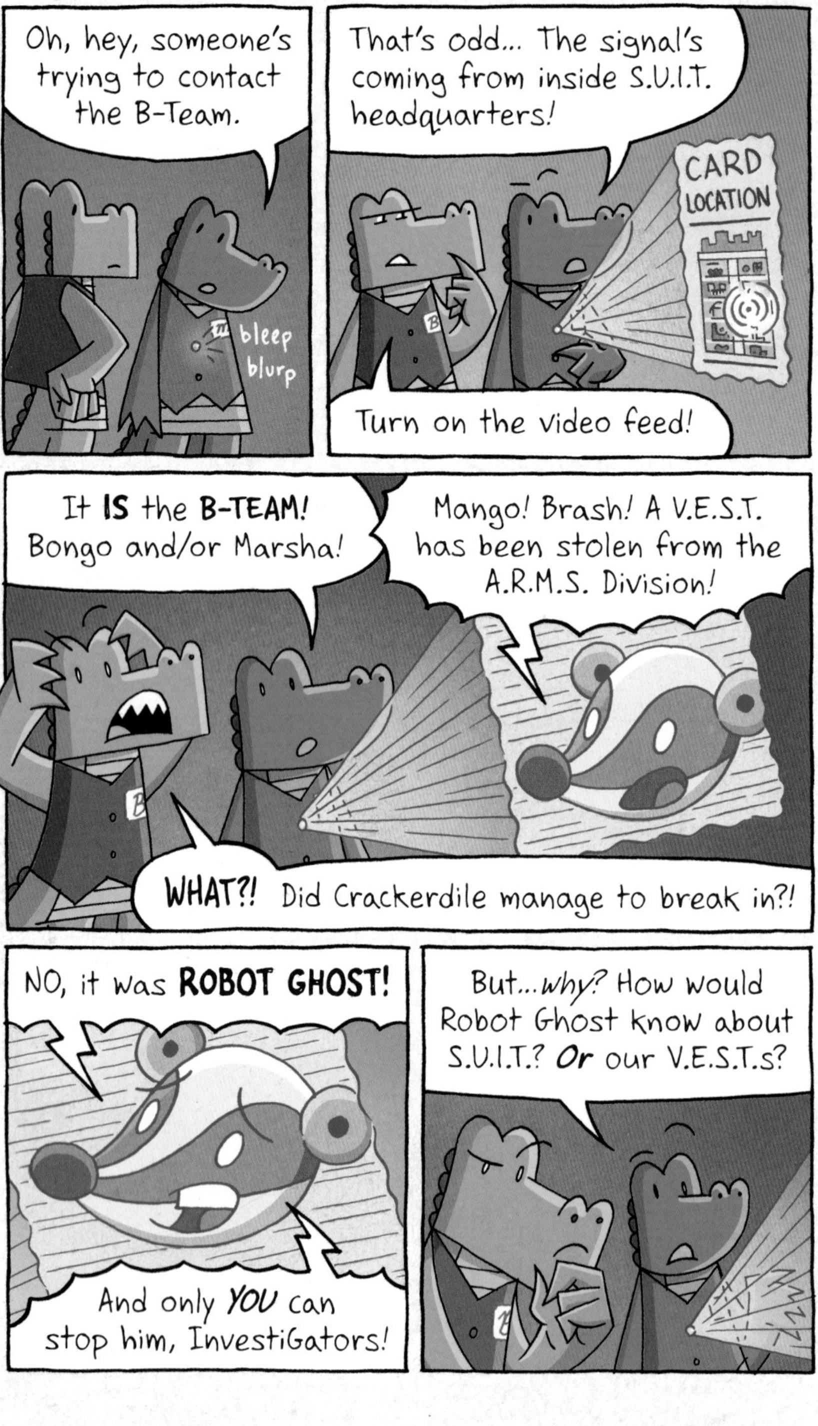
Oh, hey, someone's trying to contact the B-Team.
bleep
blurp
That's odd... The signal's coming from inside S.U.I.T. headquarters!
CARD LOCATION
Turn on the video feed!
It IS the B-TEAM! Bongo and/or Marsha!
Mango! Brash! A V.E.S.T. has been stolen from the A.R.M.S. Division!
WHAT?! Did Crackerdile manage to break in?!
NO, it was ROBOT GHOST!
And only YOU can stop him, InvestiGators!
But...why? How would Robot Ghost know about S.U.I.T.? Or our V.E.S.T.s?

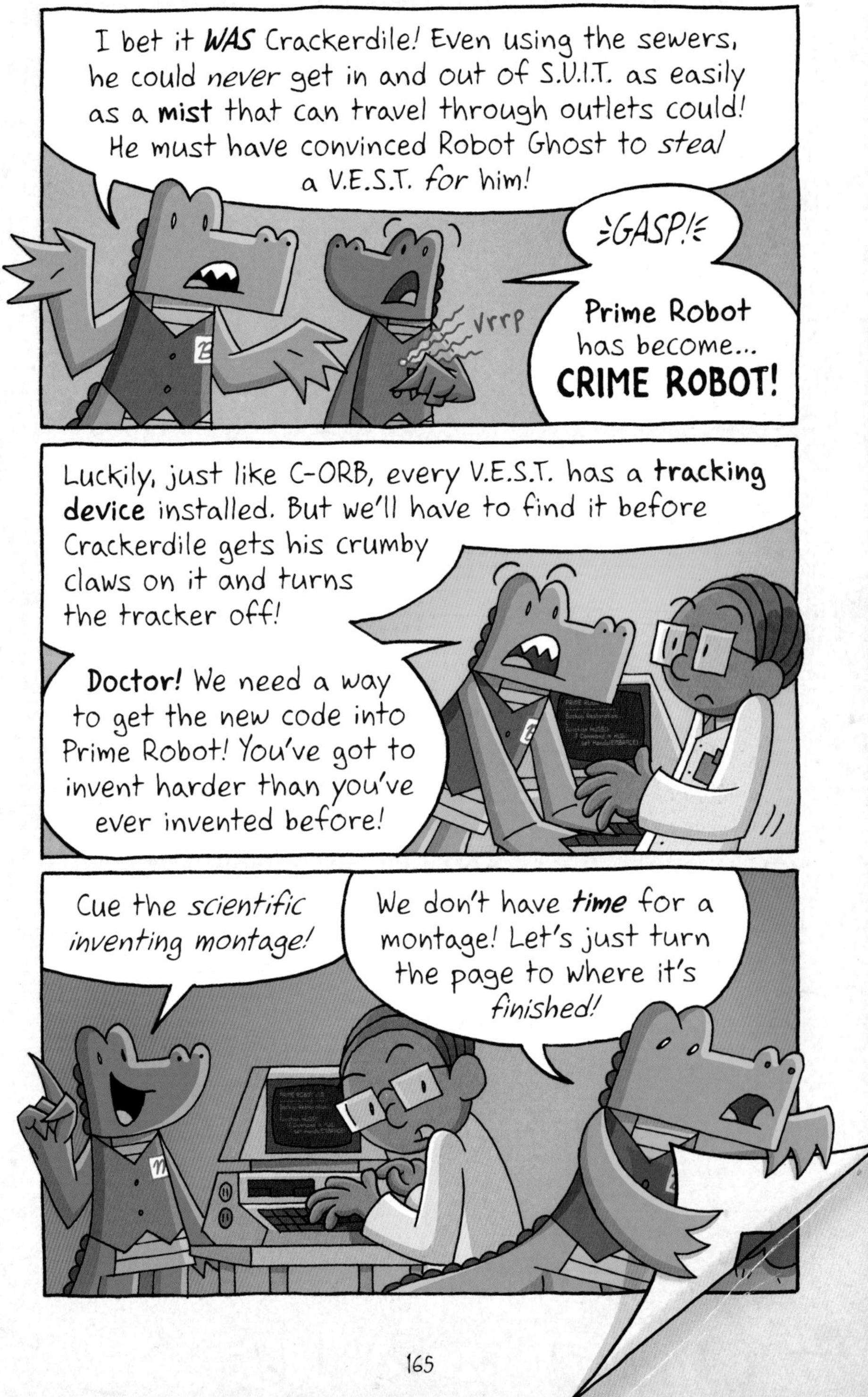
I bet it *WAS* Crackerdile! Even using the sewers, he could *never* get in and out of S.U.I.T. as easily as a **mist** that can travel through outlets could! He must have convinced Robot Ghost to *steal* a V.E.S.T. *for* him!
Vrrp
GASP!
Prime Robot has become... **CRIME ROBOT!**
Luckily, just like C-ORB, every V.E.S.T. has a **tracking device** installed. But we'll have to find it before Crackerdile gets his crumby claws on it and turns the tracker off!
Doctor! We need a way to get the new code into Prime Robot! You've got to invent harder than you've ever invented before!
Cue the *scientific inventing montage!*
We don't have ***time*** for a montage! Let's just turn the page to where it's *finished!*

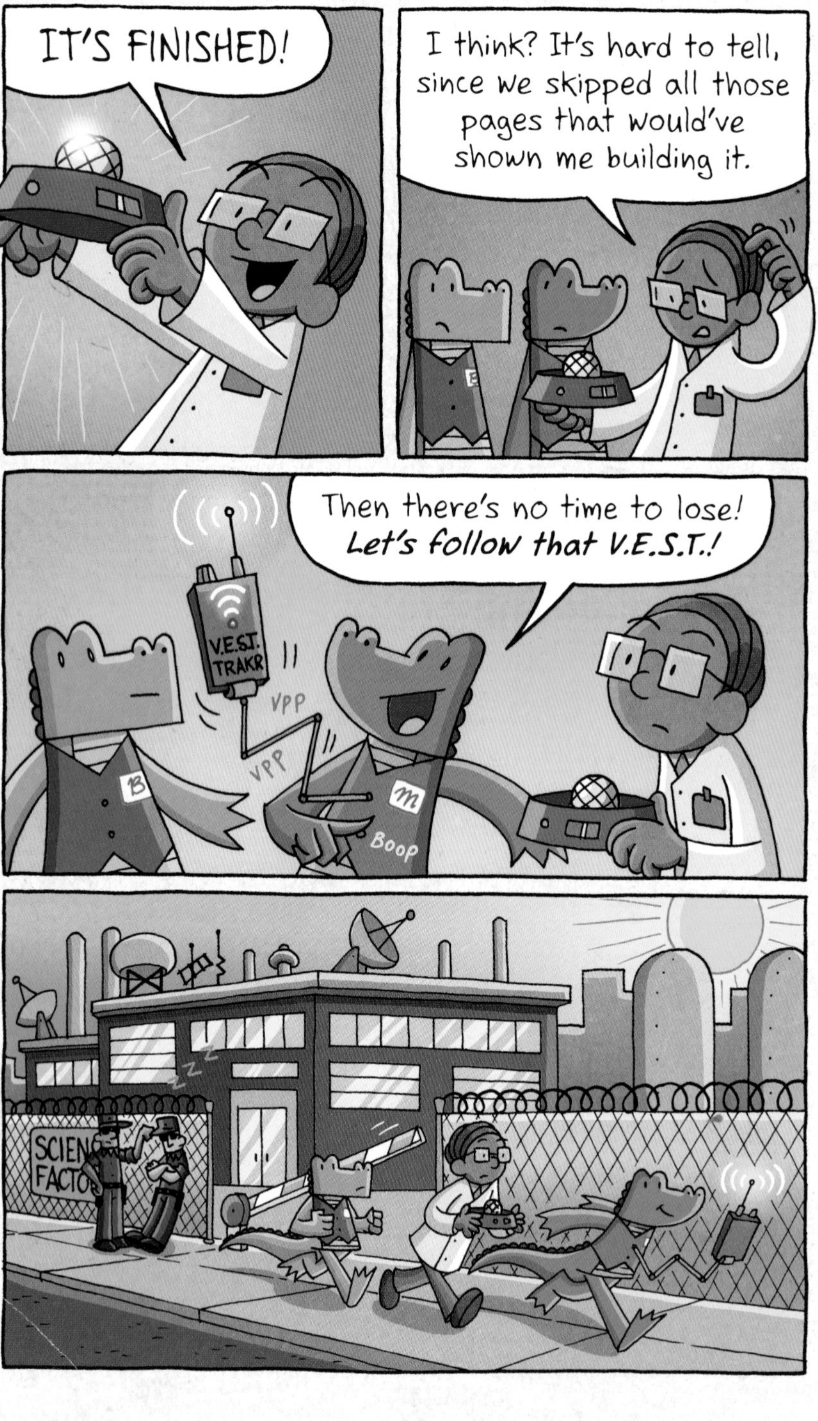
IT'S FINISHED!
I think? It's hard to tell, since we skipped all those pages that would've shown me building it.
Then there's no time to lose! *Let's follow that V.E.S.T.!*
V.E.S.T. TRAKR
VPP
VPP
Boop
SCIEN
FACTO

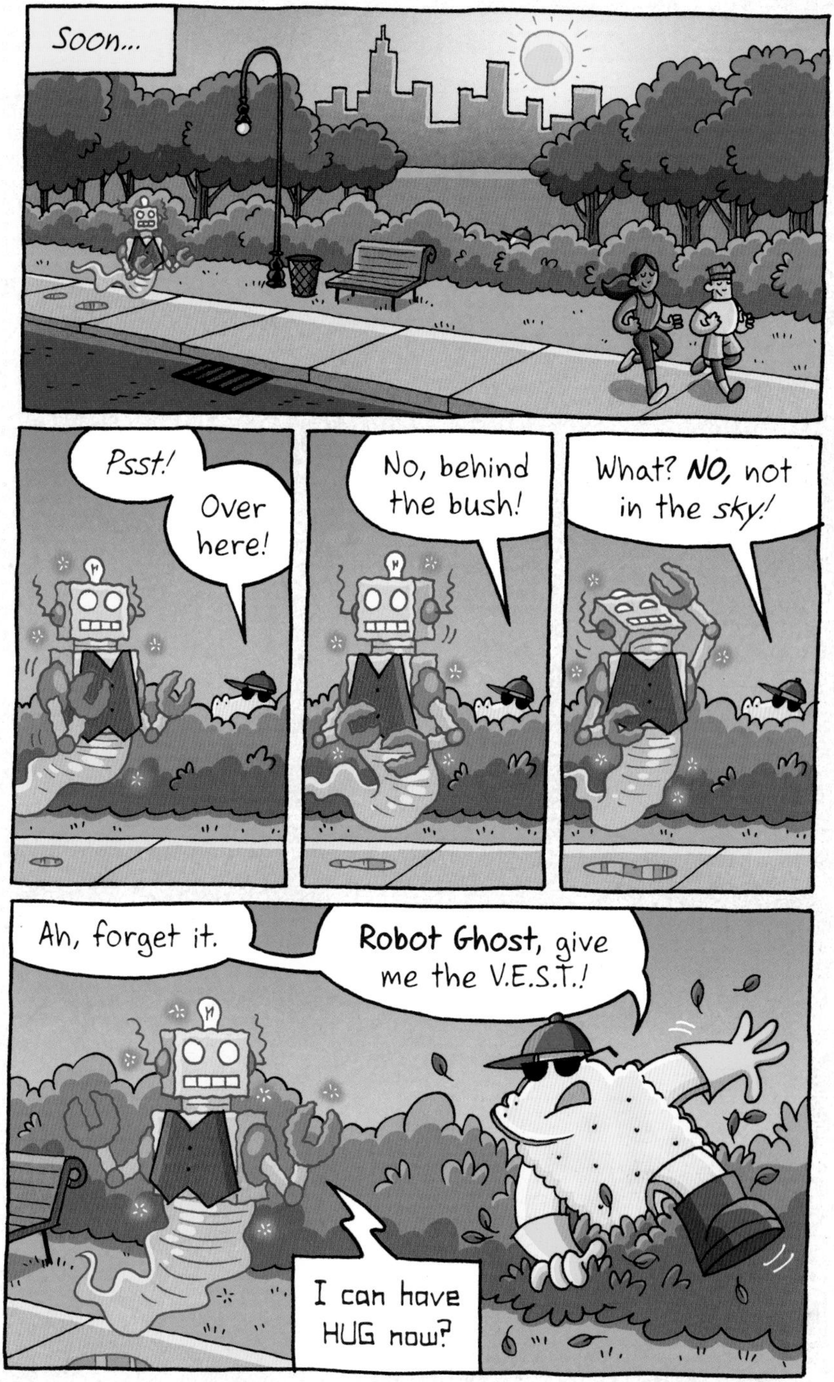
Soon...
Psst!
Over here!
No, behind the bush!
What? NO, not in the sky!
Ah, forget it.
Robot Ghost, give me the V.E.S.T.!
I can have HUG now?

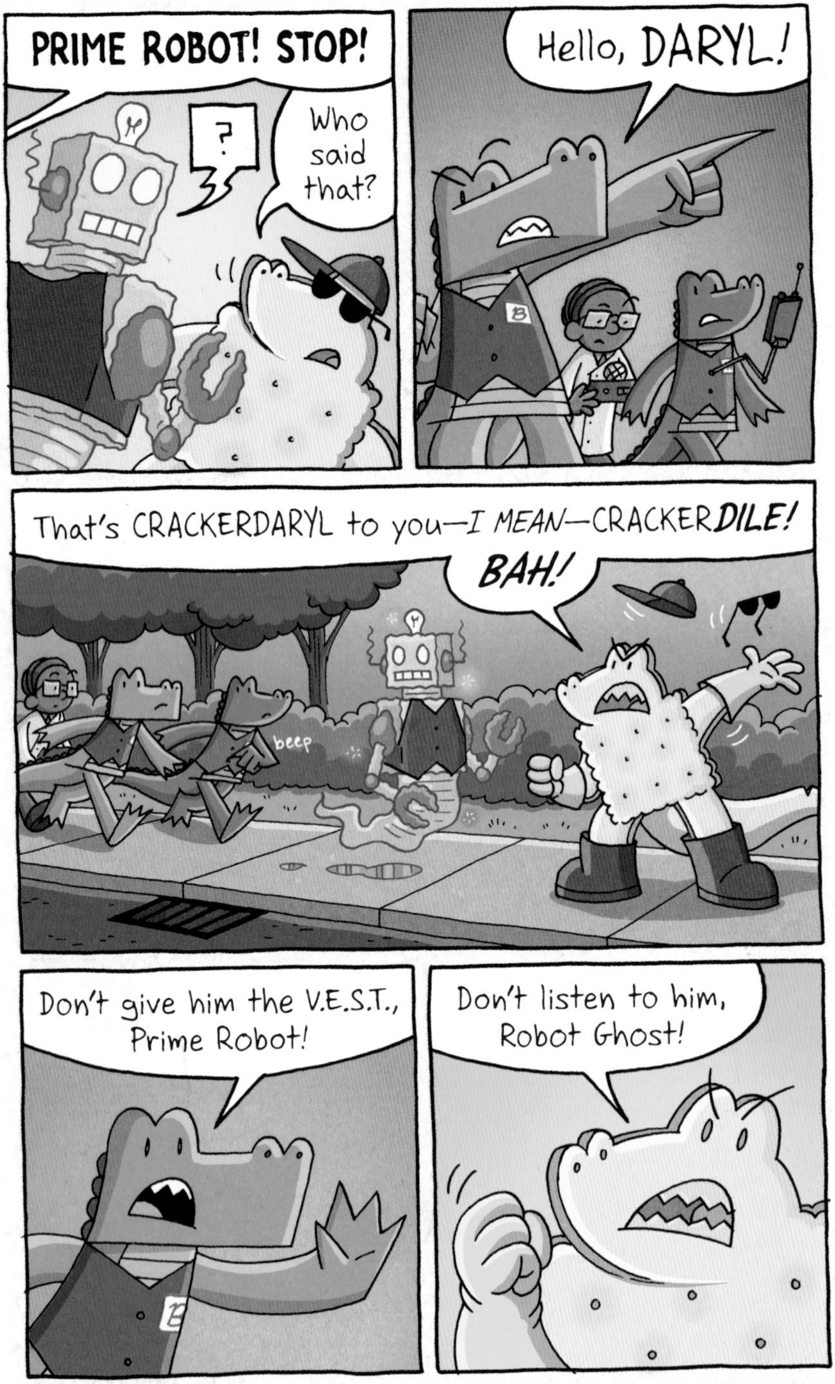
PRIME ROBOT! STOP!
?
Who said that?
Hello, DARYL!
B
That's CRACKERDARYL to you—I MEAN—CRACKERDILE!
BAH!
beep
Don't give him the V.E.S.T., Prime Robot!
Don't listen to him, Robot Ghost!

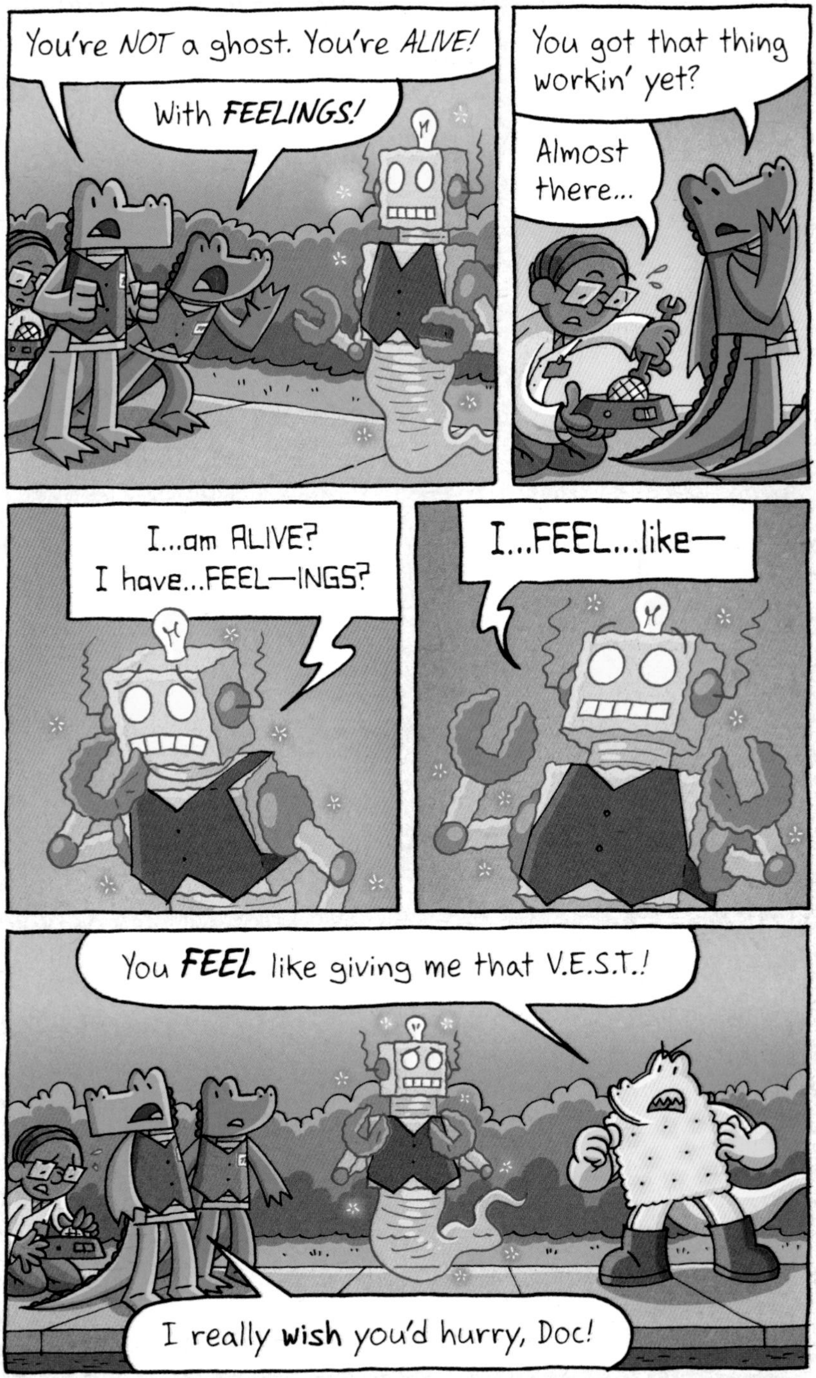
You're NOT a ghost. You're ALIVE!
With FEELINGS!
You got that thing workin' yet?
Almost there...
I...am ALIVE? I have...FEEL—INGS?
I...FEEL...like—
You FEEL like giving me that V.E.S.T.!
I really wish you'd hurry, Doc!

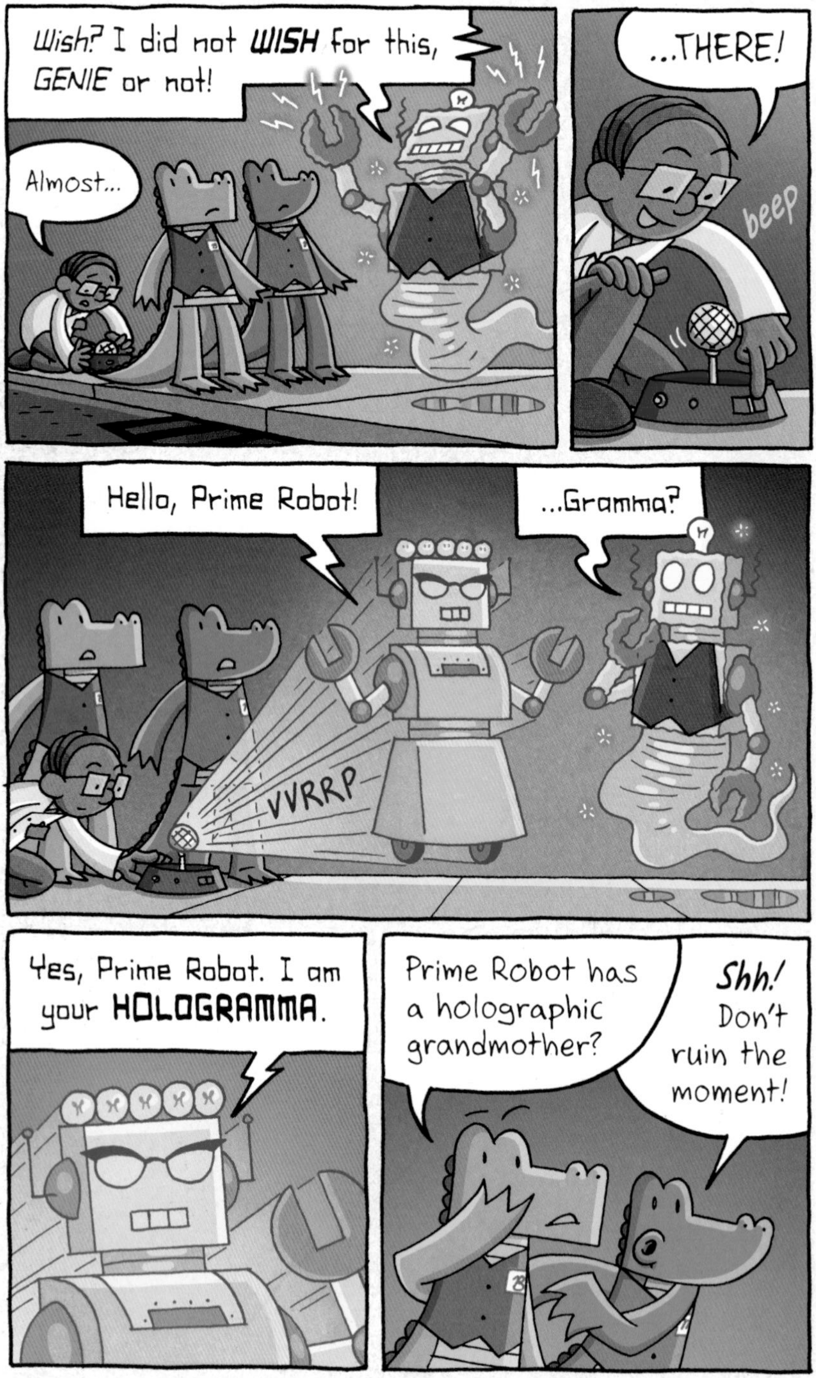
Wish? I did not WISH for this, GENIE or not!
Almost...
...THERE!
beep
Hello, Prime Robot!
...Gramma?
VVRRP
Yes, Prime Robot. I am your HOLOGRAMMA.
Prime Robot has a holographic grandmother?
Shh! Don't ruin the moment!

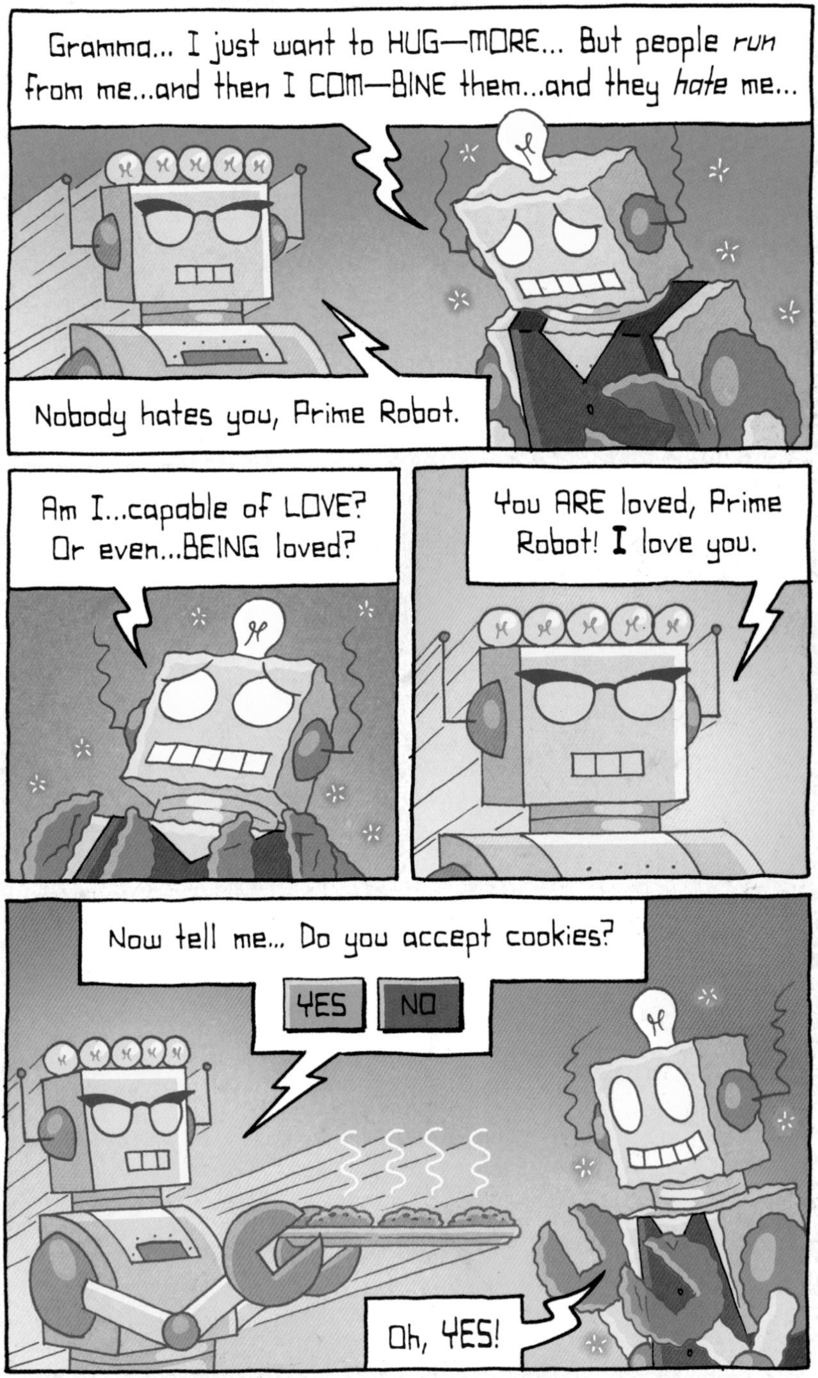
Gramma... I just want to HUG—MORE... But people *run* from me...and then I COM—BINE them...and they *hate* me...
Nobody hates you, Prime Robot.
Am I...capable of LOVE? Or even...BEING loved?
You ARE loved, Prime Robot! **I** love you.
Now tell me... Do you accept cookies?
YES
NO
Oh, YES!

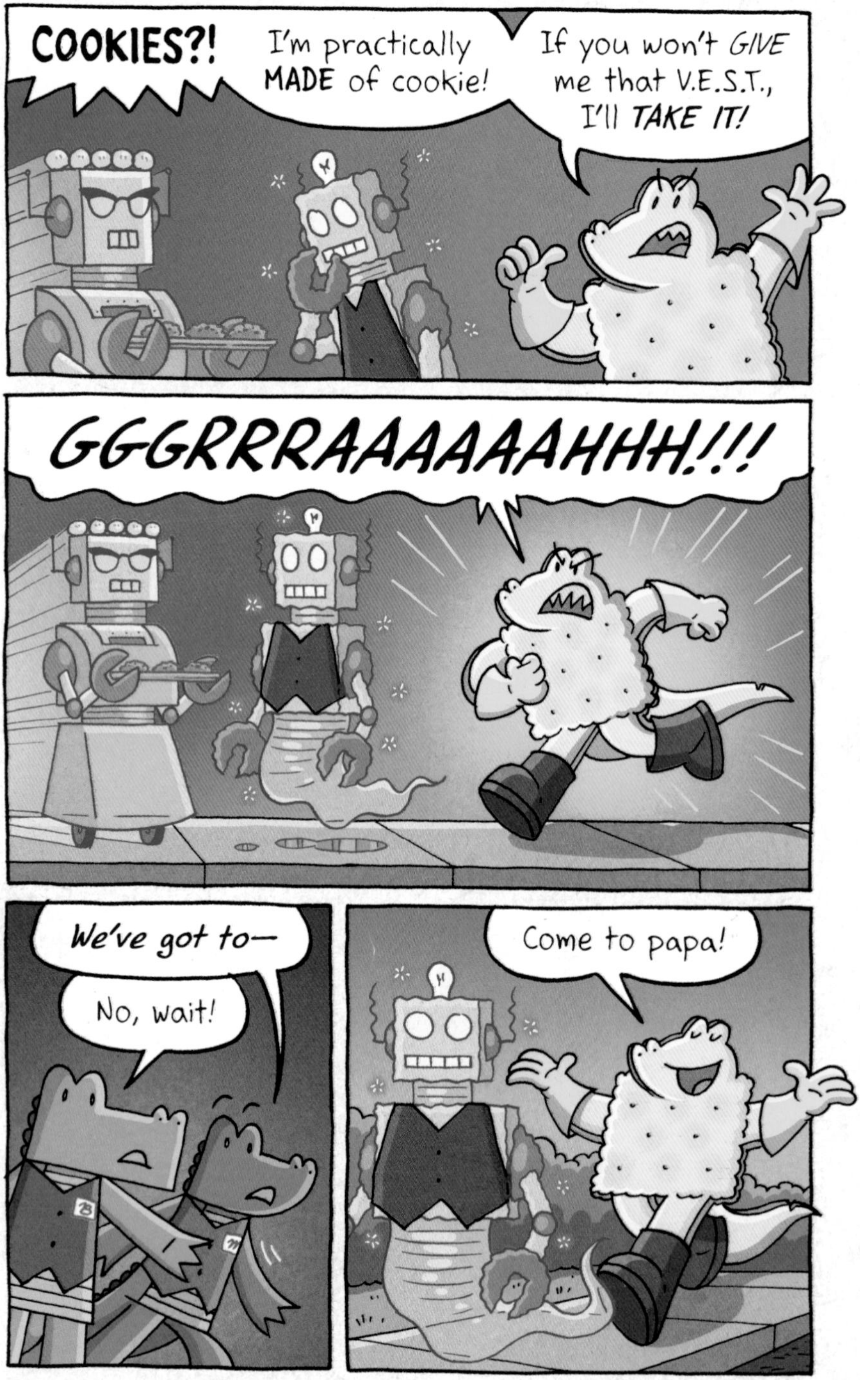
COOKIES?!
I'm practically MADE of cookie!
If you won't GIVE me that V.E.S.T., I'll TAKE IT!
GGGRRRAAAAAAAHHH!!!
We've got to—
No, wait!
Come to papa!

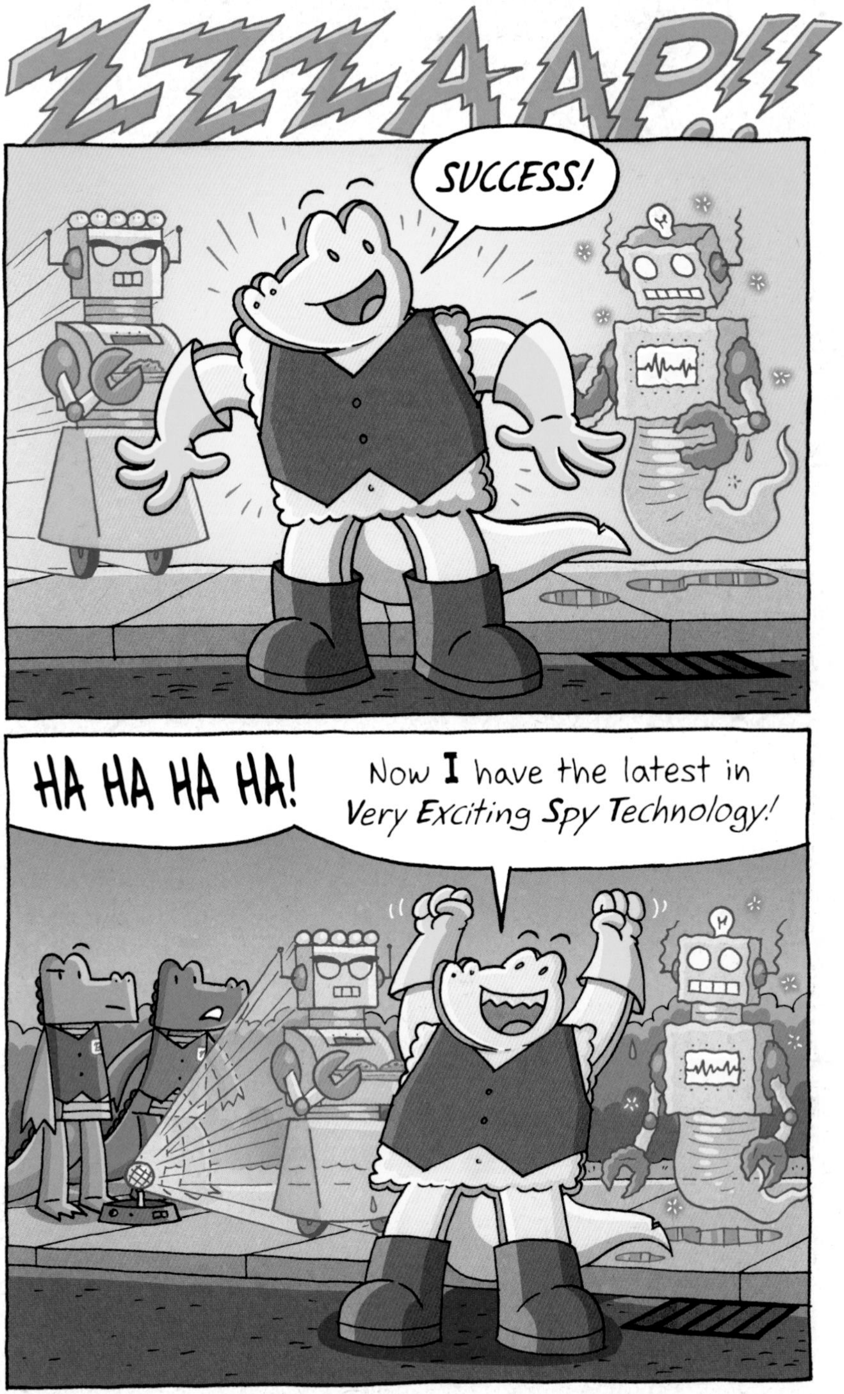
ZZZAP!!
SUCCESS!
HA HA HA HA!
Now I have the latest in Very Exciting Spy Technology!

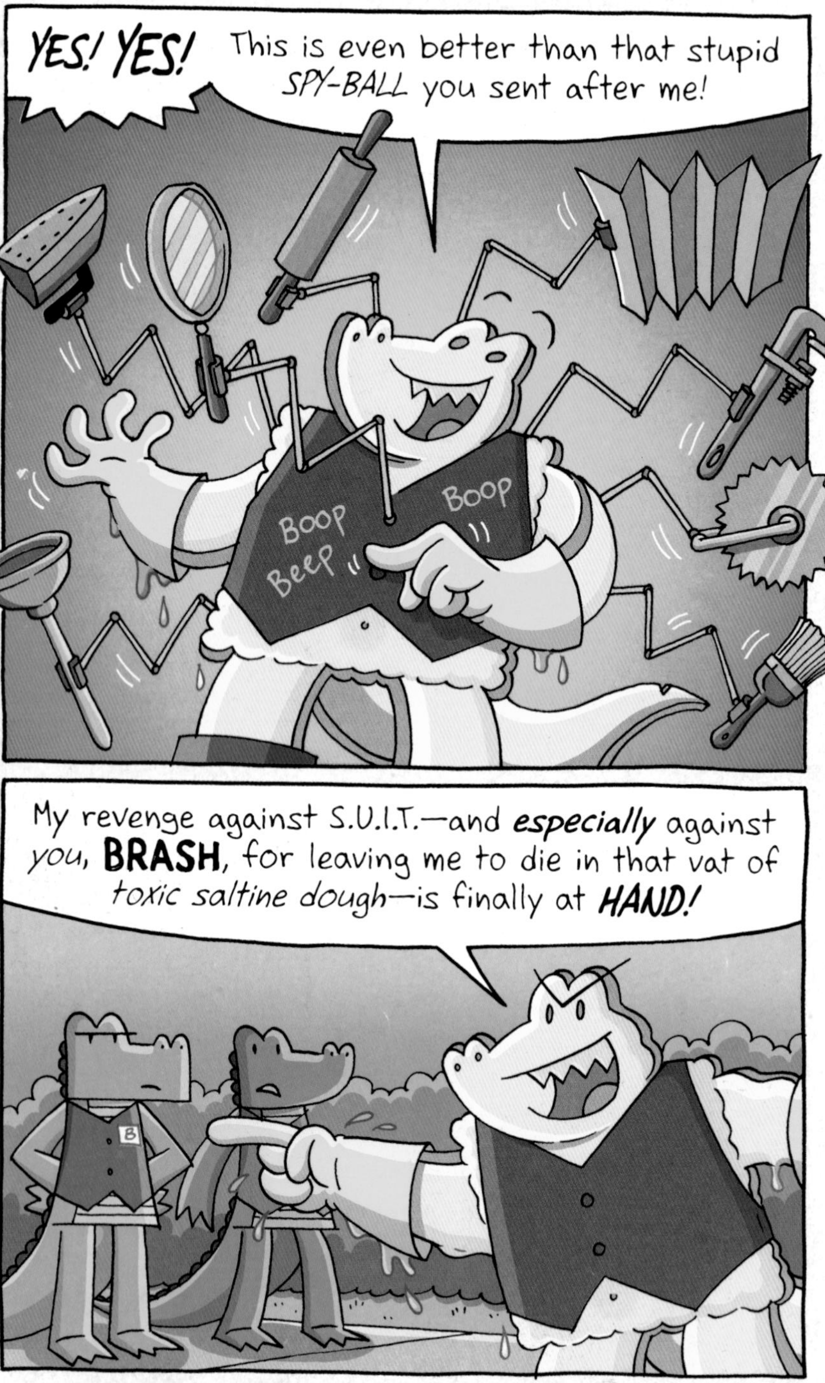
YES! YES!
This is even better than that stupid SPY-BALL you sent after me!
BOOP BEEP
BOOP
My revenge against S.U.I.T.—and especially against you, BRASH, for leaving me to die in that vat of toxic saltine dough—is finally at HAND!
B

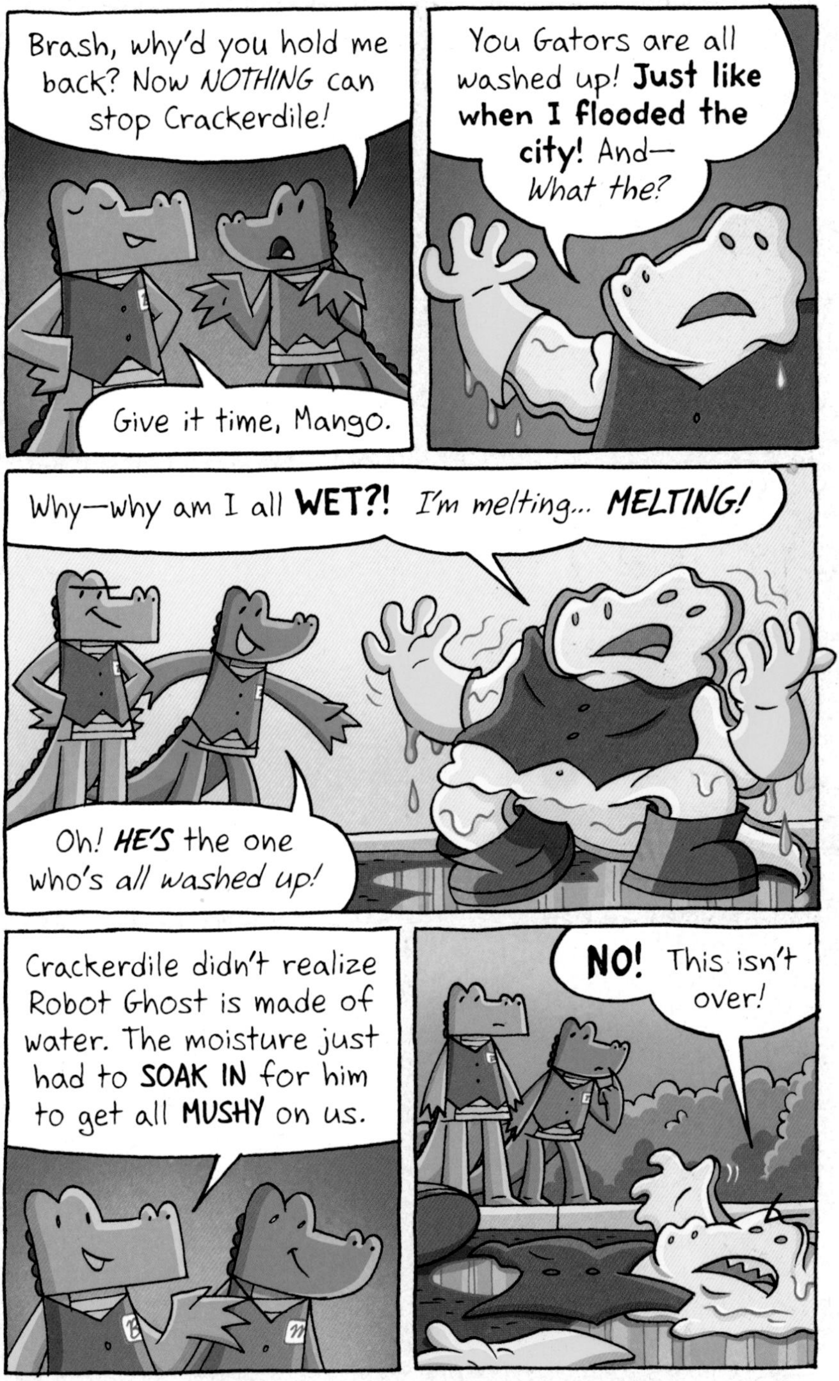
Brash, why'd you hold me back? Now *NOTHING* can stop Crackerdile!
Give it time, Mango.
You Gators are all washed up! **Just like when I flooded the city!** And— *What the?*
Why—why am I all **WET?!** *I'm melting...* ***MELTING!***
Oh! ***HE'S*** the one who's *all washed up!*
Crackerdile didn't realize Robot Ghost is made of water. The moisture just had to **SOAK IN** for him to get all **MUSHY** on us.
NO! This isn't over!

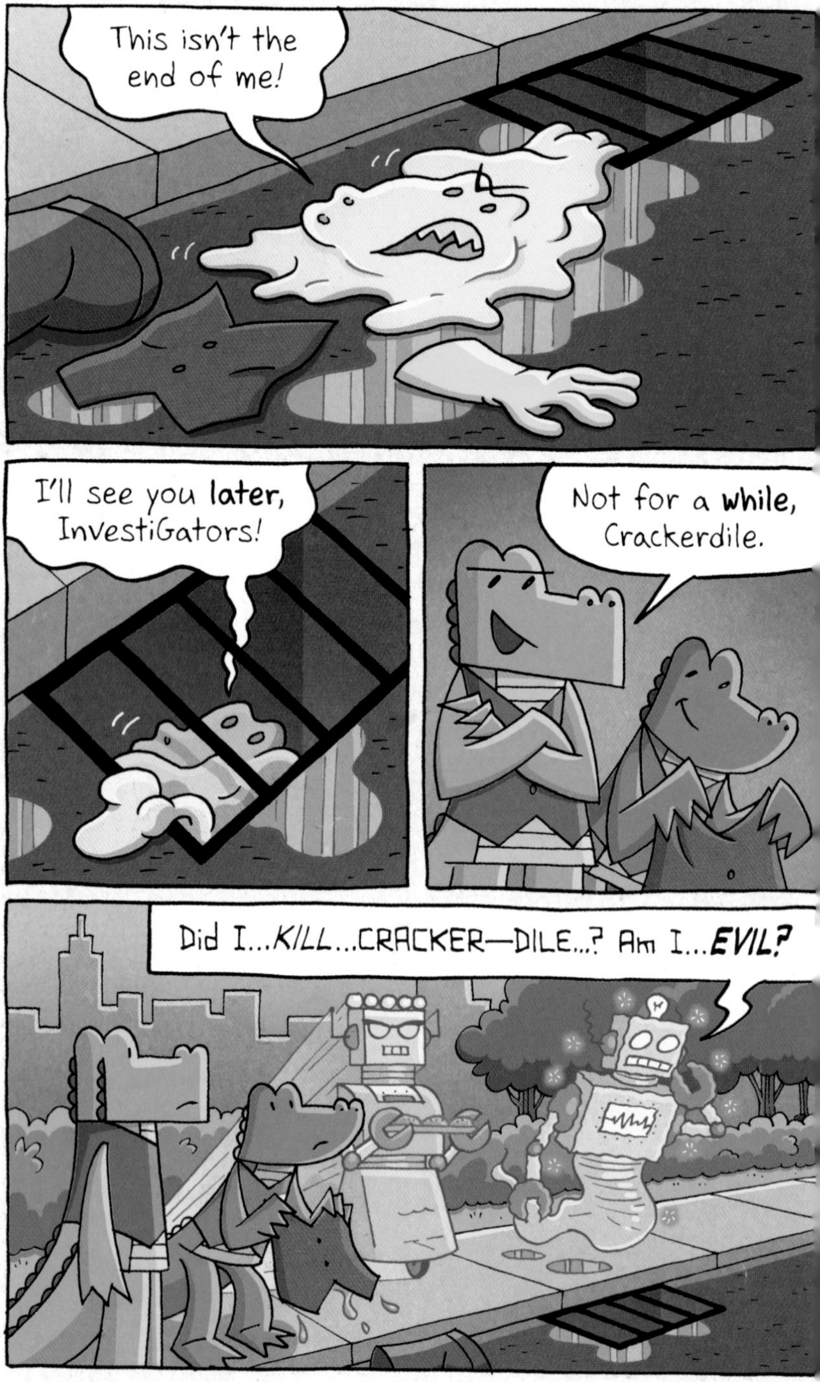
This isn't the end of me!
I'll see you **later,** InvestiGators!
Not for a **while,** Crackerdile.
Did I...*KILL*...CRACKER—DILE...? Am I...***EVIL?***

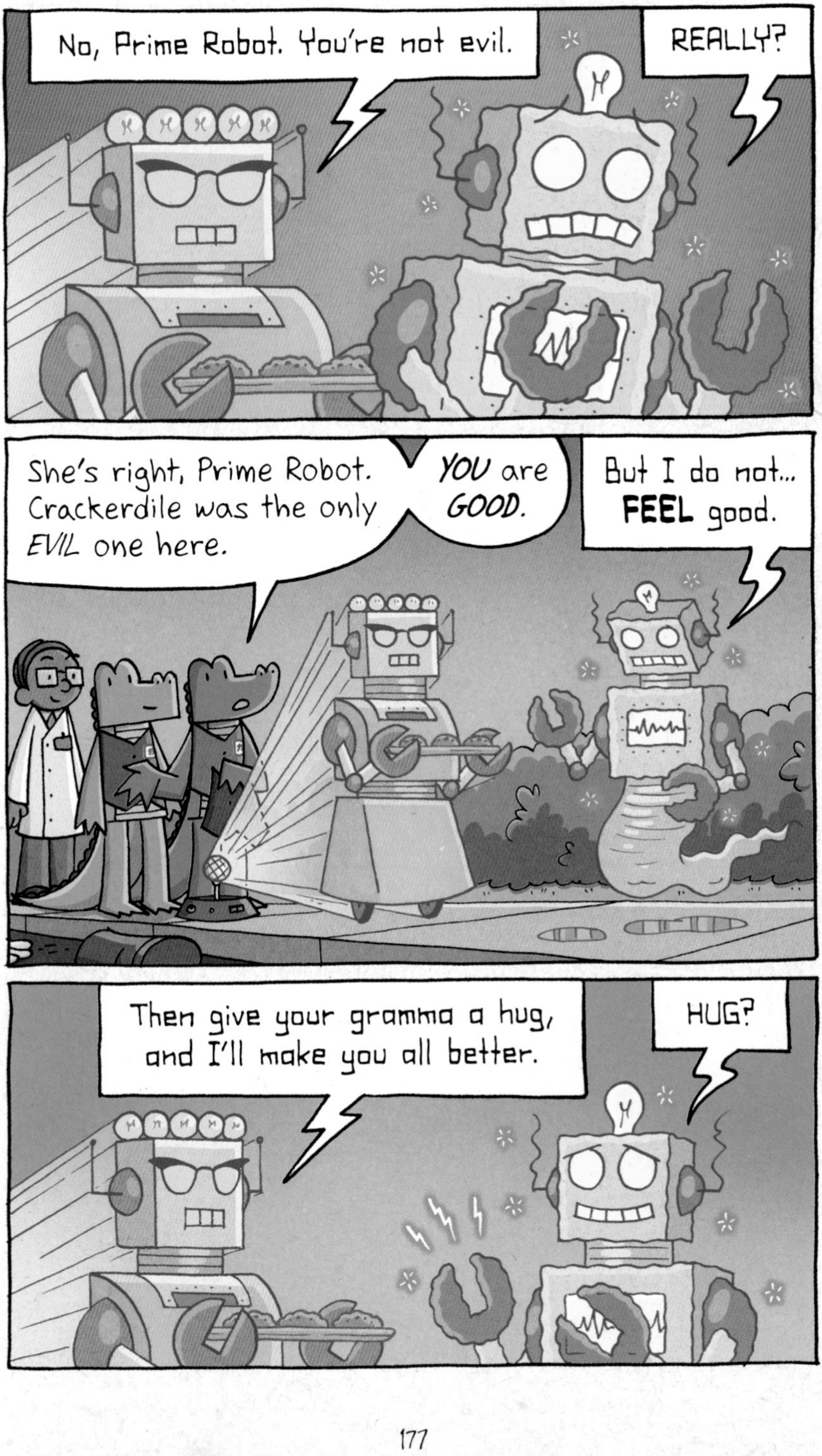
No, Prime Robot. You're not evil.
REALLY?
She's right, Prime Robot. Crackerdile was the only EVIL one here.
YOU are GOOD.
But I do not... FEEL good.
Then give your gramma a hug, and I'll make you all better.
HUG?

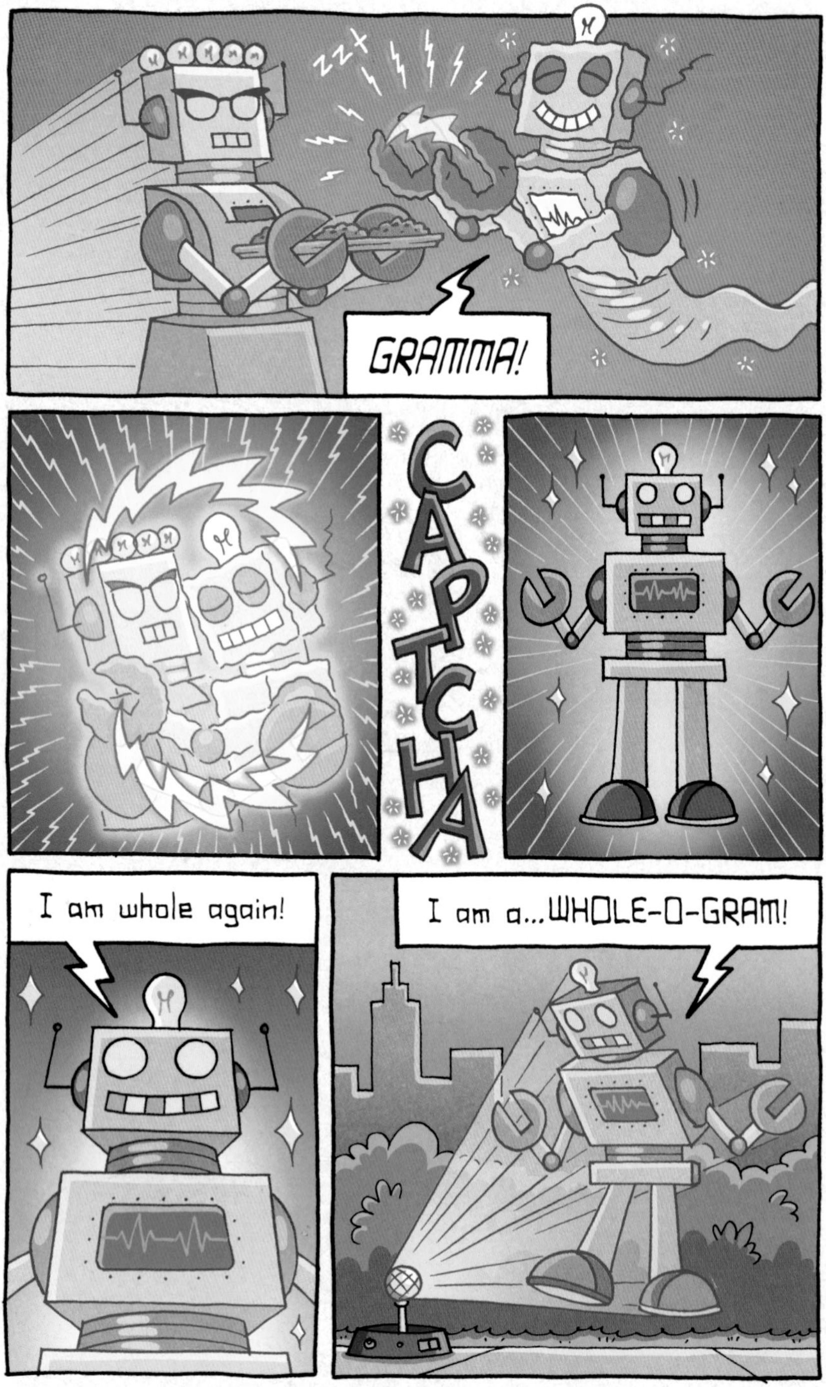
ZZZT
GRAMMA!
CAPTCHA
I am whole again!
I am a...WHOLE-O-GRAM!

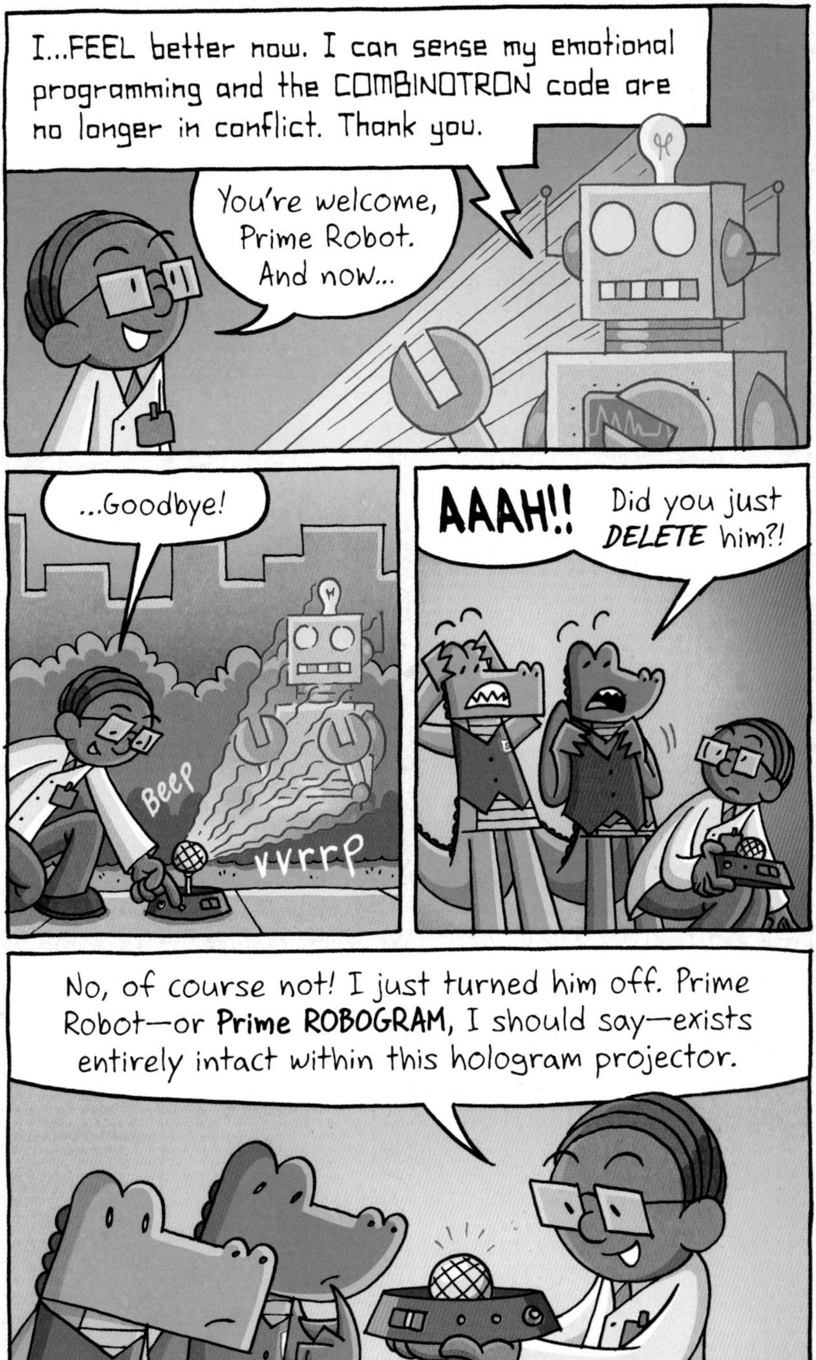
I...FEEL better now. I can sense my emotional programming and the COMBINOTRON code are no longer in conflict. Thank you.
You're welcome, Prime Robot. And now...
...Goodbye!
Beep
vvrrp
AAAH!!
Did you just *DELETE* him?!
No, of course not! I just turned him off. Prime Robot—or **Prime ROBOGRAM**, I should say—exists entirely intact within this hologram projector.

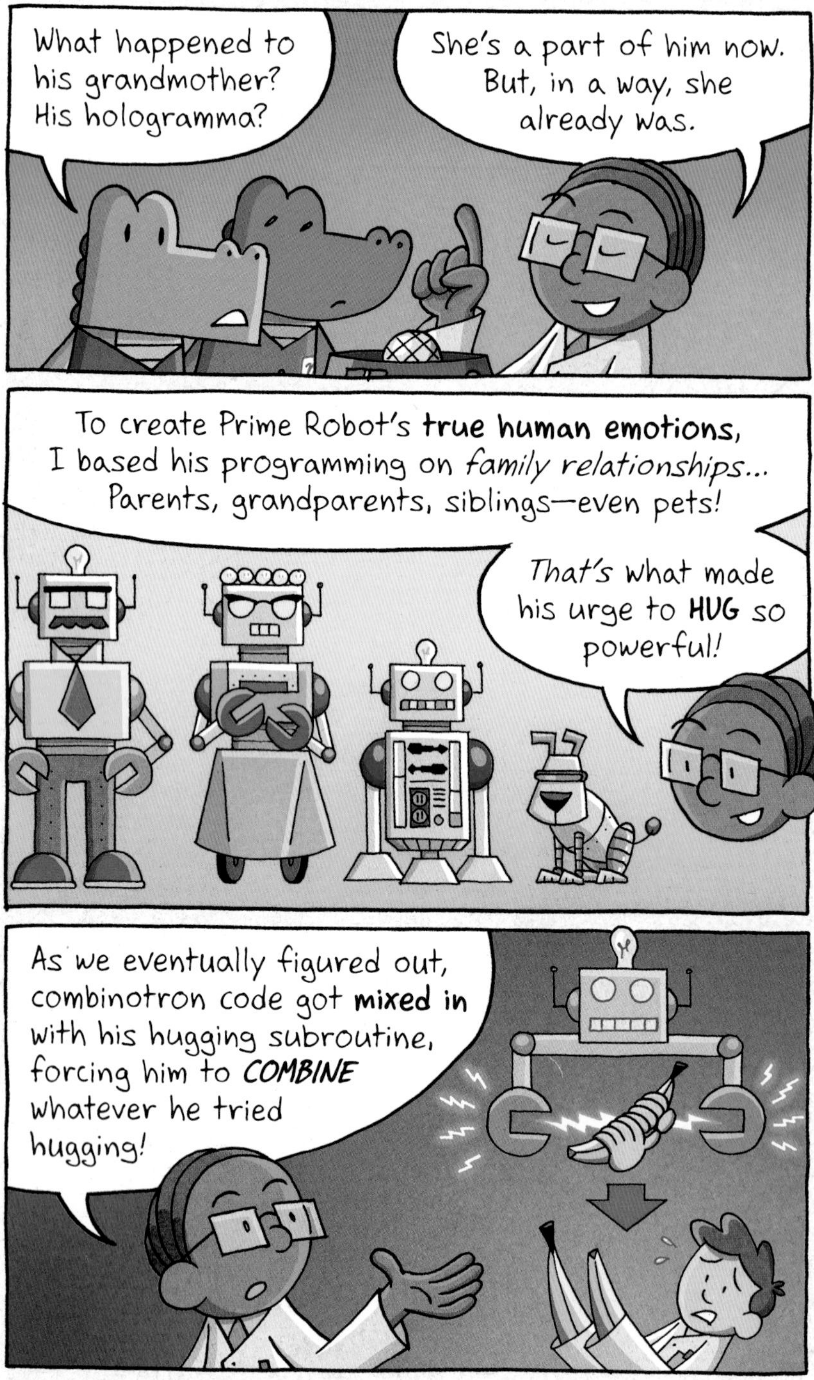

What happened to his grandmother? His hologramma?
She's a part of him now. But, in a way, she already was.
To create Prime Robot's **true human emotions**, I based his programming on *family relationships*... Parents, grandparents, siblings—even pets!
That's what made his urge to **HUG** so powerful!
As we eventually figured out, combinotron code got **mixed in** with his hugging subroutine, forcing him to ***COMBINE*** whatever he tried hugging!

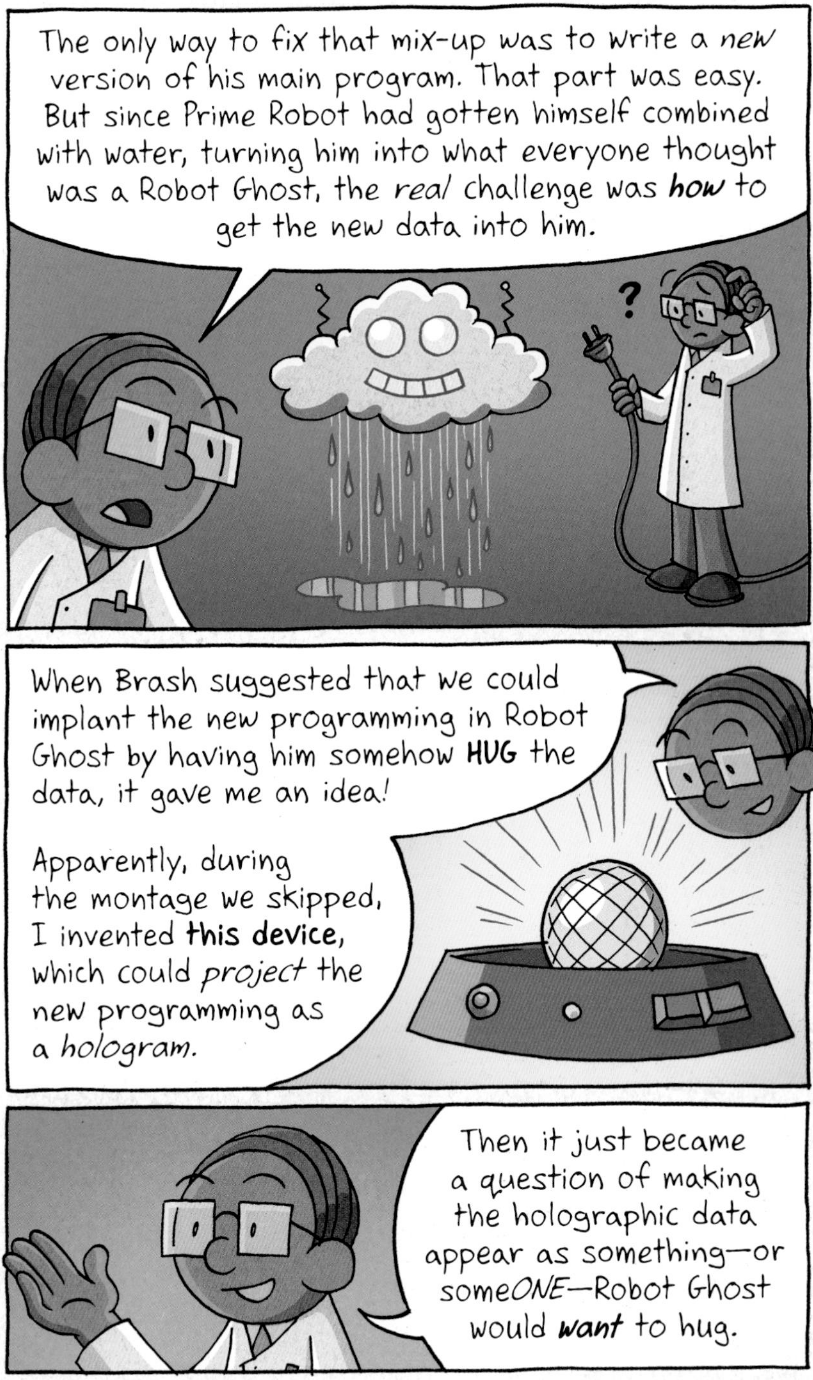
The only way to fix that mix-up was to write a *new* version of his main program. That part was easy. But since Prime Robot had gotten himself combined with water, turning him into what everyone thought was a Robot Ghost, the *real* challenge was ***how*** to get the new data into him.
?
When Brash suggested that we could implant the new programming in Robot Ghost by having him somehow **HUG** the data, it gave me an idea!
Apparently, during the montage we skipped, I invented **this device**, which could *project* the new programming as a *hologram*.
Then it just became a question of making the holographic data appear as something—or some*ONE*—Robot Ghost would ***want*** to hug.

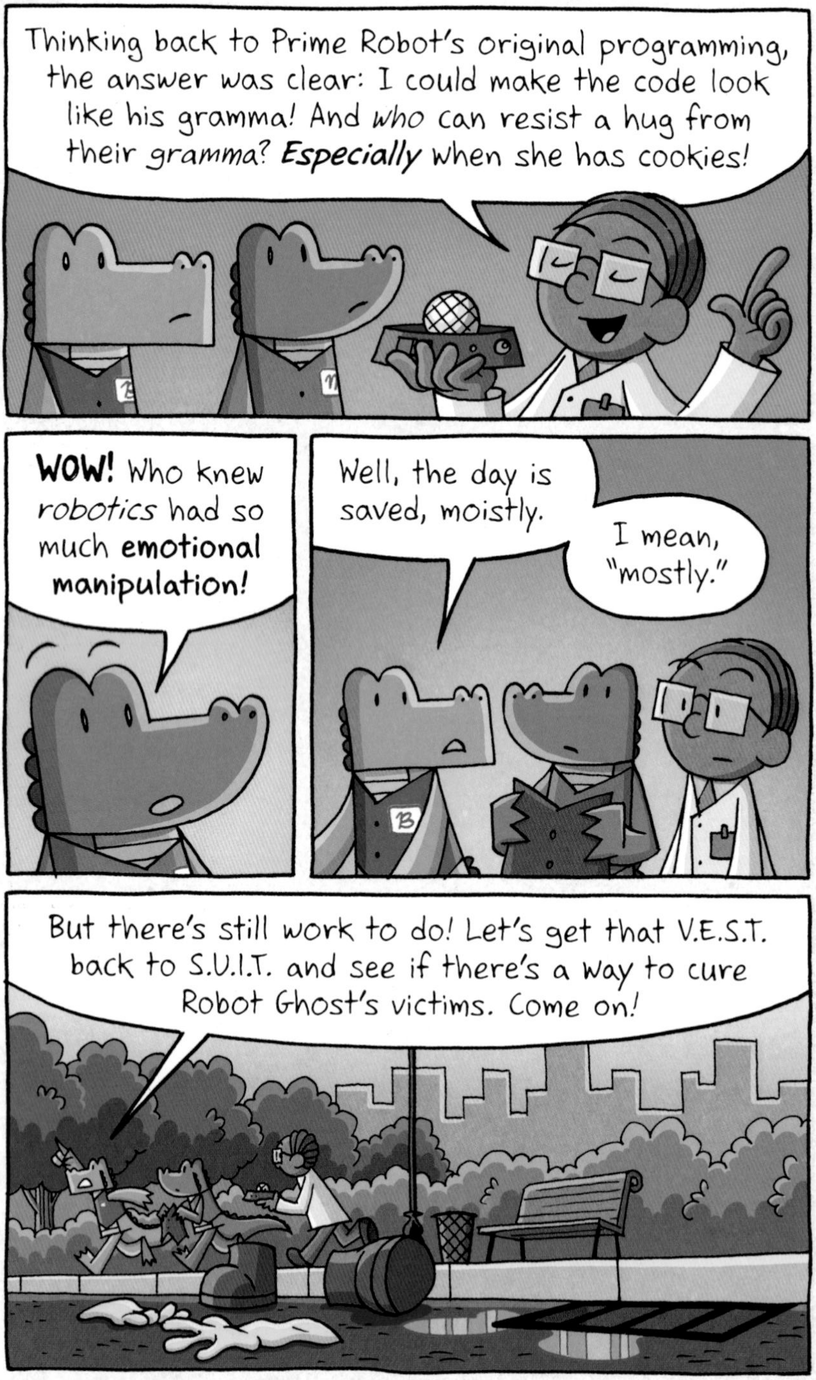
Thinking back to Prime Robot's original programming, the answer was clear: I could make the code look like his gramma! And *who* can resist a hug from their *gramma*? ***Especially*** when she has cookies!
WOW! Who knew *robotics* had so much **emotional manipulation!**
Well, the day is saved, moistly.
I mean, "mostly."
But there's still work to do! Let's get that V.E.S.T. back to S.U.I.T. and see if there's a way to cure Robot Ghost's victims. Come on!

Chapter ONE MILLION (or thereabouts)

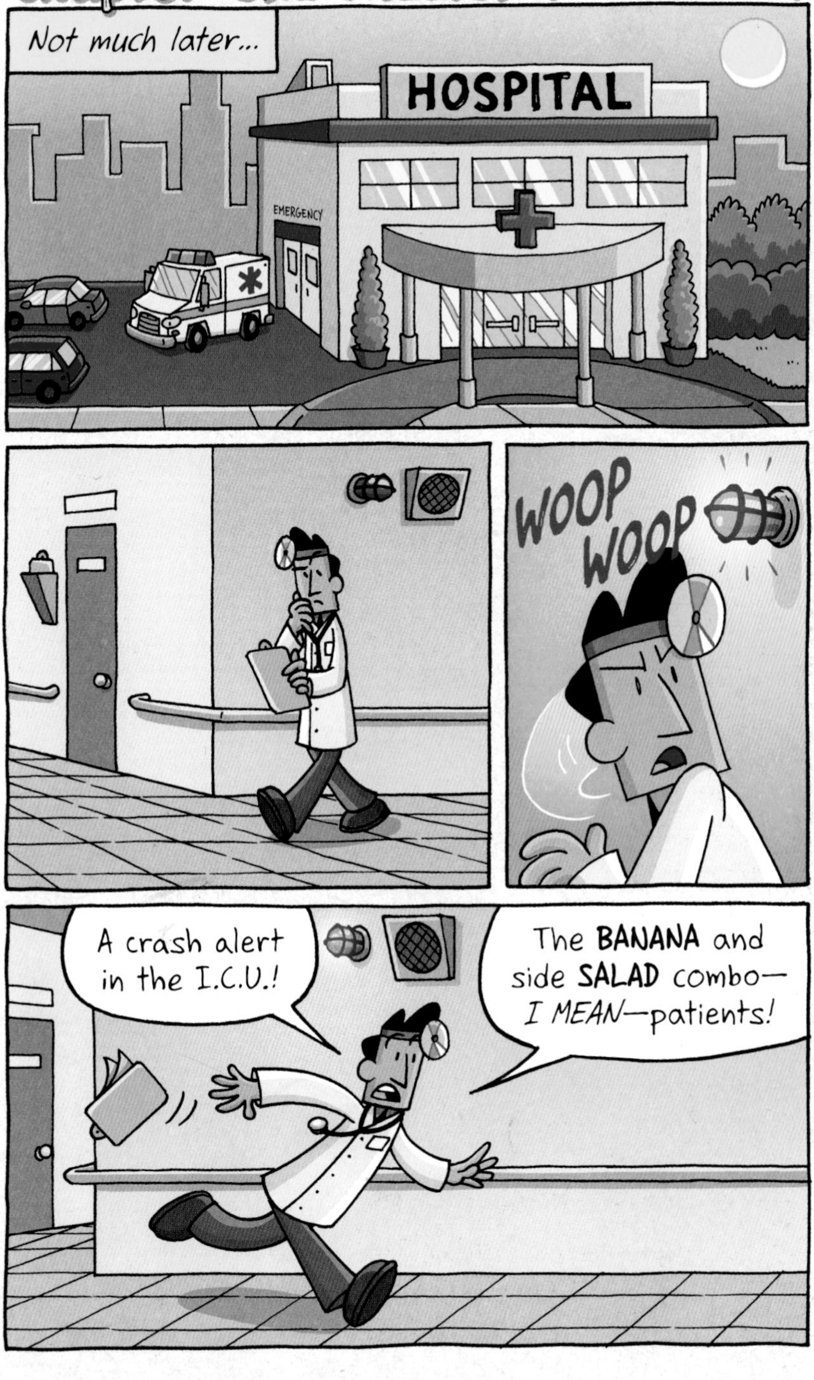

Not much later...
HOSPITAL
EMERGENCY
WOOP
WOOP
A crash alert in the I.C.U.!
The **BANANA** and side **SALAD** combo— *I MEAN*—patients!

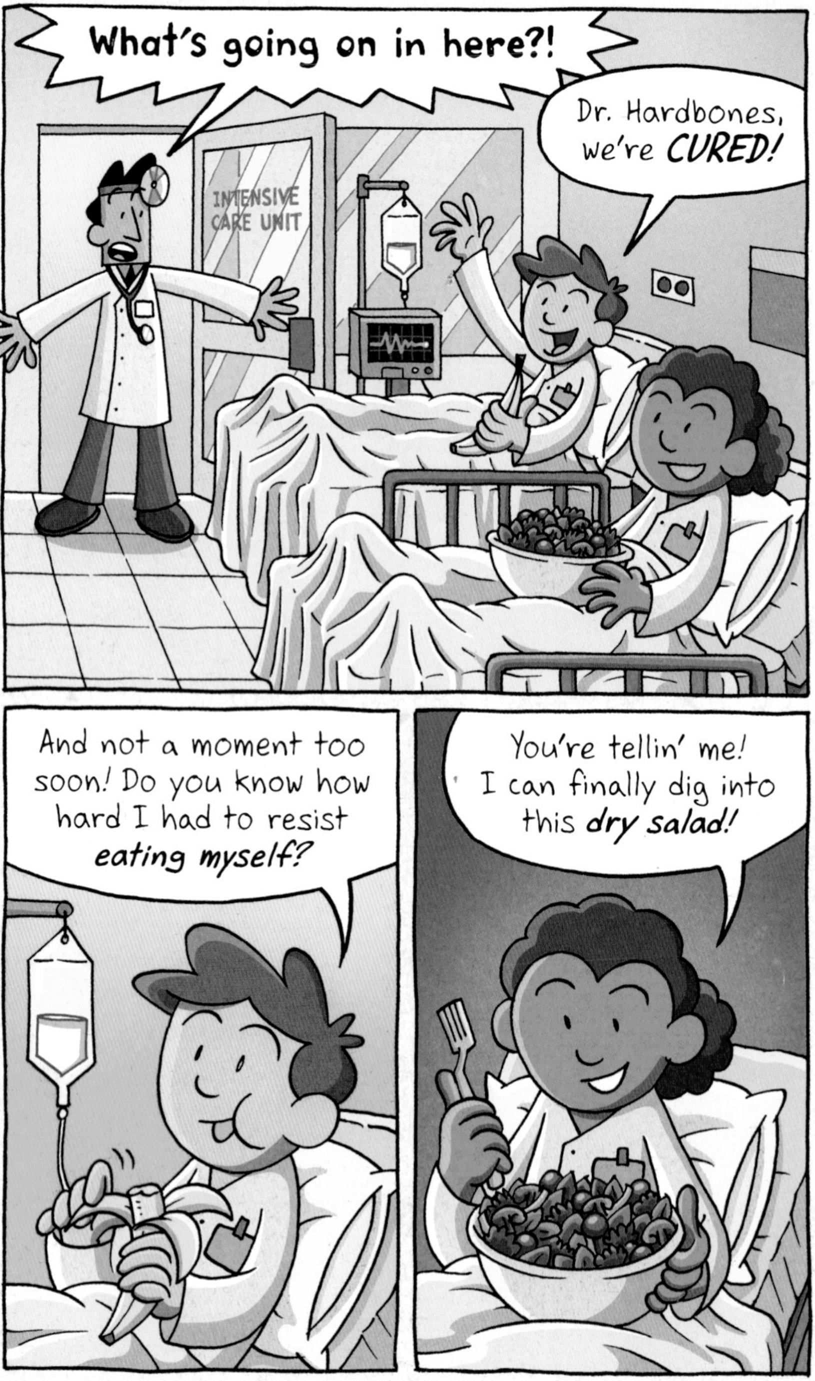
What's going on in here?!
Dr. Hardbones, we're CURED!
INTENSIVE CARE UNIT
And not a moment too soon! Do you know how hard I had to resist *eating myself?*
You're tellin' me! I can finally dig into this *dry salad!*

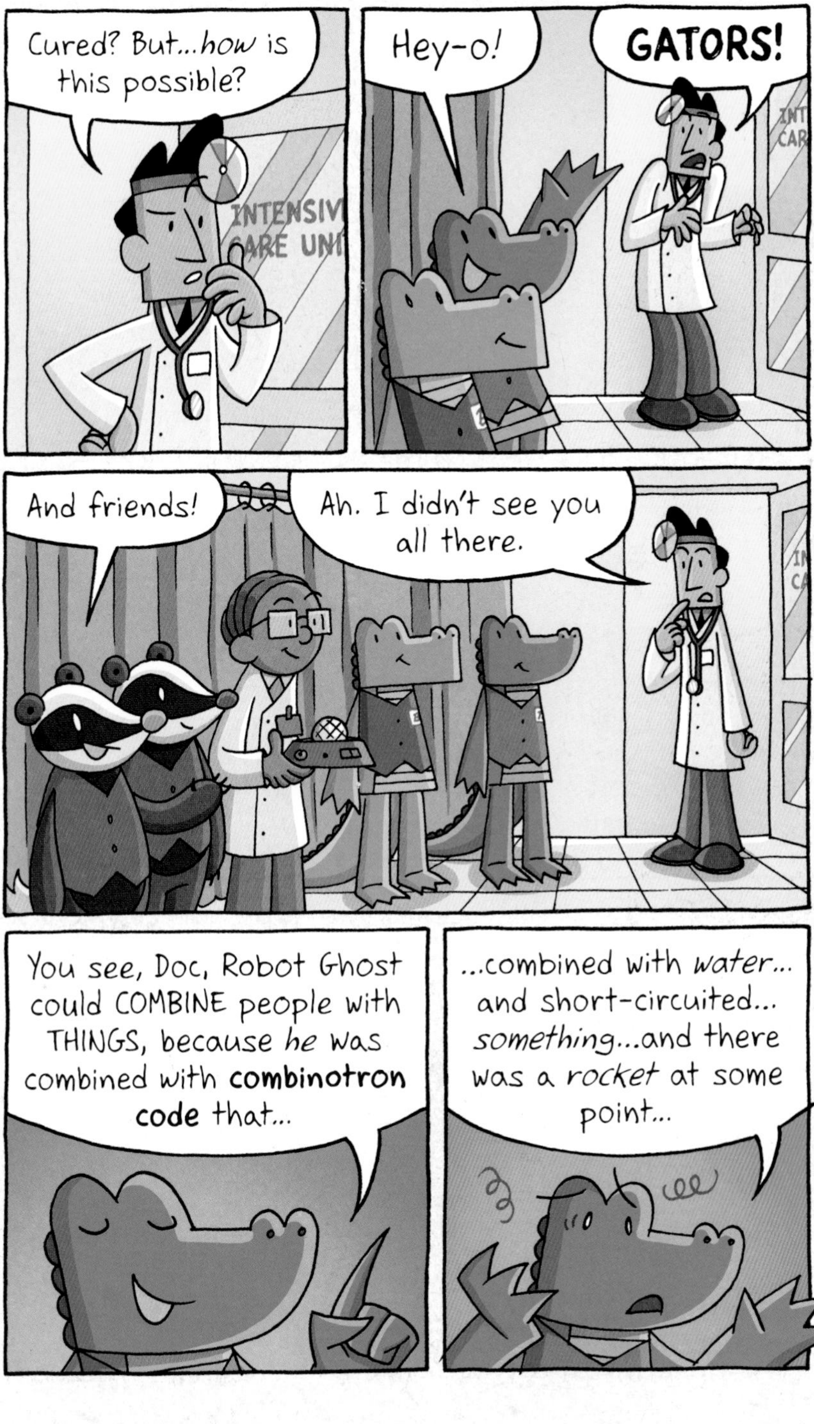
Cured? But...how is this possible?
Hey-o!
GATORS!
INTENSIVE CARE UNIT
And friends!
Ah. I didn't see you all there.
You see, Doc, Robot Ghost could COMBINE people with THINGS, because he was combined with combinotron code that...
...combined with water... and short-circuited... something...and there was a rocket at some point...

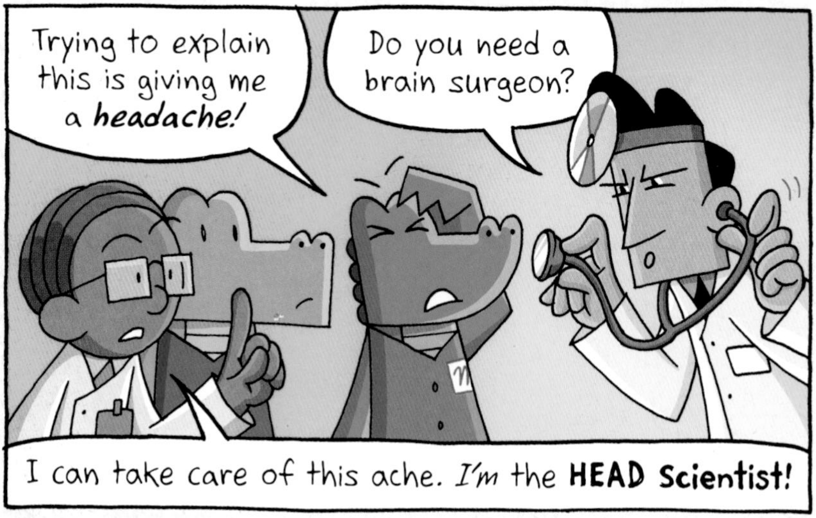
Trying to explain this is giving me a **headache!**
Do you need a brain surgeon?
I can take care of this ache. *I'm* the **HEAD Scientist!**

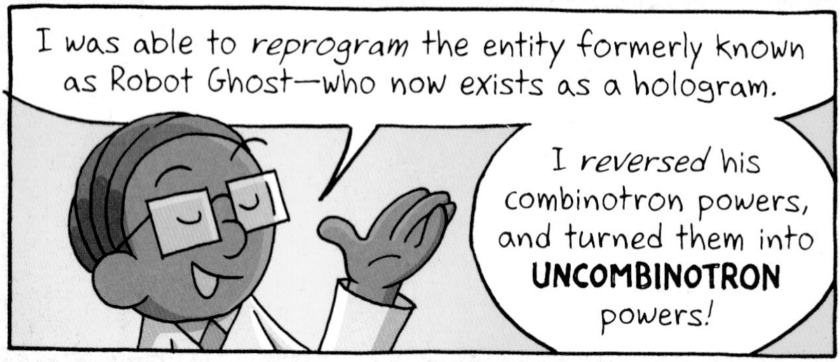
I was able to *reprogram* the entity formerly known as Robot Ghost—who now exists as a hologram.
I *reversed* his combinotron powers, and turned them into **UNCOMBINOTRON** powers!

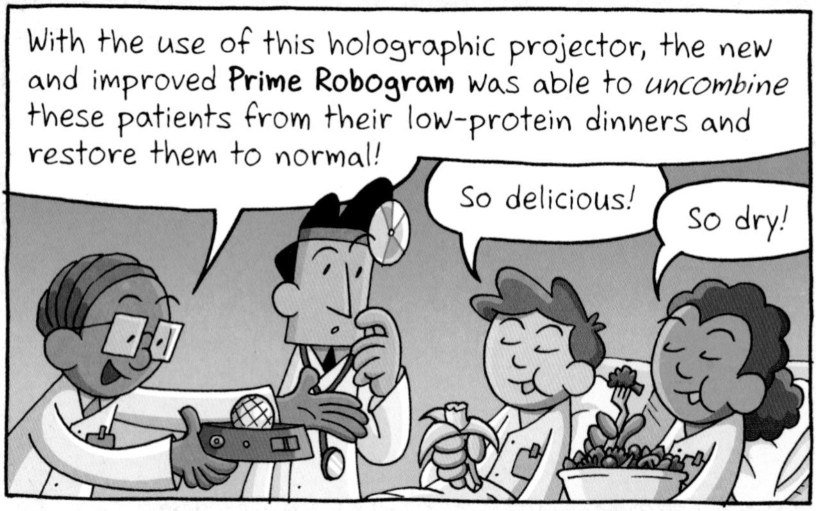
With the use of this holographic projector, the new and improved **Prime Robogram** was able to *uncombine* these patients from their low-protein dinners and restore them to normal!
So delicious!
So dry!

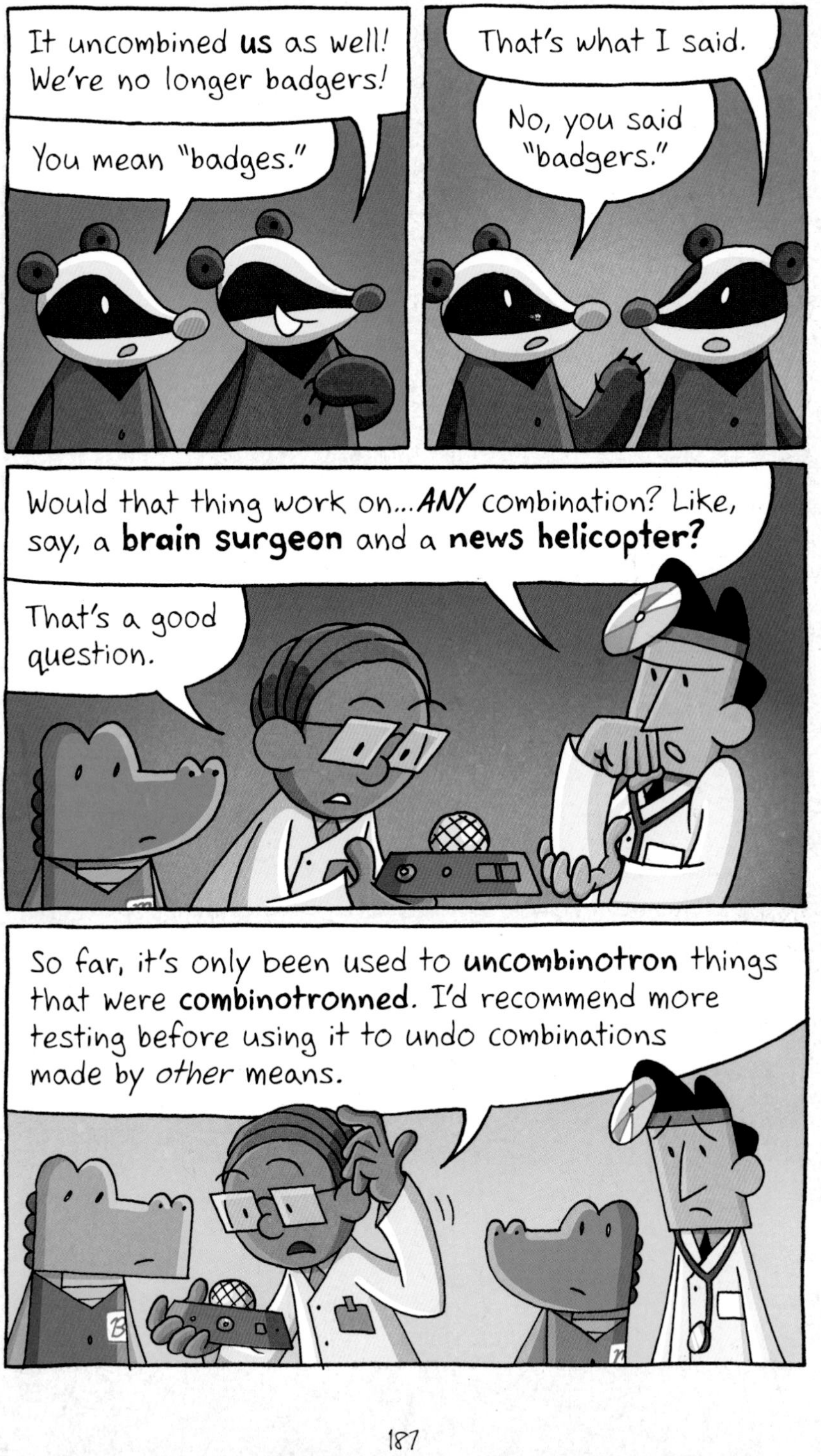
It uncombined **us** as well! We're no longer badgers!
You mean "badges."
That's what I said.
No, you said "badgers."
Would that thing work on...*ANY* combination? Like, say, a **brain surgeon** and a **news helicopter?**
That's a good question.
So far, it's only been used to **uncombinotron** things that were **combinotronned**. I'd recommend more testing before using it to undo combinations made by *other* means.

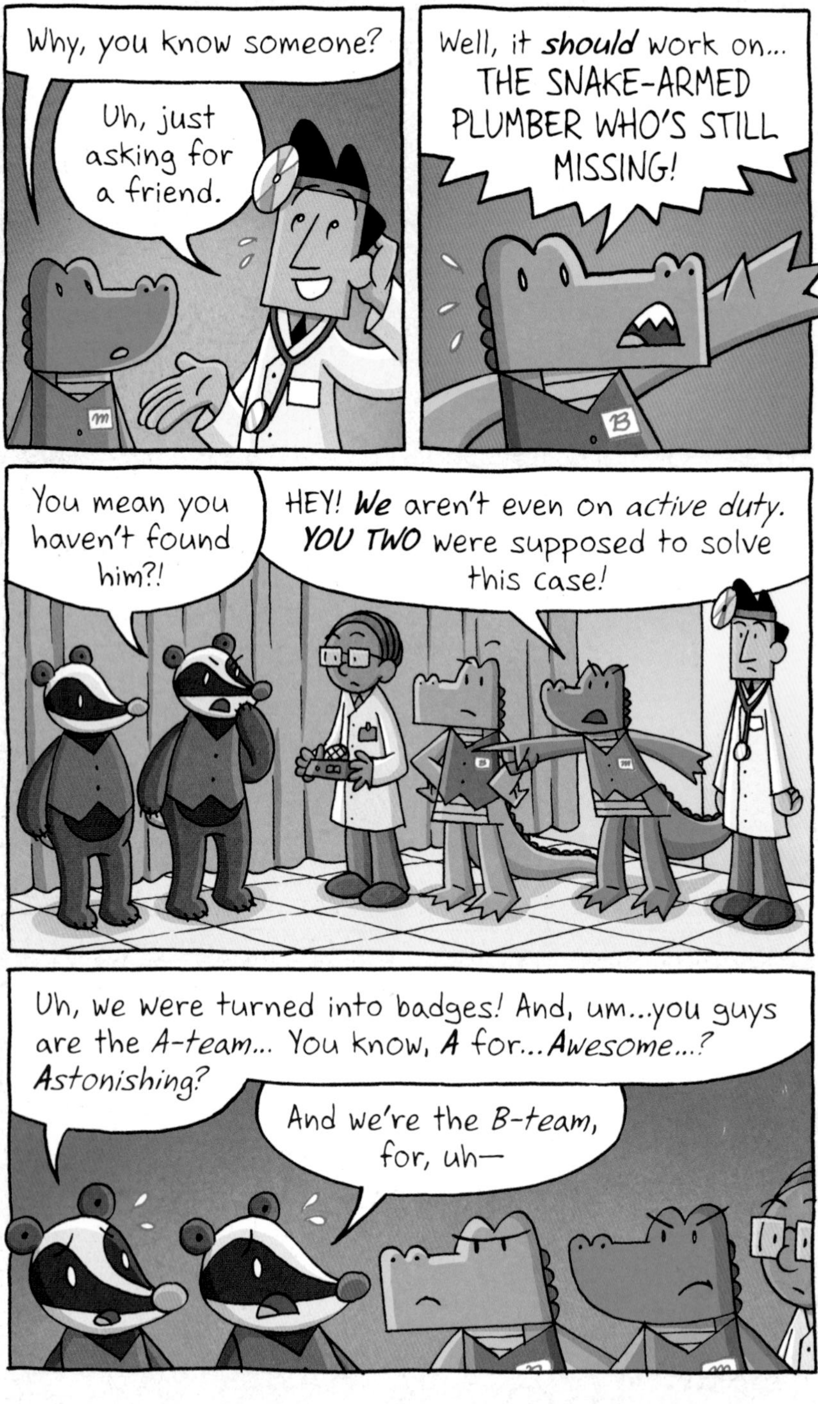
Why, you know someone?
Uh, just asking for a friend.
Well, it should work on... THE SNAKE-ARMED PLUMBER WHO'S STILL MISSING!
You mean you haven't found him?!
HEY! We aren't even on active duty. YOU TWO were supposed to solve this case!
Uh, we were turned into badges! And, um...you guys are the A-team... You know, A for...Awesome...? Astonishing?
And we're the B-team, for, uh—

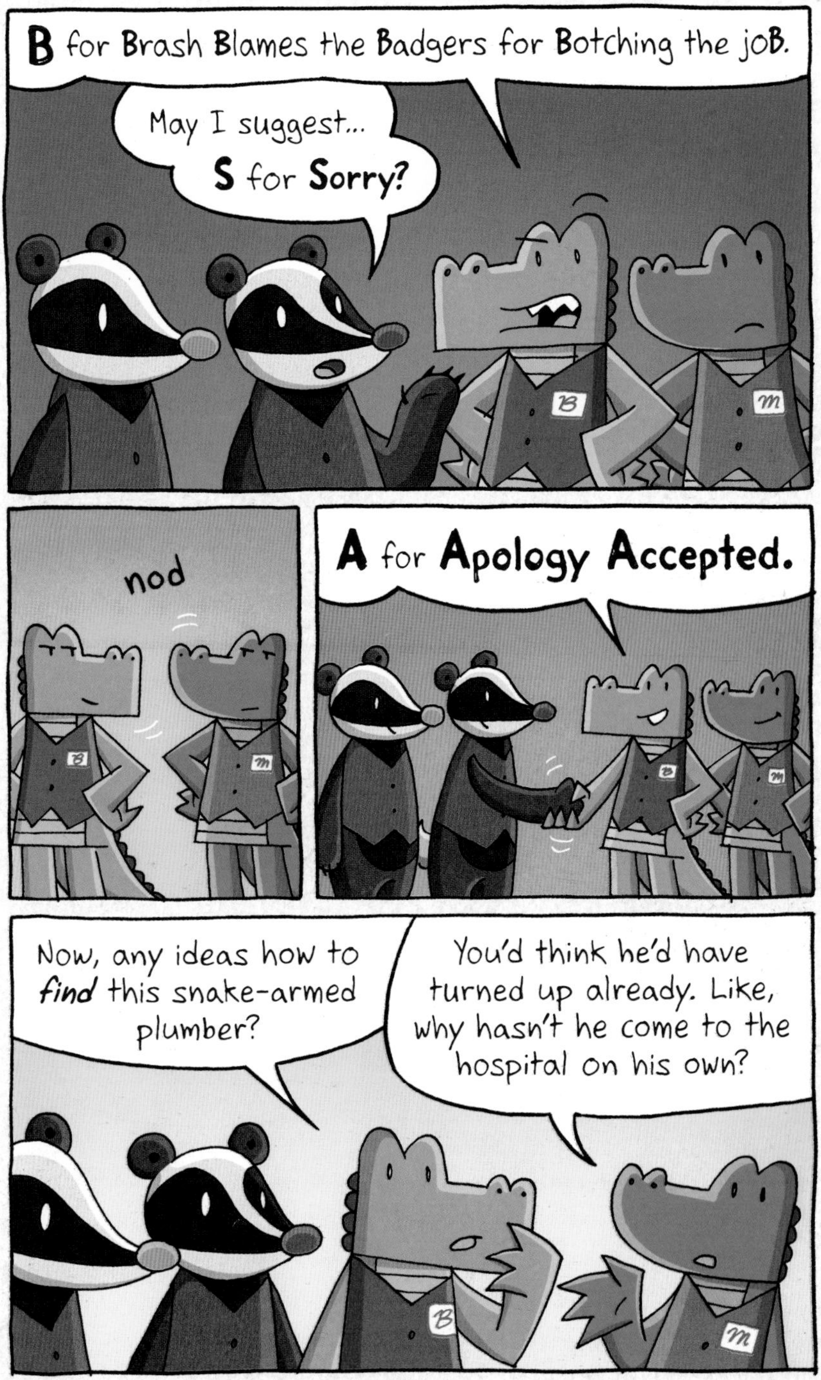
B for Brash Blames the Badgers for Botching the joB.
May I suggest...
S for Sorry?
nod
A for Apology Accepted.
Now, any ideas how to *find* this snake-armed plumber?
You'd think he'd have turned up already. Like, why hasn't he come to the hospital on his own?

Wouldn't he want to see if a doctor could get the snake off his arm?

Is the *snake* on the *PLUMBER?* Or is the plumber on the *SNAKE?*

What's the difference?

Well, all the *other* combinations Robot Ghost created were with **fruits** and **vegetables**. Which, as far as science can tell, don't have minds of their own.

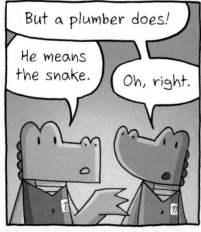

But a plumber does!

He means the snake.

Oh, right.

So the question is... which **MIND** is in control? The *PLUMBER'S?* Or the *SNAKE'S?*

Chapter S, for Speaking of the Snake...

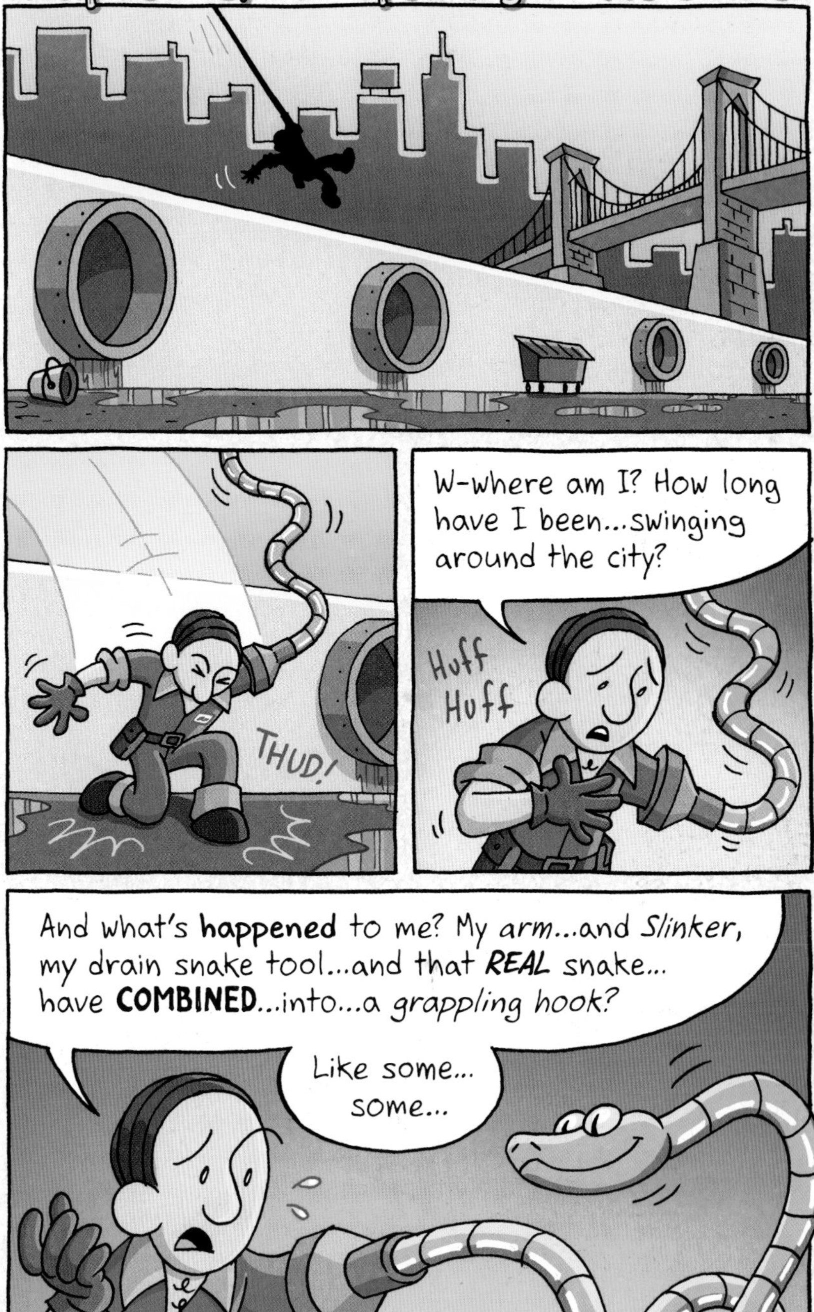

THUD!
W-where am I? How long have I been...swinging around the city?
Huff Huff
And what's **happened** to me? My *arm*...and *Slinker*, my drain snake tool...and that ***REAL*** snake... have **COMBINED**...into...a *grappling hook?*
Like some... some...

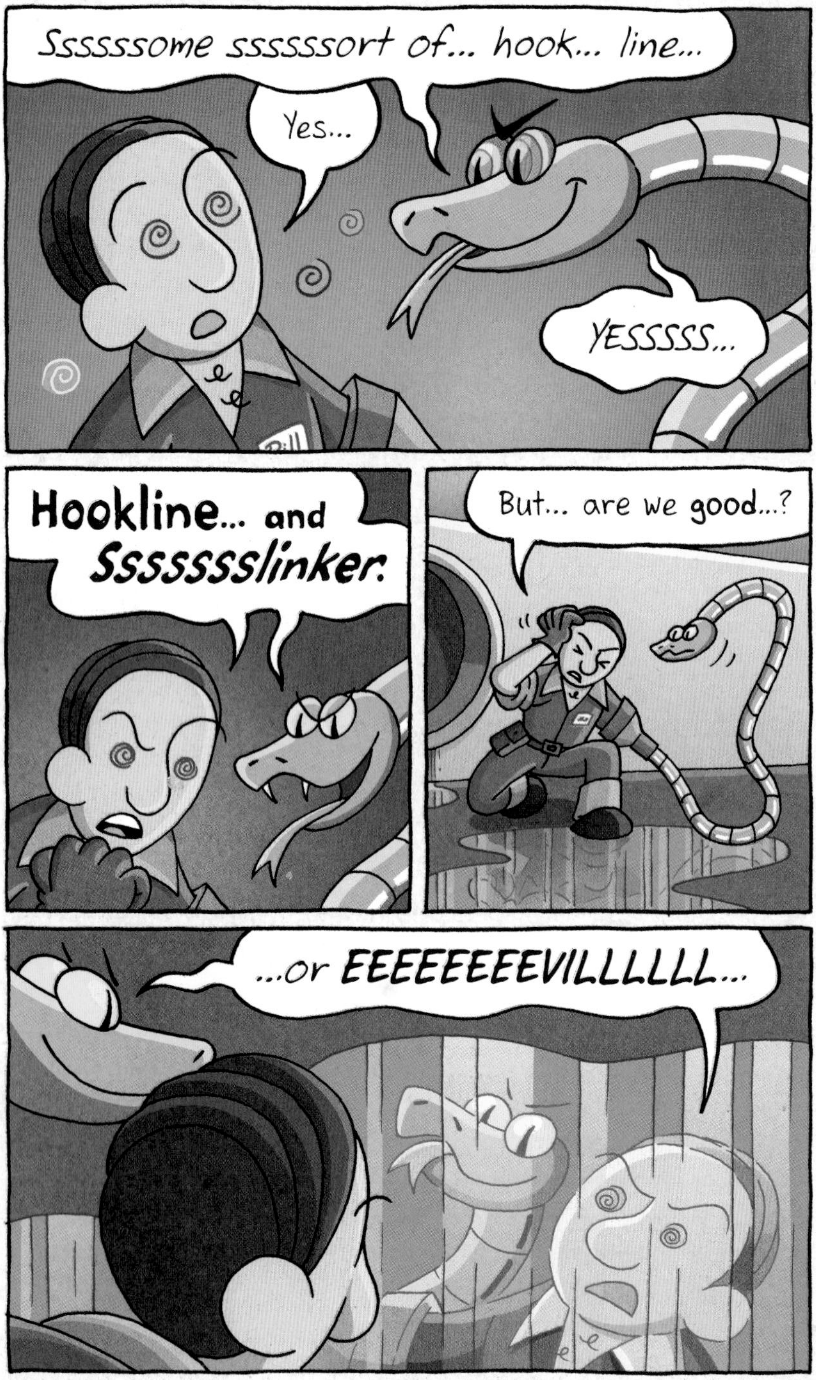
Sssssome sssssort of... hook... line...
Yes...
YESSSSS...
Hookline... and Sssssslinker.
But... are we good...?
...or EEEEEEEEVILLLLLL...

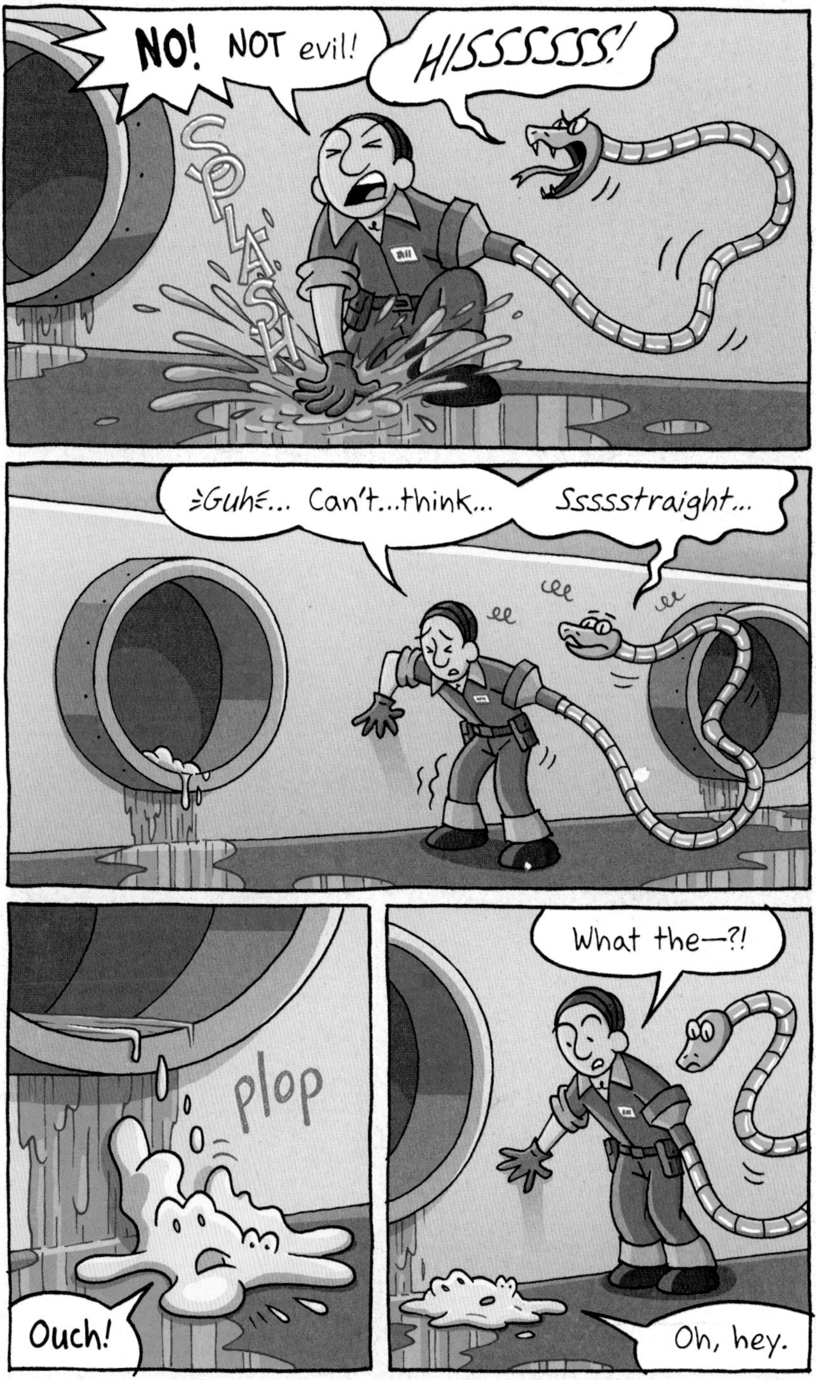
NO! NOT evil!
HISSSSSS!
SPLASH
Guh... Can't...think...
Ssssstraight...
plop
Ouch!
What the—?!
Oh, hey.

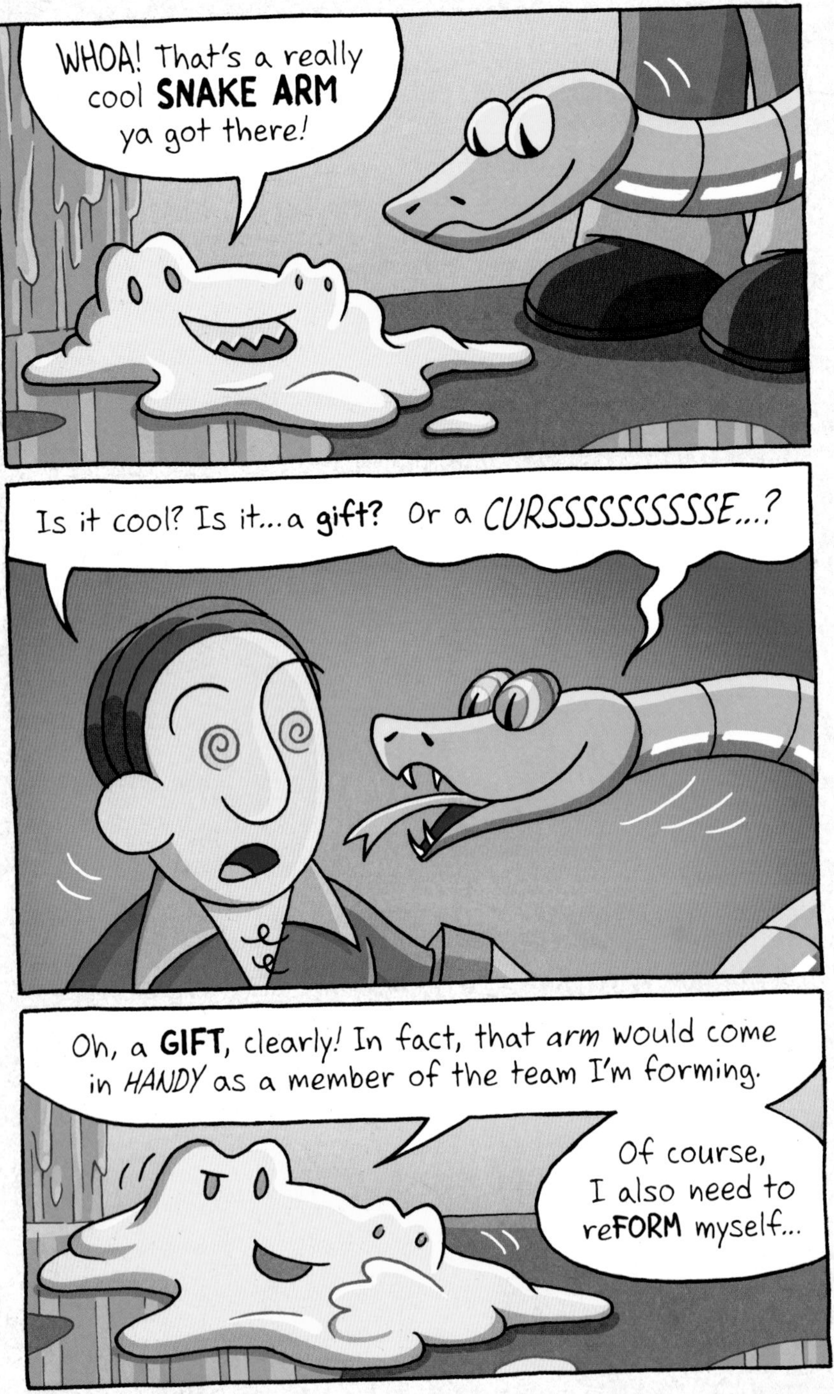
WHOA! That's a really cool **SNAKE ARM** ya got there!
Is it cool? Is it... a **gift?** Or a *CURSSSSSSSSSSE...?*
Oh, a **GIFT**, clearly! In fact, that *arm* would come in *HANDY* as a member of the team I'm forming.
Of course, I also need to re**FORM** myself...

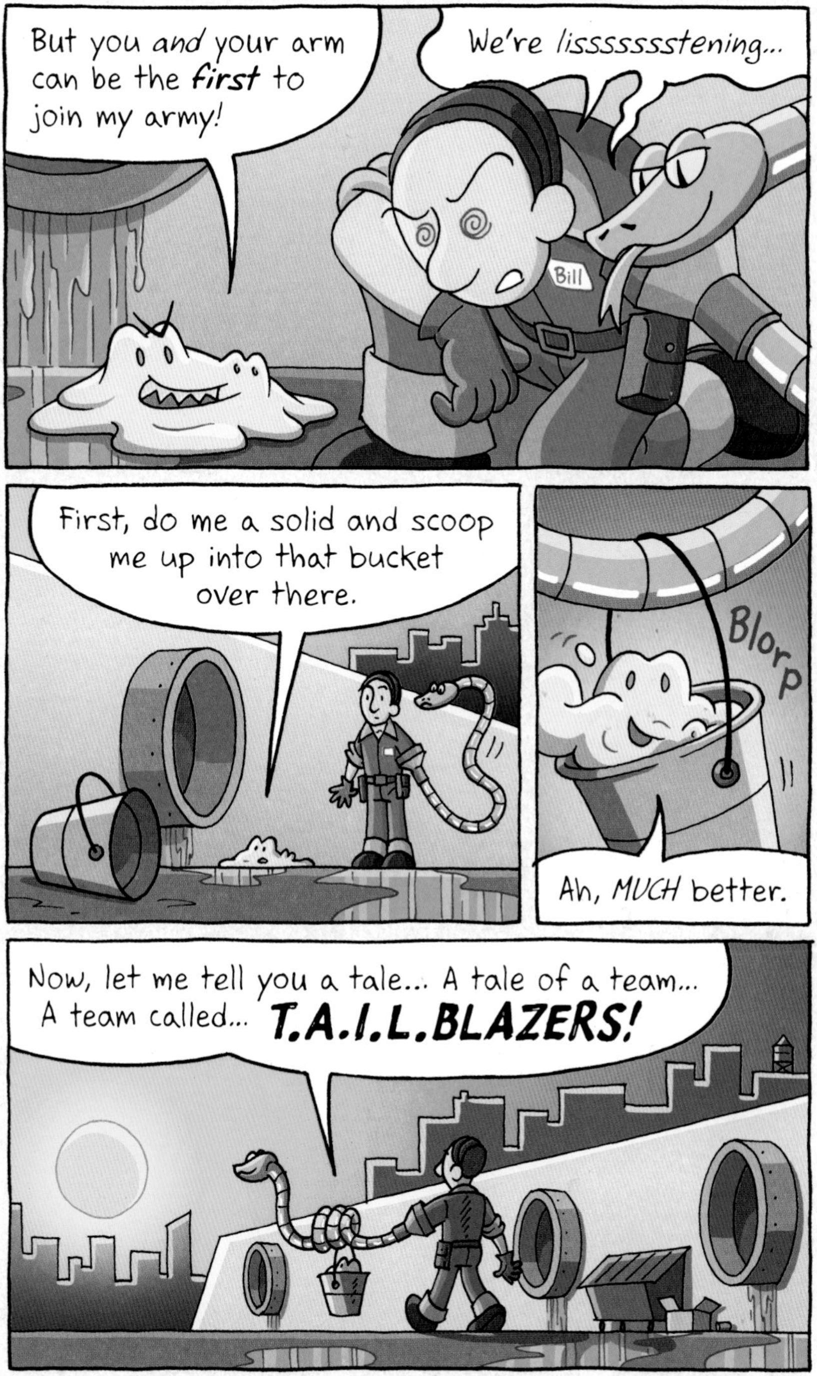
But you *and* your arm can be the ***first*** to join my army!
We're *lisssssssstening...*
Bill
First, do me a solid and scoop me up into that bucket over there.
Blorp
Ah, *MUCH* better.
Now, let me tell you a tale... A tale of a team... A team called... ***T.A.I.L.BLAZERS!***

Epilogue

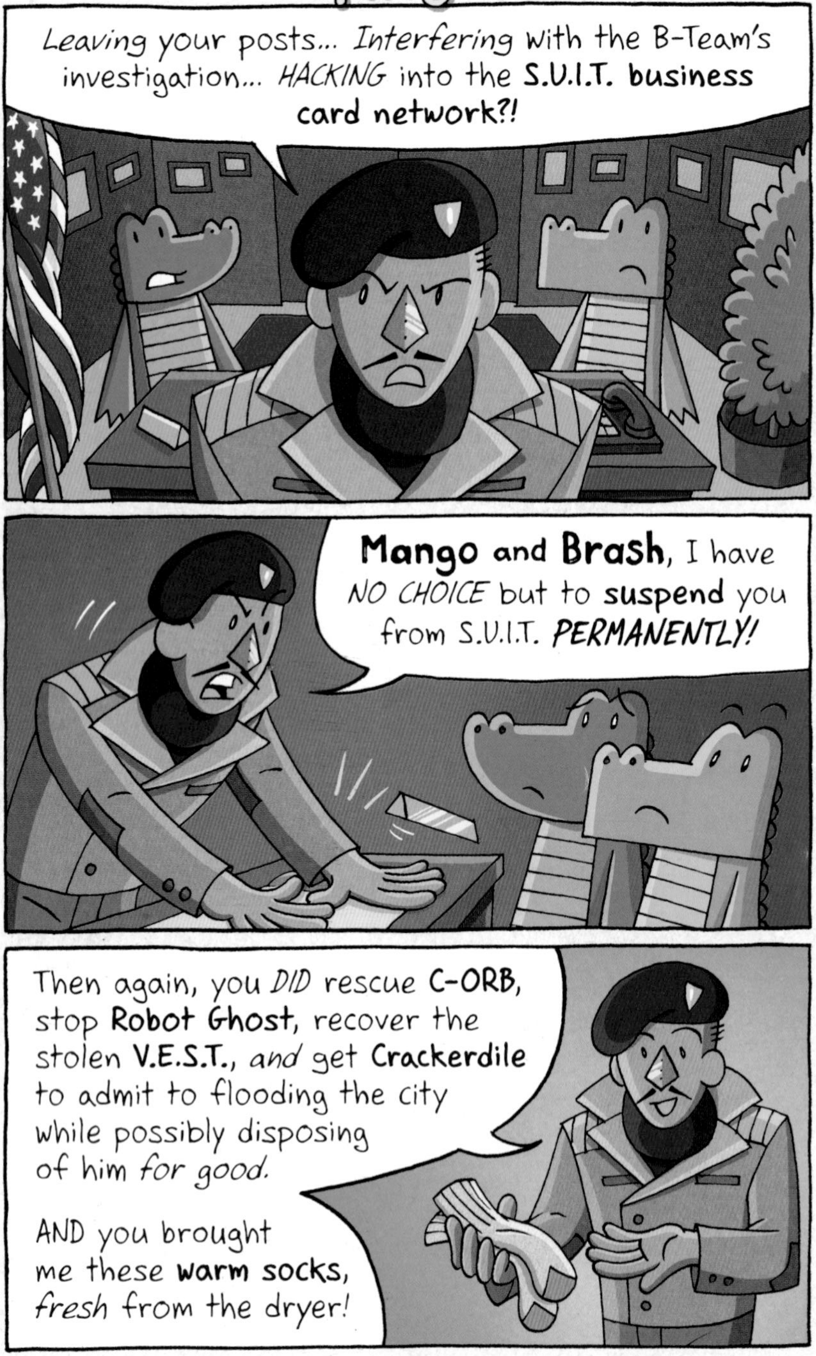
Leaving your posts... Interfering with the B-Team's investigation... HACKING into the S.U.I.T. business card network?!
Mango and Brash, I have NO CHOICE but to suspend you from S.U.I.T. PERMANENTLY!
Then again, you DID rescue C-ORB, stop Robot Ghost, recover the stolen V.E.S.T., and get Crackerdile to admit to flooding the city while possibly disposing of him for good.
AND you brought me these warm socks, fresh from the dryer!

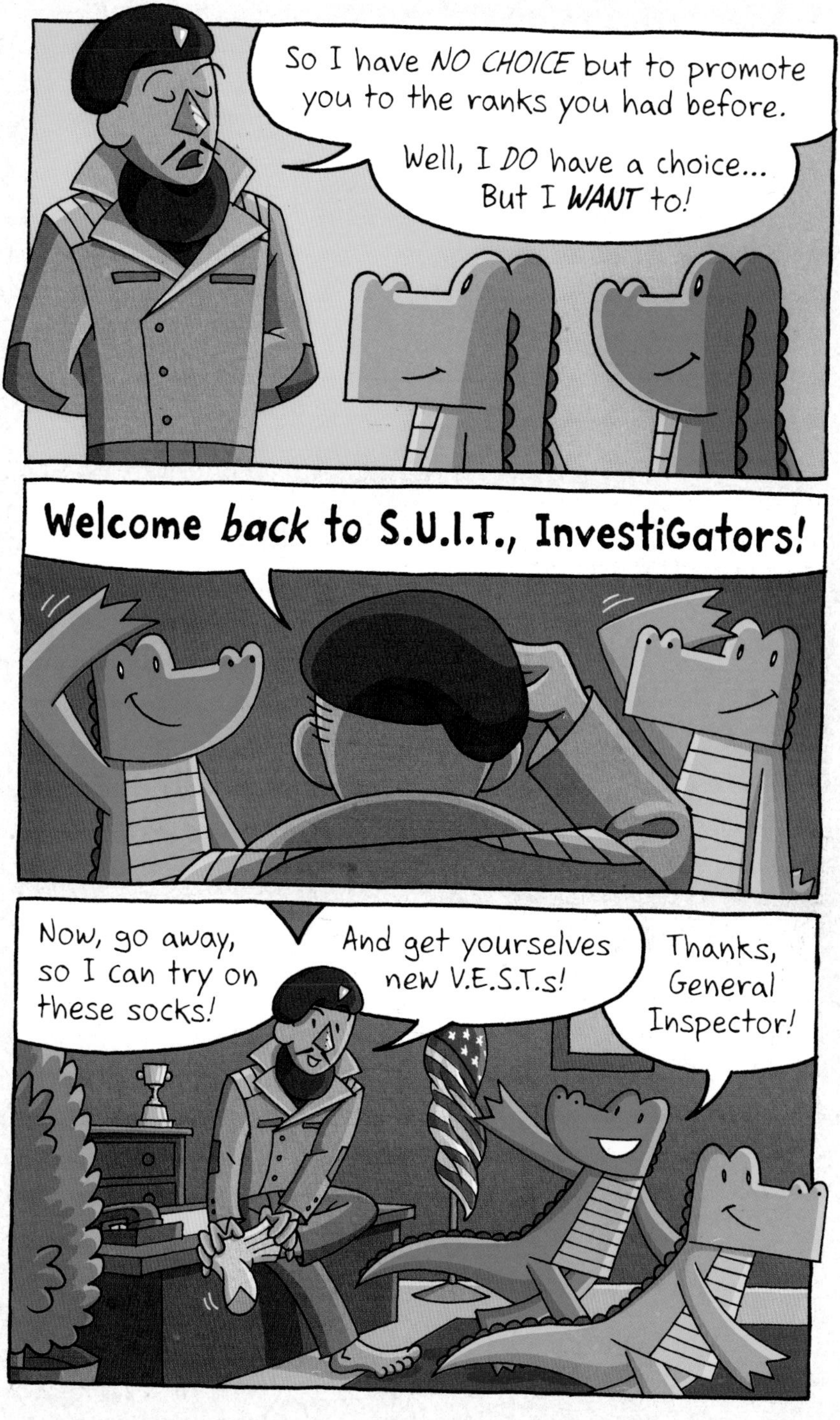
So I have NO CHOICE but to promote you to the ranks you had before.
Well, I DO have a choice... But I WANT to!
Welcome back to S.U.I.T., InvestiGators!
Now, go away, so I can try on these socks!
And get yourselves new V.E.S.T.s!
Thanks, General Inspector!

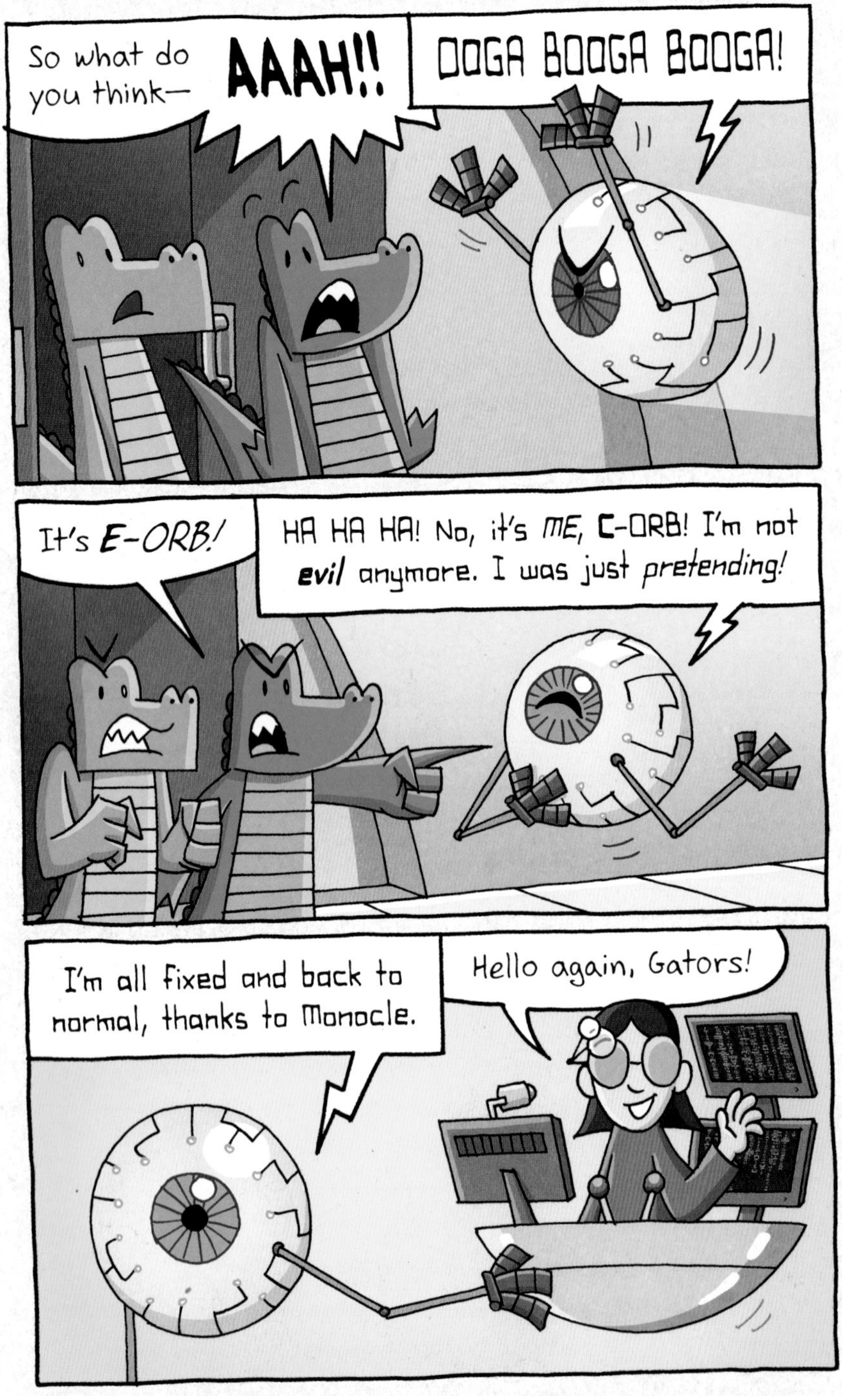

So what do you think—
AAAH!!
OOGA BOOGA BOOGA!
It's E-ORB!
HA HA HA! No, it's ME, C-ORB! I'm not evil anymore. I was just pretending!
I'm all fixed and back to normal, thanks to Monocle.
Hello again, Gators!

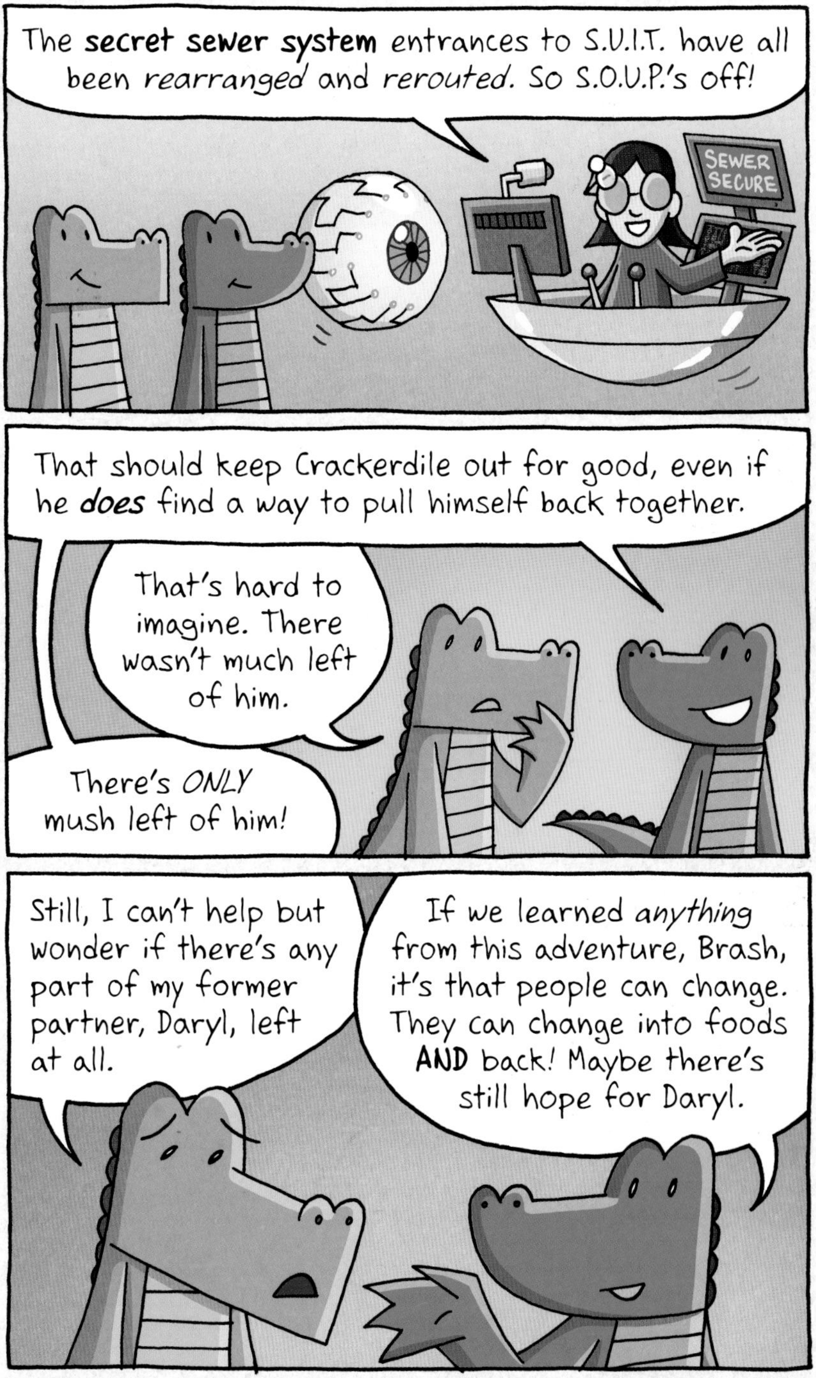
The **secret sewer system** entrances to S.U.I.T. have all been *rearranged* and *rerouted*. So S.O.U.P.'s off!
SEWER SECURE
That should keep Crackerdile out for good, even if he ***does*** find a way to pull himself back together.
That's hard to imagine. There wasn't much left of him.
There's *ONLY* mush left of him!
Still, I can't help but wonder if there's any part of my former partner, Daryl, left at all.
If we learned *anything* from this adventure, Brash, it's that people can change. They can change into foods **AND** back! Maybe there's still hope for Daryl.

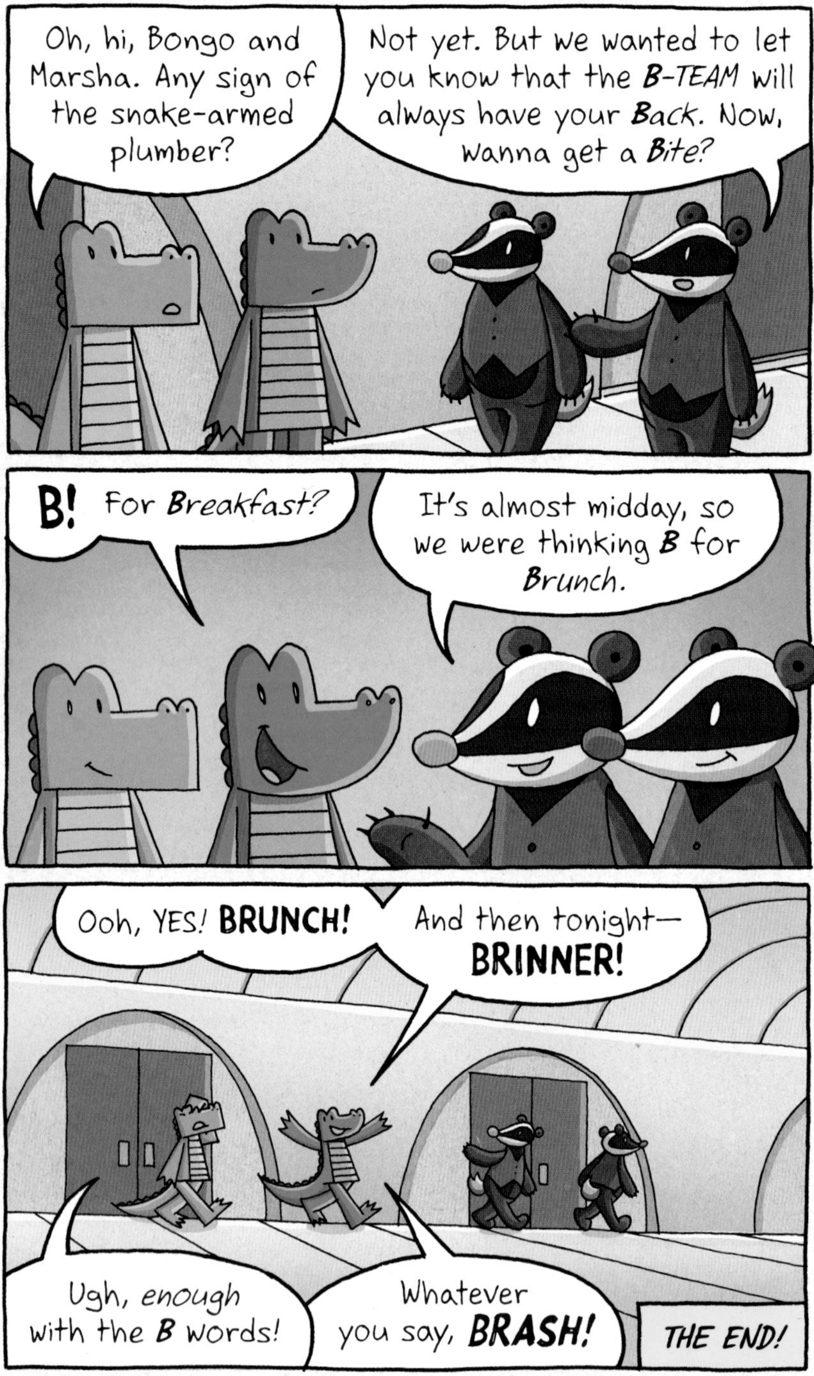
Oh, hi, Bongo and Marsha. Any sign of the snake-armed plumber?
Not yet. But we wanted to let you know that the B-TEAM will always have your Back. Now, wanna get a Bite?
B! For Breakfast?
It's almost midday, so we were thinking B for Brunch.
Ooh, YES! BRUNCH!
And then tonight— BRINNER!
Ugh, enough with the B words!
Whatever you say, BRASH!
THE END!

The Secret Agent word of the day is: ACCOMPLICE

Robot Ghost stole a V.E.S.T. from S.U.I.T., but he isn't the only one responsible for the crime. Crackerdile was his **accomplice**.

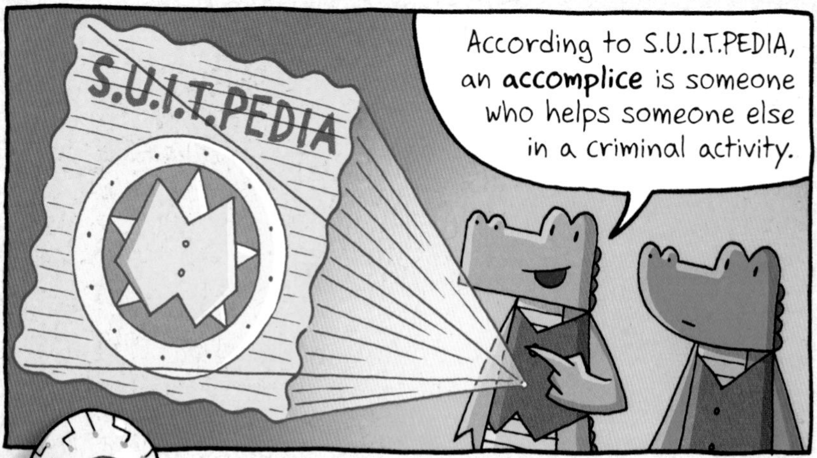
S.U.I.T.PEDIA
According to S.U.I.T.PEDIA, an **accomplice** is someone who helps someone else in a criminal activity.

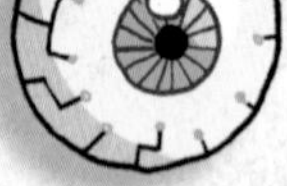

Keep an eye out for MANGO & BRASH'S next adventure!

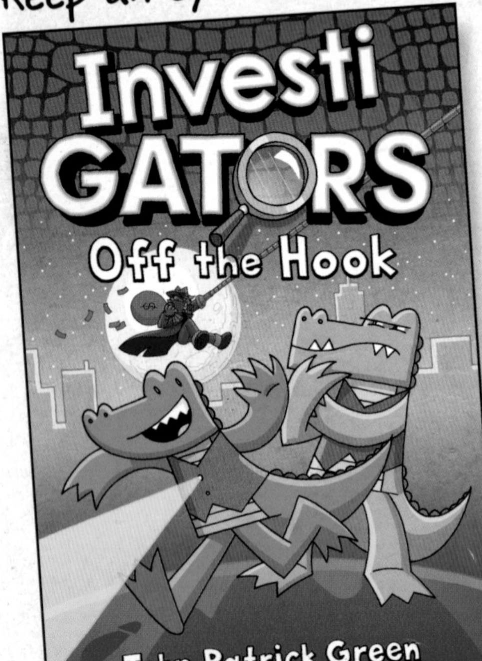
InvestiGATORS
Off the Hook
John Patrick Green

And be sure to read where their adventures began!

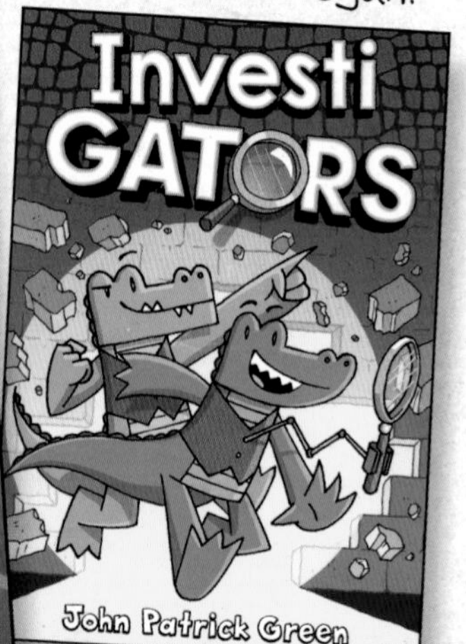
InvestiGATORS
John Patrick Green

InvestiGatorsBooks.com

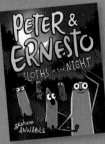

Special thanks to...

Aaron Polk and his flatters, Christine Brunson, Robin Fasel, and Rowan Westmoreland, for their amazing colors.
The usual suspects at First Second, especially my editors, Calista Brill and Rachel Stark.
Jen Linnan, my (secret) agent and demolitions expert.
Jon Roscetti, for the printer ink.
My brother, Bill, for introducing me to comic books.
Dave Roman, for reintroducing me to comic books.
And my parents, for never discouraging me from drawing.

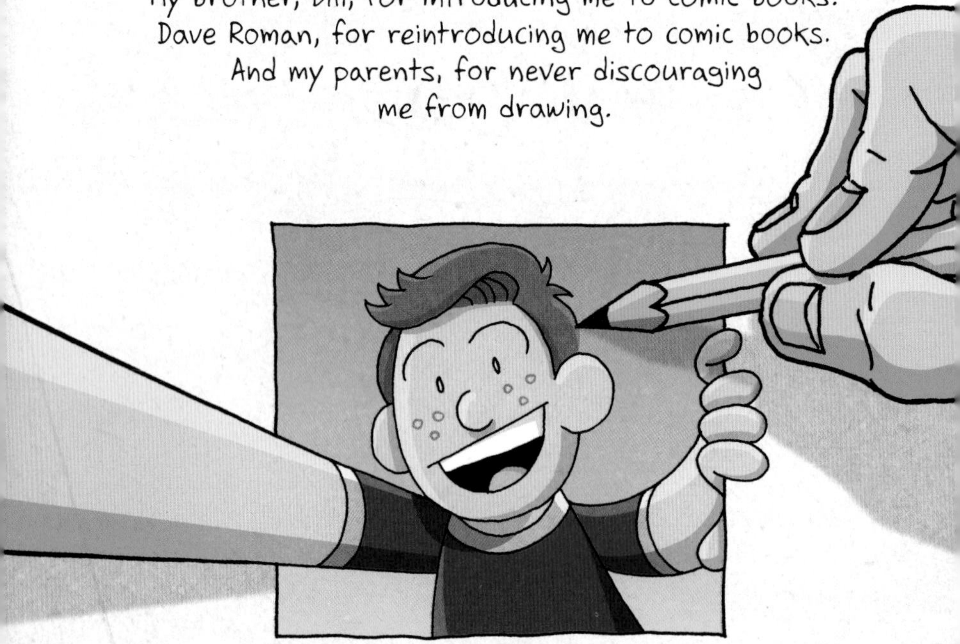

John Patrick Green is a human with the human job of making books about animals with human jobs, such as *Hippopotamister*, the Kitten Construction Company series, and now the InvestiGators series. John is definitely not just a bunch of animals wearing a human suit pretending to have a human job. He is also the artist and co-creator of the graphic novel series Teen Boat!, with writer Dave Roman. John lives in Brooklyn in an apartment that doesn't allow animals other than the ones living in his head.